PROLOGUE

MASON—AGE 21, NEW YEAR'S EVE

I tug at the collar of my shirt. It's stifling, sitting here in this room while we're pretending everything is still ... normal. When nothing will ever feel normal again. I glance around the room at my four brothers, wishing I could read their minds. Surely they all feel this too. It can't only be me who feels as though it's all kinds of fucking wrong to be doing this without her.

Elijah and Nathan stare at the fireworks through the window, watching the rest of the world celebrate when we're stuck here, in this mausoleum to her memory. Even Maddox, a party animal who can keep up with any one of us despite being the youngest, is staring at his drink like he has no idea what to do with it.

Unable to bear the suffocating tension a second longer, I speak up. "Does anyone else feel like it's weird that it's just us?"

"We could put the TV on. Watch the ball drop," Elijah suggests.

Drake shakes his head emphatically and reminds us all how she used to hate watching the ball drop because, as she claimed, the time was off by a few seconds.

Fuck, she used to get so animated when one of us tried to reason with her about it. "Remember how she'd always insist on using Great-Grandad's old Navy diving watch to determine when it was midnight instead?"

Nathan frowns. "Where the hell is that thing?"

With his eyes full of unshed tears, Maddox takes the watch out of his pocket. He holds it up, and the polished metal glints in the lamplight. It's got to be eighty years old, and it still keeps perfect time. I can almost feel the flat, polished silver of the watch's edge, worn smooth from years of use. She would rub the pad of her thumb over it absentmindedly while she regaled us with stories from her childhood in Valencia.

"Jesus, it feels so weird without her here." I gulp down my Scotch and jump to my feet, needing to be anywhere else. "Like this house has no fucking soul anymore. Let's get the fuck out of here and go somewhere."

Drake gives me an eye roll. "Like where, jerkwad?"

Anywhere that doesn't feel like the walls are closing in and suffocating me. It feels like the house grieves for her too. This house she worked so hard to make a home for us all, and without her in it ... Well, it doesn't feel like home

PLAYED
MANHATTAN RUTHLESS

SADIE KINCAID

CONTENT WARNING

This book deals with mature and sensitive themes which may be triggering for some readers. They include, but are not limited to:

Homophobia
    Self loathing and associated thoughts
    Violence
    Violent and emotional abuse of a minor
    Sexual assault of a minor (off page)

Please protect your own mental health

at all. Not anymore. "I dunno. A club or something. A place where there's life."

Maddox glares at me. "And what about me, dickface?"

Fuck, he's right. Sometimes I forget he's only sixteen. He looks and acts much older than his years.

"Nobody is going anywhere," Dad snaps, effectively shutting all of us down in an instant. "So quit your whining and drink your Scotch."

Guilt overwhelms me. I can't imagine how tough this has been on him. Or how it must feel to lose the love of your life like that. I mean, I know how much it hurts to lose someone that you thought would ...

I swallow down the tidal wave of shame and sadness that surges up from my chest. That's a completely different situation, and I won't sully Mom's memory by even thinking about comparing what he and I had to what my parents shared. My mom and dad truly adored each other.

"Sorry, Pop." I drop back down onto the couch and go on staring out the window, trying to put a lid on all the unwelcome feelings swirling around inside of me.

Dad chugs down the rest of his drink like he's trying to drown out his own feelings. He's always been someone I've looked up to. A good father. Tough but fair. As the fourth son of five, I felt a need to stand out from my brothers somehow, and from a young age, I decided that would be to learn to push Pop's buttons better than any of my brothers. Fortunately, I'm also able to sweet-talk him around again easier than they can. He's my idol though, and to see him like this, broken and defeated, tears a chunk out of my heart.

"I have a piece of advice for all you boys," he announces. "You live by this, and I promise that you'll never know a day's heartache in your life."

I bite my tongue so I don't tell him that I could have done with that advice five years ago.

It's Elijah who speaks. Elijah who's clearly trying to hold us all together while our dad falls apart. "And what's that, Dad?"

Pop takes a few seconds before he replies, and we all stare at him expectantly. Waiting for the piece of advice that's going to revolutionize our lives. He won't cry in front of us—he rarely has, apart from the day she died and her funeral, but his eyes are wet with tears.

He clears his throat and says, "Never fall in love."

I bite my tongue harder. Yeah, definitely could have used that advice five years ago, Pop. I down my own Scotch, and it burns the back of my throat. Or perhaps that's the shame again. Sneaking up on me when I least expect it.

I'll take his advice. Four words I can get behind. He's given us boys a lot of good counsel over the years, but I've never agreed with him more.

ONE

Luke's excited squeals echo around the den, making Maddox and me laugh. I guide our nephew to the sofa, my hands around his waist as I make the sounds of an engine stalling. I jerk him, making him the plane that's about to crash-land, and his shrieks grow louder.

"Now, Unca Mase, now!"

I bring us both crashing to the sofa, and his resulting giggles are loud and infectious.

"Mel is going to kick your ass getting him this worked up before bedtime," Nathan says, eyeing me and his son with amusement. He's already dressed in his tux for the second stage of Drake's wedding celebrations this evening. Like our two oldest brothers and their wives, Drake and Amelia decided to get married at our family home in an intimate ceremony. Now they're on a brief hiatus to decompress—which we all know is code for fucking—while an army of caterers and people with checklists on clipboards get the house ready for over two hundred guests.

Mel is Nathan's wife and the only person in the entire world he's afraid of. Much like Drake and Amelia, the two of them are sickeningly in love, and I'm sickeningly happy for all of them. Mel and Amelia are amazing women, and they keep my pain-in-the-ass older brothers on their toes. Safe to say I love them almost as much as I love my brothers.

"Again! Again!" Luke demands, already a pint-sized tyrant—he definitely gets the tyrant part from his dad.

"Can't help it if I'm the fun uncle," I tell Nathan with a shrug. "Besides, it's a special occasion. Surely he can stay up a little later?"

"Yeah!" Luke proclaims, not understanding what he's agreeing to given that he's not yet two, but I admire his loyalty.

"Wrong, buddy." Nathan picks up his overactive toddler, and my nephew protests loudly for a few seconds, but then Nathan chucks him beneath his chin, and Luke cuddles into his dad's shoulder. "Special occasion or not, bedtime is nonnegotiable unless we want to deal with some epic overtired toddler tantrums."

Having looked after Luke overnight on a number of occasions, I can confirm that him becoming overtired is no fun at all. I learned that lesson the hard way and haven't strayed from his bedtime routine again. Nathan expertly manages his excitable son while Luke kisses Maddox and me goodnight.

The sounds of the wedding party being set up and our family in various stages of getting ready for tonight's event filter through the house, and I sit on the sofa, wishing Luke could have hung around a little longer. I feel Maddox's eyes on me, and when I glance at him, he's staring at me with a curious look on his face.

"What?" I ask him.

"You're really good with kids" is all he says, but it seems like he's saying something more.

"Why, because I'm on their wavelength?" I default to our usual brotherly teasing, trying to avoid the deep conversation it feels like he wants to have. Maddox gets that look on his face when he's about to say something profound. Where he's deep as the Pacific, my emotional range is more akin to a puddle.

He shakes his head. "No, you're just really good with Luke."

That's because he's fucking adorable. I could sit and listen to Luke's chatter all day. For a little guy with incredibly limited communication skills, he's a whole lot of fun. I shrug. "I'm his uncle."

"Yeah, but it's just ..." He rubs a hand through this thick beard. "You instinctively know what to do and how to make him calm, or laugh until he bursts."

"Same as you, Drake, and Elijah can," I remind him.

"Of course we can. But I'm not talking about being a good uncle. I'm talking about something more."

I have no idea what he's trying to say, but I'm ready to be done with the conversation. "Well, that's because I'm the fun one, remember?"

"You're so much more than that, Mase." His intense brown eyes are locked on my face, and I can't look away. "You ever thought about having kids?"

Damn, I wish I had a drink. "Are you fucking serious? Me? Kids?"

He leans forward in his chair, hands clasped between his thighs. "Why wouldn't I be? You love kids. You're amazing with them."

I snort. "I'm also severely allergic to commitment."

"That could change though. With the right circumstances. And technically, you don't need to be in a relationship to have kids. Especially—"

I interrupt. "Because I'm gay?"

He frowns. "Especially in the times we live in, and with the support and resources available to you, asswipe."

I never should have made the gay comment, and I honestly don't know where that came from. "What about you? Have you ever thought about having kids?"

He nods. "All the time, especially since Nathan and Mel had Luke, and then when she got pregnant with their second. Today made me think about whether I'd ever get married. It's only natural to reevaluate your life choices when people close to you go through a huge life change."

"Kind of hard to have kids when you're celibate."

He arches an eyebrow. "You're really going to take a shot at my celibacy after you jumped down my throat?"

I wince. "Sorry. It's what I do. Inappropriate humor is my thing."

He hums, deep in thought, wise sage that he is. "Often the most sensitive souls hide behind humor."

I roll my eyes. "I don't hide behind humor, Mad."

"Never said you did," he says. "I was talking about sensitive souls, which we both know you're not."

Now that's more like it. He winks at me and stands. On his way toward the door, he passes by me and places his hand on my shoulder. "For what it's worth, I think you'd be an amazing dad, Mase. Or an amazing partner or husband for that matter. Maybe you could have everything you've ever wanted."

He walks out of the room, and I stare after him, wondering how the hell we ended up here. Marriage? Kids? Me? I've never heard anything so ridiculous. So what if I love spending time with my nephew? And I may have the occasional thought about what it would be like to have another person depend on me and how nice it might be to feel needed in that way—maybe by a kid or perhaps a partner or even a dog.

That doesn't mean I'm not happy with my lifestyle. I do what I want when I want, and I don't have to worry about upsetting or inconveniencing anyone else. My life is fast-paced, fun, and most importantly, easy. It's exactly how I like it. I tried the whole deep and meaningful shit a long time ago, and it didn't end well. I have no desire to ever go there again.

"THAT's another James brother off the market," Tyler says with a mischievous grin. "I can hear the hearts breaking all over New York tonight."

I hand him another Scotch. "I think Drake has been off the market from the moment he set eyes on Amelia. But yeah, it was good to officially welcome her into the family." I was shocked as hell when Drake fell for his secretary considering what a workaholic and commitment-phobe he was. But when I see the two of them dancing together on the balcony where he proposed to her on New Year's, it all makes sense. A little over five months later, they're married. New York in June makes for a beautiful wedding. Romantic bastard.

Tyler stands beside me, his arm bumping against mine, and we stare out at the New York skyline. "So that's Nathan, Drake, and Elijah all happily married now. That only leaves ..." He lets the unfinished sentence hang in the air. My oldest brother also got married this year—or rather remarried. He and his wife divorced because they made each other miserable as sin, then both realized they were more miserable without each other. Now, they're two of the happiest people I've ever seen. Another of my brothers I'm undeniably happy for. Whatever broke, Elijah and Amber definitely fixed it. "I wonder who'll be off the market next."

I take a swig of my Scotch. "Well, given the choice between me and my celibate, Buddhist monk little brother, my money's on him."

Tyler laughs. "Mine too. I can't imagine anyone ever being man enough to pin you down."

I sigh and take another swig. "Although many have tried."

He laughs again, his huge shoulders shaking with the force. "Like the bartender from that sex club."

I roll my eyes. "Jesus fucking Christ, I forgot about him." He wasn't my usual type, but when a member of the Irish mob wants to set you up with someone, it's not the kind of offer you turn down. Mikey Ryan told me about a guy who works at his club, Ben, who's around my age, hot, and also gay, and assumed we'd be compatible.

The guy was hot, but we went on one date, and it was a disaster. It's like with Tyler and me. He's Mel's cousin, and he's become as much a part of our family as she is. I'm sure most of them keep expecting us to hook up at some point, and I get why. We're both single, both into dick, and we get along great. What more could we want?

Tyler grins at me. "He didn't seem your type though. Way too alpha and very up his own ass."

I hum my agreement. "Yeah, but it was the fact he wanted to be up my ass that was the real problem."

Tyler spits out a mouthful of Scotch and doubles over, coughing and laughing, while declaring his inability to breathe.

I slap him on the back. "Jeez, buddy. You used to be able to handle your liquor."

He stands straight and wipes his mouth with the back of his hand. "Fuck!" He lets out another chuckle. "Your dating stories never fail to entertain. I swear you have the most colorful love life of anyone I've ever known."

That's probably true, although lately it's been decidedly less so. More like beige. The dating scene in Manhattan is growing old—or maybe I am. Or maybe I've already dated every unattached gay guy in the state. "Colorful? Is that a polite way of saying ...?"

"That you're a man-whore," he replies, deadpan, folding his tattooed forearms across his chest. "Have you ever bottomed though? For anyone?"

Fuck, I do not want to open that can of worms. Not even with him. And besides, it was a different life, so it's not exactly a lie when I shake my head and tell him no. "You?"

He shrugs and flashes me that grin that makes his dimples pop. "Occasionally. For the right guy."

Well, that's an interesting development. Tyler is all top energy, and I never considered that he could be a switch. On paper, he's exactly my type. Tall, broad, tattooed, sparkling blue eyes. Funny as hell. "For the right guy, huh?"

He tilts his head to the side and rakes his eyes down my body. Fuck. We have had way too much Scotch and are far too alone in this room to be having this conversation. "That's what I said."

"And how does someone find themselves lucky enough to be that guy?"

He arches an eyebrow in challenge. "Keep smiling at me like that, Mase, and you might find out."

As tempting as that offer is, and it is really fucking tempting, we can't. Tyler is hot as fuck, and those dimples could bring a man to his knees. And maybe all this talk of weddings and kids is making me sensitive. But it's his quick wit, his sharp mind, and his huge fucking heart that I love most about him, and for that reason, I would never risk losing him from my life—not even for the promise of a decent fuck, which I could definitely do with about now. He's my best friend, and that's all he'll ever be.

I step closer and take his face in my hands. He doesn't back down, instead holding my gaze. "You know I love you, don't you?" That's partly the Scotch talking, but it's also the fucking truth.

He winks at me. "Yeah, I do."

He's such a goddamn flirt. I press a kiss on his forehead. "Goodnight, handsome."

He lets out a low but exaggerated sigh as I walk away from him. "G'night, Mase."

After I go to bed, the conversation I had with Maddox replays over and over in my head. What if I could have everything I ever wanted? What would that look like? There was a time when I knew exactly how I wanted my future to pan out—and who I wanted to be in it. But like I told myself earlier when Tyler was asking me if I ever bottomed, that was a lifetime ago.

TWO

S crewing my eyes closed, I hope that when I open them again I will have imagined what I just saw. That it won't be her name flashing on the screen of my cell phone. It's so unlike her to call me, even when I go no contact for months at a time. I open one eye and peer at the vibrating phone. Unfortunately for me, it was no mirage.

I blow out a deep breath and answer the call. "Hello, Mother."

"Oh, so you are alive after all, Kyngston. I can't remember the last time we had a phone call. A visit?" Disdain drips from her tone.

I roll my neck, my eyes trained on the man across the street. Indigo Bernard—"Indy" to his friends. "That ungrateful little cunt" to his father. He leans against the red brick wall of the disused library building, his hands

15

shoved in the pocket of his hooded sweatshirt and a cap pulled low over his face, like that will stop him from being recognized. Stupid kid.

"You missed your father's award ceremony," she says.

"Yeah, sorry about that." I lie with ease. Watching a man I despise receive an award for his contribution to society is low on my list of ways I'd like to spend my time —only just above driving a nail through my own skull. "I've been busy with work." I give her my well-rehearsed excuse for my abysmal lack of contact.

Maybe one day I'll tell her the real reason I hate coming home. Her screams of horror and disgust would likely shatter glass all the way here in Chicago. A smile tugs at my lips at the thought. Shame I'm far too much of a fucking coward to actually do it.

Absentmindedly, I run the pad of my thumb over the scar on my pointer finger, tracing the rough edges. The words come back to me, like the chorus of a song you can't forget. *It's only a scratch. Stop crying. You're such a weak little child.*

"Oh, yes. Your work." She sniffs like the word is an insult. And to her, I suppose my line of work is. Yet another way I've let her and the entire Worthington family down. Not going into the family business was another slap to her surgically enhanced face. The fact that she believes my father's legacy of screwing over the less fortunate to be above what I do speaks volumes. Honestly, the woman has the self-awareness of an amoeba.

Indigo glances up and down the street, impatiently tapping his foot against the sidewalk as he waits for his drop.

I grit my teeth. If I don't get over there soon, he'll think I'm not coming. Skittish little fuck has been a nightmare to track down, and I don't have the time or energy to go through this whole charade again. "I have to go. I'll call you—"

"Your grandfather is sick." Her words cut me off at the knees.

He's always sick, but she's never called me about it before. "How sick?" I ask, my heart in my throat.

"It's terminal," she says. Cold. Unfeeling. "He has a month or two at most."

I can't do this with her right now. I focus on Indigo. The slump in his shoulders. Brown curls spilling out from under his cap. The rip in the left knee of his jeans, which are far too big and hang loose on his hips. How he picks at his fingernails, a habit I've observed in him before, noting how he favors the index finger of his left hand.

"He'd like you to come home, Kyngston."

I bristle. I hate that goddamn name, and she knows it.

Indigo pulls his cap lower and pushes himself off the wall. He's twitchy. Ready to run. Shit, I have to move. I end the call and shove the phone into my jacket pocket, ignoring the vibrations against my chest when it rings again. Ignoring everything except my target.

He glances up and sees me. I raise my hand in a brief

wave, letting him know it's me he's waiting for. He's suspicious though, rightly so. He glances up and down the street again.

"You got my money?" I ask, still a few steps away from him.

His beady eyes narrow like he's sizing me up, wondering if he can outrun me. He can't. "You're not my usual guy."

I shake my head. "Tony had some shit to take care of."

"What shit?"

"None of your fucking business, shit for brains. You want this or not?"

I step close enough that I see him trembling, but I would expect no less. I've got at least a foot on him, and I'd guess he weighs a hundred-twenty pounds dripping wet. His survival instinct is probably screaming at him to run, but the rest of him, well, that's jonesing for his next hit. "Y-yeah, I want it."

I wink at him. "Good boy."

His eyes blow wide when I pull the syringe from my pocket. "W-what the fuck, man?"

I grab him by the scruff of his neck. "This is what you wanted, right? Oblivion?"

He struggles and opens his mouth to scream, not that anyone will pay him any mind around here, but I shove a rag between his teeth anyway. Holding my finger to my lips, I tell him to shush.

His eyes are wide with fear now, and he's shaking like

a leaf caught in a storm. "Relax, Indy. This is going to feel real nice, I promise."

I stick the tip of the needle into his arm. "This is some grade A pharmaceutical morphine. Not like that usual shit you inject into your veins." I inject him with it, and his horrified expression is quickly replaced by a look of pure contentment as he slumps into my arms.

I scoop him up and carry him to my car. "Time to get you back to your daddy, kid."

THREE

KING

I greet the staff at the assisted living facility as I pass by the front desk. I know most of them by name after visiting here every other month for the past three years. In case they demand I stop by for dinner, I keep these visits from my parents, and I usually manage to sneak in and out of the city in a single day.

My grandfather's health has been declining for years, and it broke my heart to take him from his Long Island house and put him in here, but like he always does, he settled in easily and made the best of the situation.

When I get into his room, he's dozing peacefully, while a rerun of *Frasier* plays on his TV. I wrap my fingers around his fragile hand and squeeze gently, noticing how little padding there appears to be between flesh and bone. "Hey, Grampa," I murmur.

His eyes immediately flutter open, and he squeezes

back, the faintest of smiles thinning his lips. "There's my boy."

Tears burn behind my eyes, and an intense wave of guilt washes over me. Even if I don't like coming to New York because of them, I should have made more of an effort for him. "I'm sorry it's been a while, Grampa."

"No." He croaks out the word and gives a feeble shake of his head. "You don't get to feel sorry for yourself on my watch, son."

I rest my forehead against his knuckles, feeling like a sinner looking for absolution I will never find. "Are you in pain?"

"Not enough to make me want to quit," he rasps, and it sparks a coughing fit that has him grasping for the oxygen mask at his side.

I take it and press it against his face, gently fixing the elastic strap behind his head. My grandfather has been sickly for as long as I can remember thanks to a congenital heart defect, which has been exacerbated all his adult life by his six-cigars-a-day habit. He's also battled and won two previous bouts of cancer. He is anything but a quitter. He's the man I admire and respect more than anyone else in the world, and it hurts me that I've been away from him for so long. I should have been a better grandson. I should have visited more often.

When he's able to breathe again, he pulls the mask aside. "Your mother is insisting I come home," he says, despondent.

I can hardly believe she wants him home. More like she wants to get her hands on whatever money he has left after he dies. She wants to look like the good, doting daughter she most definitely isn't to her socialite friends. "And how do you feel about that?"

He shrugs. "I do like it here, but the doctors are suggesting it would be best to be with family."

"Then you can stay with me. My place in Chicago has plenty of space, and it's on the ground floor."

"I can't move to Chicago, boy." He shakes his head. "As much as I'd like to raise hell with you there … If I were ten years younger …" He laughs softly. "My doctors are here. My nurses."

"There are doctors and nurses in Chicago, Grampa."

He squeezes my hand. "I'm too old to move halfway across the country, King. Too tired. I just want a little peace."

I stare into his weary green eyes and read the defeat on his face. He is the bravest and toughest man I know, but he has battled hard for almost seventy-nine years. He, of all people, deserves a little peace. "Then I'll get a place here in New York."

"No, no. You can't upend your life like that for me," he says with as much authority as he can muster. "I can go stay with your mother."

That would be the most miserable place I can think of for him to spend whatever little time he has left. "I can take care of you. We can get you round-the-clock care. We can make it work."

"Time for your meds, Arthur," someone with a soft voice says from behind me. A second later, a nurse is standing beside the bed, holding out one of the small paper cups that are usually full of pills.

He nods obediently, the faintest twinkle in his eye when she smiles at him. "Anything for you, Amanda."

He introduces me as his favorite grandson. I remind him I'm his only one, and then I stand and give Amanda room to fuss over him. Fluffing his pillows and combing his hair, she tells him about the disastrous date she had last night. I listen with a smile as he tells her to never settle for a man who doesn't chase after her like he did my grandma. By the time she's done, he's drifting off to sleep again.

"He's such a wonderful character," she says, smiling sadly.

I lower my voice to ensure he can't hear me. "How long does he have?"

She shrugs. "Who can say? Maybe a few months, or maybe less." Her eyes fill with tears, and I can see how much she clearly cares for him. "There's nothing more we can do here. And his doctors think it would be good to spend whatever time he has left with his family ..."

I scrub a hand over my head. Depends on the family.

"Don't you?" she asks.

With me, yes. Maybe I was hasty making the offer to

upend my life and move to New York with him, but if he likes it here, and he has people like this nurse on hand, then wouldn't it be selfish to move him? "He really seems to like you."

That makes her smile again. "I like him too. He has so many fun stories, so many fun anecdotes and words of wisdom. But, well, tomorrow is my last day."

"No? You found something better than this place?" I make a show of looking around the small room, with its pale pink walls and small sash window and the faint smell of antiseptic.

Amanda covers her mouth, stifling her laugh. "I wish," she answers quietly. "No, they're making cutbacks, and I haven't been here very long." She plasters a smile on her face. "But I'll find something."

I make the decision in an instant, knowing I cannot allow my sweet, kindhearted grandfather to spend the last few weeks or months of his life living in a prison of my parents' making. "Then come work for me."

She blinks, a blush creeping over her cheeks. "Excuse me?"

"Well, for him." I gesture at Grampa. "If I get a place by the end of the week, get him all the equipment he needs, would you be his nurse?" I do some quick mental math. His insurance will cover the basics, and I have plenty of savings to cover the rest. It will put a dent in my early retirement plan, but it will be worth it to save Grampa from abject misery.

She gapes at me. "Are you serious?"

"I can't take care of him on my own, and he seems to be really comfortable with you. You'd be doing me a solid."

She glances at my grandfather and then back at me, worrying her lower lip. "I mean I would love to, but I ..." Her blush deepens. "I don't know you."

"I get that. But it wouldn't be a live-in position. And you do know my Grampa. I can advertise for a nurse, but I'd much rather use one he already likes and is comfortable with. I know it won't be a long-term job ..." The reality of those words makes grief clog my throat, and I clear it before continuing. "But you could use the time to line up something else."

"You're sure? Your mother indicated she'd be taking him home."

My mother, who visits him under duress once a month for appearance's sake? I wouldn't put it past her to play the doting daughter impeccably well when the doctors and nurses are around. "He still gets to make his own decisions though, right?"

Amanda nods firmly. "Of course."

"Then he'll be coming home with me. Give me a few days and I'll have a place sorted."

She arches an eyebrow. "Just like that? In New York City?"

I flash her a grin. "Don't worry about it. I know some people." I know a lot of people in New York. I just hope I don't have to call on the one with the most pull, because that's a can of worms I can do without.

FOUR

KING

This is a mistake. I know it is, but I pull up his number anyway. I still have some good contacts in New York, but apparently none of them are connected enough to get me a ground-floor two-bedroom apartment in three days. This is my last resort. Despite how dangerous it might be given the potential Pandora's box I could open, if I don't do this, then I let my Grampa down—not to mention his sweet nurse who, as of today, is out of a job.

I press call, hoping he hasn't changed his number since he moved back to New York. He answers after a few rings. "King? You're a blast from the past, buddy."

I smile at the sound of his voice. It feels like a little slice of Chicago is right here with me. "Hey, Drake. It's been a long time."

"Sure has. What can I do for you?"

I screw my eyes closed and summon all my courage. It pains me to ask for help, having been entirely self-sufficient since the age of eighteen and left to fend for myself from way younger than that. "I need an apartment, and fast. And I was hoping you could help me out. You know anyone who has an empty space available? I figure I'll need it for six months at most. Ground floor or something easily accessible for a wheelchair."

"In Chicago?" He sounds surprised.

"No. New York."

"Oh, I see. Who's the client?"

I run a hand over my head. "Not for a client, Drake. It's for me. Me and my grandfather."

"Shit! You're in New York?"

"Yup."

"Wait until I tell Nathan we have the best PI in the country right here in Manhattan. He's gonna want to meet you. We have a ton of—" He stops speaking and clears his throat. "Sorry, buddy, I got a little carried away there. You said you need a place. For you and your grandfather? Is everything okay?"

The only thing I hate more than asking for help is telling people my personal business. But I suck it up—for Grampa. "My grandfather is sick. He doesn't have long, so I'm moving back here for a while to take care of him."

"I'm sorry to hear that, King." He sounds sincere, and I thank him, but I'm growing increasingly impatient.

"I have a meeting in ten, but then let me make some

calls and see what I can do," Drake says. "We have a few properties, and I'm sure one of them is vacant. I'll check with my brother. He knows more about them than me."

Dread balls in the pit of my stomach. *He has four brothers, King.* There's only a twenty-five percent chance he's going to talk to *that* one.

I take a deep breath and keep a lid on my emotions. If Mason finds out I'm in New York and in need of an apartment, so be it. If I have to beg him to take pity on me, I will. Even if I don't deserve his help, I'll swallow my pride and ask if that's what I need to do. "Thanks, Drake. I appreciate that."

After I end the call, I mentally check another task from my shit list of awkward conversations to have today. Now it's time for the one I'm dreading most.

This old house is no less imposing now than it was when I was a kid—or when I walked out of it eighteen years ago, vowing I'd never set foot in the place again.

And I kept that promise for five long years, but something brought me back. Guilt, perhaps. Or maybe the fact that no matter how far I ran, I was still their son, and nothing could ever change that.

Eventually, I succumbed to my father's requests to come back and visit. I kept them infrequent and brief, twice a year at Easter and Christmas. They were stilted, uncomfortable affairs at first, but as time went on, they grew increasingly tolerable. That was until Christmas a few years ago. Ironically, it was also the Christmas when my parents told me they needed my help.

My father was mixed up with some dodgy shit, which wasn't unusual for Kyngston Worthington III, whose business dealings have always been barely legal. Despite his shady business practices, he's managed to maintain a respectable public facade. However, on this occasion, he got himself in far too deep with the Russian Bratva and had heard I'd done a little work for the Cosa Nostra and the Bratva up in Chicago, so he asked me to use my contacts to "smooth things over."

And of course I was going to help. They're my parents, and some deeply ingrained part of me has always sought their approval, particularly his. And what better way to achieve it than to help them out of a bind. I did also take a little pleasure in thinking about getting my father in a room with Dante Moretti and Dmitri Varkov and having the opportunity to watch him postulate and peacock with men who could wipe him from the face of the earth without breaking a sweat. But I was wholly prepared to help my parents. They were desperate, and I knew it— mostly because my mother managed an entire dinner with no cruel comments or withering looks in my direction.

However, when it came to it, neither of them could help themselves. Couldn't help showing their innate hatred and inherent disgust at what I am.

Grampa came for dinner too, able to tolerate my

mother for the sake of Christmas dinner, even if not my father. We were talking about fishing of all things, surely a safe topic of conversation. Grampa let it slip that his fishing buddy had sparked up one joint too many and fallen asleep on their little boat. He wasn't used to the stuff, but he'd been so stressed about his son's upcoming wedding, and it was his son who'd handed him a couple joints and told him to "chill out."

My mother asked some innocuous questions about the venue and the color scheme and remarked how beautiful a winter wedding in the city could be, and then Grampa dropped the bombshell. Entirely by accident, he let two *he*'s drop into the conversation.

My father's sneer stopped the conversation dead. "His son is marrying another man?"

My blood ran cold.

Grampa rolled his eyes. "Men can marry each other now, Kyngston. Isn't it about time you brought your views out of the Dark Ages?"

"It's disgusting and unnatural." Father spat the words, derision seeping from every cell of his body.

My mother's face twisted in an expression of disgust to mirror his. And even that slight I could have overlooked. I could have endured their disdain for two men I didn't know.

But it was the sideways glance my father gave me, filled with so much revulsion and vitriol. I'd tried to be the good son, had renounced my "mistake" and lived my whole life pretending to be someone I wasn't, had hidden every illicit interaction and came away each time feeling so much shame and guilt that it made me physically sick. Although I did all of that to please them and protect their "wholesome family values" image and their standing in their bigoted conservative circle of friends, it wasn't enough. They hated me anyway. And that look, fleeting as it was, is what I couldn't move past.

Grampa simply shook his head and went back to eating his turkey, and I left. I did smooth over my father's fuck-up because I knew I could, and I didn't want their deaths on my conscience, but I made sure they never found out I had a hand in it.

And now I'm back. Staring at the Gothic mansion and creepy-as-fuck gargoyles and wondering what the hell I'm doing here. I came back to New York for Grampa, not these two. But my mother asked to see me, and … I don't know. Maybe the impending loss of her father has made her more reflective. More … human?

The gravel crunches beneath my feet, and every step I take makes the knot of emotion in the pit of my stomach grow heavier. It's grief and dread and shame all tangled up together, and the farther I get from my bike and the closer I get to the door, the more tangible it becomes. I reach the steps. Now I can taste it. It clambers up my throat, desperate to be let out.

I swallow it down.

The door opens, and a new housekeeper I don't recognize from my last visit offers me a wan smile. "Mr. Worthington." She greets me with a polite, practiced nod.

I follow her into the lounge at the front of the house. My mother's domain. It's overfilled with expensive art: Fabergé eggs and rare nineteenth-century Spanish plates sit beside a Jeff Koons sculpture. A Degas hangs on the wall beside a Hockney.

It's like she collects them because she can. There's no pattern. No attachment to any of the things, merely a desire to have what so many others cannot. She misses the point of art entirely, because not a single piece in this room makes her feel anything.

I do like the Hockney though. It reminds me of a summer I spent with Grampa on Long Island.

My mother sits curled up in a Louis Vuitton cocoon chair with a blanket over her lap and a glossy magazine in her hands. She raises her head a little, eyes glazed. As I suspected due to the time of day, she's already polished off her nightly bottle of wine. At least it used to be one bottle. It could have increased to two or three by now. My mother is a functioning alcoholic. Socialite and investment banker's wife by day, lush by night. She would deny that flat out of course and say her evening wine is merely her way to "unwind." Perhaps anyone having to endure being married to my father needs something. I'm sure I'd be downing more than a bottle of wine every night if I had to live with him. Although *live with* is a stretch. They coexist under the same roof.

"Kyngston." She says my name like an insult—or that's simply how I hear it.

"Hello, Mother." I address her with her preferred title. I was never allowed to call her Mom. It was always mother and father. So fucking stiff and unnatural. The opposite of Grampa. How did a man like him raise the ice maiden in front of me?

He looked so frail earlier. So small and vulnerable. He's not a man big in stature, but he's always been a man who could fill a room with his presence. "I just saw Grampa."

"Oh" is all she says. No emotion. No asking how he's doing or if he's in any pain. You know, normal human responses. Not my mother.

Anger bubbles up in my chest. "He says you want him to move in here."

She sniffs like she smelled something foul. "It's for the best."

"The best for who?" I raise my voice, but she doesn't react to that either. At least with my father there's an occasional display of emotion—albeit mostly hatred and anger—but with her there's nothing. Just ... cold. It's like she's a fucking robot.

She doesn't answer me.

"He's not coming here," I insist.

She regards me coolly. "Then where do you suggest he go, Kyngston? He is too ill to travel to Chicago."

"I'll get us a place. He can stay with me."

"Don't be ridiculous. He will be coming here."

I don't bother arguing further. It's a pointless endeavor with her. She's ungoadable. Unmovable.

"Why did you invite me here?" I ask, sighing.

Her lips twitch like she's trying to force a smile but can't quite manage it. "Your father and I would like you to come home too, darling." *Come home? Darling?* As a rule, that's a term she uses only in public. When she has witnesses.

"I'm leaving, Emmeline." The vaguely familiar voice comes from behind me. And now the darling makes sense.

She manages to muster a faint smile for him. "Goodbye, Graham, darling."

I turn around and come face-to-face with the family lawyer, Graham Reese. He smiles in recognition upon seeing me. "Kyngston?" There's that damn name again. "It's good to see you." He strides into the room and slaps me on the back before grabbing my hand to shake. "How are things?"

I'm immediately suspicious. Graham has been my parents' lawyer for as long as I can remember. He has the charm of a snake-oil salesman and the morals of a shark— like a lot of lawyers in my experience. But what the hell is he doing here?

I squeeze his hand in a firm grip and let him pump mine twice before I pull it away. "Well, my grandfather is dying, so ..."

He closes his eyes for a beat and then plasters on a

sympathetic look. "I was so sorry to hear about Arthur. My condolences."

I scowl. "Aren't condolences for the dead?"

If he's bothered by my reaction, he shows no sign of it. He keeps that fake look of pity on his face and says, "I understand it's only a matter of time."

"We're all dying, Graham." I allow a little of the anger swirling inside of me to bleed into my tone. "Some of us sooner than others."

He blanches, his facade slipping. Hastily, he bids my mother and me goodnight and leaves.

I focus my attention on her again. "Why would you think I'd consider coming home?"

"For your grandfather," she says absently, her attention back on her magazine.

Without another word, I leave the parlor and go to find my father. Can't imagine any encounter with him will be more pleasant than the one with my mother, but at least he'll give me something. And that means there's a much higher chance of getting information from him. I can't shake the feeling that Graham was here for a nefarious purpose—and that his purpose had something to do with Grampa.

My father is drinking a glass of cognac when I walk into his study. The half-empty bottle of Rémy sits open on his desk, with an empty glass I assume to be Graham's sitting beside it. Cognac is my father's drink of choice when he's celebrating something. So what the hell were those two celebrating?

"Kyngston," he says, sneering. "The prodigal son has returned."

I resist the urge to walk out. "You wanted to see me?"

Immediately, his body language and facial expression change. He's less hostile. Businessman Kyngston rather than my father. He indicates the chair opposite his desk, and I drop into it. "You've seen your grandfather, I assume?"

"Of course I have. He's the only reason I came back here."

"He'll be moving in as soon as we can have the equipment he requires set up."

That doesn't make sense. They called me two days ago. Someone with my father's pull could have had that stuff set up in a matter of hours. "Why?"

He blinks at me. "Excuse me?"

"Why is he moving in here?"

"Because he's your mother's father, and he's sick." His tone is incredulous, like I'm a monster for asking such a question.

The rage that simmers beneath my skin when I'm around this man bubbles out of me. "But you fucking hate him."

"How dare you!" His right eye twitches. He wants to argue, maybe even fight me, but he knows better than to try the latter with me these days. Not now that I'm bigger and stronger than he ever was. It grinds his gears that he can't push me around the way he used to. Little does he know that every single weight I lift, every punching bag I hit, every pound of muscle I add to my body—all of it is because of him.

"But it's true, isn't it? You can't stand the man. You never cared about his health before, so why now, *Father*? What's your angle?"

He pulls at the collar of his shirt, visibly working to control his temper. Visible to me at least, the kid who spent years studying him until I learned every tell in his otherwise carefully curated cool persona. It's the mask he wears for his adoring public, but one he can't sustain indefinitely. "There is no angle, Kyngston."

I don't believe that for a second.

He glances at the newspaper on his desk. The headline grabbed my attention too when I saw it earlier today. "I see that actor's kid was finally found. He wasn't kidnapped after all, just went on vacation with some buddies. Ungrateful little upstart. I would have cut him off and left him to rot if it had been me."

Why is he trying to establish rapport in the form of verbal sparring? "Well thank fuck it wasn't you then, eh?"

He scoffs. "Who in their right mind names their kid Indigo anyway? That's looking for trouble if you ask me."

Well, nobody did ask you, you despicable asshole. They can't be worse than the kind of people who name their kids Kyngston. I don't say that to him though. He has something to tell me or something to ask me, and I'm not going to make it easy for him. The less I converse with him, the quicker he'll get to the point of why I'm here, and the quicker I can leave.

I stare out the window behind him, watching droplets of rain run down the glass and wishing I were anywhere but here. Maybe that same feeling is what drove Indigo Bernard out of his house and into the arms of an opiate addiction.

The disgusting noise of my father clearing of his throat snaps me from thoughts of Indigo.

Kyngston Worthington III looks uncomfortable. Edgy. He bristles like his clothes are itching him. And then he smiles. It's not genuine and doesn't reach his eyes, but he's smiling. At me. "Your mother and I would like you to move back here too, Kyngston. While your grandfather is here. To make the last few weeks of his life more comfortable."

So my mother was serious. Of course she was—she's never anything but. It takes every ounce of restraint I have not to laugh in his face. I simply shake my head. "No."

"Kyngston. Please," he says more than asks. "For your grandfather."

All my instincts scream at me to get out of here. He's up to something, but what? He hates both me and my grandfather, probably with equal passion. So what the fuck is his game plan? This can't be about the will. Grampa might have a few hundred grand stashed away in some bank account, but my parents have millions.

My pride wants me to tell him that I'd rather die than spend a night in this house. I'd rather die than let Grampa come and spend his last remaining time with two narcissistic sociopaths who have never shown an ounce of compassion for him.

But prudence kicks in, and I remain silent. I'll move Grampa in with me somewhere. I'll have a lawyer draw up a contract giving me power of attorney if that's what it takes to keep him out of this monster's hands.

I lie with ease. "Let me take a few days to think about it."

"He might not have a few days." His tone is laced with anxiety, but it's not about Grampa. Why is he so desperate?

I shrug. "Take it or leave it."

As I'm climbing onto my bike, Drake's name lights up my phone. I answer it quickly and let out a sigh of relief when he tells me that he spoke to his brother, *Elijah*, and they do have a two-bed, ground-floor apartment in Marble Hill available.

"I can't thank you enough, buddy. You're a lifesaver."

"Anything to help out a friend."

Emotion clogs my throat once more, and I silently curse myself for being so sensitive. What the hell is wrong with me lately? It's just nostalgia. Drake and I shared some good times back in Chicago. He's right—we are friends. Nothing wrong with that. It's not like I purposely sought him out because his last name was James. I had no idea who he was when I first met him.

"I'll ping you the addresses to the apartment and the office of our realtor, and you can pick up the keys tomorrow and make all the necessary arrangements with her," he says, bringing me back to our conversation.

I thank him again.

"You're welcome. I hope you and your grandfather are happy there. If there's anything else I can do ..."

"Actually ..." I tip my chin and look up at the starless sky. "You mentioned work?"

"Yeah?"

According to Amanda, Grampa mostly sleeps during the daytime, and she'll be there to take care of him every day. I'll need something to keep me occupied so I don't lose my mind—or do anything stupid. "I'd be grateful for anything you can toss my way while I'm back here."

He laughs. "King, I have a fuck-ton of work I can send your way. When can you start?"

"How about now?" I offer, eager for a distraction. Anything to stop intrusive thoughts and self-loathing from creeping in and eating up my insides.

"Perfect. You have the same email?"

"Yeah."

"Then I'll send you a file now," he says. "Nothing

overly exciting. It's a nasty lawsuit over some art, but the plaintiff is being very elusive, and I could use someone who knows what they're doing to help track them down."

"Sounds right up my alley. Send it on over."

After agreeing with his assertion that we should meet up for drinks soon, I slip the phone into my pocket and run through today's shit list of to-dos. Get an apartment: check. Visit with the spawn of Satan and his bride: check. Make contact with the brother of the man I should absolutely avoid at all costs: double check.

FIVE

Grampa stares at the keys dangling from my index finger, his face lit up with hope. Amanda stands beside me, hands clasped together as she lets out a squeal of delight. She has been an angel since I met with Drake's realtor yesterday. In less than twenty-four hours, she finished coordinating with Grampa's doctor to get all of the equipment he needs in place. The apartment came fully furnished, so it's ready to go.

"Are you coming home with me then, old man?" I ask, grinning.

"You got an apartment?"

"I told you I would, didn't I?"

"Right here? In New York?"

I nod. "Here in New York. Two bedrooms, fully furnished. Now get your ass out of bed and let's go."

His cackle fills the room, making both me and

Amanda smile. Nurse Hector brings in a wheelchair, and I help Grampa into it while Amanda packs his belongings in a bright pink sparkly suitcase she borrowed from her sister.

"You're really putting my prized worldly possessions in that monstrosity?" Grampa snorts.

"It was the best we could do on short notice. Quit your whining," Amanda tells him.

He flashes me a wicked grin. "It looks like a unicorn ate a tube of glitter and threw it back up again."

I nod my agreement and offer him a cheeky wink while vocalizing that he shouldn't be so ungrateful.

"I think it brings a little pizzazz to the proceedings," Amanda says as she zips it up. "Makes you look young and edgy, Arthur."

That earns her a loud guffaw. "Then it stays."

He nudges me in the ribs when I lean down to tuck his blanket around his legs. "You hear that? She said I'm young and edgy."

"Pretty sure she said the suitcase was, Grampa." I straighten and look around one last time. "I'll come back for the rest of your stuff tomorrow, okay?"

His excitement to get out of here is evident in his eager agreement, and I wheel him down the hallway. On our way out the door, all the staff on duty stop to wish him well and tell him how much they'll miss him. He's an easy guy to like, my Grampa.

"Are we getting to the new place on your motorcycle,

King?" He sounds like a little kid begging to go on his first rollercoaster.

"I think we'll take an Uber," I answer apologetically.

"You could attach this thing like a sidecar." He slaps his palms on the armrests of his wheelchair and chuckles. "Have Amanda ride pillion."

"Now why didn't I think of that?" I exclaim, dramatically smacking my forehead. "I went and left my bike back at the apartment. Dammit!"

His laugh grows louder, and Amanda shoots me a warm smile.

And I enjoy the moment while it lasts.

THE UBER PULLS UP outside the apartment building and I help my grandfather out of the car while the driver takes his chair and suitcase from the trunk.

"Wow! This place looks nice, kid." Grampa whistles, eyes wide. It's a nice red brick apartment complex with a small playground and a parking lot big enough for fifty cars. A space comes with the apartment too, so I have somewhere for my bike. "You did good."

"Yeah, I did," I agree, helping him into his chair.

Amanda wheels the suitcase. "Shall I take this inside?"

"I can handle it. It's heavy."

She rolls her eyes. "I can lift Arthur here in and out of bed without getting winded. I'm sure I can handle a suitcase. On wheels."

Grampa laughs and nudges my leg. "She's a fire-cracker, that one. You better watch her, King."

I hand her the keys and let her go on ahead while I thank the driver. Grampa's scanning the street when we're approached by a woman with long blond hair and a little girl of about three attached to her leg. "You must be the new tenant."

I tell her that I am, and she introduces herself as the super's wife and tells me to holler if we need anything. Her little girl waves at me as they walk into the building, and a man shouting behind me grabs my attention.

I spin around to find my father shaking his fist in Grampa's face. "You deceitful, spiteful, ungrateful fuck!"

Outraged, I grab him by the collar and shove him away. "Who the fuck do you think you are speaking to him like that?"

Grampa is shaking in his chair, and we're drawing attention from passersby. Kyngston Worthington III, respectable Wall Street banker and advocate of good old-fashioned family values can't have that.

"You haven't heard the last of this." He points a finger in my direction and climbs into a waiting car. It drives away, leaving Grampa and I staring after it, wondering what the hell just happened.

Amanda comes out of the apartment building and blows a strand of hair from her face, her cheeks flushed pink. Thankfully, she didn't witness my father's outburst, but she sees the aftermath: Grampa still trembling with fear and me with rage. I should drive after the heartless prick and smash his face in.

"Is everything okay?" she asks.

I squeeze Grampa's hand in mine and run a soothing hand over his shoulder. "Everything's okay," I reassure them both. "Let's get you inside."

After Amanda and I finish fixing his room, she heads to the deli on the corner to get us some sandwiches for lunch, which she assures me are to die for. Her aunt lives a few blocks away, and she knows the area pretty well, which is good for Grampa and me.

I hand Grampa a mug of his favorite English breakfast tea and perch on the arm of the couch beside his oversized armchair. "All right, Grampa," I say, keeping my tone light. "Time to tell me what the hell is going on." He's still pretty shaken, and I don't want to upset him any more than he already has been, but he's hiding something from me.

"Can't we just leave it, King? I'm here now. With you. That's all that matters."

I angle my body so that I'm facing him. "Why did my father react the way he did? I've never seen him lose his temper like that in public before. If something is going on that affects you, then it matters. Please don't keep me in the dark."

His deep-green eyes fill with tears. "I didn't want to manipulate you. I didn't mean to." A tear runs down his cheek.

I give his knee a reassuring squeeze. "You don't have a

manipulative bone in your body, old goat. But you gotta tell me what's going on."

He nods, swallowing hard. "Your parents found out about the will. I don't know how. No doubt that shark of a lawyer they have."

That explains Reese's presence the other night, but not much else. "Your will?"

"No. Your grandma's will." His eyes sparkle when he talks about her. They always do. Both my parents came from money, but in my mom's case, that money came from her mom. She died when I was a baby, and although I feel like I know her from the way Grampa kept her memory alive, I have none of my own memories of her.

They adored each other, my grandparents. I used to wonder what my life would have been like if she'd been alive while I was growing up. Grampa was deemed too unwell to take care of me permanently, but I used to fantasize about living with them in their Long Island house rather than the prison of my parent's home. When Grandma died, Grampa lived a modest if comfortable life. I remember hearing my father grumble about her missing millions, but it never meant anything to me. He grumbled about a lot of things.

"What about grandma's will?" I ask. "Wouldn't that have all been taken care of years ago?"

His face lights up. "Your grandma was a smart woman, King. And she knew I'd never spend all her money. It wasn't mine to spend, you see."

"So ... You have money?" I ask, shaking my head. "Grandma's money? That's what all this is about?"

He nods. "A little over twenty-five million, I think. My financial guy invests and such, but I don't keep much of an eye on it."

Wow! The old goat has twenty-five million sitting in a bank somewhere. But what good has it done him? I wish he'd spent more and enjoyed it. Then again, Grampa has always been the type to prefer lemonade on a beach over champagne on a yacht.

"But doesn't it all go to Mother anyway?" I recall hearing her and my father discussing his will once, when he was suffering from a serious case of pneumonia. Tasteless, much like every other thing about them.

He looks around surreptitiously, a knowing smile on his face. "That's one part of the will. Not the secret clause, which will only be read upon my death. In my will."

"A secret clause?"

He nods. "I can't change even if I wanted to. Your mom will get the million dollars that your grandma earmarked for her, but as for everything else, she only gets that on the event ..." He screws his eyes closed.

"On the event of what, Grampa?"

His eyes are full of tears when he reopens them. "My Josephine was such a caring woman, you see. She knew I'd always have my health battles. Heck, I'm sure she'd be surprised I lasted to the ripe old age of seventy-nine."

I squeeze his knee again. "Grampa?"

He sucks in a breath. "Your grandma's clause states that the family member who looks after me at the end gets the money. Your parents must have found out because when they visited last week, they insisted that I would be coming to live with them. They were all fake smiles and polished words. I saw right through them, but, well, what was I going to do with all that money when I'm gone? So I agreed." He places his gnarled hand over mine. "I'm sorry, King. And of course I've already provided for you, my boy. You know that, right?"

In all honesty, I never gave it much thought. I haven't requested a penny from my family since I left, and I assumed my parents would find a way to cut me out of Grampa's will. "I don't care about your money."

He smiles. "I know."

"So, what? You agreed to go stay with them? Was that your plan until I showed up?"

"You showing up was my only plan, King. I'm sorry." Tears run down his face once more.

"What do you mean?" Then it falls into place. My father kindly asking me to move back. Mother saying she wanted me to come home. Reese acting happy to see me. "You told them you'd only move back there if I came too."

He nods sadly. "I ... I thought they'd find a way to make me move in with them anyway. Have me declared mentally unfit or something. I didn't intend for you to upend your whole life in Chicago and get a place of your own in New York. I know I don't have long, so I thought you might be able to tolerate it for a few weeks. Because the only thing that could have made living with your parents bearable would have been to have you there. I'm sorry, son."

I wrap my arms around him, filled with regret and guilt that I haven't been there for him the way he always was for me. "You don't have to be sorry for anything, Grampa. I'm glad you got me back here. I wouldn't change this for anything."

He sniffs. "You wouldn't?"

"No. Being able to spend this time together, just you and me—that's the best gift anyone could have ever given me. I'll take that over twenty-five million any day."

He laughs and pats the back of my head, and I release him from my embrace. "Well, now you'll get both."

"You coming to live with me means he doesn't get the money? That's why he turned up here so pissed!"

"Exactly."

Well, fuck me. Pissing my parents off to the tune of twenty-five million dollars is the cherry on top of an already great day.

I slide the large envelope across the desk to Drake.

He opens it and peers inside at the collection of photographs. They're also on a thumb drive, but I prefer to go old school and print them too. Anything online can be wiped, but photographs are cold, hard evidence.

"Thanks, buddy," he says. "Nobody ever gets the job done as quickly as you."

I shrug. "It wasn't exactly taxing." I'm used to much more interesting cases than the cheating husband I caught nailing his personal trainer in the back of her Mercedes.

He offers me a sympathetic smile. "I'm sorry I don't have anything more exciting for you, buddy." He tosses the envelope onto his desk. "I'm up to my ass in corporate lawsuits and messy divorces. I have to say, my wife much prefers me doing this kind of work than the kind we did back in Chicago."

"You ever miss the place?" Before moving back to New York over a year ago, Drake headed up the Chicago branch of James and James, which was where he and I met ten years ago. James is a popular last name, and it didn't occur to me that Drake James in Chicago was connected to Mason James in New York. When it did occur to me, I'd been working for him for months and we were already friends—as much as men like us ever have friends. I figured he was in Chicago for a reason and that he'd left New York behind the same way I did. If he knew who I was, he was clearly unbothered by it, so why should I be?

He shakes his head. "Nope. Everything I love most in the world is right here. You?"

I don't actually know if it's Chicago I miss or if it's the freedom of being away from the Worthington name. Any city would probably be better than New York. "I miss the work there. You'd think New York would have a much more interesting clientele."

Drake laughs. "They do, but unlike the Morettis, our New York clients have their own super hacker at their disposal. And believe me, she needs no help from anyone."

"Sounds like an interesting setup."

Drake's lips curve and he nods. "Oh, it is, buddy."

I glance at my watch. "I have another meeting to get to. But everything you need is in the envelope. Best of luck."

Drake stands and shakes my hand. "Thanks. I promise I'll try and find something more interesting for you."

"Hey, I'm grateful for any work you can throw my way. I appreciate it."

"No thanks needed, man. As soon as you said you were in New York, I knew I needed to get you in here. There's a reason we call you Hotshot, and that's because you're the best at what you do."

I can't help but smile at the familiar nickname, although it seems like a while since I've felt like the best at anything. The shadow of my father's disapproval is far too close when I'm in this city.

"Thank you for meeting with me, Mr. Blackthorn." Curtis Jones indicates the chair opposite, and I take a seat. My new potential client is a used-car salesman. Originally from Connecticut, he now lives alone in a New Jersey townhouse. Widowed. Father of one.

"No need to thank me," I say. "Tell me what I can do to help."

He inches forward, and the lines etched deep on his face make him look much older than his forty-two years. "I want you to find my daughter."

I suspected this was the job he wanted to hire me for when I looked into him. He filed a missing persons report for Cassidy Jones thirteen months ago, and the cops uncovered a string of text messages between him and Cassidy which not only revealed they'd had a huge falling out over her choice to drop out of college and become an exotic dancer, but also that she threatened to leave the state and never speak to him again.

A week after her alleged disappearance, she paid off the remaining lease on her apartment using her credit card and gave notice she was moving out via email, which led the to the conclusion that she'd made good on her threat to leave. So they closed the case.

"I understand the police have looked into her disappearance and ..." I stop speaking. There's no delicate way to say this, and he's clearly grieving.

"Yeah, I know what they say." His nostrils flare, and he continues. "And yes, we had a huge fight. I didn't always agree with her life choices, Mr. Blackthorn, but she was still my little girl. She threatened to stop speaking to me at least once every couple of months, but she would never actually do it. We made up after that fight. She came to my place for dinner after. We were good."

"Maybe this time she did mean it. Maybe it was a farewell dinner?"

His knuckles turn white. Curtis is a man with a temper, and he appears to be clinging to his last shred of it. "She's a good kid. She would never be so inconsiderate to run away and never contact me again. Something happened to her."

I shake my head. "If the police—"

"Fuck the police!" he roars. "If she simply up and left, why is there no trace of her anywhere? Can you answer me that, Mr. Blackthorn? Yes, I know the bullshit about her lease, but someone could have easily stolen her card and sent that email if they had access to her phone. Four PIs I hired to track her down, and not a single one could find a shred of evidence as to her whereabouts. Not a credit card receipt, a doctor's visit, traffic violation, or even a paycheck. Nothing!"

"Perhaps she simply doesn't want to be found, Mr. Jones."

He snorts a laugh. "She's a twenty-one-year-old community college dropout, Mr. Blackthorn, not a criminal mastermind. We're a working-class family. She doesn't have the money to disappear like that even if she did have the know-how. That kind of ability to disappear is only afforded to those who can afford it, if you know what I mean."

The accusation in his tone makes me bristle.

His right eye twitches. "There's a reason I contacted you specifically, Mr. Blackthorn."

I'm the best at what I do, asshole. But I have a sinking feeling that's not the reason I'm sitting here today. I grind my teeth. "And why is that?"

"I know who you really are. Mr. Worthington." He keeps his eyes on my face, waiting for me to react.

My insides churn, but I don't give him the satisfaction of showing that the name gets to me. "And what? Would you like some kind of medal for your efforts? It's no secret I changed my name, Mr. Jones. Anyone could look that up."

Nodding, he places his forearms on the table and leans forward. "It's not that you changed your name that interests me though—it's why."

My hands ball into fists at my sides, but I retain my calm exterior. "And why do you think that is?"

He goes on regarding me with curiosity. "I don't exactly know, but I do know that you left New York eighteen years ago and that you changed your name shortly after. Took your mother's maiden name, I believe."

So he doesn't know why I changed my name, but why is he fishing and why does it matter to him? "And?"

"I figure a guy does that because he actually hates his father and wants nothing to do with him, rather than a kid who's simply mouthing off about it."

"Like your daughter was?" I push back.

He simply nods. "We didn't have the easiest relationship. It was just me and her after her mom died, and it was fucking tough raising a headstrong teenage girl. But we love each other, Mr. Blackthorn. She is all I fucking have."

"So you reached out to me because you assume I actually do hate my father?" I ask, still not able to put all the pieces together.

He leans closer, and the sadness in his dark eyes is now tinged with fury. "You are my last resort, Mr. Blackthorn. Not because you're good at what you do, but because of who you are."

What the fuck does that mean? I remain silent, letting him play his hand before I reveal mine.

"I hope you hate your father, Mr. Blackthorn. I sincerely hope you hate him as much as I do."

Now he has my attention.

"Because he knows something about my little girl's disappearance. I am one hundred percent sure of it."

What the fuck? I breathe in through my nose, maintaining the calm facade that serves me well in this job even as my heart pounds violently against my ribcage and my mind is flooded with questions. My father is a cruel piece of shit, but this? Could he truly be involved in Cassidy's disappearance? "And you think that his only son is the person you want looking into this? That sounds like quite the risk, Mr. Jones."

He scrubs his hands through his hair, leaving it sticking up and giving him a stronger air of desperation. "A risk I have no option but to take. I have nowhere else to turn. The cops won't do anything. And every PI runs for the hills once I mention your father's name. For some reason, he's untouchable in this part of the country, in case you didn't know that."

Oh, I fucking know it better than anyone.

Curtis's eyes narrow to slits. "But I figure you do know that, and that's why you left. And if I'm wrong ..." Defeat weighs his shoulders down. "Well, I already have nothing left to lose."

Jesus fucking Christ. I can't take this case, can I? I can't look into my own father for something like this, no matter how much I hate him. "Why is it you think my father is involved?" I ask, too curious to walk away without knowing more.

"He was the last guy she gave a private dance to in that club she worked at."

"And? I'm sure she gave plenty of guys a private dance."

Curtis shakes his head. "But he ..." His lip curls in a sneer. "He was the one. Her boss at the club told me your father really took a shine to her. He visited a few times and was only ever interested in her. He was the cause of our last argument."

"How so?" I ask.

"She'd been telling me for weeks about this man, some guy with lots of money and influence. Despite what the cops thought, I didn't hate her job. I wanted her to be safe, and I disliked that she was constantly looking for an easy way out. And when she came to see me the day before she disappeared, she told me she'd already quit her job because this asshole asked her to. She said he was gonna take care of her. Gonna set her up in her own fancy place so she wouldn't have to work again. She didn't give me his name, but now I know it was your father. It makes perfect sense."

Does it? There are coincidences, but surely that's all they are. "Because she danced for him? That's quite the leap."

He shakes his head. "No, not because of that. It was the tattoo. That's how I know it was him."

"The tattoo?"

"The day she quit, she went and got herself a tattoo, right across the top of her back." He traces his fingers over his shoulders. "It was healing when she came to visit, and I told her she was an idiot for defiling her body like that."

Aware of my own visible tattoos, I arch an eyebrow at him.

"I have nothing against tattoos. But she got a tattoo for some guy she barely knew."

I lean forward. "What was the tattoo, Mr. Jones?"

His eyes narrow. "It was a crown, and right beneath it, right across her back, were the words 'King's Princess.' Kyngston fucking Worthington."

My blood runs cold. Memories of overheard hushed conversations flicker through my mind. *I'll be there when I can, princess. I need you too, princess. Be patient, princess.* He called them all princess. That way he never needed to remember their names.

It's still a leap, but my gut tells me my father was indeed her rich guy. However, I'm self-aware enough to know that's my own bias speaking, and the straws Curtis Jones is grasping at are made of very thin paper. "There are hundreds of rich and powerful men in New York, Mr. Jones."

"Yeah, but not a lot of them go to some seedy club for a lap dance, do they? I'm sure they have higher-class, more discreet establishments they prefer to frequent. But your father just happened to visit there the day before she quit. And then she disappeared a few days after she started telling me about a guy so rich he was gonna take care of her and she'd never have to work again. That ain't no coincidence, Mr. Blackthorn, and we both know it."

"I assume you told the police all of this?"

"Of course I fucking did. But they spoke with him, and he never denied paying for a dance at the club. He denied ever seeing her before or after that though, and obviously because he's who he is and I'm some shmuck used-car salesman ..." He doesn't finish the sentence, and he doesn't have to. My father has far too much influence in this little corner of the world.

"When was the last time you heard from your daughter, Mr. Jones?"

He blinks, surprised. "You're taking the case?"

I run my tongue over my front teeth. Am I? "I'll look into it, but I want to get some more details from you to make sure they match up with what's in the report."

His entire body seems to sag with relief. "Thank you, Mr. Blackthorn."

"Call me King."

I read the headline again and scowl. "I can't believe this shit! Once is a coincidence, twice is fucking sabotage. Somebody gave them that information, Elijah. Someone at *our* fucking company."

Elijah frowns across the dining table while nodding his agreement. "The Fuller patent could have been put down to coincidence given we were all chasing the same goal, but this one was ours. Nobody knew about it. When I find out who leaked that information, I will ..." His sentence is cut off by a snarl.

Nathan takes the newspaper from me and scans the article again. We've all read it at least half a dozen times. It's the reason all of us James boys, along with our dad, canceled our weekend plans and are sitting in our childhood home on a Saturday morning. "So this is definitely a leak?" he asks, his brow furrowed.

"Nobody but key people in our organization knew about that patent. And now here it is, splashed across the *New York* fucking *Times* by Spartan." I growl the name of our biggest competitor. Before now, despite our guts telling us something different, the contracts they won over us could be explained. They're a well-established company, almost as old as ours. And while they're not as big, their relatively new CEO is some young genius entrepreneur, at least that's what Astyn Bartley was named by *Time* magazine last year. We lose out on contracts all the time—it's part of business. But this tech was ours, and the patent was being filed Monday morning. Spartan, those fuckers, filed theirs yesterday afternoon.

"I can't believe it. In our own company," Pop says sadly.

I give him a reassuring squeeze on the shoulder. "We'll find out who it was, Pop."

"And fucking destroy them," Elijah snaps.

"So what's the plan?" Drake asks. "The people who knew about that patent will also have seen this article. Everyone will be suspicious and twitchy as fuck."

"But they'll also be eager to find out whoever the fuck did this, because they've potentially put their jobs on the line too," Nathan adds.

"We'll get everyone involved in tomorrow," I say. "Don't give a damn that it's Sunday. Between us, we'll be able to tell who's lying."

"What if it's not one of the people involved in the patent though?" Maddox says as he places a plate of freshly baked chocolate chip cookies on the table. Cooking is his love language. I'd prefer Scotch at a time like this, but they smell incredible. All of us except Pop, who's watching his diet, reach for one.

I finish chewing and ask, "What do you mean?"

"You said the information was leaked? Then it could have been anyone in the company with access to your systems. Theoretically."

Elijah shakes his head. "Our firewalls are locked down tight, and we check for security breaches every day. There haven't been any reported."

Maddox takes a bite of a cookie. "I know you guys work in tech, but it's developing faster than anyone can keep up with. With the strides in AI and whatnot, who's to say it's not some disgruntled minion who got passed up for a promotion or has no morals and wants to make a fast buck."

I finish my second cookie and debate reaching for a third. Fuck, they're good. "Bro has a point."

Elijah regards him intently. "You sure you don't want to come work in the family business, Mad?"

Maddox scoffs. "Fuck no."

Our father huffs—he built that business from nothing —but Maddox flashes him a warm smile that instantly appeases the old man. It's so good to see them together after everything that happened before Maddox left. It brings a lump to my throat when I recall him storming out of this house and swearing he'd never come back. It was years before he did.

"We still need to talk to everyone involved in that project," Elijah says, bringing me back to our current problem. "It doesn't hurt to lay our cards out on the table. Make them sweat a little."

"It will have to be tomorrow," I remind him. "I leave for the conference in Philly Monday morning and won't be back until Wednesday."

Elijah signals his agreement.

"If it is a leak at Jamestech, can the security team be fully trusted?" Nathan says.

Pop sighs. "Until we find out exactly who it is, everyone is a suspect. And if this goes back to the last patent Spartan took from under our noses, it's been going on for a year at least."

"Could be longer," I add. "Who knows what other information Spartan has been handed."

Pop's lips flatten into a thin line. "Then I'll wager it's not going to be easy to find out who it is. They obviously haven't done anything to come to our attention in the monthly security sweeps."

Nathan leans back in his chair and runs a hand over his beard. "It could be someone from security."

"So we need to hire someone from outside. Someone we've never worked with before?" I suggest.

Elijah looks around the table. "Any of you know any decent PIs?"

Drake's eyes light up.

"Are you thinking Jessie Ryan would help?" Elijah asks. The Ryans are some of Nathan and Drake's biggest clients. They're also Irish Mafia.

Nathan shakes his head. "I'm not sure we need to involve them at this stage, not unless we need a hacker. And as much as I respect them, they're still the mob. Besides, Shane keeps riding my ass about them having me on retainer and not the other way around."

"And Jessie is pregnant, so they're more protective than usual," Drake adds, pulling off his tie and stuffing it into his jacket pocket. "I was thinking of someone else, anyway. He's a guy I used in Chicago."

I rest my forearms on the table and take another bite of cookie. "A good PI?"

"Better than a PI," Drake says. "I believe the Morettis call him a fixer."

Nathan rolls his eyes. "So, we're gonna jump into bed with the Italian Mafia instead of the Irish mob?"

The irony of him being the one who objects to bringing this guy on board is too good not to comment on. "More of your closest friends."

"Yeah, well," he says, shrugging. "But my point still stands. Jamestech is a legitimate multi-billion-dollar corporation."

Drake shakes his head. "This guy isn't Mafia. He's legit, I swear. He's the one renting out the apartment in Marble Hill."

Elijah frowns, and I can see him running down the extensive list of properties we own. We have a lot of properties in New York, and they're managed by a realtor, but Elijah knows more about them than the rest of us. "The guy who's looking after his sick grandfather?"

Drake nods. "Yes. See, he's a good man. And he's really fucking good at his job. Back in Chicago, they call him Hotshot."

"Hotshot?" I roll my eyes. But I guess he can't be as pretentious as his name suggests if he's looking after his sick grandpa.

Drake grins. "Don't worry, Mase, he's nowhere near as cool as you."

I return his grin and flip him the bird.

Ignoring me, he continues. "That's what people called him. He helped me out with a few really tough cases. Plus, he happens to be in New York right now, and he's looking for a case to get his teeth into."

Elijah's already nodding, the cogs turning in his brain. "Can you set up a meeting with him for Monday?"

Drake smiles and leans back in his chair. "Yeah, I don't think that'll be a problem. That okay with you, Mase?"

I nod. "Sure. Elijah can meet with the hotshot and fill me in on the details."

Drake smirks at me. "Wait until you meet him. You'll find out what I mean."

Well, now I'm all kinds of intrigued and looking forward to meeting him when I get back. Let's see exactly how *hot* Drake's guy actually is. Figuratively speaking, of course—I don't mix business with pleasure.

CHAPTER

EIGHT

KING

A bead of sweat trickles down my back, and I glance around the elegant glass reception area of Jamestech. I have no fucking clue why I agreed to this. When Drake called on Saturday and asked me to meet with his older brother because he had a case for me, I said yes before I had a chance to think it through. Older ruled out the brother I'm trying to avoid at least, even if he is COO of this company.

How the fuck do you expect to avoid him, asshole?

This was a mistake. A huge fucking mistake. I should leave and tell Drake something else came up. No hard feelings. No big deal. No chance of an incredibly tense and awkward encounter with Mason James.

I turn around to leave and come face-to-face with a slightly older and broader version of Drake. "Mr. Blackthorn?" he says, offering his hand.

69

"Elijah?"

He nods, giving my hand a firm shake. His dark-gray eyes hold mine, and we assess each other the way most alpha males would in this situation. Like me, he's probably forming an opinion in only a few seconds. From the neatly trimmed beard, the pristine and expertly tailored suit, and the lack of fine lines around his eyes, I gather that he's organized, respectable, calm under pressure. Laughs only when absolutely necessary. Of course, I also researched him thoroughly before my meeting today.

"Call me King."

He indicates the elevator a few feet away. "Shall we?"

ELIJAH'S OFFICE is like one of those you see in slick TV shows: all glass and sleek lines but filled with antique furniture. Dripping with wealth. It's as big as the entire Marble Hill apartment—an office befitting the CEO of a multi-billion-dollar tech corporation. I sit in an Elysium chair, aware my ass is encased in a seat more expensive than my bike, and listen intently as Elijah fills me in on the leak at Jamestech.

Already, I suspect it wasn't one of the four people involved in the actual project. More likely, someone who shouldn't have been able to somehow accessed the files, but I keep those thoughts to myself for now. Until I know better, every person at this company whose last name isn't James is a suspect.

When he's done speaking, he studies me while I turn everything over in my mind.

"Drake tells me you're the best at what you do, King."

"He flatters me."

That gets me a short laugh. "If you know him as well as he says you do, you'd know he doesn't do flattery. That's our brother Mason's department."

The mention of his name sends a shudder up my spine and kicks my heart rate up at least two gears. I grind my teeth, hoping Elijah doesn't notice my reaction.

He does notice. Fuck. "He runs all our marketing and PR," he explains. "Flattery is part of his job."

I know what Mason does. I read the article about him stepping up as COO a hundred times or more. And the accompanying image of him flashing that easy smile full of charm and arrogance in his perfectly fitted navy suit and white shirt is burned into my consciousness. I've read every article I could find on him in the past eighteen years, seen far too many pictures of him with whatever actor or model he was dating at the time, and always been secretly relieved when not a single one of them seemed to last more than a few weeks. The press branded him a playboy by the time he was in his early twenties, and he sure lives up to the title.

I shouldn't take this job. But it's too fucking intriguing to pass up. And perhaps this is my chance for ...

For what, fuck-knuckle? Redemption? Nothing you can ever do will get you that.

I clear my throat. "Will I be reporting to you? PR isn't really my thing."

He gives a single nod. "Yes, you'll report to me for the most part. And we'd like to keep your role here between us —that is my brothers and me. To explain your presence, all of our employees will be advised that you're under-taking an audit. Nobody else is to know why you're here."

I really shouldn't take this job.

"So are you in?" Elijah asks.

It's a mistake. I can't work for Mason James.

"King?" Elijah's voice is tinged with frustration.

"Yeah, I'm in."

CHAPTER

NINE

MASON

I never stay at the hotel where conferences are held, preferring my own privacy over having to make small talk with people I'll never see again—or worse, getting hit on by drunk tech guys who are too young to understand that Green Day is a punk-rock band and not a national holiday for vegans. But as I'm the keynote speaker at this particular event, I make an effort to attend the meet and greet on day one and speak to people before they get wasted on the free sparkling wine.

Sean Phillips, the VP from a tech company we do a lot of business with, greets me as soon as I walk into the conference center. "Mason. It's so good to see you, buddy." He doesn't bother with any attempt at a formal handshake and instead wraps me in a bear hug. "How the fuck are you?"

I clap him on the back. "Good. You?"

Smiling, he pulls his cell out of his pocket. "Fucking aces, buddy. You wanna see the twins?"

Not particularly, but the enthusiasm in his voice stops me from saying that. A few seconds later, he pulls up a fuck-ton of pictures of two cute babies, each with a shock of white-blond hair.

"They're adorable. How old are they now?"

He's still beaming, scrolling through picture after picture. "Coming up on six months. You know they change so much every day at this age. Makes me really want to reevaluate my life and the hours I'm putting in, you know?" He comes to a stop at a picture of him and his husband, Rick, each proudly holding a baby in their arms.

Thinking of my own workaholic brothers and the change in them, I agree. "Yeah. Marriage and kids will do that to you, I hear."

"Fuck. I must be boring you stiff." He slips his phone back into his pocket and offers an apologetic shrug.

He wasn't boring me, per se. We're just at very different stages of our life. It wasn't always this way. Up until about three years ago, he was terminally single, like me. But then he met Rick. They were married within the year and promptly found a surrogate who delivered them twin daughters. "Not at all."

"Tell me what's going on with you," he says, graciously changing the subject.

"No husband and kids on the horizon quite yet," I assure him.

He throws his head back and laughs like I told the funniest joke in the world. A joke I don't get. "Yeah, right." He wipes an actual tear from the corner of his eye.

"Why is that so funny?"

It must be the sharp tone of my voice that turns his smile into a perplexed frown. "You? The eternal bachelor? Married with kids?"

I bristle, feeling defensive for reasons I don't understand. Never in my life have I been insulted by anyone's assumption that I'm not the settling down kind of guy. In fact, I cultivate it, so why the hell am I getting so pissy with Sean? It has to be spending time with my nephew. Adorable little jerk. "It could happen," I insist.

Sean's demeanor changes entirely. Either he's remembered Jamestech is a primary shareholder in his company, or he's genuinely worried he hurt my feelings. Probably both. He's a nice guy, and I have no idea why I'm so rattled this afternoon. "I didn't mean to offend you. It's just that ..." He winces rather than finishing the sentence.

"Just what?"

He blows out a breath. "You remember that summer we went on a few dates?"

I remember it was a scorching hot July, and he was working in New York for a few months. My recollection of that time is that we had some fun and there were no hard feelings when he had to head back to Philly. We've stayed friends ever since. "Yeah."

"I asked you if you wanted to come see me in Philly,

and you almost had a fucking stroke. I've never seen anyone ask for a check so quickly in my whole goddamn life."

"We agreed it was a casual thing though," I say. "Didn't we?"

He winces again. "You offered casual, and I was so fucking smitten, I agreed."

I arch an eyebrow. "You were smitten? Really? Did you, a thirty-six-year-old man with a Harvard degree, really use the word smitten?"

He laughs and shakes his head. "You have no idea of the fucking tornado you are, do you, Mason James? You blow into people's lives and turn them upside down before moving on like nothing happened."

What the fuck? "I truly don't understand what you're saying. You never said you wanted more. We stayed friends all these years, and you never ..." I pinch the bridge of my nose, feeling a tension headache building.

Sean places a hand on my shoulder. "Yeah, I wanted more. But you made it very clear that more wasn't on the table. And I'm not trying to make you feel bad. I'm sorry if I have. You were one hundred percent up front about what you wanted, and I went into it knowing exactly what I was getting myself into. I welcomed the tornado with open arms, well aware I was headed for nothing but heart-break." He follows that up with a smile.

He's messing with me, surely. "If I broke your heart, then why are we still friends?"

His eyes twinkle. "The same reason most of your exes remain your friends, Mason. You're impossible to dislike. And sometimes I suppose it's for the occasional *benefit* that comes with being your friend."

"Benefit?"

"Like when we went to the cryptocurrency conference in Vegas."

When we won ten thousand dollars playing poker, got fall-down drunk, and still managed to fuck all night? That conference in Vegas?

"I met Rick a few weeks later, and he finally cured me of my Mason James habit."

Well, that's good to know. I think. "So now we're friends because ...?"

"Because you're funny and smart, and I get to be entertained by your exciting love life." He nudges my elbow. "How many of these greedy young tech geniuses have you fucked so far?" The conference center is filled with hundreds of young smartly dressed men and women who are just starting out in the careers and will no doubt be hanging on my every word when I deliver the keynote speech tomorrow. "I only got here this morning, Sean."

"Only two or three, then?" He snorts a laugh.

I straighten my tie. "I don't fuck people I work with. And you don't count because we didn't work together then."

"I do miss the freedom sometimes though," he says with a wistful sigh. "I adore Rick and want to wake up with only him for the rest of my life, but it's still quite the realization when you're confronted with the fact that this is it."

"Mr. James?" The woman who interrupts our conversation introduces herself as Dana, the VP of a new start-up that is looking for investors. She tells me what a huge fan she is and how much she's looking forward to my speech, but I'm uncharacteristically distracted.

Ordinarily, I'd be listening intently to Dana's pitch, because that's what it is, and I'd probably give her some pointers too. But I'm only half listening. The other half of my brain is replaying my conversation with Sean and dissecting everything he said.

Just because he had that experience doesn't mean I'm a tornado blowing in and out of people's lives. Does it? While I do remain friends with most of my exes, it's not for *benefits*, at least not on my part. I go over and over it, trying to think of other examples where guys have wanted more than I could offer. I'm sure there must have been some, but I'm usually checked out of the relationship before any meaningful conversations about feelings can take place. And like Sean said, I'm totally up front about my expectations, so why the hell is this bothering me now when it hasn't for years?

And then I recall what he said about only waking up with one person for the rest of your life. I can't imagine what that would feel like. Only knowing one body. One person's likes and dislikes. What makes them tick. What makes them fall apart and rebuild. It's not something I have any interest in, so why does what he said play over and over in my head all damn afternoon and into the evening? So much so that when the hot-as-fuck bartender at my hotel—who is exactly my type with a dusting of stubble and tattoos running all the way down to his knuckles—suggests we "grab a drink" after his shift finishes, I tell him I have to be up early for work. Not a lie, but also not a factor that's ever stopped me from taking a guy back to my room before.

I almost convince myself it's because I'm tired and that it has nothing to do with my chat with Sean earlier today. Almost.

TEN

MASON

"How was the trip, Boss?" Hayden asks in greeting. The human resources executive is perched on the edge of my secretary's desk outside my office like he's been waiting for my return.

Please tell me there's been no more drama in my absence. Elijah didn't mention any, but sometimes Hayden likes to filter bad news through me instead of taking it to my older brother.

"Good. Got what I needed to do done. Everything okay?"

He nods. "Yeah. I was just passing by your office and ..." He looks at the closed door. "Wondered if you were back yet, and then I saw you walking down the hall."

"Hey!" Elijah places a warm, strong hand on my shoulder from behind. "It's good to have you back. I have someone you need to meet."

I suspect it's the hotshot. He started Monday, and Elijah says he's good, so he must be. My brother isn't easily impressed. But that's all I know about the guy. Since his work for our company isn't exactly common knowledge, I don't ask for more details in front of Hayden.

I follow Elijah to his office, and Hotshot is already there, staring out the window with his back to us. His arms are crossed and his shoulder muscles bulge against the fabric of the tight white T-shirt he's wearing. Guy is fucking huge and not exactly inconspicuous. What kind of auditor wears jeans and a T-shirt and looks like a linebacker?

"Mason, I'd like you to meet King Blackthorn."

King? The shadow of a memory associated with that name burrows to the surface, and he turns around at the sound of my brother's voice. The second our eyes meet, I am assaulted by so many memories that it feels like someone has punched me in the stomach. I'm certain all the oxygen has been sucked from the room. My head spins, my heart pounding. I'm going to pass out. Or have a stroke. Through sheer force of will, I force myself to look him in the eye and not run out of Elijah's office.

"Hi, Mason." He has the gall to say my name, to speak to me like nothing ever happened. As though eighteen years ago he didn't rip out my heart and stomp all over it. And suddenly I'm that kid again, feeling worthless and used and ...

I draw in a breath and push down the hurt dredged up at the mere sight of him.

So he's going to pretend that this is all normal? That he and I don't share a deeply fucked-up history? I focus on my rage and shove aside the maelstrom of other unpleasant emotions swirling through my body. Two can play at that game, *Hotshot*. "Mr. Blackthorn. Nice to meet you." My voice is calm and even despite every cell in my body vibrating with anger.

Elijah checks his watch and winces. "I have to meet a new client. King, can you bring Mason up to speed on what you've discovered so far?" My older brother, oblivious to the suffocating tension in the room, claps me on the back. "I'll catch up with you later, and you can tell me all about Philly."

I don't answer, keeping my gaze trained on the asshole on the other side of the room, the one who's staring at me like I'm the problem. A few seconds later, Elijah is closing the door behind him. Leaving me alone with a man I'd really like to kick in the balls rather than speak to.

I fold my arms across my chest. My stomach rolls. The sooner I get out of this room and away from him, the better. But I'll be fucked if I give him the satisfaction of leaving first. We stare at each other, engaged in a twisted game of chicken.

Annoyingly, it's me who can't stand the awkward silence any longer. "So, Mr. Blackthorn. What is it you'd like to update me on before you leave?"

His jaw works. "Mason?" There's a plea to his tone, but I ignore it. Manipulative bastard.

"The update?"

He takes a few steps toward me. Instinct tells me to back away, but pride roots me to the spot. "I just want to explain—"

"I don't give a single fuck what you want to explain!" I roar, eighteen years' worth of anger and hurt spilling out into a single moment. "Give me the fucking update and get the hell out of my building."

He opens his mouth to speak, but I cut him off. "In fact, I don't give a fuck about any update, because as of right now, you no longer work here. You are no longer contracted to do whatever the fuck it is you think you're doing. And if you have a problem with that, if you think any NDA you signed will be null because you're not getting a dime of my family's money, then you're wrong. My brothers will tie you up in court for the rest of your miserable fucking life."

He clenches his jaw, his green eyes smoldering. "I have no intention of breaching any NDA." His voice is calm and soft, like rich velvet brushing over my skin. I recall it all too well. "Let me say my piece, and then, if you still want me to, I'll walk out of here and you never have to see me again."

The latter would certainly be a welcome outcome. I glare at him and will my knees to stop fucking trembling. Seems King *Worthington* still has the same effect on me after all these years. "You have sixty seconds before I have security toss you out of here."

"I know I shouldn't have accepted this job. But I worked for Drake in Chicago—"

"Yeah. He told me all about you. The hotshot? Had no idea it was you, though." Disdain drips from my tone, so unmistakable that even King, who has the emotional intelligence of a tadpole, could pick up on it. And he does.

Scowling, he takes a few more steps toward me, and now we're only a few feet apart. Again, self-preservation tells me to run, but my ego makes me take a step closer. "If you're only giving me sixty seconds to say my piece, then don't fucking interrupt me, Playboy."

Playboy? Arrogant fuck! I inhale a deep breath that has my nostrils flaring. "So speak, Hotshot."

"Drake asked me, and I ..." He scrubs a hand over his buzz cut. "I honestly wish I could tell you why I said yes, Mase."

Mase? What the hell gives him the right to call me that? I hate that my body responds on instinct when he does though. I despise remembering how good it felt when he whispered that name in my ear. How he moaned it when I made him lose control. "To torture me, maybe? To tell me how disgusting I am, just in case I forgot? I mean, it has been eighteen years, so maybe you figured I was due a reminder."

The pain that flashes in his eyes only stokes my anger. How fucking dare he act hurt after what he did. "No, nothing like that," he says. "Maybe I thought it would be my chance to say I'm s—"

"I swear to god. If you tell me you're sorry, I will throw you through that fucking window." His Adam's apple bobs, drawing my eye to the thick dusting of stubble covering his jaw and neck. "The time for sorry has long since fucking passed, King Worthington. Or is it Blackthorn now? Did you change your name in the hopes I might not recognize you?"

It's fury flashing in his eyes now. "Of course I knew you'd recognize me. For fuck's sake, we were ..." He growls and shakes his head, unable even now to say what we were to each other. Clearly he's still disgusted by it. "I changed my name because I didn't want to be associated with my father."

His father. I stagger back a step. Kyngston Worthington III. Sick, twisted fuck. Bile surges up from my stomach, burning the back of my throat.

"Mase." King's hand is on my forearm. "Are you okay?"

I shrug him off. "Don't fucking touch me." He doesn't get to pretend like he cares. I wonder if he knows what his father did. I've convinced myself that he couldn't have. It was the only way to survive it.

"Okay." He backs off, holding his hands up in surrender. "You looked a little ..."

"What?" I snarl, regaining my composure. Ten long years of therapy helped me deal with what King's father did to me, and I won't let it take up any space inside my head. Not sure any amount of therapy could fix what King broke though. "Like I'd seen a ghost? Just what the fuck are you doing here, King? No more bullshit. I'm not some sixteen-year-old kid who thinks the sun shines out of your ass anymore. Give me the truth or get the fuck out."

"The simple truth is I needed a job. I needed an interesting job that doesn't make me want to gouge out my own fucking eyes. I swear if I have to record one more dude fucking a woman young enough to be his daughter, I will lose my goddamn will to live."

"Well, being honest, that wouldn't be the worst thing in the world."

"If we're being honest," he replies, "then I also took the job because I am fucking good at what I do."

"Yeah, Hotshot. I get it."

His green eyes narrow. Good. He's pissed at me, and I'm fucking glad about it. I can't believe he walked in here and intruded on my life, thinking it was okay. "I think I can find whoever the leak is," he says. "And I already know it's not one of the people who worked on the patent."

I suspected that too, but I've worked with these people for twelve years. How can he be so sure after only two days? "How do you know that?"

"I met with them. I was granted full access to their personnel files. And I just know. I can read people."

"You can, huh? Then you must know exactly what I'm thinking right now." I smirk at him in challenge, and he takes it.

Nodding, he steps closer, leaving us only inches apart. "You're thinking about how much you want to hate me."

"I don't want to hate you, Hotshot. I actually fucking do."

He trails two fingertips across the lapel of my jacket. I should punch him in the face. "You can keep telling yourself that, Playboy, and yeah, maybe a part of you does." His voice is low and dangerous, and it sends a shiver up my spine. "But that other part of you remembers all the ways I made you come."

Holy fucking shit. My knees almost buckle. Arrogant fucking douchefuck.

"I'll be back tomorrow morning, wearing a suit and tie. You know, so I look like someone doing a health and safety audit." He arches an eyebrow. "And if I don't find the leak within three months, then you can fire me."

Or I could fire his ass right now. Actually, I just did a few minutes ago, didn't I? So why am I working out when his three-month period would be up? He's so damn sure of himself. What I'd give to wipe that smug, self-centered look from his face. But I don't.

"Fine. But you stay the hell away from me. I don't even want to see the back of your goddamn head while you're working here. Got that?"

"You won't see me," he says, holding up his hand. "Scout's honor."

I roll my eyes. "Like you were ever a fucking Boy Scout."

He lets out a soft laugh. It sounds self-deprecating, except that it's him, so it can't be. "I'll do my best to stay out of your way, Mason." He sounds sincere too, which again, can't be the real King. Not the one I remember anyway.

"See that you do." I spin on my heel and walk out of Elijah's office, blood thundering in my veins and my heart racing with every step. I barely acknowledge any of our employees as I pass them, propelled forward by my singular mission to reach my office, close the door, and have a full mental breakdown.

When I finally get there, I close the door behind me, rest my head back against it, and take deep, calming breaths until my pulse returns to normal. Then I stagger to my desk and pour myself a full glass of our "special occasion" Scotch. Two huge gulps and it's gone. The burn in my throat isn't enough of a distraction though. Neither is the slight buzz as the alcohol hits. Because it's not only King. It's everything he represents from that time in my life. The ghosts I worked so hard to lay to rest. And they all came roaring back with a vengeance. Ten years of therapy up in smoke.

I could tell my brothers what happened, and they'd never work with King again. They'd probably have his father taken out by their friends in the Irish mob, which is definitely an option to revisit at a later date. But truthfully, I don't want to open that can of worms with them. I managed to keep my relationship with King a secret from them all for the entire eighteen months we were sneaking around.

More surprisingly, I managed to keep the aftermath a secret too, although that was unintentional.

I roll my neck. I can do this. Three months, and then King is out of my hair again. No need to dredge up the past. No need to reopen old wounds that I spent a fortune and thousands of hours healing.

I place my hands on my desk. Yeah, I can do this. I survived the Worthingtons before, and that was when I was a scared kid. Now, I am Mason fucking James, and nothing and nobody will ever make me feel weak or less than what I am ever again.

Let King stay. Let him see what I've made of my life without him in it.

ELEVEN

MASON - AGE 17

"Fuck!" King's warm breath dusts over my skin. "You feel so good, Mase." He sinks his teeth into my shoulder blade. "You're my perfect little fuck toy, aren't you?"

My entire body thrums with pleasure. "Yeah."

"Yeah you are." His lips dust over my ear. "I'm really gonna miss you, baby."

I swallow past the lump in my throat. "Gonna miss you too."

He gives me a final kiss on the back of my neck before falling onto the seat beside and zipping up his fly.

I tug up my jeans and sit beside him, still riding the high of my climax. He lifts his arm, and I go to snuggle against him, our usual post-fucking-in-my-Jeep position, but before I can ...

"What the fuck is going on?" The voice is so full of rage

and disgust that I flinch. But my reaction is nothing compared to King's. His face turns whiter than snow, and he scrambles to get away from me.

We purposely use this spot because nobody ever comes out here. So who's discovered us? How? And why the hell does he sound so mad about it?

"Shit," King mutters, and what happens next happens so fast my head spins. King is pulled from the car by a very large balding man who appears to be foaming at the mouth. "I knew you were up to something. You dirty little bastard. You sick little piece of shit." He punches King in the side of the face, and my boyfriend falls to the ground.

"Hey!" Vibrating with fury, I jump out of the car and confront the mountain of rage standing over King. "What the hell do you think you're doing?"

He turns his angry scowl on me, his face only illuminated by the interior light of my car. "You perverted little shit. I should snap your fucking neck."

Instead of doing that, he turns his attention back to King and hauls him up by the scruff of his neck, shaking him like a rag doll. "Explain yourself, boy!"

"We weren't doing anything, sir," King protests.

He shakes King harder. "I can fucking smell him on you, you filthy piece of shit. Do not lie to your father. Now try again."

This is his dad? Holy shit. I take a cautious step toward them.

"I was just messing with him," King says, and I stop in my tracks. "He fucking disgusts me too."

I freeze now, my eyes darting between King and his father—Kyngston Worthington III. He releases his grip on his son who shrugs out of his hold.

"Tell him how we feel about dirty little perverts like him," his father demands.

King's face changes into someone I don't recognize. His eyes fix on mine. "You disgust me," he says, his tone dripping with venom. But that can't be for me. It has to be for his father—the man making him do this.

"King?" I plead. "You don't have to listen to him. Come home with me. We can—"

"You think I'd go anywhere with you? Didn't you hear me when I told you that you fucking disgust me? Did you think any of this was real?"

I blink at him, confused, not to mention scared of his father and what he might be capable of.

"This was a joke to see exactly how far you'd go, so that I can tell everyone about what a pathetic, needy, sick little shit you really are. I hate you. You're a fucking freak! You think any of this is real? I'm not gay. Never have been. Never will be."

I stagger back a step. He doesn't mean any of that, but it still causes a physical ache in my chest.

I can't breathe.

His father sneers at me, then directs his attention back to his son. "Let's go."

King doesn't look at me before he walks away, toward the dark SUV that we didn't hear driving down the road. We were too wrapped up in each other to notice anyone else.

I watch them drive away, overwhelmed with anger and betrayal and fear. What the fuck just happened?

"What's wrong, my sweet boy?" Mom's soothing voice makes me want to cry, but I choke back a sob and stare at the TV, pretending to be engrossed in some stupid show about college kids.

"Nothing, Mom."

She sits beside me and cups my face in her hands. "You have been crying, Mason. Now, please tell your mama what is wrong so I can fix it for you."

I wish it were that easy. "It was just a guy, that's all."

"A guy what? What did he do?" Her voice goes up about seven octaves, and then she curses in Spanish.

I'm still trying to process what happened myself. I've called King half a dozen times. Left voicemails. Sent text messages. I haven't heard anything from him in hours, and I'm starting to worry that something's happened to him. I can't face telling my mom about any of it, so I downplay it all. "It was nothing. I was kind of seeing some guy, and he broke it off."

She makes a horrified face. "Broke it off? With my beautiful, kind, sweet boy?"

Usually I wince at her over-the-top compliments, but they're more than welcome tonight. I nod.

Cue more Spanish cursing. "Do I need to take out a hit on anyone?" she asks quietly, crossing herself. "Or have his home infested with fire ants?" There's a twinkle in her soft brown eyes, but I have no doubt she would do either of those things if I asked her to.

"No, Mom. It's fine."

"I remember my first broken heart." She lets out an exaggerated sigh. "His name was Miguel Fernandez, and he broke up with me the day before Valentine's. Bastardo!"

I smile in spite of how lousy I feel.

"How about some ice cream, huh? I hid a tub of mint chocolate chip beneath the vegetables." She waggles her eyebrows at me.

I shake my head. "Nah, but thanks."

"Aw." She plants a kiss on my forehead. "This will not be your first broken heart, my sweet, sensitive boy." Then she wraps me in a hug, enveloping me in the sweet scent of her flowery perfume. "And any boy who does not appreciate the wonder that is you, mijo, does not deserve another moment of your time. And he is definitely not worth the salt of your tears."

If only that were true, Mom.

~

I BARELY SLEPT AT ALL, and as soon as I wake up, I check my phone. No word from King, and now I'm really worried. If I don't speak to him today, I might consider asking my dad if we should call the cops.

I call him for what must be the fiftieth time, and to my utter relief, he picks up. He speaks before I have a chance to. "Will you stop fucking calling me! Stop texting. Stop everything. I told you—"

"I don't fucking believe you, King. We—"

"There is no we, asshole. It was fake. Every cringeworthy, painful second of it. I don't even fucking like you. Now leave me the fuck alone. Go beg some other dirty little fuck to let you suck his cock."

White-hot pain lances through my chest. He can't mean any of this. His father must be there, making him say this stuff. "King, please, just—"

"Don't call me again. Fucking freak!"

The line goes dead.

My heart breaks.

I DON'T BELIEVE HIM. Can't believe him. What King and I had means something, and I don't care what he said, it must have been his father's influence. Only yesterday afternoon we were making plans for the future. He leaves for school next week—Harvard, where Nathan and Drake are studying too. And next year I'll be there as well, and we can stop sneaking around so much. Nathan and Drake are in an apartment off campus, and my mom and dad will let me do the same after my first year. Then King and I could have all the privacy we want. And after college ...

I shake my head, refusing to cry again. Everything couldn't have changed in the space of a few hours. It has to be his father making him say those things. He doesn't have the best relationship with his parents, and he's terrified to come out to them, a fact that bewilders me when my own parents, and my brothers, have been nothing but supportive. But having met his father last night, I can totally understand why.

Still, I'm not about to let his father ruin this for us. I'm not scared of him. Kyngston Worthington might be a big-shot investment banker, but my dad and brothers would eat him for breakfast. Obviously, King doesn't feel strong enough to stand up to him, and I'm not going to lie in bed all day and leave him to face this alone.

With that thought in mind, I grab the keys to my Jeep and head to King's house. I've never visited him there before, but I know where it is. When we first started dating, I drove past the place. The imposing mansion on the outskirts of the city looks about as inviting as a root canal.

The wrought iron gates are open when I pull up, and my tires crunch over the gravel driveway. This place is creepy as hell, and I have no idea what I'm walking into. But I glance around and note King's blue Audi, the same car where we shared our first kiss, and it reminds me why I'm here.

I climb the few stone stairs leading to the door, my legs shaking with each step, and ring the doorbell. A lady with gray hair wearing a pale gray dress and cardigan opens it and inquires who I am.

I roll back my shoulders. "I'm here to see King."

"One moment, please," she says. Then she closes the door and disappears.

I shuffle my feet, absentmindedly kicking at the stone wall beside me. I almost pass out when a stone comes loose, but before I can put it back, the door opens again.

"You!" Kyngston Worthington III booms.

I glare at him. He doesn't intimidate me—not much anyway. "I want to speak to King."

He glares at me.

"Please, sir."

His eyes narrow, and right as I'm sure he's going to tell me to leave, he opens the door wider and invites me in. Hesitantly, I follow him inside. The air is thick with the overpowering scent of disinfectant, but what's most stark is the lack of any noise. I've grown up with four brothers, and even when nobody else is home, it seems our house is never silent. This place is like a mausoleum.

"This way," Kyngston orders, and I follow obediently, my anxiety spiking with each step I take.

"Where is King?" I ask, hating the slight tremor in my voice.

"Kyngston is out," he replies coolly, opening a door and gesturing for me to walk inside. I peer into what looks like a study, and against my better judgment, I step over the threshold. I want to see King, and as uncomfortable as this is, I'm not going to get to unless I at least pretend to be polite and respectful to this guy. Not that he deserves it.

He closes the door behind him, and I shift uncomfortably. The faint smell of cigar smoke and brandy lingers in the air.

"Mason, is it?" he asks, his eyes narrowed on my face.

"Yes, sir."

"And where are you from, Mason? You don't go to Kyngston's school, which is the most prestigious in New York. And you drive a seven-year-old Jeep, so I'm guessing your parents like to appear well-off but are not particularly rich, correct?"

Wrong, asshole. I don't go to the same school as your son because I go to the same one my father attended, the same one as my brothers. And I drive a seven-year-old Jeep because it's Elijah's old limited-edition Wrangler. I loved it so much that he gave it to me when I passed my driving test, even though Mom and Dad offered to buy me a new one. But I don't tell Kyngston that because he's an arrogant douche-knuckle and I honestly don't give a shit what he thinks about me.

"So where did you and my son meet?"

"At Nero's pizzeria."

He runs a hand down his double chin, scrutinizing me

in a way that makes my skin crawl, and then he simply sneers.

"When will King be home?" I ask.

"Later. But you will not be here when he returns." His tone drips with venom. "You will stay away from my son, and if I ever find out you have tried to make him stray from the path again, I will not show any mercy, Mason." He spits my name from his mouth like it's a dirty word. "You are an abomination, and Kyngston wants nothing more to do with you. Do I make myself clear?"

I tip my chin. "Maybe he should say that to my face."

His lip curls. "Maybe I should teach you a lesson about what happens to filthy little sinners who should have been smothered at birth." He steps around me and locks the door. And somehow, only now does it register how much bigger than me he is. Taller than my dad and built like a WWE wrestler, he radiates menace, and I recall how cruel he was last night to his own son. How roughly he hit him and pushed him to the ground, not caring that King hurt himself when he fell.

My cell is in my pocket. I should call my dad. Or Elijah.

But I'm frozen. My heart hammers in my chest and my mouth goes dry. I can't speak. I want to say words. I want to punch him in the face, but I suspect that might provoke him further, and my instinct to survive kicks in. Right or wrong, it tells me to do whatever the hell he wants and then get the hell out of here.

When Kyngston unbuckles his belt and unzips his pants, I still don't move. He licks his lips. "On your knees."

When I still don't move, he rests a meaty palm on the top of my head and forces me to the floor. "I said, on your fucking knees."

MY KNUCKLES ARE WHITE. Head throbbing and eyes burning from holding back tears. Bile surges up the back of my throat, and I taste him. Swerving to the side of the road, I pull over and lean my head out the window just in time. Vomit spews from my insides, burning my esophagus.

I need to get home. Then everything will be okay. I'll tell Mom and Dad what happened, and they won't care that I let it happen and didn't try to fight back. They'll know I had no choice. And they'll insist on calling the cops or send some of Dad's security. Either way, Kyngston Worthington is going to regret ever laying a finger on me.

It takes forever to get home. My hands fumble with the key in the lock, and I take a deep breath. I'm here. I'm safe. Kyngston Worthington is going to get what's coming to him as soon as I tell my family what he did.

I head for the kitchen, the place my mom will surely be. Tears burn behind my eyes. Seventeen years old, and I need a hug from my mom. But she'll make everything feel better. I can almost smell the scent of her perfume and feel her soft lips on the top of my head.

"Mase?" Maddox's pained cry stops me in my tracks. I spin on my heel and see tears streaming down his twelve-year-old face. My own pain is forgotten.

He runs straight into me, and I wrap my arms around him. "Mad? What is it, buddy?"

Then Nathan walks out of the den. What's he doing here? He's supposed to be at the Hamptons with Drake and their friends, enjoying their last week of summer before going back to college. Nathan comes closer, and it's only now I see his eyes are filled with tears. My stomach drops through my knees. Nathan never cries. Ever. What the hell is going on?

My older brother wraps an arm around my shoulder and hugs me tight, while Maddox's head is still buried against my chest. "I'm sorry, Mase. We've been trying to get ahold of you all day. I didn't want you to hear like this."

Hear what? What the hell is he going on about? Why does he think I've heard anything? And then I remember I must look like shit. I've been crying the entire drive home.

"Mom wanted to wait to tell us all together, but we were all freaking out, and Dad's fucking crumbling—" His voice catches on a sob.

My legs tremble. Part of me doesn't want to know whatever terrible news he's about to tell me, because then I can go on living in my state of ignorance and believing that the worst thing to happen to me today is what Kyngston Worthington III just did. But the other part of me needs to know why Maddox and Nathan are acting like their worlds have fallen apart. "What's happened, Nathan?"

He blinks at me. "Mom's cancer is back. It's spread too much for them to ..." He sucks in a breath.

My knees buckle, but he holds me up and wraps both me and Maddox in his arms. "It's okay," Nathan whispers. "We'll all be okay."

I cling to him, my fingers trying to find a grip on the back of his T-shirt. Mom is sick. It took so much out of her to beat cancer last time. But we were all certain she'd done it for good.

"Hey." Elijah's soothing voice washes over me. "Are you guys okay?"

"Have you told him?" Drake asks.

Nobody answers. None of us speak. Elijah and Drake join our huddle, and they all just hold onto Maddox and me. Like they can protect us from the awful truth. Mad's hot tears soak through my shirt. This is what families do, isn't it? We protect each other. And right now, Mom is our priority. What happened to me was fucking awful, but telling them all about it will only bring more pain. We can deal with Kyngston Worthington III some other time. When Mom is better.

I scrub the tears from my cheeks and steel myself to go see Mom and Pop. They need all of us at our strongest, and that's what I'll be for them. Strong. Dependable. The easy kid who never gives them any trouble.

TWELVE

MASON

"Scotch for you thirsty fucks, and an OJ for you, Mad," Drake says, placing the tray of drinks on the table.

Amelia, Mel, and Amber attended a luncheon for Amber's charity today. From what Elijah told me, they were full of laughter and headed out for mocktails afterward. Not to be outdone by their wives, my brothers insisted we meet up for drinks at our favorite bar after work.

Which is the perfect distraction for me after the unwelcome slice of my past I ran into today.

"How's King doing?" Drake asks. "He found your leak yet?"

I bristle at the mention of him. Now Drake calls him by his name. Had I been advised of his actual name, I may have connected those dots and saved myself a minor cardiac event earlier today. There are not many people with the name Kyngston. Unfortunately, I've met two of them and hate them both with equal fervor.

Thankfully, Elijah answers for me. "He hasn't found out much yet, but it's only been three days. He's good though. Efficient. Discreet. Someone from HR asked who he was and what he was doing there today, and his spiel about doing some kind of health and safety audit rolled right off his tongue."

Yeah, that sounds like him. He's an incredible liar.

"What did you think of him, Mase?" Drake asks.

He's an arrogant, heartless douchebag with the emotional intelligence of a fire hydrant. I shrug. "He was okay."

Drake arches an eyebrow. "Just okay?"

"Yes, just okay, Drake. Is there something wrong with that?"

Nathan puts a calming hand on my shoulder. "Relax, Mase. You're usually much easier to please than Elijah, that's all."

"Hey!" Elijah protests, but quickly quiets down when we all remind him this is true.

"I would've thought he'd be right up your alley, to be honest," Drake says with a smirk.

That snaps the remainder of my already thin patience. "What's that supposed to mean?"

"Did you see him? All muscles and tattoos and a square jaw. He seemed exactly your type is all I meant."

"Well, *I* don't fuck around with my employees, Drake," I bark.

"Ouch," Nathan mutters.

"Jesus fucking Christ, Mason." Drake frowns, understandably hurt by my words. He met Amelia before she was his secretary and is hopelessly in love with her, and she him.

My anger shifts to self-loathing, and I drop my head into my hands. "I'm sorry. It's been a long day."

Nathan slaps me on the back. "We've all been there, buddy. Have a drink and cool down."

Someone pushes the glass of Scotch into my hand. I look up into Drake's dark eyes. "Sorry, bro," I say again.

"It's okay. I didn't mean anything by it. I just wondered if he might be gay, and you usually know about these things."

I frown now. "Why would you think he's gay?"

He shrugs. "No idea. Never saw him with a girl though."

He didn't? Part of me assumed King would be married with a wife and a couple of kids by now. Trying his best to prove to the world that he's a straight dude-bro capable of procreation. "Did you ever see him with a guy?"

He sips his Scotch, considering my question. "Also no."

"So why assume he's gay?" I ask, incredulous.

Maddox looks me dead in the eye. "Why do you assume he's not?"

Fuck. He's got me there. "Yeah, well, straight, gay, bi, or pan, he's not my type."

Elijah arches an eyebrow. "Am I going to have to separate you two when you're in the office?"

I take a gulp of my drink. "Don't be ridiculous. Just because I didn't think about fucking him"—that's a dirty rotten lie—"doesn't mean I can't be around him."

Elijah smiles. "Good to know, because I really want to take Amber to this spa place I found in the Seychelles next week."

"The Seychelles? Dude, you got back from Spain a few months ago."

He winces. "I know. But it's super exclusive, and they do this hot salt therapy she loves, and they emailed me earlier to tell me they had an opening. I cleared my schedule and will do what work I need to remotely. I know we have this leak, but we have you and King on it. Nathan and Drake can step in if we need to take any legal action. I'm sorry if it puts you in a bind, but I didn't take a single vacation with my wife for ten years."

"Yeah, on account of him always looking after us," Nathan reminds me.

It's true that Elijah put his life and his marriage on hold for our family and the company. He helped build Jamestech into the behemoth it is today, and I can't in good conscience deny him the opportunity to take his foot off the gas a little now just because I'm uncomfortable with our newest contractor, can I?

"It's only five days, Mason," he says.

"Fine. Go get some salt rubbed over your ass in the Seychelles then. I'll hold down the fort."

"You're sure?" he asks, but the dude is already picturing his wife on a beach in a string bikini, I know it.

In spite of my shitty day and the horrible memories it dredged up, I truly am happy for him and Amber. "I'm sure," I promise.

"I'll tell King to report to you then," he says, pulling his phone out of his pocket.

I sink the last drop of my Scotch. Fuck my goddamn life.

THIRTEEN

MASON

I stare out my office window, admiring the incredible view of the Hudson. It's the kind you could get used to when you see it almost every day, but when you really pay attention and look at it, it will take your breath away. I've been lucky enough to travel the world, but there's nowhere quite like New York.

There's a knock at my open door, and my secretary says, "Mr. Blackthorn is here to see you, sir." Deborah only calls me sir when I have an unfamiliar visitor. Outside of that, we're very informal.

"Show him in."

I brace myself and turn around. True to his word, he's wearing a suit and tie. I expected him to look out of place, maybe a little uncomfortable given how well he rocked the laid-back vibe yesterday, but he looks just as good in a suit. Damn him.

He glances around the room like he's expecting an ambush. "I thought I was reporting to Elijah?"

"Elijah has taken a last-minute trip, so you'll be dealing with me. You think you can handle that?"

He arches an eyebrow. "Do you think you can?"

Looks like he's still the same cocky fuck who humiliated me eighteen years ago. The fact that he has the nerve to walk in here like nothing happened was proof enough of that. I sit at my desk and he takes that as a cue to sit opposite me.

"So what's your strategy?" I ask.

He licks his bottom lip. An unwanted and incredibly inappropriate memory flashes through my brain.

"You have four hundred employees," he says. "I'm going to comb through all of their work emails and—"

"All the emails for all four hundred of them?"

Smirking, he raises his eyebrows. "I have a program I use. I'll input some specific keywords, and then I'll use that to narrow down my suspect pool."

I want to ask how exactly he'll do that, but frankly, I don't have time and I don't want to appear too interested in what he does in the event it's misconstrued as interest in him. Which it absolutely is not.

King Worthington, now Blackthorn. Who came back to New York to look after his sick grandfather. Drake has never seen him with a woman or a guy. He's not married. No kids? Yeah, I have no interest in him at all.

His rich voice cuts through my racing thoughts. "Anything else you'd like to know, Mason?"

I clear my throat. "What about after you narrow down your suspects?"

"I'll be spending a lot of time here at the office, getting to know people, their habits, their personal lives. Anything that will give me clues as to who they really are."

"You said you're good at reading people."

He nods. "I am."

Conceited douchebag. "And you think that will be enough? Sounds like what any PI might do. Drake said you were better than most."

He leans forward, his eyes burning into mine. "I am, Mason. I'll be doing plenty, don't worry about that. You don't need to question my methods, but I can promise you results."

God, he is such a cocky fuck. How is it he's sitting in my office, the one that my company owns, yet I still feel like he's the one in charge? I roll my neck and remind myself who I am. I've dealt with much more powerful and intimidating people than King. "You'll report to me with updates on your progress every day."

He smirks. "Whatever you wish, Mason."

I wish you'd get the hell out of New York and crawl back to whatever hole in Chicago you slid out of. I jerk my chin at the door and say, "That will be all."

He bristles. I lock my hands behind my head and smile. Welcome to my world, King.

THIS IS NOW the sixth time King has sat across from me at the end of the day, giving me an update on his progress. Elijah's back from the Seychelles, but for some reason I have remained King's point of contact. Neither of us has objected or made any attempts to change the status quo, which either makes both of us masochists or completely fucked up.

His eyes rake over me, and his hungry gaze feels like a caress on my skin. I stare back at him just as intently. At the bulging muscles of his biceps straining for freedom against his shirt sleeves, at the dark ink etched on his skin, visible beneath the stark white fabric. The shadow of stubble on his jaw that gets at least two shades darker by the end of the day.

This has to be wildly inappropriate, the way we sit here eye-fucking each other. But as long as neither of us acknowledges that it's happening, then we can both pretend it's not.

King has made clear progress on the case, but I'm impatient. I want to know who the piece of shit is that betrayed me and my family. Who used their trusted position to sell our hard work.

It frustrates the fuck out of me, and I clearly don't disguise it well because he says, "I know it feels slow and laborious, and I guess it is, but it's going to take time."

"You said it would take less than three months."

"It's been less than two weeks, Mason."

Annoyance bubbling over, I push back my chair and go to make myself a coffee. And like he's done the past three days, King comes to stand beside me. Not too close, but close enough that I feel his body heat.

"You want one?" I grumble. I didn't offer him one the first few days, but my inherent good manners must have gotten the better of me, and by Monday of this week, I was offering him a cup. He refused. He agreed on Tuesday, stood beside me and watched on Wednesday, then helped by pouring his own sugar yesterday. And now we sound like we're trapped in a Craig David song.

I still hate King, even if I do find him absurdly attractive, but I'm not an animal. I can suppress my baser desires for a few weeks. And I suppose if I'm going to have to work with him for the foreseeable future, I can at least be civil.

"Yeah," he replies to my offer of coffee, his voice so low it's almost a growl. His fingers brush the back of my hand when he reaches for the sugar, sending heat traveling up my forearm. I bite down on the inside of my cheek and pray I didn't show any outward reaction. It's simply muscle memory, that's all. Nothing more.

He reaches for the spoon next, and it happens again, our little fingers brushing together, creating a palpable crackle of electricity. He did that on purpose.

He gives me a sideways glance. "Cream?"

Motherfucker.

He pours a splash into each of our mugs without me having to answer, and I stir before handing him one. Like the past three days, we drink our coffee in silence, eye-fucking each other over the rims of our mugs now rather than across the desk. I definitely do imagine what it would be like if I had a real fuck-it moment and threw my mug on the floor before pinning him to the wall by his throat. I'd hold him in place while I let my mouth and hands wander all the places my eyes do. Especially his cock, which I already know from experience is huge and lined with thick, lickable veins. I don't let my eyes wander there often, but when I do, fuck if I don't see the outline of that monster in his suit pants.

He drains his mug and places it back on the tray. And then he stares at me, his top lip trapped between his teeth like he wants to say something. Or maybe he's thinking about pinning me to the wall by my throat, and that scenario isn't any less appealing to me than the one I've been playing out in my head.

"I guess I'll see you Monday" is what he eventually says. All that thinking to tell me he'll see me Monday?

Swallowing my disappointment, I nod.

"Goodnight, Mason." Is that disappointment I hear in his voice too? Or am I imagining it?

He walks out of my office, and I let out a long breath and scrub a hand through my hair. Whatever that was, his leaving is for the best. Even if my body remembers how good we were together, my brain will never let me get past the hurt he caused. I can never trust him like that again.

My dick is just going to have to get with the program. King Blackthorn's perfect body and monster cock don't negate the fact that he's a giant douchebag and therefore totally off-limits.

CHAPTER
FOURTEEN

KING

I wake up with a raging hard-on, and as usual, my thoughts immediately turn to Mason James. What I wouldn't give to have those sinful lips wrapped around my shaft. I wrap my own hand around it instead, picturing his dark eyes when I tug hard. He was in good shape when he was younger, though much skinnier than he is now. But I've already gleaned enough about his routine to know that he works out six days a week, and I can only imagine how good he looks beneath those tailor-made suits of his. I can practically feel the taut muscles of his ass and how good it would feel to dig my fingers into them. To sink my cock into him.

"Fuck!" Precum weeps from my slit, and my balls draw up. I picture him the whole time. Imagine him on his knees for me, or with my tongue in his mouth, or have him bent over that damn desk he uses like a shield.

Light splinters my vision as hot jets of cum streak over my hand. I sink my head back into the pillow and blow out a breath. If only I had the balls to say something last night when we were drinking coffee and pretending we weren't thinking about getting the other one naked. He might have told me to go fuck myself.

Or he might have ended up right here in my bed, with my cum inside him. That surely would have been worth the risk of rejection.

I'm not blind—I know he wants me. And he no doubt knows I want him every bit as much. But I suspect it's a line he's unwilling to cross without some significant pushing. I'm just not sure I have the right to push after what I did.

I roll out of bed and head to the shower. Amanda is taking a rare Saturday off, and I'm determined to get Grampa out of the house today for some sunshine. I'm equally determined to put thoughts of Mason out of my head for as long as possible.

"I DON'T KNOW why I need fresh air," Grampa croaks, then immediately starts coughing.

I stop pushing his chair and gently attach his oxygen mask, giving him a pointed look. "Really? I'll give you three guesses." His eyes tell me to go to hell, but he doesn't have the breath or the energy to tell me with his words.

"Seriously Grampa, being cooped up in that apartment all day isn't good for you. Now quit whining and let's have a little fun, you old goat."

Ignoring his protests, I go back to pushing his wheelchair along the sidewalk. "Where are we going?" he huffs, arms folded across his chest.

"For ice cream."

He makes a lip-smacking sound. "Can I get rum and raisin?"

"Yeah."

"And whipped cream?"

"Yup."

"And sprinkles?"

"Of course, Grampa." Personally, I think rum raisin ice cream with sprinkles sounds revolting, but he can have whatever makes him happy.

GRAMPA GRINS AT ME, and I dab a smudge of rum raisin from his chin with a napkin. "Did you enjoy your ice cream?"

He purses his lips like he's giving his response a lot of thought. His mask hangs on the armrest beside him. Today is one of his better days. He's survived much longer than the doctors predicted, and we've settled into a routine together. And today is definitely a good day. The sun is shining. We got to eat some delicious ice cream. It's the smallest things that make the biggest difference. "I've had better," he finally declares.

I arch one eyebrow. "Oh you have?"

He nods. "It was 1972 at a movie theater in Kentucky. Best rum and raisin ever." His green eyes twinkle, and I drop a brief kiss on the top of his head that makes him cackle.

And when I straighten up again, bam! I'm looking right into the dark-brown eyes of Mason James, who's staring at me like I have an extra head. Self-conscious, I wipe my mouth with the back of my hand. If there was any leftover mint chocolate chip on my face, then he has nothing else to gawk at me for. But he goes on staring anyway. And it seems like it takes forever for one of us to speak.

"You need something? A picture maybe?" I snap before he does. But I feel vulnerable here with Grampa, and I hate that, especially around Mason.

"I-I," he stammers for a second before his cool facade slips back into place. "Just didn't expect to see you at an ice cream shop is all."

"I could say the same about you. Especially here in Marble Hill. Little out of your comfort zone, isn't it?"

His jaw tics. Grampa is craning his neck and trying to get a look at who I'm talking to. "Introduce me to your friend, son," he demands.

With a sigh, I spin him around until he too comes face-to-face with Mason James. All six foot two of toned muscle and charm wrapped up in obscenely well-fitted jeans and a casual shirt, which look as good as his suits. "Grampa, this is Mason. Mason, meet my grandfather."

Grampa extends his hand. "Arthur Blackthorn. Nice to meet you, son."

Recognition dawns on Mason's face at Grampa's last name, but he quickly plasters on a smile and shakes his hand. "It's great to meet you too, sir."

Grampa glances between the two of us. He likes being addressed with respect, and I know Mason has already won him over. "How do you boys know each other?"

"King works for me," Mason replies before I get a chance to.

"Oh, so he's your boss?" Grampa asks, eyes on me now.

He's an asshole is what he is. I grind my teeth. "Not exactly."

Mason cups his hand at the side of his mouth and makes like he's whispering to my grandfather. "I pay him to work for me, but he gets a little touchy about people calling me his boss, Mr. Blackthorn."

"That's because I'm my own fucking boss," I snap.

Mason winks at Grampa. "See. Touchy."

Grampa laughs out loud. "I was exactly the same at his age. And please, son, call me Arthur."

Mason smiles at him. It's his genuine smile, the one that makes my cock twitch in a way it definitely wasn't a few seconds ago. It also reminds me of the guy I lost.

"What the hell are you doing this far from Manhattan,

Mason? Don't you burst into flames once you cross the district line in daylight or something?"

He tilts his head, and the way his brown eyes rake over me does nothing to ease the situation going on in my jeans. I thank fuck for Grampa's wheelchair right in front of me. "Marble Hill is part of Manhattan, Hotshot. And I'm here to meet Maddox. He works in the vegan café around the corner."

"Is Maddox a friend of yours?" my grandfather asks. "Or is he someone special?"

Fuck, Grampa. Why not just outright ask him if he's gay?

Mason's smile widens. "He's someone very special, Arthur. He's my kid brother."

"I had a brother once," Grampa says sadly. "Died when he was only a few years old."

Mason's expression softens, and he crouches down, bringing his face level with my grandfather's, and rests a hand on his knee. "I'm really sorry to hear that, Arthur. We almost lost Mad once." There's a crack in his voice that I haven't heard for a very long time. I had no idea about that. "Not a day goes by that I'm not grateful to still have him."

Grampa nods, a tear rolling down his cheek.

"He'll be wondering where I am if I'm late, so I have to run, but it was great to meet you, Arthur."

"You too, son."

Mason stands tall, his eyes a little softer when they meet mine again. "Good to see you, King."

He walks away, and I watch the overtly admiring glances of the people he passes. Men and women. He has the kind of energy that people are drawn to. Whether it's charisma, pheromones, or something else, Mason James has it by the truckload. That's why I keep watching him.

"He's gay, right?" Grampa asks matter-of-factly.

"Why does that matter?"

"Doesn't." He shrugs. "I just consider myself to have a well-tuned gaydar. I knew about my buddy Leonard's son before he did."

I roll my eyes. "How do you even know what a gaydar is, old man?"

He huffs a laugh. "I'm a man of the world, young pup." He coughs, and I replace his mask again before we head for home.

After a few minutes, he pulls it aside and says, "So, am I right?"

My mind is still on Mason and work, and Mason at work, and how each time I see him, it takes all of my willpower not to touch him. "Right about what, Grampa?"

"About your boss being gay."

"He's not my boss," I remind him.

He waves a hand dismissively. "But I was right, wasn't I?"

"Yeah, Grampa, you were right."

He grins with triumph and beckons me closer. I crouch

down, resting my hands on his knees. His green eyes are always so full of life even when his is fading. I wish there was more I could do for him. He rests his hands over mine, gnarled fingers gripping mine as tightly as his frail health allows. "From the day you were born, you have been the light of my life."

Tears burn behind my eyes, and I don't want to cry in the street, especially with Mason in the near vicinity. "You getting sentimental on me, old man?"

He squeezes a little harder, with all the strength of a small child. "You are a special boy, King. Never let anyone tell you differently. Never let anyone stop you from being who you are. You understand me?"

Do I understand? Is Grampa ...? Does he know about me?

"Never pretend to be less than who you are to please anyone, my boy, especially not your parents. And never let them stop you from finding love."

I press my forehead to his knuckles. Of course he knows. "How long have you known, Grampa?"

"Probably longer than you have." He cackles, and it's the perfect way to both preserve and break this tender moment. I'm not prone to displays of emotion in the middle of a crowded city street.

I look up at him and grin. "You think, huh?"

He taps his temple and winks. "Like I said, finely tuned."

"You're a lovable old goat, you know that?" I stand and drop a quick kiss on his forehead.

"Must be where you get all your charm from."

If I have any charm, then I'm in full agreement with him. The idea of my grandfather having a well-tuned gaydar makes me smile in spite of the lingering awkwardness from my encounter with Mason. That he saw Grampa and me together isn't ideal. I don't ordinarily share my personal life with my colleagues, and for good reason. But somehow Mason meeting Grampa feels like it was meant to be. Like it was long overdue.

FIFTEEN

MASON

Maddox is sitting in a booth when I get there. Two green shakes sit on the table, and I pull a disgusted face when I slide into the seat across from him.

He rolls his eyes. "You're such a fucking neanderthal, Mase."

I pull out the straw and let a blob of the green mulch fall from the bottom of it back into the glass. "No, but I'm also not a Buddhist monk like you. What the hell is this shit?" I pick out a piece of greenery. "Is that a fucking leaf?"

"It's mint, dickface. You know, like you get in your mojitos?"

I wrinkle my nose. I can detect a hint of mint, but it mostly smells like grass. "Yeah, but mojitos taste good."

He sighs and slurps his through a straw. "Chicken."

I peer into the glass and shake my head. "Nope definitely not chicken, Mad." That gets me a laugh from my baby brother, and I drop my voice to a stage whisper. "Are you even allowed to say that word in here?"

"Only when referring to asshole big brothers who are scared to eat a vegetable—not when referring to the delightful little feathered creatures some people like to roast on Sundays."

I laugh now too. "They're also good in a curry, I hear. You know, like that one you cooked for us last weekend."

He grins. Maddox might work in a vegan café, but he's still a carnivore like the rest of us James boys. He just thanks the animals for their service before he cooks and eats them. "Well, I'm glad you agreed to drop by and have lunch with me."

Maddox and I grab food together a lot, but I prefer eating in places that serve animal products because he's right—I am a neanderthal. However, as he works here and is proud of his job, I came to him today. Against my stomach's better judgment.

This definitely isn't my kind of joint. Far too hipster for me. Full of young people wearing beanies and baggy clothes. I like to imagine the chef is an aging hippie who grows his own lentils and eats mushrooms while he cooks. "You said the coffee here was amazing," I say, glaring at the green drink accusingly.

"It is. But I figured you could use one of these too. It's very cleansing."

"So are the sauna and steam room at my gym."

He takes another sip. "This stuff cleanses your soul."

I peer into the glass again and pick out what looks like a piece of eggshell but obviously can't be. "What's in it, holy water?"

"No. That shit would burn your insides if you drank it, you heathen."

True. "What makes you think I need my soul cleansed?" Does he know I've been having inappropriate thoughts about someone I shouldn't? Someone who is technically my employee. That same someone who nearly knocked me on my ass in the street minutes ago, figuratively speaking of course. Seeing him with his "Grampa" was like witnessing an entirely different King. I have seen that side of him before, but it was a long time ago. Besides, that was all an act back then. At least according to the last conversation we had before he left—a mask he wore for whatever sick thrill he got out of messing with me. Today though, that was real. How he tenderly kissed the old man's head.

It brings a lump to my throat.

"Not your soul, no. But you haven't seemed yourself lately. Everything okay?"

I stare at Maddox, his soulful brown eyes boring into mine. He and I have a unique relationship. Maybe it's because he and I are closer in age and our older brothers had all but moved out by the time he was a teenager, but we bicker and squabble more than the others. In a lighthearted way, of course. I guess it's our love language.

But he was my annoying kid brother for so long, and although I tease him relentlessly about his monk status, it's easy to forget how deep and soulful he truly is. He sees things other people don't. While I'd take a literal bullet for any of my brothers and I adore them all equally, Mad and I are closer to each other than we are to the others.

As the oldest and the one who had to become like a second dad once Mom died, Elijah has been out on his own for so long, and Nathan and Drake have been a double act since birth, which was solidified when they started their law firm together.

So it was Mad and me. He had so much shit happen to him, and like I told Arthur, we almost lost him, which was terrifying and shameful—the latter because we couldn't stop his spiral.

"I think I just have a lot going on at work, you know," I tell him, which is not exactly a lie.

"You always have a lot going on at work. This feels like more."

In an attempt to avoid the conversation, I take a gulp of the ridiculous green shake. It tastes like the scum you might find on top of a pond, and I gag.

"Such a fucking drama queen, dude," Maddox mutters.

I wipe my tongue with a napkin. "How can you call me both a queen and a dude in the same sentence?"

He grins. "Speaking of queens—my friend Yanko tells

me you haven't been to Xylophone in the last couple of weeks."

I forgot one of his drag friends is a bartender there. "You and your spies, man."

"I have them everywhere. Little brother is always watching you." He widens his eyes and tilts his head like a cobra, and it makes me snort-laugh so hard I taste the green stuff again. Fuck, what was in that thing?

"Seriously though, Mase. It's not like you to not be out partying. Is there something else going on?"

"You mean have I become a paragon of virtue like your good self?" Maddox is sober, which I one hundred percent applaud and admire. I understand that part of him, and I'm grateful he has the strength to remain so because it means I get to keep him in my life. He's also celibate, which I don't understand. Objectively, he's handsome as hell, and he works out so frequently he has barely an ounce of body fat. He's smart and kind and funnier than anyone I know. Women and guys stare at him with undisguised desire, and he fucking ignores it. It's not like drugs or alcohol—sex didn't almost kill him. He abstains because he chooses to, and that's the kind of sacrifice I don't understand.

He doesn't respond to my jibe, recognizing it as the attempt at deflection it is. "You don't have to tell me, but know I'm here if you need anything. Okay?"

I consider telling him all about King. I really do. I even consider telling him about everything that happened in the past with King and his sick fuck of a father. Of all the people in my life, Maddox would be able to relate to that kind of pain. That's why I nearly told him thirteen years ago when he came home from a party one night and found me sitting in the den in the dark, half a bottle of Scotch in.

He slumped in the chair beside me and asked what was wrong. He assumed it was about Mom, and I snapped and told him not everything was about Mom. And then I felt guilty as hell, but even at the age of seventeen, Maddox was insightful. Constantly high, but deep as the ocean. Living with our mom's illness affected us all in different ways. So he didn't make me feel guilty. He sat with me. Quiet. Steady. I was about to tell him, but then he got the phone call that changed the course of his life forever.

And maybe that's why I don't tell him now. Because my wise-as-a-sage baby brother will listen intently, and then he'll expertly guide the conversation in such a way that I'll come up with what I should do next. And it will be what I should do, of course, because this is Mad, and he always does the right thing. And once I decide what to do about King, it will eat me up until I do it. It's better—easier—to go on living in this hellish limbo of wanting him and not being able to have him.

"Thanks, Mad," I say sincerely. "But you know what I could really use? Some of that coffee you promised me. The one that will have me buzzed for days, if you're to be believed."

He glances forlornly at my green shake and his shoulders slump. "Fine. Be right back. I'll grab our lunch too." He slides out of the booth and heads into the kitchen.

Left to my own devices once more, my thoughts predictably return to King. The man I saw today has dredged up far too many unwelcome feelings. Feelings I don't have a fucking clue what to do with.

Nah, I know just what to do: Bury them in a vat of Maddox's buzzed-for-days coffee and keep on pretending that everything is fine. I have a date to get to after this.

CHAPTER
SIXTEEN
MASON

I check my appearance in Jack's bathroom mirror, running a tongue over my teeth and making sure there's no stray greens from our early dinner date. His bathroom is tidy and elegant, with expensive grooming products neatly displayed on a shelf.

I like a guy who takes good care of himself, and Jack Donnelly definitely falls into that category. He's a regular at my gym, and we've been eyeing each other for weeks. Last night, he finally asked me out, and as luck would have it, neither of us had plans for this evening. The guy is built. He has muscles on his muscles and tattoos covering most of his chest and arms, not to mention a killer smile. He's funny too. Also terminally single. In short, he's exactly my type.

So why aren't I fucking ecstatic about what's about to happen? Inviting me to his apartment for a drink is code for fucking, and we both date enough to know it. Yet, I'm ... I'm not exactly nervous, but I'm not thrilled either. And I should be. This is what I do. I hook up with super attractive guys for meaningless but fulfilling sex. If things go well, we might date for a few weeks, and then we'll move on.

I wash my hands and give myself a pep talk. This has nothing to do with King Blackthorn walking back into my life. And absolutely fuck all to do with the memories seeing him has dredged up. Get it the fuck together, Mase.

Pep talk administered, I head back into the open-plan living space. It's a nice apartment. Clean, orderly, tastefully furnished.

Jack has fixed us drinks, and my Scotch and his vodka sit side by side on the coffee table in the center of the room, but from the look in his eyes as he prowls toward me, I'm not certain we'll be drinking them any time soon.

He comes to a stop in front of me, and we act on instinct, our mouths crashing together and hands roaming wildly.

He pulls back, breathless. "I've been thinking about what it would be like to be fucked by you from the second I set eyes on you, Mason."

I arch an eyebrow, tugging his head back with my hand fisted in his hair. His eyes are dark with hunger. "Yeah?"

"Yeah. You're hot as fuck."

His T-shirt strains against his hard pecs, and my

mouth waters at the thought of running my tongue over his skin.

"Can I taste you?" he pants.

"Knock yourself out, handsome."

He drops to his knees and makes quick work of my belt and jeans. My cock hardens at the touch of his skilled fingers, thickening in his grasp. He murmurs appreciatively, then his tongue darts out, flicking over my crown. I groan, pleasure building in my core. I grab his hair again and guide him onto my waiting cock. He takes all of me until I hit the back of his throat. Then he looks up at me, tears being squeezed from his eyes.

A memory takes hold, and I shake my head, trying to shake it loose. But it's too late. It's no longer Jack's mouth on me; it's mine on *him*.

I'm on my knees. Choking. Crying. My head is held still. He tells me how disgusting I am to be enjoying what he's doing.

I screw my eyes closed, willing the memory to slink back to the deepest recesses of my brain where it belongs. But it's a stubborn little fucker.

And now I can taste him. Smell him. My stomach rolls.

I stagger back a step, sliding from Jack's mouth. "I can't," I mumble.

Jack's staring up at me, blinking.

"I-I ..." My eyes dart around the room. I'm in Jack's apartment, but in my head I'm in Kyngston Worthington

III's study. All I can smell are cigars and cheap brandy. And him. Stale piss and dried cum.

I balk.

Jack jumps to his feet. "Mason. Are you okay?"

I slam my hand over my mouth and mumble against my palm. "Must be something I ate."

He comes closer, trying to reassure me or maybe help me, but I wave him away and hurriedly do up my pants. I need to get out of here. Need to get home. Need to get safe.

I make a hasty apology and a hastier exit, and as soon as I make it out into the busy street, I suck in a lungful of New York air.

I'm still sweating. Still feel like I'm about to throw up. I decide to walk home, needing the fresh air.

Out of nowhere, like a gift from the heavens, I bump into my baby brother, and everything feels better. I wrap my arms around him like he's a life raft in the storm that's become my life. "Maddox! What are you doing here?"

He hugs me back, holding me tight, giving me exactly what I need. "I've just been to a meeting after my shift."

I nod, my head still spinning. "Of course, yeah." Maddox attends regular NA meetings, and one of his favorites takes place in a church near here. Still, it feels more than serendipitous to bump into him now.

"Everything okay, Mase?"

Shit. I must look a mess or at least not my usual self. I nod again though. "Yeah. Yeah. Just happy to see you. You headed home?"

He smirks. "Where else would I be headed on a Saturday night?"

"You want to stay at my place?" I could really use the company tonight—anything to distract me from the disastrous date I ran out on.

Maddox is a nomad, and although he has his own place in Queens, he often stays with me, our dad, or one of our brothers, so it's not unusual for him to spend the night at my penthouse. Still, I'm glad when he immediately agrees with no questions asked.

We walk through the city, and he's quiet, which I know from experience is a strategy he uses to get me to talk. After our brunch this morning, I know he suspects there's something up with me. "How was your meeting?" I ask.

"Great." He smiles, expertly dodging a mom with a double stroller who gives him a brazen once-over.

"Can I ask you something?"

"You can always ask. Doesn't mean I'm gonna answer." He winks.

"You've been sober for over seven years, but you never miss a meeting. Why do you still go?"

"Maybe I'm still sober because I never miss a meeting."

I shake my head. "I think you'd be able to do it on your own now, no?"

He laughs. "But I don't have to, so why would I? And besides, apathy or overconfidence—whichever makes people stop thinking they need help—are addicts' biggest downfalls. The moment you start thinking you don't need a meeting, you're in trouble."

"You think you'll go every week for the rest of your life though?"

"Maybe. Maybe not." He shrugs. "For now, the meetings are a big part of my life. A meaningful part of it. I don't only go for myself; I go to support my peers too. People get a lot from hearing others' stories, and what if my story is the one to help someone else choose sobriety? Then isn't it worth it?"

"Yeah, I guess it is."

"And as much as I love you and Dad and the guys, and as much as I value your support, nobody understands an addict's journey better than another addict. The struggles or the triumphs. There's something remarkably healing and awe-inspiring about being in a room full of people who've been where you are—or where you were."

I never considered it like that, nor how difficult it must have been for my baby brother to admit he needed help. It takes guts. "That makes a whole lot of sense."

"That's probably how any support group works," Maddox goes on. "The people who've been through it are often the easiest to talk to about it."

"Are there other kinds of support groups for people struggling with something?" Like men who freak out while having a hot guy suck their cock because of something that happened a lifetime ago.

He nods. "In New York, I bet you could find a support group for anything."

There's every chance I'm about to reveal something I don't want to, but I trust Maddox enough not to push me if I do. "Theoretically speaking, is there a group for people who ..." I swallow the words, not able to bring myself to say them. I shift tactics. "A friend of mine ... Something happened to him when he was a kid. He was ... forced to do something he didn't want to do. Is there a support group for that?"

The time between my question and Maddox's response seems to stretch into eternity. My heart is beating in my throat. Surely he knows I'm not talking about my friend. He knows it's me who's fucked up.

"You mean sexually assaulted?" is all he asks.

I nod.

"Yeah," he says. "There's a few actually. One meets every other week in the same place as my Tuesday NA meeting. I'll write down the details when we get to your place and you can pass them on to your friend."

"Thanks, Mad. I'm sure he'd appreciate that."

"No problem. I'm sure he'd be interested to know that almost twenty-five percent of men experience some form of sexual violence in their lives."

I had no idea the figure was that high. "That many?"

"Yeah, and over fifty percent of male rape victims experience it before the age of eighteen."

Definitely didn't know that either. But why does my

brother sound like he's giving a presentation on sexual violence? "How do you know all this?"

He shrugs. "I read a lot. And I support a lot of sexual assault charities, for both men and women."

Of course he does, after what happened to his high school girlfriend, Yasmin. Jamestech donates to a designated charity every year in her memory, and I make a mental note to add a charity for male victims to our annual donation list.

"Male sexual assault is rarely discussed openly, and I'm sure a lot of victims, like your friend for instance, think they're alone. Unfortunately, they're not." He gives me a sad smile.

What would a support group for men who've been sexually assaulted look like? Would I have anything in common with any of them, aside from the obvious? I spent ten years in therapy and did all the work, got my pat on the back, and graduated. That should mean I'm fixed.

Maddox and I are quiet for a while, and I don't know how to stop feeling so fucking tense and awkward.

Of course, he expertly lightens the mood with a change of subject. "Are we watching *Top Gun*, then?" I have never been happier to have him by my side than I am at this moment.

"Only if we watch the original," I reply.

He scoffs. "Have I ever insisted otherwise?"

"Yes. Two years ago on New Year's Day. I had an epic hangover, and I recall it vividly."

He rolls his eyes. "That's only because I hadn't seen it yet."

We're quiet again.

"Do you have popcorn?" he asks.

"Of course I have fucking popcorn. What kind of heathen do you think I am?"

Laughing, he throws an arm around my shoulder. "I can guarantee you don't have any green tea though."

"Because it tastes like ass. I have soda—the appropriate accompaniment to popcorn."

That gets me another eye roll.

"Fine. We can stop by somewhere and I'll get you some of your ass tea."

"Good." He gives me a side eye. "And I would have thought you enjoyed the taste of ass."

I laugh so loud that the people around us stop and stare. This is exactly what I need—not some support group full of strangers who don't know my name.

SEVENTEEN

MASON

Running my fingertip over the crease of the scrap of paper in my hand, I scan the carefully written details in Maddox's neat handwriting for what must be the thousandth time. I refold it and return it to the pocket of my jeans while looking up at the Episcopalian church. Two guys, one wearing a baseball cap and the other in a suit and tie but both carrying a Starbucks cup, walk past me and go inside. Are they here for the support group?

Am I here for the support group? Until today, I would have said no. Yet I find myself here anyway, wondering if it might do something, anything, to help me never picture that evil fuck's face ever again.

I've been loitering around the building for ten minutes now, and I wouldn't be surprised if someone calls the cops soon. I have no idea how I would explain my being here.

Would anyone buy me being in the heart of the Bronx for an important business meeting on a Tuesday evening? I could claim I'm here for a hookup. That would be more believable. The reminder of my disastrous hookup on Saturday night has me taking a step toward the building. I should at least go in there and see what it's like. It's probably not for me, and it's unlikely I'll have anything in common with anyone in there, but I won't know unless I give it a try.

What have I got to lose, except for my dignity?

Taking a deep breath, I steel myself and walk inside. There's a hand-written sign in the entryway that reads *MSASG* with an arrow pointing to a set of oak double doors. My heart hammers as I approach them. My fingers tremble as I grip the handle. When I pull open the door, I'm hit by the smell of coffee and cleaning products layered over a faint odor of rubber and plastic. Nope. This isn't for me. It's not too late to leave.

"Come on in," someone calls. "Grab yourself a seat."

Shit! Too late. Should I pretend I've walked into the wrong place? The owner of the voice, maybe late forties with ginger hair and a thick beard, smiles at me. "You're in the right place," he says softly. "It's hard to walk through these doors for the first time, but it will get easier, I promise."

Tentatively, I step into the room and note the other two dozen or so men in here. Some sit in plastic chairs that form a circle in the center of the room while others mill around a table along the far wall, getting coffee and what look to be brownies. "I'm Chris." The guy holds out his hand, and I shake it.

I consider giving a false name, but for some reason, I don't. "Mason."

"It's good to meet you, Mason. Would you like some coffee? Homemade brownie? They're salted caramel, my wife's specialty."

I shake my head. "I'm good, thanks."

"Then please take a seat." He gestures toward the chairs, and I choose one that has a vacant seat on either side. Crossing my legs and arms, I feel like the new kid at a school where I don't belong and don't want to be. This was a mistake. A huge mistake. And now I have to sit here for the next hour and feign interest in the Men's Sexual Abuse Support Group.

Once everyone is seated, Chris gives a brief speech to remind us of the need for confidentiality and to welcome the new faces, which are me and a guy named Isaac who's in his early twenties and looks even more uncomfortable than I feel.

The group starts with a brief check-in for those who want to update, and I am already certain this is going to be no help to me at all.

Then the first person shares his story. Jeff is a construction worker, which he told us in his update because he started a huge job yesterday and is feeling tired. A fifty-eight-year-old grandfather, Jeff spent over forty years of his life trying to forget the fact that his uncle raped him when he was fifteen. It was only when his second grandson was born and his daughter wanted to name the baby after her grandfather—who happened to have the same name as Jeff's uncle—that he couldn't lie any longer.

Faced with the prospect of his grandchild sharing a name with his abuser, he told his wife and daughter what had happened to him. They were supportive and showed him nothing but love, but he still struggles to talk about what happened and is dealing with the shame of never standing up to his uncle. Tears stream down his face as he thanks the group for being there for him and for letting him say whatever he needs to say without judgment.

My own eyes are full of tears by the time he's done talking, and I join the rest of the group in applauding his bravery. Next, we hear from Jason, who was sexually assaulted by his boss when he was an intern. Most of the attendees speak, some only for a minute and some for longer, but each of their stories are unique yet hauntingly familiar. And all of them, including Peter the plastic surgeon and Max the war vet, share common themes of overwhelming guilt and shame as well as the belief that they should have somehow been able to stop what happened.

When nearly everyone in the room has spoken, Chris asks if the new people would like to share tonight, and Isaac shakes his head. "Mason?" Chris says softly.

Do I want to speak? I've never told anyone but my therapist what happened to me, and that was in the safety of her office with a wall full of credentials that promised confidentiality. I'm not sure I really want to divulge my darkest secrets to a room full of strangers. Strangers who might recognize me and sell my story to the highest bidder.

"You're safe here, Mason," Jeff tells me.

Everyone else signals their agreement.

The words pour from my mouth. "I was sexually assaulted by my boyfriend's dad when I was seventeen. He caught me and his son together, and he was a homophobic piece of shit. Being forced to suck his dick was my punishment for being a pervert." When I'm done speaking, I find everyone in the circle watching me. Not with pity in their eyes, but with understanding. Every man in this room knows what it's like to be powerless, to be filled with shame for something we have no business being ashamed of.

I'm surprised to find that I feel lighter. I feel seen and understood, and I realize I haven't truly felt those things in a very long time.

AFTER THE MEETING IS OVER, I hang back to help clear the chairs, and I thank Chris for being so welcoming.

"I hope you'll come back," he says. "It really does help. Some of the guys here have been coming for years now, and the change in them is stark. You did good speaking on your first visit." He claps me on the back and goes to help Peter clear away the coffee mugs.

The other newcomer, Isaac, sidles up beside me. "That was brave telling everyone your story like that. I kind of wish I had now."

I have no idea what the protocol is here, but part of me wants to encourage him to share now. Maybe invite him for coffee and a chat, but I suspect that wouldn't be a good idea. I'm not sure I'm ready for facing these kinds of issues out in the real world. "Next time, then. You're going to come back, right?"

He wrinkles his nose and shrugs. "Maybe. I dunno. Groups aren't really my thing, but my girlfriend—she's super smart. She's also pregnant with our first baby."

"Congratulations, buddy," I say.

A faint smile tugs at the corner of his lips. "Thanks. Well, she said I should really find some help for what happened before I become a dad. And, you know, it was comforting hearing other people's stories. Fuck, that sounds awful. Like I'm happy that other people went through the kind of shit that I did."

"No, it doesn't," I assure him. "I understand what you mean."

"Will you come back?" Isaac asks.

"I will if you will," I promise, holding out my hand.

He shakes it, his lips slightly curved. "Deal."

CHAPTER
EIGHTEEN

KING

Laughter drifts through the open office door. Unrestrained laughter, the kind that only happens between two people who have a connection. It's after six, and most of the building has cleared out, so it probably isn't work. Does Mason have a guy in his office?

I haven't seen him since Grampa and I bumped into him on Saturday, and as much as I hate to admit it, I've missed him. He hasn't been here for our usual update the past two nights either and I have no idea why that is.

I brace myself for what I might find when I walk in. He knew I was coming here tonight because I told him so via email. So is this some kind of punishment? Does he want me to see him with whichever guy this is? To witness someone else sharing something with him that I never will again because I lost that right a long time ago.

The door is wide open, so I walk in without knocking. Mason is still laughing, and the guy next to him—big, tattooed, stacked, exactly Playboy's type—is smiling back at him like he's landed the most incredible man in the world.

My research on Mason has led me to the conclusion that he doesn't go short of offers, yet he remains terminally single. But perhaps that's a cover. Maybe being New York's most eligible bachelor is simply an image he likes to curate. Maybe he and this guy are actually living together and have two puppies and an old one-eyed cat they rescued from a sewer drain.

They're doing nothing more than sitting next to each other on the large sofa, but they may as well be fucking for the way jealousy courses through my veins. Their thighs are touching. They're close, and not just literally.

Mason looks up, and all too suddenly, his laughter halts. There's not even a hint of a smile on his face now. It fucking stings, but I swallow down my anger the same way I always do. One of these days, it's going to be the cause of a massive heart attack or something.

"I'll catch you later, Ty," Mason says stiffly. I can't help but feel like he doesn't want me to see that side of him—the vulnerable, open side.

Ty squeezes Mason's shoulder and offers me a polite goodbye before leaving us alone.

"That your boyfriend?" I ask as soon as he's out of

earshot, and I'm annoyed at myself for being so damn obvious.

"Would it bother you if I said yes?" Mason is standing right in front of me now. "Disgust you to think about my hands on his cock? Make you feel sick to imagine me fucking him? Right here. Over my desk." He jerks his head at his desk, and the willpower and restraint I've been holding onto for the past two weeks snaps like a tightly wound rubber band.

My hand is wrapped around his throat before I can think through the consequences of what I'm doing. I yank him forward and his chest crashes against mine. "The only thing that makes me feel sick, Mason, is imagining anyone's hands on you." I slide my free hand over his cock and suppress a growl at finding it semi-hard already. "Anyone's but mine."

His pupils blow so wide it's hard to see the sparkling brown of his eyes. I squeeze him over his suit pants and he groans. "Fuck you, King."

Keeping a firm grip on his throat, I dust my lips over his jawline until I reach the spot beneath his ear. "I bet you'd like to. But I'm the one who does the fucking, or have you forgotten that?"

His cock stiffens at my touch, and I fumble for his belt and tug it open. Mason's breathing grows faster and heavier. I unzip his pants, and the sound is full of promise and temptation. My own dick strains at my zipper. Slipping my hand into his boxers, I wonder what he'd do if I simply spun him around and bent him over that desk. Fucked him the way I've dreamed about for eighteen long years.

When I wrap my hand around the base of his thick shaft, he groans. "You always were such a good boy for me, Mase."

He grinds into my hand. "I said fuck you!"

"You are fucking me, baby. Fucking my hand like you've been desperate for me to touch you." I flick my tongue over the shell of his ear. "You are desperate, aren't you? My needy little fuck toy."

He grunts something unintelligible.

I work my hand up and down his solid length, reveling in the feel of him, hot and smooth. Swiping the pad of my thumb over his crown, I collect the precum there and use it as lube to work him over. And while I do, I grind my aching shaft against his hip, feral with need for him. Eager for him to touch me the way I'm touching him or to sink myself into any part of him. Mason James is unraveling me. Every time I have any contact with him, it pulls at another loose thread. Soon, there will be nothing left of me but a mess of desire.

"Tell me how good it feels to have my hands on you after all this time," I growl in his ear. "I've waited so fucking long to touch you again."

His hands rake over my scalp while he fucks my hand. "Jesus, fuck, King," he cries, spilling warm ribbons of hot cum over my fist.

Panting for breath, he staggers back and glares at me. "Get the fuck out of my office."

Fuck. Did I push him too far? He did want that, right? "Mason, I'm sorry, I just ..." I wipe my hand on my shirt, staining it with his cum.

"Get the fuck out, King!" he bellows.

Filled with remorse and anger, I walk out of his office and make a vow to never go back. This job was a mistake, and jerking off my boss in his office was a bigger mistake. One I won't make again.

NINETEEN

KING

You fucking disgust me! I hate you. You're a freak. An abomination against God. I should have smothered you at birth. The words of Emmeline and Kyngston Worthington III ring in my ears for the whole ride home. It's like they're trapped inside my bike helmet and I can't get them out.

And then I hear Mason screaming at me to get out. I recall the hurt expression on his face. The fear in his eyes. Was he scared of me? I would never hurt him.

Except I did.

Now it's my own words playing over and over. The ones I said to Mason after my father caught us together. *Didn't you hear me when I told you that you fucking disgust me? Did you think any of this was real? This was a joke to see exactly how far you'd go, so that I can tell everyone about what a pathetic, needy, sick little shit you really are. I hate you.*

You're a fucking freak! You think any of this is real? I'm not gay. Never have been. Never will be.

I blamed him for corrupting me. Me—the one who was older and bigger and stronger. The person who should have protected him. Instead, I fed him to the wolves. I made him feel as small and worthless as I'd been made to feel my whole life. And I never went back and told him it was all a lie. A lie told by a scared little boy who still craved the love and approval of his parents. I left as soon as I could a few days later, and I let him go on believing I meant every word.

When I stop at a light, I open my visor and scrub the tears from my eyes so I can see properly.

By the time I get to Marble Hill, I've cleared my head enough that I can face Amanda and my grandfather without them worrying something has happened. The last thing I want to do is burden either of them.

My heart sinks at the sight of Dr. Lichtenstein's car parked outside the apartment, and I turn off my bike engine and race inside.

Amanda is crying on the sofa.

Now I can't breathe.

She looks up. "King! I left you a voicemail. I had to call the doctor an hour ago. I called your parents too, but they said they d-didn't want to c-come." She sobs loudly.

I pull out my phone and see her voicemail from a little over an hour ago, the time it took me to get here in New York traffic. I'm scared to ask ... "Is he dead?"

She shakes her head, and I almost drop to the floor with relief. At that moment, Dr. Lichtenstein walks out of Grampa's room, a solemn look on his face.

"Doc? Is he okay?" I plead. His breathing was a little more labored than normal this morning, but he was here. He was alive. He laughed at a stupid joke I told him.

"He's comfortable, but he's not conscious. He doesn't have long left, Mr. Blackthorn. If there is anyone who would like to say their final goodbyes, then I would suggest you call them immediately."

Pain twists my insides into a knot. This is it then. "Thanks, Doc."

He offers me a faint smile and rests a comforting hand on my arm. "He sure is a fighter. I'm going to miss him."

All I can do is nod my thanks before he leaves.

Amanda sniffs, scrubbing at her cheeks with the sleeve of her cardigan. "I really wish I could stay but ... I look after my nephew on Thursday nights for my sister ... and she can't ..." A sob steals the rest of her sentence.

I pull her into a hug, probably needing the human contact more than she does. "It's okay. You've done more than anyone could have expected. He truly loved spending time with you. Thank you for everything."

She glances at the open doorway to his room. "Can I go say goodbye?"

"Of course."

I watch her walk into the room and remain outside while she sits with him, speaking quietly. After a few minutes, she gives him a kiss on the forehead and walks out, her cheeks soaked with tears.

She grips my hand tightly. "He's not in any pain, you know. That's important, I think."

I nod my agreement. "It absolutely is."

She plasters a sad smile on her face. "Hey, he beat out those doctors though, huh? Four weeks, they said."

"He sure did. Stubborn old goat." We both laugh, but it's hollow and sad. Something to replace the dreadful silence of his impending death.

"Will you call me ... if ... you know. So I know?"

"Of course I will," I promise.

"Would you like me to try your parents again? Maybe if I explain—"

"No, it's okay. Really," I tell her. Not only would it be a waste of her time, but I don't want them here anyway. Just because I would permit their presence doesn't mean I welcome it. They would only taint his final hours with their hostility and disapproval.

"You're sure there's no one I can call to come sit with you?"

Immediately, and for reasons I can't fathom, my thoughts turn to Mason. I dismiss them as quickly as they arrived. "No. There's no one else." Those words hang solemnly in the air. Nobody but me and Grampa.

She glances at the clock. "I really have to leave." She hurries to his bed, gives him one last kiss on the cheek, and whispers something to him that I don't hear.

And then she's gone, and it really is just me and him. The way I spent the best parts of my childhood. Even if they were far too infrequent, all of my favorite memories are of him. His cigar smoke and his rattling cackle. His frailty and his strength. He taught me all I know about being a man.

I sit beside him and rest my forehead on his knuckles and talk about all the things I should have talked about when there was time. I tell him about Mason, how we met, how I fucked it up, and how much I wish I could make up for it now. I tell Grampa how much I love him and how much I'm going to miss him and how the world will be a little duller without him in it. I tell him I'm sorry for all the time I spent away, and I'm saddened beyond belief that he won't sit up and scold me for it.

When he passes, it's quiet and peaceful. I expected something more. A final gasp of breath. A squeeze of my hand to let me know he was on his way. But he left this life the way he lived it, gently and without a fuss.

I call Amanda in a haze of confusion and console her when she sobs down the phone. I call my parents, and our conversation is brief and detached. Once he's been taken away, I remove his sheets from the bed, dislodging the scent of cough drops and lavender that is so much him that it makes me stumble. But I don't fall. I carefully fold the linens and place them in the laundry room, ready to be washed tomorrow. Or perhaps I'll never wash them, and they'll be a constant reminder of his presence here.

I wander around the apartment in a daze—a place that only felt like home when he was in it. Thunder cracks and lighting splits the sky in two before rain begins to hammer against the windowpane. It's as though even the heavens know he's gone.

"Bye, Grampa," I whisper.

CHAPTER

TWENTY

MASON

How the fuck could I be so weak as to let him anywhere near me? I slam my beer bottle down on the kitchen counter. As soon as he put his hands on me, I lost all ability for rational thought.

I hate that I told him to get out, and even more, I hate the look on his face when I did. It was nothing less than he deserved, but it wasn't fair. He's not a mind reader. I wanted what happened, but it was easier to blame him for my loss of control, although I could have told him to stop at any point. I could have pushed him away. I should have punched him in the face.

But the truth is I didn't want him to stop. It felt too good to have him touching me, to have him make my body respond the way only he's ever been able to. He somehow knows exactly what I want when I want it. When to speed up and slow down, when to be soft or when to be rough. And I hated myself for the way I felt, so I took it out on him.

Now I feel like the world's biggest asshole and everything is fucked because I came all over his fucking hand like that awkward teenager who was obsessed with him back in high school. Is that why he did it? To prove he still had some control over me? To prove he still holds all the power?

I grab another beer from the fridge and lean against the kitchen counter. King was right. I am fucking disgusting. Just not for the reasons he believes I am.

My cell vibrates on the countertop beside me. Think of the devil. I shouldn't answer it, but my fingers twitch against the granite—itching for me to pick up and find out why the hell he's calling.

With a frustrated sigh, I pick it up and put him on speaker. The sound of the rain is deafening, and I glance outside at the storm. What the hell is he doing out in this? When he doesn't speak, I do. "What do you want?"

"I'm outside." He sounds small. Lost. Not at all himself.

Between the rain and the fact that I'm thirty floors up, I don't expect to be able to see him. Still, I walk to the window and peer down at the street below. How does he know where I live? "What the hell are you doing here?"

The rain hammers against the pavement and parked

cars, but I can't see him. "Your d-doorman won't let me in." He sounds like he's shivering.

Of course he won't. Still doesn't answer my question. "What do you want, King?" I press my forehead to the glass, hoping for a glimpse of him. Not much can be seen from up here other than the streetlamps.

"I don't ... I dunno, Mase. He's ... and I didn't know ..." He sobs.

Fuck, is he crying? Panic bubbles up in my chest. "King, what's happened?"

"He's dead, Mase."

Is he talking about his grandfather? After seeing them together, it's hard for me to imagine that he's close enough to anyone else to be this upset about their death.

"I didn't know w-where else to go," he adds.

Fucking hell. My heart cracks in two at the desperation in his tone. "My doorman will let you in. Go hand him your phone."

There's a shuffling sound, and a few seconds later, I speak to Bill and ask him to show King to my private elevator.

The line goes dead, and without thought for the fact I'm wearing only my shorts, I jog out into the hallway in time to see the light indicating the elevator is traveling up. My heart beats in my throat while I wait for him. He sounded so distraught, and he must be to have come here. To have come to me, of all people.

The elevator doors open, and he steps out, shoulders

slumped and his dripping T-shirt plastered to his skin. He looks up, his dark-green eyes full of tears when they meet mine. "He's dead."

"Arthur?"

He gives a single nod.

"Shit. I'm sorry, King." I take a few steps toward him.

"I didn't know where else to go. I didn't ..." He screws his eyes closed and shakes his head, sending droplets of rain flying from his head. "I'm sorry, I shouldn't have come here. I shouldn't have ..." His shoulders shake, and he pinches the bridge of his nose. "Fuck!"

If King is here, that must mean he has nowhere else. Nobody else. I have no idea how painful that must be. Losing my mom was devastating, and it ripped out my heart, but I still had my brothers and my dad to turn to. Instinct takes over, and I rest a comforting hand on his shoulder. "It's okay that you're here. Come on in and I'll get you something to drink. You can get dry and then you can talk. Or you can just sit. Okay?"

He opens his eyes again and nods, and he looks so vulnerable and un-King-like that it's easy to forget how mad I was at both of us a few minutes ago. He follows me through the open-plan space, and I gesture for him to sit at the kitchen island while I pour him a Scotch.

After checking he's okay, I leave him to grab some dry clothes. He decides to change out of his wet clothes right there in my kitchen, and I distract myself by pouring a bag of chips into a bowl, anything to avoid staring at him while he undresses. Anything to avoid him catching me staring.

By the time I've set out the chips and some dip, he's wearing my sweats but has annoyingly left the T-shirt on the kitchen island, and now I'll be forced to stare at his chiseled physique while we talk. Great.

He rolls his neck. "It's kind of hot in here. You don't mind if I don't wear that, do you?" He looks to the folded T-shirt.

It is hot in here. I like it hot because I enjoy walking around here in only my shorts, like I am right now. Fuck, if I knew he was coming over, I would have turned the thermostat down forty degrees and left my suit on. He's finished his Scotch, so I pour him another and take a seat across from him. "I'm sorry about your grandfather."

He knocks back his drink and drops his head, scrubbing his hand over the back of his neck. "Thanks. I'm sorry I turned up here like this. I guess I didn't want to be alone, and I didn't know where else to go."

"You don't have to apologize."

He glances around. "I haven't interrupted anything, have I?"

I shake my head. Unfortunately, since you walked back into my life, there has been very little to interrupt. Wisely, I keep that thought to myself. "Your grandfather seemed like a real nice guy," I say instead, steering the conversation to safer, less likely to give me an inappropriate hard-on, territory.

"He was."

"He was your mom's dad, right?"

King nods vigorously. "Yeah. My dad hated him. And vice versa."

Well, now I like the late Arthur Blackthorn even more. "Do they know?"

He snorts a laugh. "Yup. Couldn't give a fuck. His own daughter didn't come see him when he was dying. How fucked up is that?"

"Pretty fucked up." I take a sip of my Scotch, and when I put my glass down on the counter, King is staring at me intently.

"I'm really sorry, Mase," he says, his voice thick with emotion.

I swallow hard, unsure what he's apologizing for.

"For what happened today. But also for what I did eighteen years ago. All the things I said. Leaving the way I did."

I don't go near the whole eighteen-years-ago thing because everything is already raw and emotional enough. "You don't have to apologize for what happened today. I shouldn't have reacted the way I did. It was ..." I take a deep breath. "It was a lot to process, and it took me by surprise. But I wanted what happened, and I'm sorry if I made you feel like I didn't."

"I appreciate you telling me that." Now his deep-green eyes rake over me unashamedly. "You know, I think I do know why I came here." His voice is dark and seductive, and that inappropriate hard-on situation is becoming more real by the second.

Fuck me, this just got a whole different kind of intense. Memories of today—of how good it felt to have his hands on me, how easily he manipulated my body—fill me with both shame and desire. "And why is that?"

"I think ..." His Adam's apple bobs in his throat as he swallows. "I think I needed to be around someone who loved me. Even if it was a long time ago." Tears fill his beautiful green eyes again, and I have to take a deep breath as the force of his admission hits me. He downs his Scotch. "I also think it's dangerous to admit something like that to you."

"Dangerous how?"

He walks around the kitchen island. "Talking feelings with you is dangerous, Mason. Don't you think?"

It's not talking about feelings that scares the hell out of me where he's concerned. It's acting on them. Still, I inch closer, hyperaware of the heat from his body. King Blackthorn is fire, and it seems like I'm looking to get myself burned. This is a dumbass move—I know it and so does he. We're going to regret this tomorrow, but as idiotic as it is, I can't seem to stop myself. I'm hypnotized by those dark-green eyes, rock-hard abs, and gray sweats. I glance down. Yeah, definitely by the gray sweats, or more likely by the outline of the impressive semi-hard cock I can clearly see in them. Fuck me. I think I just lost fifty IQ points.

He sits on the stool directly beside where I stand, facing me and daring me to make the next move—after my reaction in my office earlier today, I can't blame him.

"No, but I think it's dangerous to have you sitting in my kitchen like this." I trail my fingertips over his jawline, my fingernails rasping against his thick stubble.

He grabs my hips and pulls me between his spread thighs, and I don't try to stop him. "Like what?" His voice is low and full of gravel, and each word feels like a caress on my skin.

"Half drunk and half dressed."

He tilts his head to the side. "I'm not drunk. Not even a little bit. Are you?"

Nervous energy sizzles along my spine. I know exactly where this conversation is headed, and I'm powerless to stop it. Powerless to stop him. "Not drunk, no."

He breathes heavily, his warm breath dusting over my skin and making me shiver. His fingers flex on my hips, digging into the muscle. He drags his bottom lip through his teeth and groans. "You are so fucking sexy. Do you know that?"

I don't reply. Can't form a word. All my effort is being directed into not smashing my mouth against his and then begging him to fuck me.

"Yeah, you know that already, right, Playboy?"

"Fuck you, Hotshot."

He tugs me forward until my hips are pressed against his thighs. I know if I look down his cock will be as hard as mine is, so I don't. He leans closer, his mouth inches from my ear. "No, but I'd really like to fuck you."

I groan. Actually fucking groan. God, I'm ashamed of myself.

He pulls back a little, and I'm left staring into his deep-green eyes. "I need you, Mase. Please?"

I can't believe this is real and that he's saying these things. Would I be taking advantage of his grief and the fact that he's seeking comfort? Would any warm, willing body do, or is it specifically me he needs? I realize I don't fucking care, at least about the latter. Not right now at least, with his hands on me and my cock aching for his touch, not to mention the need coursing through my veins like it's my life force. But I do care about taking advantage of someone who's not thinking clearly. "This is your grief speaking. You're not gay, remember? You'll regret this, if not tomorrow, then when you're thinking straight."

He huffs a dark laugh. "Mason, I am one hundred percent gay, even if I'll never admit it openly. And this isn't my grief talking. This is me wanting you the way I have since you walked into your brother's office a few weeks ago and tore me a new one. Nothing more and nothing less." And fuck me, but I want him too, no matter how much I should hate him. He palms my cock over my shorts, and it stiffens further at his touch. "You want me too. I know you do."

I can hardly deny that fact when I'm hard as fucking iron. "If we do this, it's once, King."

He wraps a hand around my throat and squeezes lightly, and pleasure snakes its way up my spine. "Of course it is. I'm not looking for anything serious, Playboy."

I glare at him. Condescending jackass. "I top now."

He smirks, tightening his grip on my neck. "Not with me, baby."

There's no time to tell him to go to hell because his mouth crashes against mine. He drags me closer and his tongue is in my mouth while his free hand is on my ass, and it all feels so fucking good that I go with it, melting into him and letting him kiss and touch me like he owns me.

How the hell did I wind up naked in bed with a man I'm supposed to hate hovering over me, his cock slick with lube because he's about to fuck me. He works his finger inside me, opening me up, and I groan at the unfamiliar sensation.

His hot mouth rests against my ear. "How long has it been since you let someone fuck you, Mase?"

I hiss out a breath. "Eighteen years."

"Jesus fuck," he mutters, running his nose over the back of my neck. "Am I the only one?"

I don't answer. Admitting that to him makes it sound like he was special, and although he was, neither of us need to be reminded of that.

He presses a soft kiss beneath my ear. "Am I?" His tone has lost all of that cocky arrogance, and maybe that's what makes me tell him yes.

"Spread a little wider for me." Full of impatience, he nudges my thighs apart with his knees before I have a chance to comply. And then his chest is flush against my back, pressing me into the mattress while I tremble with anticipation. "Relax, baby. I know exactly how you like to be fucked."

"The fuck—" My retort is cut off by a loud moan as he finds my prostrate and massages it with expert fingers.

"Yeah, you like that, baby. I remember."

I remember too. And it's too much and also not enough.

We shouldn't do this.

But it's only once. I can give into this one time. And then we'll go back to being barely civil colleagues. "Fuck me, King."

"Oh, baby. I love it when you beg for me." He drops a kiss on my neck and pulls his fingers out of me. The crown of his thick cock nudges at my ass. Somewhere in the darkest recesses of my consciousness, the place where I keep all my memories of King, I remember how to breathe through the burning pleasure of that first push inside me.

Recall how to relax my muscles so that he slides in without resistance.

"Fuck, Mase." He rests his lips in the crook of my neck. "You feel good. So. Fucking. Good, baby." He sinks all the way inside, and his hips slam against my ass.

His forearms are on either side of my head, pillars of muscle lined with thick veins. I drag in a harsh breath as the pleasurable sensations wash over me. He feels good too. As good as I remember. "Jesus fuck." I grit out the words as he slides out and sinks back in.

He grunts in my ear and nails me to the bed, pushing me closer to the edge with every move he makes. My aching cock rubs against the duvet, grinding into the soft material with each thrust of his hips.

He sinks his teeth into the muscle at the nape of my neck. I'm going to come. Fucker is going to make me come like this, with his cock stuffed in my ass and his mouth on me. My entire body trembles. "That's it, baby boy," he groans. "You're gonna come for me."

"Fuck!" I bite down on my pillow as the orgasm slams into me with the force of a fifty-ton truck.

"Good boy."

I should tell him to go to hell for calling me that, but I don't care. I'm fucking boneless. Melting into the bed as he grinds his own release into me. When he's done, he rests his head between my shoulder blades and catches his breath, skating his fingers along my ribcage. The same way he used to.

The moment is way too intimate. Way too familiar. Too much of what we absolutely cannot be. He must sense it as well because he grumbles something unintelligible before pulling out of me and jumping out of bed.

I roll onto my back while he gets rid of the condom. The familiarity is already gone, replaced by an awkward silence that neither of us appears to know how to break. It's King who finally speaks. "I should go."

That's definitely for the best. I have no idea what we were thinking, letting ourselves get carried away like that. "Your clothes will be dry. I'll go get them."

He shakes his head. "No."

His tone is harsh and clipped and I wince at my own stupidity. Should never have opened the goddamn door to him.

"I'll go get them. And then ..." He glances over his shoulder at me. "I'll get out of your hair and let you get yourself cleaned up."

His desire to leave so quickly stings more than I expected it would. As for me getting cleaned up, I'm not sure anything in this world could cleanse me of King. He doesn't look at me again before he walks out of the room, and I try my best not to stare at his annoyingly fine ass as he does. I don't get up to use the shower until I hear the elevator doors and I'm certain he's gone. Was I hoping he'd come back? No, of course not.

A minute later, I'm standing in a scalding-hot shower with my head bent low, letting the water run over me. I can still smell him. Still feel his mouth on my skin and his hands on my body. My muscles ache with the memory of what we did. I have no idea how long I stand here for, but as I suspected would be the case, I could stand here forever and use all the soap in the world, and it still wouldn't be enough to wash him off me.

TWENTY-ONE

KING

"Morning, Mr. Blackthorn." The name of the junior assistant escapes me, but I nod a greeting as she leans over me to grab a banana from the bowl I'm standing in front of.

I have no idea how long I've been stirring my coffee and contemplating the stupidity of what I did last night.

How did a simple walk in the rain lead me to Mason James's apartment building? Why the hell did he let me in?

I know the answer to that one. Because, behind all of his arrogance and easy charm, he's a good guy. A really good guy. He's also technically my boss and the man I fucked last night.

It felt good though. Sinking into him was incredible. Familiar and new. Running my hands over his chiseled body was like heaven. He's fucking spectacular, but I'm still an idiot for doing it. Which is why I ran out of there as soon as it was over. I'm such a coward.

"Any plans for tonight?" She's so close I feel her breath on my face, reminding me of her presence. Her eyes rake over me while I'm thinking of her boss's boss's boss's hot ass.

"None that I'd like to share." I give her a tight smile and walk away. I've made a point of not cultivating any relationships with the employees here. That gives them less opportunity to ask questions and discover something about me they shouldn't.

I'm here undertaking a health and safety audit. Nothing more. Certainly don't want to make friends with any of these people, although I think being friends was the last thing Chanel was looking for. Yeah, that's her name. Chanel. Like the perfume. I head down the hallway in time to see Hayden from HR go into Mason's office.

Hayden has been on my radar since day one. For one thing, he spends far too much time in Mason's office. Why the hell does the HR manager have that much face time with the COO? Two possible reasons: He wants to fuck him or he's trying to get information he shouldn't have. Or both. He definitely wants to fuck him though. It's obvious from the way his eyes linger on Mason's ass whenever he thinks nobody else is looking. I'm always watching though.

I lean against the wall, blowing on my hot coffee and watching the door for Hayden's exit. He never remains in there for long, so maybe Mason is onto him too. My cell vibrates in my pocket, and I fish it out.

> We need to discuss your grandfather's will.

A text from my mother. No condolences. No emotion. Cold. Detached. Emmeline Worthington all over. I expect them to contest the will, and maybe they have every right to. My grandma made that thing over thirty years ago, so maybe it won't hold up now.

Sliding the phone back into my pocket, I decide that I don't give a fuck at this moment in time. Grampa is gone. Nothing will change that. While I'm grateful for the time we spent together, I'm also aware that it has made his loss more acute. There's a gaping hole in my life now and nothing for me to fill it with. In the past, I used work as an escape, but this kind of hole can't be filled with anything but more of the same. More connection. More feeling.

I spoke with the funeral director this morning, and as per his last wishes, Grampa will be cremated and there will be a small celebration of life with only a few select guests. Amanda and me, his fishing buddy Leonard, and my parents—if they choose to attend. As it's a public opportunity to air their grief and garner some sympathy, no doubt they will.

I sip my coffee and go on staring at Mason's office. It's been ten minutes. What the fuck are they doing in there?

I'm considering going to find out for myself when the door opens and Hayden walks out, a sheepish smile on his face.

Fucker.

I place my empty mug in a plant pot and stride across the hall. Deborah isn't at her desk for some reason, which is probably why that sneaky little fuck got to stay in there for so long, but it's also why I can walk straight in without knocking. It's rude and disrespectful, but I'm acting on instinct. I need to see him. I need to make sure last night didn't fuck everything up. I need him to look at me and not feel guilt or shame. What we did was reckless and stupid, but it was also something incredible.

He's sitting behind his desk, brow furrowed as he stares at his computer. I close the door, and the sound gets his attention. He immediately starts chewing on his bottom lip. I wish I could tell what he was thinking. That look in his eyes could either mean he wants to punch me in the face or suck my cock.

"I wanted to thank you for last night," I blurt out.

He arches an eyebrow.

Shit. "For letting me up, and you know, listening." I run a hand over my neck. It's so fucking hot in here. Why does he need everywhere to be the same temperature as the surface of the sun? "Not for the other thing."

"You're not thanking me for the fucking?"

I glare at him. "Do I need to?"

He smiles. My knees almost buckle. The fuck is wrong with me? I sit in the chair opposite him before my legs give way entirely at the sight of those dimples. "You don't have to thank me for any of it, King."

Then why do I feel like I should? "Well, you didn't have to let me come up, so ..." I shrug, feeling awkward.

"You think I'd leave you standing in the rain after you told me your grandfather died?" He sounds hurt.

"It's probably no less than I deserved. Could have been the perfect revenge." I laugh, but the poor attempt at a joke doesn't land well.

"How are you doing?" he asks, his voice full of concern now.

I shake my head. "Kind of numb. There's so much to do. The funeral. The will."

"Yeah, it's a lot. You need any help?"

I blink at him, confused.

He clears his throat. "I mean lawyer wise. I'm sure Drake would help out."

"Honestly, I don't know yet. Gonna have to take each day as it comes."

There's a knock at the door, and Hayden is back. "What is it?" Mason asks with a sigh, like he's annoyed at being disturbed, which is unlike him. He's the kind of boss who always has plenty of time for his employees.

"Just wondered if you needed any help," he offers breezily. "You know, with Deborah being sick today."

"I'm sure I can cope for one day. And I'm in a meeting." He gestures at me.

Hayden looks flustered. "Sorry, sir."

I suppress a smile at his dismissal of Hayden. He's never done that to me when I've interrupted a meeting, which I've done both purposely and accidentally.

Mason leans forward in his chair. He has his shirt sleeves rolled up to the elbow, and he rests his forearms on the desk. I distinctly remember trailing my tongue over a thick vein there last night. "Did you mean what you said?"

Fuck, he wants to talk about that? Maybe if I feign ignorance ... "About what?"

"About the reason you came to my place."

I could lie, but I owe him the truth. "Yeah. I meant it."

He doesn't reply but simply nods and leans back in his chair. As we stare at each other, the room grows thick with unspoken words and sexual tension. While we agreed to one night, I know we both want more.

I can tell by the way his dark eyes keep drifting over my torso, his pupils blown wide. By the slightest change to the rhythm of his breathing.

He loosens his tie and unbuttons his shirt, and I stare at his neck. The place I had my mouth last night. The sweet, salty taste of his skin has my dick aching to be let out of my pants.

"You know we can't do this, right?" His voice sounds pained.

"Why not?"

He pinches the spot between his brows. "I just can't. We agreed it was one time. We both said that."

I know I hurt him, but fuck, that was eighteen years

ago. How long will he make me pay for it? "Fuck, we were kids, Mase." The moment the words leave my mouth, I regret them.

The light in his eyes dulls. "Yeah. You're right, King. We were kids. It meant nothing. Right. You told me that already." He's hurting now too. I can hear it in his voice.

"I never said that," I growl, my temper flaring. "I only meant ... How long can you go on punishing me for something I did eighteen years ago?"

"How long?" he repeats. "You say that like you didn't ghost me for eighteen fucking years and then walk back into my life a few weeks ago expecting me to forget everything that happened. And you know what? I wish I could forget it. I really fucking do."

I don't understand him sometimes. He's so full of compassion and forgiveness, but he refuses to get past this one thing. I fucked up. I hurt him. But how can he not see that I always loved him?

"I think you should leave. You're good at that, right?"

I take a deep breath and stop myself from telling him to go fuck himself. Stop myself from kissing him until we can't breathe. Neither of those scenarios are likely to end well.

So I do what I do best.

I leave.

CHAPTER
TWENTY-TWO

KING

I spent the better part of yesterday and today visiting the remaining tattoo shops in New York. It's taken weeks to get through them all, and it's been a time-consuming pain in the ass, but there are some parts of this job that need to be done in person. Unfortunately, it's also been fruitless. Not a single one of them recognized Cassidy Jones or remembered giving anyone a "King's Princess" tattoo over a year ago. Most of them asked for a photograph of the ink, saying they'd recognize their own work, but unfortunately, the only evidence of the actual tattoo is Curtis's description of it.

Thanks to that lead going nowhere, I'm already in a bad mood when I arrive at Graham Reese's office building. I agreed to meet my parents here to discuss Grampa's will, but I already sense this was a mistake. Their lawyer's office isn't exactly neutral ground.

They're huddled up with Graham on the other side of the glass conference room, looking conspiratorial. If I'm honest, I really don't give a fuck if I'm not entitled to Grampa's money, but I do give a fuck about those two sycophants getting a cent of it. I'd rather donate it all to charity.

His secretary announces my arrival, and my parents take a seat while Graham comes out to greet me, all fake smiles when he tells me it's good to see me.

"King?"

I turn toward the familiar voice and see Nathan James headed my way. I've met Mason's other older brother a few times at Jamestech since I started working there. "What are you doing here?" he asks.

"Here to discuss my grandfather's will. You?"

"Had a meeting." His eyes narrow on Graham, and the two men don't share any kind of greeting, although I get the sense they know each other. "Is the will being contested?"

"Seems so," I tell him.

He doesn't ask who's doing the contesting or what the issue is. Instead, he says, "You need any representation?"

"That won't be necessary," Graham blusters.

"I think we'll let Mr. Blackthorn decide that, don't you, Reese?" His tone drips with ice. I've heard of Nathan's ruthless reputation but have only ever found him to be pleasant in our interactions. This must be the side of him his adversaries see—the one that earned him a reputation as a shark in the courtroom. He looks to me. "I have an hour free, and it's all yours if you want it."

"Actually, you know, I could use some representation after all."

Graham scowls at us both, but there's not a damn thing he can do about it.

THERE ARE moments in life that stay with us forever, and the looks on my parents' and their sleazy lawyer's faces while Nathan James systematically destroys their argument in a few sentences is one such memory I intend to revisit often.

My father is foaming at the mouth while my mother stares at us with her usual air of coldness and Graham blunders his way through objection after objection.

Nathan rests his forearms on the table. "You have nothing, and you know it. There is not a single legal reason this decree does not stand as it is currently written, word for word. You wouldn't even get it in front of a judge. And if you waste any more of my client's time with this nonsense, I will sue you for harassment. Do you understand me?" Without waiting for an answer, he stands, fastens up his jacket, and indicates we're leaving.

My father shouts obscenities while Graham tries to appease him, and my mother simply glares at us like she's wishing for our imminent death.

I'm glad to get out of the room and into the elevator. "Thank you for that," I tell Nathan.

He nods, his brow furrowed in a frown. It's a minute before he speaks. "They have absolutely no grounds to contest that will, and Reese must be aware of that."

"They think they do though. My parents believe they're entitled to my grandfather's money," I explain.

"As often happens with families, but that will is airtight. And while I don't particularly like Graham Reese, he's a good lawyer. So it strikes me as odd that he didn't advise his clients of that fact."

"Maybe they assumed I'd roll over." It's not like they don't have grounds to reach that conclusion, although I don't say that to Nathan.

His frown deepens. "Maybe. Or maybe the stakes are higher than you think."

Now it's me frowning. "How so?"

"Your parents strike me as pretty desperate to get their hands on that money, King. Have you not picked up on that?"

I pride myself on being a good reader of people, and it pains me that I missed something he picked up on so quickly. "I figured it was their usual sense of entitlement."

He nods. "No doubt that's a factor, but I would wager there's more at stake than that. Are they experiencing any financial issues?"

"Not that I'm aware of. My mother's art collection

alone is worth millions, her jewels are worth more than most trust funds, and their house is worth at least ten million. They still have a housekeeper. I can't imagine they're struggling to any significant extent."

Nathan's hums like he's still thinking, still working through the details of the meeting. "Houses can be mortgaged, jewelry replicated from paste, and art collections can be copied and then sold. Their behavior would make more sense if they were broke is all I'm saying."

He makes valid points, but the idea of my parents being broke is ridiculous. There's no way to squander the kind of wealth they had. "I don't know. I've never looked into their financial situation. But they sure put on a good front if they are broke."

"I could be wrong, but it's worth considering. This may not be the last you hear of this. Even if they don't pursue it through legal means, they may try and use some other underhanded means."

I definitely wouldn't put it past them. "Such as?"

"The good old guilt trip for one."

I laugh. "Well, that one won't work on me."

"I wouldn't be so sure. We often have blind spots when it comes to our parents. Just be on your guard." The elevator reaches the ground floor, and we both step out. "That will is rock solid. I couldn't have written it better myself. But don't hesitate to reach out if you need any more advice."

I thank him and tell him where to send my bill, but he

insists on offering his time for free. After agreeing that I'll at least buy him a nice bottle of Scotch, we shake hands. When I climb on my bike, Nathan's words are still playing on my mind. Are the Worthingtons broke? And if they are, what the fuck have they done with all their money?

TWENTY-THREE

"I'm so sorry for your loss. My condolences, Emmeline." I listen to those words over and over again, and my mother soaks it all up.

She shed a single, solitary tear during the service, allowing it to run all the way down her cheek before she daintily dabbed it away with her napkin. She is center stage today and loving it. She thrives on the attention. Predictably, my father uses the opportunity to network and connect with his old cronies. They make me sick.

We've barely uttered a word to each other since the meeting at their lawyer's office a few days ago, and they have given me nothing but contempt all day long. I suspect they wouldn't have allowed me here to pay my respects if it wouldn't have made them look bad. But it was a mistake coming to their house after the service. There were three people present today who actually loved my grandfather—Leonard, Amanda, and me. They both left after the service I planned, declining the offer to come to the exquisitely catered wake at my parents' house.

I can barely stand to be here a second longer. I only came because it felt disrespectful to Grampa to not show my face. But none of these people knew him. None of them gave a damn about him.

Without a word to anyone, I jump on my bike and head back into the city. Maybe it's instinct that takes me to the Jamestech building. It's only a little after six. He's probably still in there. And I don't care if it's stupid or that we're pretending we don't have feelings for each other. I need him.

That's why, a few minutes later, I find myself standing in the doorway to his office. Thankfully, he is still here, sitting behind his desk with his sleeves rolled up and his eyes glued to his monitor. Uncharacteristically for me, I knock.

I'm sure he smiles when he sees me, but if I'm right, he quickly hides it. "Hey."

"Can I come in?"

He pushes back his chair and rests his hands behind his head. "You don't usually ask."

I walk inside and, out of habit, close the door behind me. Not because I expect anything from him. Avoiding my usual seat opposite him, I wander over to the coffee machine and run my fingertips over the handle of a mug.

"How was today?" His deep voice washes over me, comforting and familiar.

Tears well in my eyes. "Fucking awful."

"I'm sorry. Funerals suck. You okay?"

I stare at the wall, not wanting to admit that I'm not. Not wanting to look in his eyes and let him unravel me.

When I don't answer, he pushes his chair back and his footsteps grow closer until I can feel him standing behind me. "You want to talk about it?"

I shake my head.

He skims his fingertips over the back of my neck, and fuck, it feels so good. Pleasure skitters down my spine. I turn around and come face-to-face with his intensely dark eyes and the face that haunts my every waking thought, not to mention my dreams. "I just wanted to ..." I swallow, the rest of the words refusing to form.

He takes a step closer. "What do you want, King?" His voice is husky, his warm breath dancing over my skin. He slides his hands inside my jacket to grip my waist.

"This," I whisper.

He dusts his lips over mine, taunting me with the faintest hint of a kiss.

"I want to feel connected to someone." My voice cracks.

And so does he. He seals his lips over mine and slips his tongue inside my willing mouth. I moan at the contact and he swallows the sound, greedily exploring with his tongue. I fist a hand in his thick, dark hair, unable to stop myself from wanting control. I tilt his head and tongue-fuck him back, flicking my tongue in the dark recesses of his mouth as I devour him. He feels like everything I need.

"You taste like cheap brandy," he murmurs.

I kiss him again. "You taste like mine."

"Fuck, King," he groans, and I love the way he says my name. All need and hunger. I unzip his pants and wrap my hand around the base of his shaft.

He does the same to me as I push him back against the wall. Our mouths explore each other, throat and jawline, ears and forehead. We kiss and bite and suck while we work each other over, jerking each other off to the same punishing pace. When I'm close to the edge, I capture his lips with mine once more, kissing him so deeply that I feel like I'm going to pass out from lack of oxygen.

I break the kiss and suck in a ragged breath. "Come with me, baby boy."

He curses in Spanish as hot ribbons of cum spurt over my hand. He grips me tighter, giving me a final tug that has me coming right along with him.

I press my forehead to his and we catch our breath.

"Was that enough of a connection for you, Hotshot?" he says, laughing.

"I'd have preferred to come in your ass, but yeah, it was enough, baby."

"You drive me crazy, mi rey," he whispers.

That's what he used to call me, a lifetime ago. *My king.* And despite what we just did and how far down his throat my tongue was, that was the connection I've truly longed for.

Before it can take root, he breaks it, pulling away and zipping up his pants. "I'll go get some paper towels."

As he disappears into the bathroom, I tell myself not to take it personally. It's his instinct to protect himself where I'm concerned, and I can't blame him. I lied to Mason eighteen years ago when I told him that I never loved him. I loved him more than anyone or anything in this whole goddamn world.

The truth is I still do.

CHAPTER

TWENTY-FOUR

MASON

The headline about Astyn Bartley makes me snort: "Tech wiz who's about to take the AI world by storm."

More like "Tech wiz who somehow stole Jamestech's patent and is getting all the credit." Nothing but a fucking fraud. I scroll down to his picture and shoot daggers at him through the screen. There he stands in front of his Bugatti, wearing a sweater tied around his neck. Who the actual fuck dresses like that? Pompous jackass. He's smiling, and I can tell they're not his real teeth. Porcelain veneers I'll bet.

I scroll to the message at the bottom of the email. *This goes live tomorrow. Thought you'd want to see it first. Shelby xoxo*

I went to college with Shelby, and we once got so drunk on tequila that we were arrested by campus security for stealing a bust of Shakespeare from the library. For the rest of our time there, we were inseparable. She's a journalist now. A top-class one who reports on important stories, like wars and presidential elections, but she keeps an ear to the ground for the kind of stuff that she thinks would be on my radar. She's a good friend.

I fire off a quick thank-you email, then shoot a text to King, asking him why he hasn't found my leak yet. It's been three weeks, and he doesn't seem any closer to the truth. While I'm willing to cut him a little slack given his personal tragedy, the article has really shined a light on the importance of getting answers. Thus far, King's updates have consisted of who the leak is not.

Funny thing is I used to respect Astyn as a contemporary, even with his pretentious name and diabolical taste in fashion. We were rivals, but I never begrudge people anything they earn through talent and hard work. Now I see he's nothing but a fraud, and it's annoying that I ever admired the guy.

Less than two minutes after I sent my text, my secretary shows King into my office. Despite him looking nothing like any health and safety auditor I've ever met, I will admit he's done a good job of fitting in here. We run a casual office, and most of our male employees don't wear a suit and tie every day. King has adapted his uniform accordingly, and it now consists of slacks and a fitted white shirt with long sleeves, which he obviously rolls up. Why hide those beautiful tattoos if he doesn't have to? He looks more comfortable than he did in a suit. He looks fucking hot.

And I wish that having him relieve my bad mood by asking him to relieve me wasn't the first thing that popped into my head when he sauntered into my office. Pretty sure yesterday's mutual masturbation isn't helping the whole situation. Also sure it was a violation of at least one health and safety policy. And if it wasn't, then we should probably write some. I can see the fine print now: *Senior management will absolutely not administer handjobs to—or receive handjobs from—their employees or any contractors.*

He drops into the seat across from me, brow furrowed. "You wanted to see me?"

"I want some answers. Who is our fucking leak?"

He clears his throat. "I'm working on it. You have over four hundred employees. If you want this done discreetly, then it's going to take time. You know how difficult it is to hack into someone's personal emails?"

"You're hacking into people's personal emails?"

His scowl deepens. "You think they're gonna be stupid enough to sell company secrets using their work ones? Of course I started with those, because I do my due diligence. But that's not where I'm going to find the answers and we both know it."

I screw my eyes shut. "How about you don't tell me about your highly unethical methods and just find me my leak? That way I can claim ignorance when one of our employees sues us for violation of privacy."

He laughs, dark and dangerous. "You seriously under-estimate me if you think anyone will ever detect my methods, Mr. James."

My eyes snap open and I scowl. "Mr. James? Seriously?"

He smirks. "Thought that might be more appropriate when you're chewing me out for not doing my job. Something piss you off this morning?"

I push my chair back and begin to pace. I need to move. To think. To do something to sate this constant feeling of being on edge. "An article about Astyn Bartley taking the AI world by storm," I grumble.

"Ah, that'll do it." He jumps up from his seat and walks toward me, stopping my pacing. "I promise I'll find your leak. I promise I'll get you the evidence you need to bury Bartley if that's what you want to do. I know you don't trust me on a lot of things, but please trust me on that." He sounds sincere. Sincere and concerned, and I wish that the sound of his voice alone didn't have the power to soothe me. But fuck, it does. Soothe and ignite.

I take a half step closer so we're within touching distance. Kissing distance.

He glides his hands inside my suit jacket, and his fingers dig into my waist as he pulls me closer. "Do you trust me?"

I swallow, need already working its way through my veins. "About that, yeah."

"And what's it going to take for you to trust me enough to let me fuck you again?"

Keep talking to me like that, and trust won't matter. I chew on the inside of my cheek to stop myself from saying that out loud. But the truth is the other night at my apartment was incredible. Doesn't mean I want to open up all those old wounds and be his submissive little fuck toy again though. Hell no.

"What if I tell you that's never going to happen, Hotshot."

He glances down and smirks. "No? You wanna tell your dick that?"

"Well, my dick is a fucking idiot. I mean it. Not a single brain cell in his head."

"Don't insult him like that." He trails the fingertips of his right hand over my zipper. "He's sensitive."

"He's a jerk. Seriously."

King's tongue darts out to wet his bottom lip. Predictably, my slutty idiot dick stiffens, and I picture King's tongue running over the crown, licking the precum I can feel collecting there. "Quit playing games with me and let me fuck you," he says.

"This all feels very one-sided," I argue. "Surely there has to be a little give and take."

His pupils are blown wide, his chest rising and falling with each labored breath. We've been doing this dance for far too long, and he wants it as much as I do. He swallows. "What kind of give and take are we talking about, Mase?"

Mase? I bite on my own lip to stop myself from groaning. Plenty of people call me that, but the way he says it ... Fuck, it does something to me. Something feral. How far can I push him? "Suck my cock. Then I'll let you fuck me again."

His pupils grow larger, and his breath hitches in his throat. God, I fucking love having him on the back foot for once. I narrow my eyes, drinking in every slight change in his usually confident expression. "You do still suck cock, right?" He was never seriously into it when we dated back in high school, but he did it. And he was damn good at it too.

Moving tantalizingly slow, his tongue runs over his lips. The wicked glint in his eyes and his veneer of confidence, bordering on downright arrogance, are firmly back in place. "Better than anyone else you've ever had."

"That's quite the claim to make."

He tilts his head to the side, scrutinizing me. Testing me. "Not a claim. More like a promise."

I shake my head, a laugh bubbling from my lips. "You're a cocky fuck, you know that?"

He shrugs and inches closer, eating up the remaining empty space between us. "Just sure of my talents."

I palm the back of his neck and run my fingers over the short hair at his nape. "How about you stop talking about how good you are, get on your knees, and put that smart mouth to much better use."

His narrowed eyes rake over my face. I sense a

moment's hesitation, and it's clear he's not used to being spoken to like this. At this point, I'm not entirely sure how things are going to play out. Maybe he won't be able to handle me after all. Perhaps that would be for the best, given our complicated history and our newfound professional relationship.

But he sinks to his knees, and every drop of blood in my body, not to mention common sense, heads south.

He unbuckles my belt, and there's something oddly Pavlovian about the way my already stiff cock jumps at the sound. His fingertips brush my zipper, and I tip my head back and let out a groan that makes King chuckle.

"You're so impatient for my mouth, baby."

"Because you're moving slower than anyone in the history of blowjobs has ever moved," I snap.

That gets another dark laugh, but to my relief, he finally lowers my zipper, allowing my aching cock some room. But instead of taking pity on me, King mouths me through my boxers, sucking and licking until his saliva is soaking through the fabric.

"Fuck!" I grunt, rocking my hips against him.

He keeps a tight grip on my thighs, preventing me from moving too much, maintaining the control he seems to crave. "You know that sucking cock means you have to actually touch the skin, right?"

He digs his fingertips into my quad muscles. "Such a fucking brat sometimes, Mase." Before I can reply, he tugs down the waistband of my boxers and runs his warm tongue up the length of my aching shaft. Lord have mercy, it feels like fucking heaven.

I moan, running my fingers over his buzz cut.

When he takes me into his mouth a few seconds later, fireworks explode inside my brain, synapses misfiring left and right as he takes me to the back of his throat. When I'm sure I haven't passed out and woken up in an alternate reality, I look down at him. The sight unravels me—King Blackthorn on his knees with my cock stuffed in his mouth, making soft humming noises while he sucks me off. I almost blow my load right here and now.

The fact that my secretary is right outside the door, that Elijah could possibly burst in here at any second, makes it hotter. Not that I want either of them to see or hear, but the fact they might adds to the thrill of it all.

When I think it can't get any hotter or the sound of King greedily sucking on my cock couldn't get any filthier, he slides a finger into my ass, and I have to shove my fist into my mouth to stop myself from roaring his name.

He works his finger inside me while his tongue flicks over my crown, and the fireworks are back, more colorful and explosive than before. Electric pleasure races through my veins.

"Gonna come." Shuddering, I empty my release into his willing mouth. He holds my gaze and swallows it all.

My legs are trembling when he slips my dick from between his lips, and I lean back against my desk for support. He wipes his mouth and stands, eyeing the desk behind me with wicked intent in his eyes.

I shake my head. "No. Not on my desk."

He steps forward, bringing our bodies flush. "Yeah, your desk. Every time you sit there, I want you to remember how well I'm about to fuck you on it."

Before I know it, I'm telling him there's condoms and lube in my gym bag and leaning over my own fucking desk for him. He pulls off my jacket and quickly works my pants down. His powerful hand between my shoulder blades keeps me pressed to the wood while he preps me. I groan his name, and he showers me with praise.

He slides inside me, thick and hard, and I have to bite my forearm to stop myself from roaring his name loud enough to be heard all over the building. It shouldn't feel this good to be used by him. My entire body comes alive, singing with pleasure as he drives into me, whispering filthy promises in my ear. When he gets close to the edge, he wedges his hand between me and the desk and grips my hard length.

"Hard for me again, baby. So eager to come again, my little fuck toy."

"Please, King."

"I got you, baby boy." He jerks my cock and drives into me until we both fall over the edge one after the other, and I am once again covered in my own cum.

I pant, totally boneless and breathless, King still

leaning over me, his hot mouth at my ear. "You're such a good fuck, Mase."

Reality comes crashing back down. A good fuck— that's all I ever was to him. All I will ever be. And while that never bothered me with any other guy I've been with, it does with him. This isn't only about sex with us, and it never can be. As fun as it is, and as incredible as he makes me feel, this has to stop. Because I'm already catching feelings for him.

Or maybe I never let them go to begin with.

I nudge him away and stand. "I have a meeting I need to get cleaned up for."

"What? Oh. Uh, okay." He runs a hand over his buzz cut and blinks, confused. If I didn't know him better, I'd say he looks a little hurt, but I do know him. All too well.

He removes the condom. "Can I use your bathroom?"

"Yeah." I avoid his gaze while I fasten up my pants. I don't have a meeting, and the sneaky little fuck has access to my calendar. But I'm the chief operating officer. I can have meetings that come out of nowhere and aren't on my schedule.

After the water shuts off, he emerges a few moments later, looking far too handsome for his own good. "Maybe we can go over that stuff tomorrow, then?"

I nod, distracted. "Yeah."

"Everything okay?"

I should say everything is fine and let him leave, but I

am clearly a masochist. "No. It's not. You can't keep fucking doing this."

His brow furrows. "I can't keep doing what, Mason? Because if you're referring to what just happened, you were a very willing participant."

"I was. I know that we can't keep doing this, but also you—yeah, you. You come in here and you ..." I stop talking. He what? He dominates me? He leaves me covered in my own cum? Fuck, I sound like an idiot. "You make me feel like that stupid sixteen-year-old kid again."

His frown deepens. "What's wrong with that?"

"I don't like him, King. I did everything in my power to stop being that guy. That needy little fuckboy who craved your attention."

Hurt flashes over his face. "You were never that to me. You were—"

"Stop!" I cut him off. "It can't happen again. At least not like this."

"What do you mean not like this?" His pleading tone sparks something in me, reminding me I'm not that needy teenage boy desperate for his affection. I'm Mason fucking James.

I move forward until we're inches apart and I'm looking him in the eye. "If we do this in the future, it will be me fucking you. That is the only way this happens again."

His lip curls. "Then it will never happen. You know I don't do that."

I do know that, and it stings like a motherfucker. If I can be that for him, why can't he do the same for me? I won't let him see how much it hurts me though. "Then I guess this is it," I say, shrugging.

He growls, opens his mouth like he's about to say something, then stalks out of my office, slamming the door behind him on the way out. When he's gone, I sink into my chair and let out a long, slow breath. Looks like that's the end of me and King Blackthorn. Again.

It hurts, but not as much as last time. I'm tougher now. Stronger in every way. I keep telling myself that while I go through the applications for our new vice president of marketing role. Combing through the sea of willing and eager young potential employees is as good a distraction as any.

CHAPTER

TWENTY-FIVE

KING

I read the words on the screen again. This must be my third attempt at the same email, and the content still isn't sinking in. Frustrated, I shake my head and command myself to stop thinking about Mason fucking James and get my mind back in the game.

Cassidy Jones deserves so much more than what I'm giving her. But he is so damn distracting. Everything about him gets under my skin in all the worst and best ways. Every time I see him, all I can think about is having my hands on him or my cock inside him. I'd give him another blowjob if that's what it took to be close to him, and that should tell me all I need to know about how bad I have it for him. Because I get head; I rarely give it.

But Mason ... The mere thought of swallowing his thick cock makes my mouth water. What in the ever-living fuck is wrong with me? I have no idea how much longer I can go on working with him and not end up buried inside him. But he has made it abundantly clear that his ridiculous ultimatum still stands. It's been a week since he made it, and despite us being alone and in close proximity at least half a dozen times since then, he's been nothing but professional, and curt with it.

My cell vibrates, and the message that lights up on the screen does nothing to curb my frustration or clear my head.

> We need to discuss this will and come to some arrangement that will suit everyone.

No hint of affection. No loving kiss. Not that I should expect anything like that—she's only the woman that gave birth to me. The woman whose body I ruined, as she reminded me countless times when I was growing up. Why would anything change now just because her father is dead and I'm the only living blood relative she has left in the world?

Fucking hell, get ahold of yourself. My mother being a robot with less warmth inside her than the cold heart of a lizard is not a new development. I need to stop feeling sorry for myself and grow the fuck up. With a final glance at the screen in front of me, I close the laptop. Maybe a visit to my parents' house is better than combing through the last year of Cassidy's emails anyway. So far all I've found are complaints to her landlord and annoying newsletters from various chain restaurants and beauty websites. Not a lot of personal stuff on there at all, which isn't too surprising given that most people under the age of forty no longer use email as a form of personal communication. Everything is WhatsApp and Snapchat now, and those servers are much harder to access than email.

Some good old-fashioned detective work in the form of talking to Curtis Jones's prime suspect is the way to go.

I find my father in his study, puffing on a cigar.

He urges me to take a seat, and I comply out of habit. "Where is Mother?"

"In bed with a migraine."

I refrain from rolling my eyes. More like she passed out following the bottle of wine she drank after having to endure the agony of texting me.

"I didn't expect a visit from you today," he says, eyeing me with suspicion.

I shrug. "I got a text from her. I came to talk."

"Ah." He stubs his cigar out in the black marble ashtray on his desk. A present I bought him when I was fourteen and trying to appease him for something. It doesn't exactly surprise me that he's hung onto it. I bet he tells visitors that his son bought it for him, making out like he's a contender for father of the year. "Your grandfather's will."

"His airtight will," I say, reminding him of Nathan's words.

"Let's not sully this with lawyers and paperwork, son. We're family."

Son? Despite everything and as much as I hate to admit it, that word still means something to me. I see right through his scheme to get me on his side, but I still bend. "What exactly did you want to discuss, Father?"

He runs his tongue along his top teeth. "Your grandmother meant for that money to go to your mother, her daughter."

I shake my head. "That's not what Grampa or the will says."

"Your grandfather was a sick man. If he'd known your mother was—"

"If he'd known she was only going to get the million she knew about, you mean? He did know that. He knew all about it. Yeah, his body was sick, but his mind was sharper than anyone else I know. Don't you dare try and tell me he didn't know how this would pan out."

His right eye twitches and anger radiates from him like heat from the sun, but he keeps a lid on it. Which tells me he's eager to keep me here and talking because any other time he would simply let it rip and tell me what a constant disappointment I am to him. He clears his throat. "What could you possibly need twenty-five million dollars for, Kyngston? We could come to an agreement. A few million, even five, would set you up for life."

"You and Mother are living in a mansion filled with her pretty stuff. What the hell do you need twenty-five million dollars for?"

His jaw works. "Will you at least consider coming to some sort of settlement, son?"

The fuck I will. But saying that would put a swift end to this conversation, and I have things I want to know. I change the subject instead. "I heard you earned the former mayor a fortune on the stock market. So work must be going well?"

My father walks the fine line between morally bankrupt and respectable enough for his services to be courted by the rich and powerful from all walks of life—city officials to drug lords. At least in his working life, he's all about equal opportunity. It makes for as many enemies as friends, but he has enough powerful people in his debt and in his pockets to drift through life without consequence.

"It's good. As always. It's a shame you didn't take the same path, Kyngston. You could have made something of yourself."

I ignore the barb. "I like my job."

"Oh, yes. A private investigator." He manages to make the title sound like an insult, but I'm immune to his disdain.

"Yeah. It's interesting. The case I'm working right now, for instance. It's a real head-scratcher."

He takes the bait, too curious not to. "And what is

that?"

"It's a disappearance. Cassidy Jones."

If he recognizes her name, he doesn't show it outwardly, but he's always been a master at hiding his true emotions when he needs to.

"Young girl. Daddy issues. Cops seem to think she up and left to get away from him."

His right eye twitches again. His only tell. "Yes, well, some children are ungrateful little shits like that."

I don't let that barb get to me either. The man taught me all of his best moves in that regard, I'll give him that.

"Thing is, she has no history of running away. No evidence that would support her leaving and starting over somewhere else."

"So maybe she changed. Maybe she hid her intentions well." He shrugs, staring at the portrait of his father hanging on his study wall as though it's the most fascinating thing he's seen all year.

"That would take some planning though, right? And there was no evidence of that either," I say, folding my arms and following his gaze. It's a well-painted portrait at least, of a man my father hated almost as much as I hate him. I have no idea why it hangs in here, but he stares at it now to avoid my gaze. "No evidence of hidden bank accounts. No evidence of a boyfriend anywhere. Well, anywhere except for this rich guy in New York she told her father about."

He rolls his eyes. "Why are you boring me with this, Kyngston?"

"Oh, I assumed you'd be interested. You know, because the cops spoke to you about her. You were the one of the last people to see her alive, weren't you?"

The vein in his neck pulses, and he grinds his jaw before quickly reschooling his features into nonchalance. "Ah yes, I remember being spoken to about that. I'm not sure about being one of the last people to see her alive, considering she is neither missing nor presumed dead."

"Well, technically you were, because I can't find any record of her being seen by anyone since. And as for whether she's missing or dead, that all depends who you speak to. Her father for sure thinks she's the former, but me ..." I tilt my head, scrutinizing him for any hint that he knows more than he's admitting. "Well, seeing as it's been fourteen months, I'd say the latter, wouldn't you?"

He sucks on his top teeth, a sure sign of his irritation. "I think I'd go along with New York's finest and their professional assessment that she is neither." Anger bleeds into his tone now too. He's unable to keep a lid on his temper for too long when provoked—at least when he's provoked by me.

"She say anything to you about her plans? You know, when she was giving you your lap dance?"

That vein in his neck bulges now. "Why do you insist on pushing me, Kyngston?"

"Because I'm working a case, and you were definitely

one of the last people to see her in New York. Possibly the last person she had any meaningful form of conversation with."

He sneers. "You think I was interested in conversation with some whore while she had her tits in my face, son? Then you really don't know me at all."

I know you all too well, you misogynistic, homophobic asshole. "She never mentioned anything to you then?"

"No."

"Not even when you took her back to her place and fucked her?"

He moves quickly, much faster than I would have given him credit for. His hand is wrapped around my throat and his teeth bared as he snarls at me, telling me everything I need to know. Kyngston Worthington, who regards himself as calm and collected—and he can be, at least on the surface. And at least until he feels confronted and vulnerable.

Had he not taken Cassidy home and done what I accused him of, he would have brushed me off. And the real kicker is he knows that too, which means he also knows he's revealed far too much. "How fucking dare you accuse me."

I pry his fingers from my neck and twist them enough to make him wince before pushing him away. "Not accusing you, *Dad*. Just aware of your nature. Pretty little brunettes are your type, right? I'd be disappointed if you hadn't taken her home and fucked her."

His eye twitches again, and he glares at me. Pissed because he's not strong enough to subdue me anymore and no doubt wondering how far I'd go to see him burn. And the truth is ... I don't know. At this point, I have no idea what I'll do if I find real evidence that he had something to do with Cassidy's disappearance. It's a strange concept to hate one's parents as an adult yet still have an inner child that craves their approval and affection.

There's a soft tapping at his office door, and when he barks for the intruder to come in, the housekeeper pops her head inside. "Will you be joining us for dinner, Mr. Worthington?" It takes me a second to realize she's talking to me.

My father curls his lip. "No, he has plans."

She mumbles an apology and disappears back into the hallway. For once, his dismissal of me doesn't sting even a little. I have no plans at all, but I would rather stick needles in my eyeballs than endure a dinner with my drunken mother and my cruel, narcissist father. I make a show of checking my watch. "I suppose I'd better get going then."

"Seems that would be for the best." His tone is back to ice-cold calculation. No hint of the temper he lost with me a moment ago. "As would be you leaving that case the hell alone, Kyngston. If you know what's good for you." It's a threat, and we both know it. We also both know it means there's something for me to find, but he already revealed as much when he lashed out the way he did. Even when he beat me as a kid and chained me in that goddamn base-ment to try to "get all the evil out," he rarely showed anger. Only stone-cold cruelty, which made him all the more terrifying. He only loses his temper when he's scared.

And I scared him. Cassidy Jones's name scared him.

And I am going to find out why.

TWENTY-SIX

MASON

It's only been eight days since I issued my ultimatum, and while that's not a long time, it feels like a lifetime where King is concerned. Although I knew that he'd never go for my suggestion, a stupid, fucked-up part of me still hopes he will cave every time he strolls into my office, which he continues to do with alarming regularity. That he'll sink to his knees and tell me he's got the worst case of blue balls that have ever occurred in the history of all humankind and beg me to fuck him.

Unsurprisingly, that life-altering event has not occurred. And I'm the one with a chronic case of blue balls. No matter how many times I jerk off, it's not satisfying at all. The past three times, I couldn't even summon the will to finish the job.

I can talk to my brothers about guy stuff, and frequently do, but never anything deep. Nothing that involves actual feelings, at least not my own. And talking about King when all except Mad know him would feel too messy. I could talk to Mad, but he's working tonight. He's been working a hell of a lot lately, but it keeps him busy and he seems to enjoy it.

There's only one man I can think of who'll have good advice regarding how to get out of my King funk. And that's how I find myself lying on my sofa with Tyler on speaker while I confess a hell of a lot more than I should. I don't tell him the whole truth. Only enough about the way King left eighteen years ago to provide context about the situation I'm in.

"So he just disappeared?"

"Yeah. Didn't even go to Harvard like he'd planned. He vanished off the face of the earth. He did such a good job of it that I thought something awful had happened to him when he didn't show up to college. Stupidly, I hired a PI to find him. A few weeks later, he showed me photos of King sitting outside a pizza joint in Idaho with some girl. They were laughing." The look of pity on that PI's face still makes me cringe. How fucking pathetic I must have seemed. And yeah, my eagerness to make sense of what had happened made me pathetic. It was then I realized I was the only one hurting. That King had truly moved on. As though our time together meant nothing.

I've never felt so worthless—so fucking empty. Even what his father did never hurt as much as the realization that I was so easily discarded by the same guy I would have willingly died for. And that was the moment I swore nobody would ever leave me feeling like that ever again.

"Wow. Sounds like he was a douche. But he was what, eighteen? Maybe he was struggling with who he was. Could be he's changed."

"I don't know, Ty. One thing I am sure of is that he has me all fucking kinds of messed up."

"You need to ask yourself whether you want to be with him or not," he says, cutting through the bullshit the way only he can.

I let out a weary sigh. "That's the problem though. I do want to be with him, but I don't want to want that. It's like craving extra butter *and* cream in your mashed potatoes, or that last shot of Scotch, even though you know you're going to regret it because it's bad for you, or it's gonna make you throw up."

"Fuck me," he mutters. "This King guy really did a number on you."

I snort a laugh. "And then some."

"Then I really don't know what to tell you, buddy. I've never known a guy to get under your skin like this before, and only you can determine if that's a good thing or a bad thing."

"Oh, it's definitely a bad thing."

"Okay," he says, but he doesn't sound convinced. Which makes sense because I don't believe it myself. "So, if you can't go fuck the guy you can't stop thinking about, and what you're saying you want is to not want this guy, then go do something about it."

That's far too many *want*s for one sentence. "What do I do, Ty?"

"The thing every jilted, star-crossed, or broken-hearted lover does to get over the object of their affection—you get under or, in your case, on top of someone else."

I blow out a breath. If only it were that easy.

Tyler laughs. "I can practically hear you thinking."

I can't help but smile. "Oh yeah, so what am I thinking, buddy?"

"Well, firstly, you're thinking you wish I was there so we could go out together and I could be your wingman."

"True," I admit. "You are the best wingman ever."

He laughs again, and I'm reminded how easy our friendship is. Relationships should be like this too. Easy, uncomplicated. "And secondly, you're thinking what if you fuck someone else and this guy is still in your head after."

I snort, refusing to admit he's right on both counts.

"And I'd say there's only one way to find out."

"You think I should go fuck someone else?" I wince at the incredulity in my tone. What the hell is that about? Ty's suggestion is a perfectly valid one. It's the way I'd move on from any other relationship where any suggestion of catching feelings was involved.

"Better than sitting at home alone beating yourself up. You and this guy aren't exclusive, so what's stopping you?"

How about the fact that I'll be picturing King if I do end up balls-deep in some other guy. "We're nowhere close to exclusive. Not even dating. Not anything. Not even able to be seen smiling at each other in public."

"Right. You said he's not openly gay," he murmurs like he's talking to himself.

"Nope, he's firmly in that closet."

I pace the room now, chewing on my lip and arguing with myself in my head. Tyler remains frustratingly silent. "Is that your best advice, then? Go fuck someone else and get him out of my system?" I'm short with him, and he doesn't deserve it, but he responds before I can apologize.

"I never specifically said that, jerkwad."

"You told me to get on top of someone else," I remind him.

"I believe I suggested either fucking the guy you really want or fucking someone else." I can picture his smiling face, those dimples popping. I really do wish he was here. It sucks that he travels so much for work.

I find myself smiling too. "But fucking is your only solution?"

"Isn't it always, buddy? When in the history of humankind has a good fuck ever not been the answer?"

"Um. Off the top of my head, the gunfight at the O.K. Corral?"

"If all those guys had just fucked each other, they would have resolved that conflict a whole lot faster," he says, laughing harder.

"You're an asshole."

"An asshole who's always right."

I chew on the inside of my cheek. He is usually right. And what the hell am I doing pacing my apartment on a Thursday night, pining over a guy who doesn't deserve a second of my time? A guy who has made it abundantly clear that I'm good for nothing but a clandestine fuck? I could be out having fun. Thursday nights at Xylophone are full of hot, single guys looking for casual hookups. Maybe that is exactly what I need.

I hear a voice in the background and remember that Tyler's waiting for his date to show. "That your date now?" I ask.

He hums in response, and I take that as a yes and also that he's lost for words, which is either a very good or very bad thing.

"How hot is he?"

"Surface of the sun," he answers quietly.

Good for him. Tyler deserves the best. "I'd better leave you to it then. Have fun. Be safe."

"Always, buddy. You too, okay? Call me if you need me."

I know he means that. I could interrupt his hot date

and he'd answer the call because he's that good of a guy. The opposite of King Blackthorn, who simply wears the disguise of a good guy when it suits him.

Tyler's right—I need to get over King.

He's also right about the best way to do it.

TWENTY-SEVEN

My chronic lack of a social life is more acute than usual tonight. I have nothing to do but sit in my apartment and think about Mason and what he might be doing. It's either that or bury myself in work, and the latter holds no appeal to me at this moment.

The fact that my father was somehow involved in Cassidy's disappearance is obvious to me now, and I need some time to sit with that and figure out my next steps. It will take careful digging to not aggravate him too much now that he knows I'm onto him. He might be a weak man and a coward, but he's powerful in all the ways that matter. He knows a lot of the right people in the right places and has enough money to make almost anything disappear. Including poor Cassidy Jones and any evidence there might be connecting him to her. If I don't tread carefully, I may never get the answers Curtis needs.

Without work, my thoughts are back to my only other source of frustration—Mason James. I doubt he's sitting alone at home, staring at a blank TV screen and eating cereal from the box. No, I bet he's out somewhere fancy. Maybe on a date with some guy whose abs are like cut diamond, who's fucking salivating over him. Jealousy burns hot in my veins.

It's an invasion of his privacy, I know, but I check his phone location anyway. And immediately regret it when I discover where he is. He's at Xylophone—the place he goes to pick up guys. What the fuck. I guess he was serious about the whole this-can't-happen-again thing. Except that's not exactly what he said, is it? It can happen again, so long as I ...

I must have thought about his offer at least a hundred times since he made it. And each time it gets a little more tempting, which worries me. I don't get fucked. I fuck. Period.

Sucking in a breath, I try to calm the anger that's threatening to spill out of me—anger I have no right to feel. Mason and I aren't together. He has every right to go pick up some guy tonight. To kiss him, let his hands wander over those unbelievably sexy abs, his firm ass. His gorgeous fucking dick.

With a groan of frustration, I grab my coat and keys. Looks like I'm headed to Xylophone too.

. . .

I KEEP my eyes on the floor as I weave through the mass of warm, hard bodies on the dance floor. *Nobody knows you here, King. Nobody knows you.* I repeat the mantra to myself over and over. I'm sure there's no danger of running into anyone I know from my past life in here. Nobody except Mason fucking James, anyhow.

I ignore the offers to dance or buy me a drink as I make my way to the bar, the place I saw him standing when I walked in. Talking to some fucking guy. Rage and jealousy burn through my veins, and no matter how many calming mantras I chant to myself, none of them fucking work. Nothing works. Nothing except him.

In a move he won't realize has done wonders for his future health, the guy talking to Mason is already walking away by the time I reach him. Mason blinks at me, as shocked as I am to find me in a place like this.

"Who the fuck is that asshole?" I jerk my head in the direction of the guy now headed toward the bathroom.

The smug bastard has the fucking nerve to grin at me. He knows exactly how pissed I am to see him with his hands on some other guy. "First of all, that's none of your fucking business, Hotshot. And second, he's not an asshole. His name is Dax, and he's actually very sweet. Not to mention hot, funny." He leans closer, his lips resting dangerously close to my ear. "Submissive. You know the type, right?"

Yes, I know the fucking type. I want Mason to be that type—for me. Only for me. I want every single part of him for myself. What the fuck is wrong with me?

"I think the more appropriate question is what are you doing in here? Aren't you worried someone might see you in here with all of us gays? They might start doing some math and realize you're not who you say you are." He's goading me, and I'm a heartbeat away from pinning him to this bar and showing every person here exactly who I am, not to mention exactly who he belongs to.

His dark eyes sparkle with mischief and sin. Mason James is trouble, and I can't seem to stay the fuck away from him. "I came looking for you." I glance in the direction of the bathroom. "Wanted to make sure you didn't get yourself into any trouble."

His brows knit in a frown. "Your concern for my well-being might be touching if you weren't such a massive jackass. How did you even know I was here?"

I'm pretty sure telling him I track his phone will earn me that mojito he's holding thrown in my face, so I simply shrug and tell him I have means.

"Well, however you found out, I don't give a fuck. Go do your thing and stay the hell away from me."

If only I fucking could. All of this would be a whole lot easier.

Maybe it's the four shots of Scotch I had before I left home. Maybe it's the thought of him with anyone else. Or maybe it's the fact that fucking Mason James is currently occupying all top ten spots in my usually diverse highlight reel that makes me say "Take me home with you."

His laugh, deep and sexy, has my dick stiffening in my jeans. When he's done, he blinks at me again. "You're fucking serious?"

Don't I look fucking serious? I lick my lips and count to ten, determined to avoid starting an argument and causing a scene right here at the bar. "Deadly."

"I told you last time we hooked up, King, that the only way it would happen again ..." His eyes sparkle as they bore into mine, and he doesn't finish the sentence. He doesn't have to. We both know what he told me. I recall with startling clarity every word he said—and how many times since that night I've considered taking him up on his offer.

I grab his hip, fingers digging into his taut muscle as I pull him closer. He doesn't resist. His wickedly sinful lips twitch at the corners as he goes on staring at me. Taunting me. Jesus Christ, I could fuck him right where he stands. "You'll have a much better time with me than with Dax, and you fucking know it." I lean closer, inhaling his intoxicating, masculine scent. My mouth dusts along his jawbone to his ear. "You know that nobody will fuck you better than I can, Playboy."

"Maybe." His voice drops an octave. "But I'm not looking to be fucked tonight, asshole. So you're fresh out of luck."

Stubborn little shit. My cock is hard. My mouth is

watering. I'm in a club full of hot, willing bodies. I could go home with plenty of the other guys in here, but I only want Mason. I want him more than anything I've ever wanted in my life. Enough to ...

"The line was crazy." Dax suddenly appears at Mason's side. His face is lit up by a smile. Tall and muscular, ripped jeans, tattoos, a hint of stubble. Yeah, I know the type. I see why Mason is attracted to him. He's not my type though. Although it seems my type has become incredibly limited of late and consists only of the arrogant, smug-as-fuck billionaire playboy standing in front of me.

"You ready to go?" Dax asks hopefully, smiling into Mason's handsome face and casually resting a hand on his shoulder.

The fuck he is. Dax is going to have that hand ripped off and shoved up his ass if he touches what's mine again. "He's here with me," I say, snarling.

Dax flinches and takes a step back. Mason glares at me. "What the fuck, King?"

"Hey, he told me he was free. I didn't know I was interrupting something here," Dax says, waving his hands between us.

"Well, you fucking are," I growl.

"No, you're not," Mason snaps.

Dax shifts from one foot to the other, sizing me up and no doubt wondering whether the man we're both hoping to take home tonight is worth the effort. He most definitely is worth the effort, but Dax here will never know that. "Fuck off, Dax," I say, but my eyes are now firmly fixed on Mason's scowling face.

Mason's lip twitches in the hint of a snarl, his deep-brown eyes flickering with anger. All of his attention is on me, exactly how I like it. Fuck, I love provoking this kind of reaction from him. What the hell is wrong with me?

"Yeah, I think I'm gonna leave you both to do ... whatever it is you're doing," Dax announces before he wanders off and disappears into the crowd.

He can find some other willing body to go home with tonight. Mason is leaving with me.

"You're such a fucking asshole," he says, nostrils flaring. "What the hell do you think you're doing?"

I'm still burning up with jealousy. Still irrationally pissed that the man I can't have—the same man I rejected all those years ago—is looking to get his rocks off with someone else. "You seriously want to go home with that guy when I'm standing right fucking here practically begging you to take me home?"

He folds his arms across his chest and lets his gaze roam my body. Hungry. Feral. Despite his annoyance, he wants me as much as I want him. And I do want him. So fucking much. "I haven't heard anything close to begging. And I already told you that's not happening again. Not unless ..." He raises an eyebrow, always fucking challenging me.

He's right. I haven't begged. I haven't begged for

anything since I was a teenager, but this is as close to it as I've come. "Mase ..." That's all I say, all I can manage.

His eyes soften a little, and he gives me wicked grin. That one that makes me want to smash my mouth against his. "Thought so. Have a good night, King."

Then he turns around, looking like he's about to head off into the crowd in search of Dax, but I catch him by his wrist, stopping him before he can.

He tries to wrench free, but I pull him closer, pressing his firm body against mine. Images of him lying beneath me, at my mercy and full of my cock, burn themselves into my brain and have me aching to fuck him again. What the hell am I doing?

"I'll do it." I hear the words leave my mouth even as I'm sure I'd never say them aloud. My traitorous throbbing cock is running the show for the rest of tonight, and he wants Mason James any damn way he can get him.

Mason blinks at me. "You'll do what?"

I suppress a growl. "You know what. Don't make me say it in the middle of this club."

Realization dawns on his face. Those brown eyes darken with undisguised desire. "Don't fuck with me, King."

I take a deep breath. "I'm not fucking with you. I want this. Take me home."

His eyes narrow, his grin wicked. "Not until you say it."

A growl rumbles in my throat. I shake my head. He's enjoying this. Torturing me.

He places a hand on my chest and skims it down my abs, stopping dangerously close to the waistband of my jeans, where my aching cock is bursting to be let out. To be inside him. "Tell me what you want, King. Consent is very fucking important to me, and I need to establish yours."

I chew on the inside of my cheek. Motherfuck. Why does he have such an effect on me? Why can't I get him out of my goddamn head? I close my eyes so I don't have to look at his smug face when I say it. "I want you to fuck me."

His hand disappears, and when I open my eyes, he's making his way across the dance floor, through the swirling mass of bodies. He's heading out of the club. A second later, I'm hot on his heels.

TWENTY-EIGHT

KING

We take a cab from the club to Mason's penthouse, and I don't know if the Scotch from earlier has worn off completely, but I'm nervous as hell. And I'm never nervous about fucking. I have no idea what to do in this situation. I'm always the one in control.

Mason places his cell phone and black Amex on the coffee table, then stuffs his hands into the pockets of his dress pants and simply watches me, his dark eyes roaming my body, like he's enjoying how nervous I am. Maybe this was a huge fucking mistake.

"Come here," he says in that deep, soothing voice I imagine he uses when he's convincing billionaire investors and buyers to do whatever he wants.

I take a few steps closer, wanting to reach out and grab him. Resisting the urge to smash my mouth against his and kiss him until neither of us can breathe—before I bend him over his sofa and fuck him into submission. I curl my hands into fists at my sides and let out a shaky breath.

Mason's eyes narrow. "You don't have to do anything you don't want to do, King. I'm not that much of an asshole. The door's right there." He glances over my shoulder.

He's not even a little bit of an asshole, but I'm not nervous because I don't want this. I'm scared as hell because this is a big fucking deal to me. I shake my head. "I'm not going anywhere."

"Good to know." He slides one hand to the back of my neck and holds me possessively as he rests his forehead against mine. "I know this is a big deal." He presses a soft kiss on my lips. "But it's still just me and you. And we've done this plenty before. Whatever happens, I've got you, okay?"

I don't deserve this level of concern and comfort from him. Not after the way I treated him. But that's one of the things I admire most about him—he is a genuinely good person. He'd never willingly cause someone pain. He'd never humiliate or betray them. If I'm going to do this once in my life, then it should be with him. My shoulders drop, tension slipping out of my muscles. "Yeah."

"Good boy." He flashes me a wink that has my cock twitching. "How about I get you nice and relaxed first though." Without another word, he drops to his knees and his deft fingers make quick work of my jeans.

"You been hard since the club, huh, Hotshot?" he teases, gripping my aching shaft.

I thread my fingers through his hair, feeling more in control already, which I'm certain was his intention. "I'm always hard around you, Playboy."

He hums with his lips against the crown of my dick and sends vibrations of pleasure shooting through me. "Yeah you are." His tongue darts out, and he sweeps it over my engorged head, causing me to groan his name.

I dig my fingers into his scalp. "Jesus, you're so fucking good at that."

He chuckles, his breath caressing my skin. "Just wait until I fuck you."

There's no time to process those words because I'm hit with a lightning bolt of pleasure as he takes my cock into his expert mouth, his tongue flicking the underside of my shaft.

He swallows all of me, his throat flexing around the tip of my cock. Motherfucking fuck. He is so goddamn good at that. With my hands on the back of his head, I thrust my hips, driving my cock deeper. He sucks greedily. I risk a glance at him, and the sight almost undoes me. His eyes are cast upward, shining with moisture, full of hunger and ... trust? You have to trust a guy to let him fuck your throat like this. And it's a trust I don't deserve, least of all from him, but I am undeniably grateful for it.

I swipe away a tear that's squeezed from the corner of his eye. "You look good with my cock in your throat, Mase. Fucking perfect."

He swallows again, and precum weeps from my slit. How does he have a mouth so sinful, yet so fucking heavenly? Mason James is my addiction. The one thing I can't seem to live without, no matter how bad he is for me. His fingers dig into my quads through the denim, gripping my muscles tight. Euphoria shuttles through my veins, pleasure coiling at the base of my spine. I give one last thrust and empty my load into his throat. He doesn't even gag. Perfect little fuck toy.

One hand still fisted in his hair, I pull back a few inches, letting him breathe and swallow every last drop. He's still looking at me, eyes never leaving my face, watching me as he unravels me thread by thread.

With a deep breath, I slide my spent cock from his mouth. He licks his lips, gaze hungrier than ever. We both know what happens next. My legs are trembling, and not only from the mind-blowing orgasm he gave me. He stands, bringing us face-to-face.

The pleasure still coursing through my body mixes with panic. "My turn, Hotshot," Mason growls, and the sound travels straight to my balls. My fingers are still threaded through his thick hair, my grip no less possessive and controlling than it was a second ago, but he's no longer submissive. Not even a little. He's all top energy, his deep-brown eyes sparking with a dangerous glint. His grin wicked—wolfish. This is the real him. The man he lets everyone else see. That other side of him—the side that had him on his knees taking every inch of my cock—that's only for me. I hold onto that reassuring thought, because this is a part of me that will only ever be for him.

He cups my jaw in his hand, squeezing firmly, letting me know he's as powerful as I am. Not the skinny kid from high school, back when I had sixty pounds and a few inches on him. No, he's more than capable of knocking me on my ass, and he wants me to know it. What the fuck have I let myself in for?

Before I can overthink this and run, Mason crashes his lips against mine. His tongue slides into my willing mouth, and I taste myself on him. Like it always used to, the taste of my cum on his tongue is enough to have my cock hardening again. He guides me backward until the backs of my knees bump up against something. His bed.

He slips his hands under my T-shirt and glides his warm palms over my abs and up my chest as he pushes the material higher, exposing my skin to the cool air. He removes my T-shirt, my jeans, my socks and shoes, my boxers, taking his time with each one, fingers and lips skimming the flesh he exposes. How can he be so unhurried, so leisurely in his movements when he's hard as fucking stone? My cock is hard again, leaking at the tip. Desperate for him. Eager for his touch. He grazes his fingers across the crown, and I shudder, causing a dark laugh to tumble from his lips. Then his mouth is at my neck, nipping and sucking. I clench my hands into fists at my sides to stop myself from tearing off his clothes and pinning him to his bed. Because then I'd fuck him. Raw and hard. No condom. Nothing between us.

The thought sends ripples of desire skittering up my spine.

"You're being such a good boy for me, King."

I snarl instinctively. "Don't fucking push it, Mase."

He laughs again. He's in complete control, and while I don't love it, I don't hate it either. Definitely don't hate when his hand slips between my thighs and he squeezes my balls, already heavy with the need to cum again. Don't hate when he shoves me backward onto the bed. I especially don't hate watching him remove every scrap of his clothes, revealing his perfectly toned body. All rippling muscles and olive skin. Not to mention his thick cock, hard and lined with thick veins, weeping precum from the slit. He's a work of fucking art. My mouth waters. I've never been that into sucking cock—I'm too fucking selfish—but with Mason ... I would sell a kidney to have him in my mouth right now.

He grabs a condom and some lube from the nightstand and tosses them on the bed beside me. A stark reminder that my mouth is not where he intends to sink that monster cock tonight. My ass cheeks clench, and I take a deep breath. As much as this is freaking me out, I want it. I want him.

Mason kneels between my spread thighs and slides his slick fingers between my ass cheeks. "You okay, Hotshot?"

I nod, my tongue darting out to wet my dry lips. The tip of his finger dips inside me, and my muscles tense. He lies over me, his mouth resting against my ear. "Relax, babe. You can take me." He pushes in deeper, and the strange sensation makes my balls draw up. I definitely don't want him to stop.

"Fuck, Mase," I groan.

He adds a second finger and works them a little deeper, prepping me for his cock. And fuck, he's a magician with those fingers. My cock is weeping with the way he's massaging my prostate. And when I'm moaning and grinding into the mattress, he slips his fingers out of me and pushes himself up.

With one hand gripping the base of his shaft, he tears the condom open with his teeth and rolls it on. Every move he makes is so slow and deliberate. He's a fucking master at building anticipation. No doubt he's enjoying making me wait as long as possible.

He works his hand up and down his thick shaft, covering it in a generous coating of lube, although I suspect no amount could be enough.

He drops onto his forearms and checks in with me again. "You ready?"

I nod, my bottom lip caught between my teeth. I want this with him more than I've ever wanted anything, but I don't feel close to ready. I suspect it's going to hurt like a motherfucker before it feels anywhere close to good.

My fingers clench, twisting in the sheets. He runs his nose over my jawline, notching the crown of his cock at my asshole. "Relax, King. This will feel good, I promise."

I release my hold on the bedding and rest my hands on his shoulder blades. His powerful muscles flex beneath my palms as he holds himself back. I trust him, and that's all that fucking matters. This only goes as far as I want it to.

Mason inches inside me, pushing through the tight ring of muscle. "Jesus fuck," he groans. "You're so tight."

I take a deep breath while he murmurs words of encouragement in my ear and pushes in a little deeper. The sensation of him filling me is strange but deeply satisfying. It feels better than good. Jesus fuck, it feels amazing.

My eyes roll back in my head. "I want more." I grunt out the words, and he smiles against my skin.

"You sure?"

"Yeah."

"Greedy boy." He chuckles but sinks deeper.

My legs shake, and light explodes behind my eyelids. "Fuck!"

"You're taking me so well, babe." He hisses out a breath before he pulls out and drives into me again. "Your ass was made for me. And nobody else will ever fuck it. Nobody but me, right?" He drives in harder.

I throw my head back into the pillow, bearing down so I can take more of him, enjoying the moment far too much to argue and remind either of us that this is nothing more than a casual hookup. But he's right. Mason is the only guy I've considered this with, and as amazing as it is, it's amazing because it's with him.

My fingertips dig into the taut muscle of his back. His teeth and lips lash against my neck as he fucks me. I don't care that he's in control. I don't care that he could unravel me with a single word. I focus on the delicious sensation of being full of his cock, of having his hard body nailing mine into the mattress. Of having him all over me. I'm made up entirely of need now, chasing another orgasm despite the amazing one he just gave me.

I wedge my hand between our sweat-slicked bodies, grasping wildly for my aching cock, but he grips my wrist and presses it to the mattress. "Nuh-uh. Let me make you come like this." He presses his lips against my ear. "I can feel how close you are. You love my cock in your ass." He drives harder and I see stars. "Don't you?"

Motherfucker! I'm pinned by him, unable to move and unwilling to be anywhere but here, with Mason James nailing me to his bed.

"Don't you, King?"

"Yeah," I pant, squeezing my eyes closed as the most intense orgasm I've ever experienced in my life tears through my body like wildfire. Every cell in my body trembles with the force of my release as it spurts across my chest.

"Good fucking boy," he growls.

I'm too spent to tell him to stop calling me that. His hips thrust once, twice, and he goes still and moans my name. He murmurs something unintelligible, possibly in Spanish, his chest heaving as he pants for breath.

The tender kiss he presses on my forehead has tears burning my eyes. He gently slips his dick out of me. "You okay?"

Worried my voice will crack and betray me, I can only nod. Mason and I have crossed a huge fucking line—at least I have. That wasn't a hookup. It was so much fucking more. Thankfully, he rolls onto his side and gets rid of the condom, and it gives me the opportunity to get myself together.

But he doesn't stray far, and a few seconds later, he wraps an arm around my waist and tugs my body against his. "I'm gonna get you cleaned up as soon as I can feel my legs."

For the briefest moment, I let myself fall under his spell. I imagine him taking care of me, wrapping me up in his arms until I fall asleep. And then maybe we'd do everything all over again when we wake up tomorrow.

Pity I can't let that happen. I'm not a bottom. Not submissive. No longer someone who cuddles after sex. Not even for him. "I can clean myself up." I force myself out of his arms and grab my boxers off the floor.

"I know you can. I was just being—"

"Just being what?" My head snaps up, and I glare at him, trying not to let the hurt on his face get to me. If I think for a split second about what a douchebag I'm being, I'll crawl back into that bed and let him do all the things he's thinking of right now. And that can't happen.

"A decent fucking human," he says, his handsome features marred by a deep frown.

I avert my gaze, unable to stand that confused, pained expression any longer. After a quick scrabble around the floor, I find my jeans and pull them on, my chest still covered in my cum.

"Where are you going?"

I don't look at him, making a show of searching for my shirt instead. "Home." The ice in my tone makes me shiver.

"Jesus Christ." He rolls onto his back and throws an arm over his eyes. "Just get the fuck out, King."

He's hurting. I fucking hurt him. We shared something incredible, and now I'm running away like a coward, and he knows it as well as I do. But it's better this way. He and I can never work. We're from two different worlds. And surely a little pain now is worth it to save us both a fuck-load of it later.

TWENTY-NINE

KING

There's something I've always loved about walking in the rain. Maybe it's the idea of it washing everything away—the dirt and grime of the city, the shame. Maybe it's because nobody can see the tears running down a person's face when it's raining. I've never cried so fucking much in my whole life as I have these past few weeks. I hate it.

Mason James has made me soft.

Mason ... The look on his face when I left. What if I misread it? There's every chance it didn't mean all that much to him. He could have had as good a time with Dax from the club. Maybe he was being a good guy and giving me a few minutes to recover. It's not like he explicitly asked me to stay the night, even if that was the vibe I got.

I growl my frustration, because as much as I try to

convince myself this was a casual thing for Mason, I know in my gut that it wasn't. Not for either of us.

I've walked eight blocks from his apartment building. It would still be quicker for me to turn around and go back than it would to get home. I should go back. But then what? Can I admit to him that I'm scared out of my mind of what we shared tonight? Admit that I'm falling for him so hard that I'm terrified I'm going to lose myself—that I fell in love with him when I was sixteen and haven't stopped loving him a single second since?

I blow out a heavy breath and shake my head. No good would ever come from a conversation like that. There's nothing I could ever truly offer him. I'm not brave enough to tell the world who I really am, and I never will be.

Glancing up at the night sky, I let the rainwater wash over me. I need to forget about Mason James. I need to move back to Chicago and cut all ties with New York. But first, I need a drink.

There's a dive bar on this block. My favorite kind of place. Spit and sawdust and real, honest liquor. The kind of place Mason wouldn't be caught dead in.

I step inside and shake off the excess rain. My T-shirt and jeans are soaked, and the warm air and warmer scent of aged spirits are more than welcome. Ignoring the curious glances of a few patrons at a nearby table, I head straight for the bar.

"King? What the hell are you doing in here?"

"And why do you look like you just crawled out of the Hudson?"

Shit. I spin around toward the direction of the voices and come face-to-face with Nathan and Drake. Double shit. I plaster on a smile and run a hand over my soaked head. "What are you two doing in here? I wouldn't have thought this was your kind of place."

Drake makes a show of glancing around, a goofy smile on his face. "Yeah, I know. Elijah told us about it. They have the best Scotch this side of Central Park." He holds up his near-empty glass in a toast.

Nathan gives me a knowing smile and pats his younger brother on the back. "He won a huge case today."

Drake downs his drink and indicates the empty seat at their table. "Join us."

It would be rude not to, what with everything they've done for me. That's what I tell myself, but in truth, I like these guys. I especially like that they're related to the one man I can't stop thinking about. Being close to them makes me feel closer to him, which is all kinds of fucked up considering how I ran out on the guy.

Nathan orders another round of exorbitantly expensive Scotch, and after the waiter has set it down, he asks me how things are going at Jamestech.

I take a swig from my glass and enjoy the burn and slight buzz it gives me. "Good," I say.

Drake sips his Scotch. "Elijah can be a bit of a hard-ass, but he's a teddy bear underneath. Find his leak and he'll make sure you're never short of work again. Guy has more business connections than LinkedIn."

I like Elijah. Yeah, I can see why people think he's a hard-ass, but from what I've seen, he's a great CEO.

"He just expects results," Nathan says. "I wouldn't say that makes him a hard-ass."

Drake snorts. "That's because by your standards, nobody's a hard-ass. You make drill sergeants look like kindergarten teachers."

Nathan rolls his eyes and shakes his head, an amused expression on his face as he regards his younger brother. Then he turns his attention back to me. "It was a *really* big case."

I smile, finding an unexpected comfort in their back and forth. "Actually, I mostly report to Mason."

"Ah, Mase." Drake smiles. "Don't let him fool you either."

I lean forward, resting my forearms on the table, my interest piqued. "Fool me how?"

Nathan gives his brother what appears to be a warning look, but Drake ignores it. He downs the rest of his Scotch and leans in too. "Mason likes to pretend he's the fun uncle, but he's not. Not really."

Another eye roll from Nathan, and he takes Drake's empty glass from in front of him. "I'm cutting you off and getting you a cab."

But I'm eager for any insight into the man who's

currently the subject of my every waking and sleeping thought. "Fun uncle?"

Drake smirks and jabs a finger into his chest. "I'm the fun uncle." Then he stares at me, grinning. In all the time I've known Drake, I've never seen him drunk before, no matter how much liquor he slammed.

I look at Nathan. "A huge case, huh?"

Nathan winks. "Massive."

I sense something more is going on, but I don't push. Drake's personal life isn't my business. Their brother on the other hand ... "I find it hard to believe that Mason isn't the fun uncle."

"Oh, he is." Nathan takes a drink, and I'm convinced that's the end of the conversation, but he continues. "That's not all he is though."

I don't speak, worried I'll appear too eager and cause suspicion. To my relief, he keeps going. "Mason has more charisma and charm in his little finger than most people have in their entire bodies. But that often makes people underestimate him. They think the easy charm and fun-loving playboy persona he cultivates is who he is. But he's all heart, my little brother. He hides it well, but he's one of the most loyal and honest people you'll ever have the privilege of meeting."

He stares at me over the rim of his glass while he sips more of the aged blend. Why is he telling me this? Does he know I already know these things about Mason? Mason, who's probably lying in bed, wondering why the hell I ran out on him like he did something wrong.

I'm such a fucking asshole.

I make my excuses, gulp down the rest of my drink and, over their protestations, throw fifty bucks on the table to cover the cost of one shot. Once I'm back outside in the rain, I take off in the direction of Mason's place, determined to tell him that tonight meant something to me. That he means something to me.

As luck would have it, another resident of the building is getting home, and I duck in the door behind him as it's closing. The concierge immediately spots me.

"Hi, Bill. Can you let me up?" I glance behind him at the private elevator that leads to Mason's apartment. The one that can only be accessed by a keycard, which Bill has in his inside pocket.

He shakes his head. "I can't."

"But I was up there a few hours ago."

"And then you left, and Mr. James hasn't advised me of any further visitors this evening."

I scrub a hand down my face. My buzz is wearing off, and I'm halfway to feeling like a fool for coming back here. But I'm more of a fool for leaving in the first place. "That's because he doesn't know I'm coming. I called, but he won't pick up."

Bill arches an eyebrow. "Sir, you're drunk and you are trespassing. If you don't leave, I'll call the police and have them remove you."

"Fuck, Bill. I was here a few hours ago. You said good-night to me," I protest, but Bill isn't budging. So I try a different tactic. "Then you call him for me. Call him on the intercom thingy." I know he has one because I've seen it. It lets him get a look at any unexpected visitors in the lobby.

"Sir, please." He gestures toward the door I snuck through a minute ago. "Leave."

"Just call him, and then I'll leave. Please, Bill. I'm begging you. Have you ever made a huge mistake and needed someone to help you out? Please. I need to tell him one thing, and then I'll leave."

He shakes his head. "I'm sorry, sir."

"Fuck," I mutter, glancing at the elevator again. But I don't think Bill is the kind of guy to make idle threats, and I could do without getting arrested for trying to break into Mason's penthouse.

So I leave, and I call him instead. To my surprise, he picks up. Bill probably told him I was here as soon as I walked out of the building.

"Mase?" My tone is desperate and pleading, and if I weren't drunk, I'd probably hate myself for it.

"What do you want, King?"

"I'm outside."

"I know."

"Can I come up?" I ask.

"Nope."

"Mase, please."

He sighs. "Go home. It's late, and I'm really fucking tired."

I'm certain he doesn't mean physically tired. No doubt he's tired of this constant back and forth between us. I know I am. "Let me say one thing before you hang up."

He doesn't reply, so I take my shot. "I'm sorry I walked out before. But I was scared. That ... What we did meant something, and I freaked out. I've never been good at handling my emotions, and I'm sorry. Now, would you please let me come up so I can make it up to you in person?"

"Is that all?" he asks, his tone weary.

"No." I gulp. "You told me that I make you feel like that sixteen-year-old kid, and it scares you because you don't like him. But for the record, I loved that kid. I still do."

I hear him swallow. "Goodnight, King."

The line goes dead.

And so does my heart.

THIRTY

MASON

I wake up to a notification that I have a voicemail from King along with a whole fuckload of guilt and regret. Why is it that he can act like a prize jerk, but I'm the one who feels like shit about it?

I'm not a lovesick teenager who'll come running because he flashes that killer smile.

I glare at the phone screen while I make my morning coffee, refusing to listen to his excuses. No doubt that whatever he has to say will piss me off and set me up for a shitty day. As if I don't feel crappy enough about him running out of here like the apartment was on fire. Not to mention the fact that I lay awake for hours after his drunken visit, feeling like a complete asshole for not letting him in. For not letting him use me. Again.

I glance at the notification time stamp. The voicemail was left at 5:37 a.m. He's either had a chance to sober up or spent the night getting more wasted. I'm not sure which of those options would be better. Regardless, I can guarantee his voicemail will ruin my day. I should delete it and pretend I didn't see it. So, why can't I? Why are my fingers twitching to play it?

Making the decision to put myself out of my misery, I press play, leaving it on speaker so I can listen to his pathetic excuses while I finish making my coffee.

"Hey, Mase." His voice is quiet, and my heart jumps into my throat. "I'm sorry I left." Silence. "I'm sorry I came to your place after I'd been drinking. I know you think I was drunk, but ..." More silence. I lean on the counter, staring at the phone. Excitement, anticipation, dread—they all bubble up from my stomach. "I wasn't that drunk, Mase. I meant everything I said."

Holy fucking shit. My knees buckle, and I brace myself on the counter. Is he still drunk?

"This is me—stone-cold sober—telling you that every word was true."

Frantically, I rack my brain to recall every word he said. The order he said them in. Whether I misheard or filled in a blank. Because he couldn't have said the things I think he did and meant them. He's playing with me. Messing with my head. For what? Some sick joke, like back in high school? Except we're not in high school anymore. And King isn't the same fucked-up asshole he was back then. Is he?

"I'd really like to say it all to your face though. Can I

see you tonight? My place at seven? I'll text you the address. Please ... Please give me a chance." The voicemail ends, and I blink down at my phone. Confused, elated, suspicious. Nervous as fucking hell.

Last night after he left, I was clear. I was cutting King out of my life for good. Now, I have no idea what the fuck I'm going to do.

I KNOCK on the half-open door of Elijah's office before popping my head in. Instead of my brother, Amber is inside with her feet crossed on his desk, revealing the distinctive red soles of her pumps.

She spots me before I can duck back out unseen. Our relationship is a complicated one, and while it's infinitely better than it was, she's not a person I'd ordinarily seek advice from. But I've played King's voicemail at least twenty times today, and it's driving me to distraction. I need to talk to someone about it. Anyone ... including Amber.

"If you're looking for Elijah, you've just missed him," she says. "He stepped out to get us dinner."

Since they were remarried a few months ago, Elijah has made a conscious effort to reduce his work hours and pay more attention to his wife. Seeing how happy that change has made him, I really don't want him slipping back into old habits. Out of concern for him, I step fully into the room. "You're eating dinner in his office?"

She returns my frown with a smile and slips her feet off his desk. "Yes. He's helping me write a bid." She nods to the paperwork in front of her. "And we're almost done, so we figured we may as well carry on here until it's finished."

I blow out a breath and nod, relieved.

"Did you need him for something?" she asks, her brown eyes locked on me like she's trying to read my mind —or steal my soul. Could be either with her.

I could really use some advice. But Amber? "Is there anything I can help you with?" she says now, and damn if she doesn't inject a little of that Southern honey into her voice. The kind that could make a serial killer feel at ease in a courthouse. She would have had an incredible career in the FBI.

I'm not sure if it's her charm or sheer desperation that makes me say, "You any good with narcissistic commitment-phobes who are far too handsome for their own good?"

She sits up straight and flashes me the sweetest smile. "I've handled you for the past twenty years, haven't I, honey?"

I set myself up for that one, but I refuse to give her the satisfaction of confirming I'm that self-aware. It would ruin my carefully curated shallow-as-a-puddle image.

Instead, I drop into the seat opposite her and run a hand through my hair. "You think I'm handsome?"

She wrinkles her nose, but her sparkling eyes belie her feigned disgust. "Too handsome for your own good. You James boys all look alike. Those looks are wasted on someone with such a ..." Pausing, she hums. "Disappointing personality."

That garners a snort of laughter from me, and she smiles again, still pinning me in place with her curious gaze. Leaning forward, she rests her chin on one hand. "So, what can I help you with? Please tell me it's man trouble."

She's teasing me, a fact which is confirmed by the look of surprise that settles on her face a few seconds later when I haven't replied to tell her that no, of course it's not man trouble and to stop being so ridiculous. And it is ridiculous—I can admit that. Never in my adult life have I sought the advice of my brothers over "man trouble."

And technically, I'm not now either. I'm seated across from my sister-in-law. A person who has historically been one of my least favorite people. And here I am, about to spill my guts like we're besties at a sleepover.

King Blackthorn, what the fuck have you done to me?

"There's this guy ..." I wait for her reaction, half expecting her to do the whole clapping her hands and squealing thing for dramatic effect, but she simply watches me, waiting for me to go on. "I knew him a long time ago, back in high school, and he hurt me. Not like a teenage heartbreak, I mean he really ..." My adrenaline spikes from thinking about it, but Amber is still staring at me, so I swallow down my anxiety. "He really fucked me over. And it kind of fucked me up for a long time." Again, I anticipate a remark intended to cut me off at the knees, something about how I'm still fucked up, but none comes. Still, I can't bring myself to tell her any more about what happened.

"You were together in high school? You and this guy?"

I nod. "We didn't go to the same school though. And he was in the closet. Like so fucking far in the closet he could have sold package tours to Narnia. Still is."

A smile flickers over her lips, and I'm sure it's thanks to the C. S. Lewis reference. Amber's a big reader like me. "And he's back in your life now?"

That's a complicated fucking question. One I'm not sure of the answer to. "Maybe. Kind of." I shrug. "I guess he could be, but ..."

"He's still in the closet?"

"Yeah, but that's not the issue. Not the whole issue, anyway. I mean this isn't a long-term, settle-down-and-have-kids kind of gig, you know? I can live with him keeping his sexuality a secret."

Her brow furrows.

"What?" I ask.

She gives an almost imperceptible shake of her head. "It's just that you're so open about who you are—as you should be. I assumed that dating someone who isn't would be a deal-breaker for you."

I shake my head. "Not everyone has it as easy as I did. I came out when I was thirteen, and it was no shock to any of my brothers or my parents. Unfortunately, not everyone's family is as supportive as mine. His certainly isn't."

"No, I suppose you're right."

"So I can live with that, but it's ..." I run a hand through my hair. For a man who makes a living off saying the right things at the right time, I'm sure as shit no good at it right now.

She waits patiently, her gaze never leaving my face. I pull at the collar of my shirt. Is it hot in here? "What if he doesn't deserve to be forgiven?"

She presses her lips together for a moment before responding. "I suppose that would depend on what he did. Did he physically hurt you?"

I clench my jaw and can still recall the ache in it that night when I lay alone in my room. But that part had nothing to do with King, and I've never told anyone except my therapist and the guys at the support group. As much as I surprisingly trust Amber to keep my secret, I'm not going to tell her either.

"He didn't lay a finger on me. But what he did hurt more. He walked away, Amber, like I meant less than nothing." His words—and the hurt they cause—are as fresh today, nearly twenty years later. *There is no we, asshole. It was fake. Every cringeworthy, painful second of it. I don't even fucking like you. Now leave me the fuck alone. Go beg some other dirty little fuck to let you suck his cock.*

Amber's soothing voice pulls me from the painful memory. "So why does he deserve a minute of your time now, honey?"

"Well, that's the million-dollar question, isn't it? All I can say is it was a long time ago. I think he's different now. He says he's sorry, and I almost believe him."

She lifts an eyebrow. "Only almost?"

Only almost because as much as I want to, I can never be sure. I thought I was sure of him eighteen years ago. King's right, we were only kids back then, but has anything really changed? What would he do if someone found out about us now? What would he do if his father found out? After he came to me when his grandfather died, I got the impression he and his parents still aren't close, but I have no idea how much influence Kyngston Worthington III holds over his only child.

My stomach rolls at the thought of that depraved piece of shit. A bead of sweat trickles down my forehead.

"Are you okay, Mason?" Amber asks. It's too much to hear the pity in her voice. I don't need anyone's pity. I dealt with all this shit a long time ago.

I roll back my shoulders and look her in the eye, forcing a tight smile. "You know my Pop always says I'm too quick to forgive. I don't hold grudges, and I thought that was a good thing, but—" I stop talking when she gives me a sardonic look, grateful to her for defusing the growing awkwardness with one raised eyebrow. Deliberate or not, I don't entirely know, but I suspect it is.

I hold up my hands in defense. "Hey, I never held a grudge against you. I just didn't like you. There's a distinct difference. And note the use of the past tense there."

She clasps her hands to her chest and flutters her eyelashes. "Oh, Mason. Are you saying you like me now? Like really, truly like me?"

I roll my eyes. "If I admit that I no longer think you're a she-devil incarnate, can we get back to my problem?"

Her lips curve. "Of course, honey. I'm sorry. You were saying?"

Wow, she's really good at knowing where to add light and shade to awkward conversations. "Am I being a pushover for this guy? Is he ..." My emotions threaten to spill out into my words. I hate feeling like this—vulnerable and open. And I haven't allowed myself to feel this way since ... Well, ironically, since the last time King Blackthorn was in my life.

"Is he what, Mason?" Her tone is softer now, gentle even. And her brown eyes are full of concern as she waits for me to reply.

Anxiety and shame ball themselves into a thick knot in my throat, and I force myself to swallow past it so I can admit one of my deepest fears. I might be a man-whore with commitment issues, but I am always one hundred percent clear with everyone I have any kind of sexual encounter with. Never do I let anyone believe that I'm looking for anything more than casual fun. The idea of taking advantage of someone is abhorrent to me. "Is he just using me?"

"Oh, honey." She rests her hand over mine on the desk. "You are smart, successful, and yes, far too handsome. But you're funny and kind too. I can see why anyone would want to be in your orbit. And if you choose to forgive this man and let him back into your life in any meaningful way, then that would say a whole lot about the kind of man you are. If he throws that back in your face, it only speaks to the kind of man he is."

"I ..." I blow out a breath. "I don't want to feel like that again, Amber. I promised myself I'd never let anyone make me feel that way again, least of all him. And now he ..."

"Now it feels like he has all the power?"

I nod and let out a deep, exaggerated sigh. "Aren't relationships supposed to be easy?"

That makes her laugh. "Oh, bless your heart. Who told you that?"

"TV? The movies? Gay porn?" I offer.

"I'll let you in on a secret. The best relationships are the ones we have to fight for. The people who challenge us most are the ones who make us the best version of ourselves. Loving someone is easy, but staying with them through the ups and downs of life—that's the tough part. But it's also the part that knits your souls together."

Her words resonate, but as usual when I feel something too deeply, I cover it with inappropriate humor. "Jeez. Have you been hanging out with Maddox?"

She rolls her eyes but isn't fazed. "Can I tell you something about Elijah and me that I think might help?"

"Please do." I could use anything to cling to right now.

"When we were separated and we were still sneaking around behind everyone's backs, I used to worry that he had too much power and influence over me. Sometimes it felt like he held all the cards, you know? But I realized that simply wasn't true. We can't always choose who we fall in love with, but we can choose who we allow to let into our hearts. Only you can decide whether he gets to be a part of your life. That power is all yours. If he stomps all over that, or if it fails because of some other reason, it doesn't mean you failed. And if it does fail, what have you lost? A little time? A little pride? A little piece of your heart? But god, wouldn't it all be worth it for a few days, weeks, or years of the kind of happiness that lights you up from the inside?" She stops speaking, her cheeks flushed pink and her eyes sparkling, and it hits me: The ice queen has well and truly melted.

I honestly couldn't be happier for her and Elijah. They found their way back to each other.

But King and me ... Our history is a lot more complicated than theirs. Isn't it?

"I know it's hard to forget, even when we can forgive, but only you can decide whether he's worth it, Mason."

Fuck, I'm more conflicted than before. But Amber is

right—all the good advice in the world isn't going to help me. Only I can decide what to do next.

Not now, though. I'm too wrung out to think straight. Too overwhelmed with the gamut of emotion King evokes in me. Guilt. Anger. Shame. Happiness. Jealousy. Lust. And maybe that other L word I'm not going to say in full. You name it, he makes me feel it. I default to my usual setting —sarcasm. "So, in a nutshell you have absolutely no helpful advice for me?"

Amber doesn't react, at least not the way I hoped. There's no sharp-tongued, lightning-fast barb from her in response. Instead, her eyes soften, crinkling at the corners, and she pats my hand. "I know it's hard, but what can I say? Personal growth is a bitch."

"Fuck, you're not wrong there." I look up into her face once more. "Oh shit, does this mean I'm growing as a person?" I make a horrified face that has her giggling. And fuck me, but it makes me laugh too. And it's exactly what I need.

We're still laughing when Elijah follows the scent of Thai food into the room a minute later, a brown paper bag in his hand. "What's all this?"

Ignoring my growling stomach, I stand and straighten my jacket. "I was asking your wife here for a little advice."

His face is a picture of surprise, which he quickly hides behind his cool-as-a-fucking-cucumber CEO facade. "Well, she does give great advice." He drops the bag on the table and a kiss on top of her head. "Anything I can help you with?"

"No, I think we got it covered. Thanks, bro. Enjoy your dinner."

He glances between me and Amber, a huge smile on his face. It makes me sad that she and I spent so long at odds with each other when we could have been good friends. But things were a lot different then. For all of us. What matters is where we are now.

With that thought in my head, I head out of the building and grab a cab to King's place.

THIRTY-ONE

KING

top watching the fucking clock, King. Stop checking your goddamn phone. He hasn't called or texted in the past seven seconds.

I take a slug of my beer and stare at the door of my apartment. Mason hasn't contacted me at all since he told me to go home last night. While I appreciate that me turning up half drunk wasn't the smoothest move, I hoped to get some response to my voicemail this morning. I woke up with a headache from Satan himself and a gut full of remorse and shame. But my remorse is all due to my actions before drinking with Nathan and Drake and nothing to do my confession. What I regret most was walking out on him in the first place.

Despite my determination not to, I glance at the clock again. He's two minutes late. More likely, he's not coming at all. But it's not like seven was a definite time. Maybe he'll still show up.

This is a repeat of the conversation I've been having in my head all day long. I could hardly focus on the job for longer than ten minutes without rehashing some variation of it or running through scenarios of how tonight might play out. In some, he's going to be here, all smiles and charm telling me he loves me. Others, he's never going to speak to me again. And everything in between. Predictably, my pessimistic ass leaned toward the not-showing-up end of the spectrum.

Not that it stopped me from picking up two cuts of prime rib on my way home.

It's four minutes after seven now. Fucker's not coming. The loud knock at my door stops me with my beer raised halfway to my lips. I put it down and wipe my mouth.

Shit! What if he sees the bottle and thinks I'm drunk again? That I need alcohol to be able to tell him how I feel? The truth is it's a habit. I come home from work and open a cold one before dinner and that's it. But tonight, I should have thought about it before I automatically followed my usual routine.

It might not be him though. That dude down the hall could have lost his cat again.

Another knock has me jumping up from the sofa. Fuck Mason James and whatever he's done to me to have me acting like this. I'm not a thirteen-year-old waiting for his first date. I twist my neck from side to side and walk to the door, preparing for the worst and hoping for the best.

When I open the door and see him standing there in one of his absurdly expensive suits, looking sexier than any man in the world has any right to be, I can't help but smile. "Mase. You came."

He nods. "You said you had something to say to me?"

Dammit, he's not going to make this easy on me, is he? I open the door wider and invite him inside. He stands, looking a little awkward and unsure as he waits for me to close it. His eyes drift to the half-empty bottle of Bud on my coffee table. "You want a beer?" I ask.

He shakes his head. "Just here to listen to what you have to say."

I run a hand over the back of my neck. Where do I fucking start? I recall exactly what I said to him last night. Every single word. But it was much easier to say to his phone than it is to say to his face. A machine can't reject me.

His eyes narrow on my face, and I realize I have to do this. If he does reject me, at least I'll know. I won't live the next eighteen years of my life wishing I had told him the truth. "I'm sorry I ran out on you last night. It was a shitty thing to do, and I only did it because ..." My vocal cords seize. His dark eyes are still laser focused on my face. But if I trust him enough to do what we did last night, then surely I can trust him enough to say this. "I was scared."

He takes a step closer, and our bodies are less than an

inch apart. The heat from him seeps through my shirt, warming my skin. "What are you scared of, King?"

Fear surges in my chest and lodges itself in my throat. I close my eyes and force myself to swallow past it. "Scared of how much I want you. Of how fucking good it feels when I'm with you."

"How about you have the balls to look at me when you say that?"

I open my eyes to find his boring into me like he's trying to read my mind. Trying to figure out if I'm telling him the truth. "I want you, Mase. I can't stop thinking about you. I want to spend every second of every day with you, and it scares the shit out of me."

His nostrils flare as he takes a deep breath. "And?"

I blink at him. And fucking what? Have I read this all wrong? He's a renowned playboy, hence the fucking nickname. What if this is all one-sided? What if I'm nothing more than a good fuck?

He inches closer, and our bodies are touching now. His hand slides to the back of my neck, palming it possessively. I almost melt into the carpet and I don't even care. "And what exactly do you want to do about that?" he asks. "Why did you ask me here?"

I lick my lips. I want to fuck you into oblivion, and when I'm done, how about you do the same to me? And then eat, sleep, repeat. That's what I want, but that's not what I say. "I just want to see you."

He arches an eyebrow. Cocky fuck is too goddamn sexy for his own good. "Like date me?"

Shit. I shake my head. "Not that exactly. I can't be out. Not yet. I'm not ready. But I want ..." Fuck, what exactly is it I have to offer New York's most eligible bachelor?

He presses his forehead to mine. "Fucking tell me, King. Stop worrying about what you think I'm going to say or do and give me the truth."

I grip his waist under his suit jacket. "I know it's unfair to ask you to hide any part of yourself or to see me in secret, but that doesn't stop me from wanting to be with you. If that's something you can live with, I just want to be with you. Whether we're eating or working or watching TV or fucking ... I just want it to be with you."

"What about my family?" he says gently. "I don't care about hiding us from the rest of the world, but my family's different."

I screw my eyes closed. The thought of anyone knowing I'm gay is terrifying, but I already trust Drake and Elijah. And Nathan seemed to suspect something last night. "Will they all be discreet?"

He places his hands on my face until I open my eyes. "I promise you they will take your secret to their graves if I ask them to."

What would it feel like to have a family willing to protect me that way? I push those thoughts aside and focus on him and how good it feels to have him here, with my hands on him and his on me. How good it's going to feel in the morning to wake up beside him in my bed. "Then we can tell your family."

His smile makes my knees tremble. "Then I'm yours, Hotshot."

Relief and desire wash over me. "Yeah you are." I push him back against the wall and crash my lips on his. I expect him to fight for control, especially after last night, but his mouth yields to mine in an instant. I flick my tongue against his, grinding my stiff cock into him and moaning into his mouth. It would be so easy to spin him around and fuck his perfect ass right here and now. The number of times I've sat on my sofa and imagined doing exactly that is bordering on obsessive. But his stomach growls loudly.

I pull back, a grin on my face. "You hungry?"

He winces, a smirk playing over his full lips. "Haven't eaten a thing since breakfast."

"I have a couple steaks. I could do some potatoes too. Nothing fancy like you're used to, but it's good food."

He trails his knuckles down my cheek, and I find myself leaning into his touch. "First off, Hotshot, you have no idea what I'm used to. And second, you cook?"

"I've lived alone for eighteen years. Of course I fucking cook."

His eyes twinkle with amusement. "Clearly you can sustain yourself, but I assumed you lived on protein shakes and gym-bro granola bars."

I bite the inside of my cheek and try my best to glare at

him—and fail miserably. He wrinkles his nose like he's trying to stop himself from laughing. "What the hell are gym-bro granola bars?" I ask.

"Granola bars for gym bros." He tips his head to the side and smirks.

My hands still on his waist, I drag him closer and rub my cock on his, stifling the groan that elicits in me. "You should really learn to curb that smart mouth of yours, Playboy, or I might have to teach you some manners."

"I don't mind a little etiquette lesson. But we should definitely eat first."

I press a final long, messy kiss on his perfect lips before going to cook me and my boyfriend some dinner.

THIRTY-TWO

MASON

We sit on opposite ends of the sofa, satisfied but not overfull from the exceptionally good steak and potatoes King cooked. I did offer to help, but he insisted that I do nothing more than drink beer and look good, which I excelled at. I enjoyed watching this giant hulk of a man maneuver nimbly around his kitchen with a dish towel slung over his shoulder and his biceps straining against his T-shirt.

It's obvious he's at ease in a kitchen, but here and now, with nothing to focus on but me and him and whatever this new thing is between us, he's clearly uncomfortable. I'm not exactly a relationship kind of guy, but I've been on enough dates to feel comfortable sitting like this. Not King though.

I slide my bare toes beneath his muscular thigh. "How many relationships have you actually been in?"

He sucks on his top lip before he answers. "Only two, I guess."

"Were they serious?"

He shrugs, taking a sip of his beer. "Yeah. I was engaged to one of them."

I almost spit out the swig of Bud I just took. "Engaged? To a guy?"

He scowls. "Of course not a guy."

His unguarded reaction hurts despite me knowing how deep in the closet he is. "Obviously. I just didn't realize you were bi."

He scrunches up his nose, and it makes him look fucking adorable. "I don't think I am. I can fuck a woman, but I'm not really into them, you know?"

I nod, impressed and shocked by his honesty. "Why did you get engaged to one then?"

"I was nineteen and trying to convince myself I was straight. It was a huge mistake. She got pregnant, and I was fucking terrified. But then she lost it, and as painful as that was for both of us, I also felt relieved. I realized I couldn't live a lie my entire life. So I ended it. She was heartbroken, although I think that had more to do with the miscarriage than me. She married some guy a year later, and they have five kids now."

I'd love to unpack the sorrow in his tone, but I get the sense it would be better not to push too far too fast. "I'm sorry about the baby," I say.

He shrugs and takes another slug of his beer.

"And the other one?"

He frowns. "The other what?"

"The other relationship? You said there were two."

His frown deepens. "You, Mase." He says it like it's the most obvious thing in the world.

"You mean back in high school? That was serious for you?"

He pulls back, blinking rapidly. "It wasn't for you?"

His tone is accusatory, and I'm pissed that I can't stop tears from filling my eyes. "We were together for eighteen months. You were my first kiss, my first ... everything. Of course it was fucking serious for me."

His face clouds with confusion and sadness, and he shifts to his knees on the sofa and palms the back of my neck. "Every single thing I said to you after my dad found us was a lie. Everything before that was the truth. You have to know that."

"But I never knew that, even though I told myself that it couldn't possibly be true. I didn't want to believe it so much that I convinced myself something awful must have happened to you. I was fool enough to hire a PI, and he found you a few weeks later, having pizza with some girl and living your best life in Idaho. And as relieved as I was that you were okay, I have never felt more worthless and insignificant in my entire life as I did at that moment. So, yeah, eventually I believed you meant every word of it, King."

He shakes his head. "I hate that I made you feel that

way. But I wasn't living my best life. I was living a fucking lie."

"You fucking broke me," I croak.

He presses his forehead to mine. "I know, baby. And I'm so fucking sorry."

I try to wrench from his grip, but he holds me tighter. Why the fuck did we have to dredge up these old hurts right when we got to a good place? "Mase, please listen to me," he pleads. "I loved you then, and I never fucking stopped."

He seems as shocked by his admission as I am. "Are you telling me you love me?" I ask.

He licks his bottom lip, his eyes never leaving mine, and I wait for what feels like an eternity for his answer. Because I want him to love me. I need him to. "Yeah, I am," he finally says, his breath warm on my face. "You are the only person I have ever loved, Mason James. And I don't see anything ever changing that."

This is what I wanted to hear, but it scares the hell out of me. I still love him too, but he doesn't get to know that. Not yet. Not when I can't trust him not to run as soon as things get a little tough. Thankfully, he doesn't wait for me to say it back. He presses his lips over mine, demanding a kiss that I readily give.

It doesn't take long for us to find our way to his bed, naked and urgent. We paw at each other, grabbing, biting, sucking, and licking. Hands and mouths taking and giving as we devour the other. Before long, he has me pinned to the bed, one hand on the back of my neck, and he pushes his thick cock inside me.

Fuck, it burns even with all the lube, but it's everything I need.

"Nobody has ever felt this good," he says with a growl. It's true for me too. I've had plenty of incredible sex over the past eighteen years, but it's always been different with him. He rests most of his weight on top of me, his mouth pressed against my ear. "You've always belonged to me, and you always fucking will."

"Yeah." It's supposed to be a challenge, but it comes out as a moan of agreement.

"Yeah." He pulls out and sinks back inside me, causing white-hot pleasure to sear through every cell of my being. "You're the only guy I've ever fucked bare, Mase. What will it take for you to trust me enough to do that again?"

Keep doing what you're doing and you can fuck me any way you want. Fortunately, my brain kicks in before my dick can make me vocalize that response. "Prove you're clean and we can talk," I pant out.

His lips dust over my skin. "Good boy."

Jesus fuck. "And I'll do the same for you."

"Of course you will." He goes deeper, stimulating my prostate and making stars flicker behind my eyelids.

"I'm gonna fuck you again, King," I moan.

He laughs, and his breath ruffles my hair. "I know, baby. I can't fucking wait. But right now I'm fucking you, so bite down on that pillow real hard for me and my neighbors won't hear you screaming my name when you come."

I sink my teeth into the soft foam without protest—having some guy scream out his name in the throes of ecstasy isn't exactly conducive to us keeping this thing a secret, and he fucks me so hard and so thoroughly that I almost pass out from the force of my orgasm. If it wasn't for the pillow, the entire building would know King's name.

IT'S BEEN a long time since I've woken up in someone else's bed. Even longer since I've done so with a massive bicep draped over my chest and not freaked out about it.

King is still sleeping, and I try to slip out from under his arm to make some coffee, but he opens one eye and yanks me closer. "Where are you sneaking off to?"

"I need coffee."

He snuggles into the pillow, contented little noises coming from his lips. "I'll make you some coffee soon. Just five more minutes."

"Or I can make my own coffee, and you can sleep for as long as you want," I suggest.

He nuzzles my neck. "I don't want five more minutes of sleep, Mase. I want five more minutes of this."

Oh. Well, fuck. "Could you stop being so fucking adorable for one minute? This is a complete one-eighty from you, and to be honest, it's making my head spin."

He smirks, his eyes remaining closed. "No, I can't."

"Jeez," I mutter, unable to stop the grin spreading across my own face. I stare at the hairline crack in the ceiling and listen to the sound of his breathing and my own heartbeat.

He shifts his position, and his morning wood rubs against my thigh. "So you think I'm adorable, huh?"

"Not adorable enough to go without coffee. I know it's Saturday, but I still have to be at work in an hour, and I have to shower and change first."

He hooks his leg over mine. "Oh, yeah. I heard you got a whole department working overtime this weekend for the big Fortnam deal. But you can shower and change at your office."

"And walk past my secretary and my staff in yesterday's clothes? Smelling of your cologne and hot sex?"

He opens his eyes. "Does hot sex smell different than regular sex?"

I roll on top of him and skim my nose along his throat. "Yeah, very fucking different."

He groans, his hands running down my back to my ass. "But we showered last night after I fucked you."

I hum my agreement. Fuck, he always smells so good. "I know, but now I'm gonna fuck you, Hotshot."

His fingers twine in my hair. "While I would love that, we have no condoms left."

"Motherfucker," I growl, making him huff a laugh.

"It's okay, baby. I can still make you smell like sex for work." He grips both of our cocks in his huge hand. His palm glides along our shafts, and he collects our precum with his thumb and smears it over our skin. Using it as lube, he works us over together.

"Fuck, King." I hiss out a breath, resting my mouth against the crook of his neck.

"You're gonna smell like me all day. When that douche from HR makes up some bullshit excuse to be in your office, when that fuckboy barista smiles at you when he passes you your coffee. Any guy who gets anywhere near you and thinks he has a shot is gonna know you're mine."

Possessive asshole. Can't deny that I love it though— not only that he bothered to learn so much about my workday but the way he says *mine*. It makes me feel ... so many fucking things. Wanted. Needed. Safe. He always used to make me feel safe.

I rock my hips, grinding into his hand, fucking him the only way I can right now.

"Fucking hell," he says. "You feel so fucking good doing that. You're desperate to come, aren't you?"

"As desperate as you."

He grunts, working us both faster, his grip getting tighter. His free hand coasts down my back, and he slides a finger into my asshole. "Come with me, baby."

"Jesus, fuck," I murmur against his neck right before he tips us both over the edge. Warm ribbons of cum coat our stomachs and chests, and the deviant fucker rubs it into my skin like lotion.

I roll onto my side and stare at him. He has his eyes closed and a shit-eating grin on his face. Whatever this thing is between us, it can't last. He'll never admit to the world who he really is. But I can live with that. I just won't let him break my heart this time.

THIRTY-THREE

I pull out my cell phone and dial Mason's number, already regretting not heading straight to his office after my meeting with Kendra McIntyre, the owner of Matrix, the club where Cassidy Jones worked. It was a productive use of my time though. The owner gave me insight into the clientele and confirmed my father wasn't a regular patron. He only ever seemed to be there when Cassidy was working.

Matrix is closer to my apartment, but the latter is missing one vital thing—Mason fucking James.

"Hey, calling to check in," I tell him. "I don't have anything significant to update, but I'm not going to make it to your office."

"Where are you?" he asks.

The door to my apartment snaps shut behind me. "I literally just got home."

"Fuck." He lets out a sigh. "I wish I was there with you. I have back-to-back meetings until seven. Remind me to pass our European clients to our new marketing VP when she starts."

I kick off my boots. "I wish you were here too, Playboy. I fucking miss you."

He laughs, and I smile at the sound, loving that he laughs so easily with me. "You saw me six hours ago. But yeah, I miss you too." With those last few words, his tone changes from light to deep and husky. Predictably, my cock twitches in response. "I have a favor to ask, actually. Well, not so much a favor as a request."

"Okay. Shoot."

"I totally forgot I agreed to go to a play tonight," he explains. "It's starring an old friend of mine, and it's his first Broadway show. He usually does movies, so he's kind of nervous, and he sent me a couple of tickets. I promised I'd be there. You want to come with me? We could grab something to eat after."

My skin itches. "Like a date?"

"No. Like two people going to see a show together and getting some food afterward. I promise to be a gentleman and not even try to hold your hand. I'll only refer to you as bro or dude if that makes you feel better."

Fucking Smartass. "A Broadway show though?"

Mason's laugh fills my ears. "Relax, Hotshot. It's not *Starlight Express*. It's a serious play. So will you come with me or not?"

I really fucking want to, but the idea of someone seeing us together and somehow guessing what we are to each other scares the hell out of me. "I don't think it's a good idea, Mase."

It's a few seconds before he speaks again. "Okay. It's no big deal. I'll see you tomorrow." The disappointment in his voice guts me.

I hang up the call and drop my head back against the sofa. Why did I say no? It's not a date—just a show and drinks. Plenty of people do that kind of thing with friends.

Is this old friend an ex of his? Mason dated a string of high-profile actors, and it wouldn't surprise me if he's remained friends with some of them. Who am I kidding? I can pretend tonight's not a date, but we both know it would be. Because Mason James is mine.

And I'll be fucked if I let some A-list actor drool all over him.

I call him back, and he picks up on the second ring.

"I'll come to the play with you."

"Good. I'll send a car for you at— "

"I can make my own way, Playboy."

He laughs. "Fine. We'll meet inside the theater to avoid any press. I'll text you the address. There's a bar on the second floor. I'll see you there at quarter to eight."

"See you then."

We end the call, and I lean back against my sofa again, a whole lot happier this time. I'm going on a date with

Mason James, and I'm equal parts terrified and excited. I focus on the latter.

HOLDING onto my glass of Scotch like it's a comfort blanket, I spot him walking up the stairs of the theater bar. He smiles when I catch his eye. Dressed in a fitted white shirt with dark dress pants, he looks fucking edible.

I will my legs to stay still and not run in the opposite direction. It's only a show. There are hundreds of people here, all with friends, family, and partners. Nobody is paying any attention to us. Well, except for the usual admiring glances he always attracts.

Mason winks when he reaches me, a rolled-up program in his hand. "That looks good." He nods toward my drink.

I didn't think to get him one—another stark reminder of how rarely I do anything like this. "I probably should have gotten you one too." A bead of sweat trickles down my back. "You want a sip?"

He laughs. "Seems like you need it more than me. Relax, okay? It's only a play." He nods toward the doors. "You ready?"

I down my drink and place the glass on a nearby table. No, most definitely not ready, but I follow him inside the theater anyway, and we take our seats. I've been too nervous to pay attention to the name of the show or who's starring in it, but as soon as I look at the program Mason is reading through, I recognize the name of the star performer—Tommy Castle.

"Didn't you used to date this guy?" I ask through clenched teeth.

Mason shrugs, still poring over the pages. "A lifetime ago, yeah."

An unexpected growl rumbles in my throat, and that gets his attention. His eyes narrow. "That's not why we're here, King. He's a friend."

I roll my neck, feeling uncomfortable. We're in the front row, some of the best seats in the house, and I feel on display. "I know. I just ..."

The house lights dim, and he gives my thigh a subtle squeeze. "It will be fine."

It's more than fine. The play is engrossing. Tommy gives a great performance, confirming he's much more than an action-movie hero. But sitting here with Mason is the most incredible part. His warm thigh rests against mine, and the occasional brush of our hands ignites the constant spark between us.

When the play ends, Tommy gets a standing ovation. We join in, and Mason whistles for his friend. Tommy flashes him a wink.

"You want to come backstage to say hi?" Mason asks.

"To Tommy?" Your ex? The guy who eye-fucked you from the stage? I don't voice those last two things. "I thought we were going for food. I'm starving."

"We will," Mason promises. "It will only take a few minutes, and then we can get out of here." He weaves expertly through the crowd, and I follow close behind. A hefty-looking bouncer with half a dozen facial piercings stands at the stage door. He recognizes Mason and waves us through to Tommy's dressing room.

There are several people in here already, but as soon as Mason walks in, Tommy makes a beeline for him. "Mason, you came!" He's beaming, and who can blame him? Mason James has that effect on people.

Tommy looks like he's about to hug him, but Mason holds out his hand to shake. "Of course, Tom. I wouldn't miss it."

Tom takes Mason's outstretched hand and then glances at me, and I realize I'm probably scowling. Mason introduces me as his buddy, which pisses me off. Yeah, it's exactly what I asked for, but I didn't know I'd be meeting his fucking ex.

"Did you enjoy the show?" Tommy asks me.

"Yeah. It was really great. Congratulations."

He nods. "Thanks, man." He refocuses on Mason. "You guys want to come to the after-party? It's nothing huge. Just the cast and a few select people." I don't miss the way his eyes rake over my boyfriend. It's obvious he'd much prefer to attend a party that involved only the two of them.

Mason shakes his head. "Can't. I have an early meeting tomorrow. But thanks for the invite."

Tommy's eyes dart between the two of us before fixing on Mason once more, and he raises an eyebrow. "It's not like that. We're just friends," Mason assures him.

Tommy licks his lips. "Shame about the party then. Maybe next time?"

"The play was incredible, Tom. I'm really pleased for you," Mason says, expertly dodging his question. "We'd better get going."

We say goodbye, and a few minutes later we're being let out of a back door into a quiet alley. "You didn't want to go to their party, did you?" Mason asks.

"No. But did you?" There's no cause for the accusation in my tone. Mason gave zero inclination he wanted to do anything with his ex, but the guy is a Hollywood star with abs of steel and an ass that looks like it's been carved from marble—I've seen it in movies.

He stops in his tracks. "You know I didn't, King."

I chew on the inside of my cheek. He's standing close, his hands by his sides, and I can tell he's trying hard not to touch me. It's every bit as difficult for me. I want to push him against this building and remind him that he's mine, but I can't. Not even in this quiet alley. "I hate that I can't touch you," I whisper.

He hums. "You want to go home?"

"No. You said food." I grunt my response like a neanderthal.

He stares at me for a few seconds and smirks. "I know just the place."

. . .

Mason made a call, and a cab ride later found us taking a private elevator to an exclusive restaurant in Manhattan. A maître d guides us to a private room that comfortably fits a dining table for two. Music plays softly through speakers built into the wall, and there's a small bar off to the side, stocked with top-shelf liquor. One wall is entirely glass, the kind that allows us to see out into the main restaurant and bar area but, I'm assured, doesn't allow anyone to see in.

We order the Kobe filet and roasted vegetables, and it's as delicious as one would expect from a restaurant that doesn't list prices on the menu. As is the Ballantine's, which also doesn't have a price attached.

While we eat, Mason and I talk about mundane shit that doesn't really mean anything, but it feels easy. Every so often, I glance at the glass wall and fidget in my chair.

"Relax. Nobody can see us," Mason assures me. "Not that there's anything to see. We're just eating dinner."

Just eating dinner right now, but spending time in each other's company usually only ends one way. Is that why he brought me to a place where nobody can see us? "How many guys have you brought here?" I ask.

He tilts his head to the side and studies me before answering. "Enough. And while I adore your possessive streak at times, it's completely unnecessary. This place is discreet, so yeah, I've been here plenty. But if I avoided all the spots I've ever taken a guy, we'd have a pretty limited pool of places we could go."

"I don't care that you brought guys here. I care if you brought Tommy here." There it is. The thorn that's been jabbing me in the side all night long.

He shakes his head. "I never needed to. We were both very open about our brief relationship."

I recall. They were splashed all over the gossip columns for the short duration of their fling. I can't help but compare our relationships. Theirs, open and easy—ours, the exact opposite.

"Tommy is a friend, and I should have told you he was an ex before springing tonight on you, but it was eight years ago. I don't think of him like that. And there's nothing between us, I swear."

I recall the way Tommy looked at him earlier. The seductive tone of his voice when he invited Mason to that party. "He'd like there to be though."

Mason shrugs. "I don't know about that. But even if he does, I don't. And I'm sorry if it made you feel uncomfortable."

"It didn't."

He frowns, confused.

"He didn't make me feel anything, but I hated that you introduced me as your friend."

His frown deepens to a scowl. "But you said—"

"I know what I said, dammit. And I didn't want to be outed in front of an A-lister and his entourage, but ..." I scrub a hand over my face. "Fuck, it still hurt. And I know that's completely irrational and all my own doing, but I still fucking hated it."

He simply stares at me.

It doesn't surprise me that he's confused, because I am too. I'm not ready to be out, but I do want everyone to know he belongs to me. What kind of twisted logic is that? "I know it's unfair, and I'm not blaming you for calling me your friend. I'm just trying to be honest about how it made me feel."

He takes a slow sip of his Scotch. "And I do appreciate that. I would much prefer to introduce you as my boyfriend. Just say the fucking word."

I swallow the thick knot in my throat. "I really enjoyed tonight, Mase. I loved sitting next to you in that theater and doing stuff normal couples do. But I hate that I couldn't bring myself to touch you. I hate how fucked up I am. I wish I could let it all go and be me, but I ... I fucking can't." I drop my head into my hands.

He pushes his chair back and crouches at my side, his hand on the back of my neck. "Hey," he says softly. "It's okay. You'll get there when you're ready."

"What if I never get there?" My voice cracks.

"Then we'll deal with it."

"I want to be the kind of man you deserve. The kind of guy who doesn't break into hives at the prospect of holding your hand in public."

He stands, and I hear a few buttons clicking. The music

changes to something with more bass. Immediately, I recognize the opening beats of "Boulevard of Broken Dreams"—a song we used to make out to in Mason's bedroom.

"Have you ever danced with a guy, King?" Mason's voice is dark and dangerous and sexy as fuck.

I look up at him. Is he serious? The look on his face tells me he is. "No."

He grins. "There's a first time for everything."

"What, here?"

"I told you, nobody can see through the glass." He holds his hand out to me.

"I've never danced, period. Not with a guy or a girl."

"Then it's definitely about time you tried. I'll be gentle." He winks, and it makes my dick twitch in my jeans.

Tentatively, I take his hand and allow him to pull me up. His arms snake around my waist, and he pulls me closer. "I don't know what to do," I admit.

"You can't get it wrong, babe. Just do whatever feels right."

It's awkward, at least at first, but I grab his hips and concentrate on his hands on me, the way his hips grind against mine, the subtle sway of his body. My pulse races from both anxiety and desire, my mouth dry. But I move with him, and the awkwardness disappears, and all that's left is me and him—two people who've known and loved each other so many times before that their muscles instinctively know how to do this.

Mason's hand slides to the back of my neck. "You're doing so well, mi rey."

His lips brush mine, and he kisses me, slow and tender, matching the rhythm of our bodies as we sway to the music. His free hand glides up my back, over my shoulder, and along my neck until he's gently cupping my jaw, angling my face exactly where he wants me. There's no urgency to his movements or in mine as I let my hands roam his muscular back and ass. Our tongues dance in a delicate tempo, exploring and adoring. It feels like I'm seventeen again, and it's fucking heaven. We kiss and dance and kiss some more until we're too breathless to continue.

He rests his forehead against mine. "Dancing with you might be my new favorite thing to do."

I breathe him in. "Mine too. Tonight has been incredible. Thank you."

"You're welcome." He rubs the pad of his thumb over the back of my neck, sending shivers down my spine. "So was this your first date, Hotshot?"

"I thought this wasn't a date. Just two friends catching a show and grabbing some food, right?"

He grins. "You kiss all your friends like that?"

I dust my lips over his again, feeling so much, yet still not enough. "I've never kissed anyone like that. Nobody but you."

"Me neither."

Our lips meet again, our tongues sliding together. We continue kissing and dancing for I don't know how long, but songs begin and end, and we don't stop. And I know that this is exactly what I want. What I deserve.

What we both deserve.

But I'm still not sure I'm brave enough to take it.

THIRTY-FOUR

MASON

"Is Mr. James available?" King's deep voice travels through the crack in my office door, and like it's done every day for the past four days this week, it stops me in my tracks. I tip my face to the ceiling and groan, willing my dick not to get hard from the sound of his goddamn voice. That would be incredibly inappropriate. But as usual, my dick has no common sense at all when it comes to King.

"He's with HR right now, but let me check for you," Deborah replies in her honeyed Georgian accent.

I can picture the scowl on King's face at her response and suppress a smirk. I am with HR, but it's not a private meeting, hence the open door. Hayden "dropped by" to get my input—something I realized he does a lot after King pointed it out. Today it's about a new policy the team wants to implement, which I do need to be briefed on, but it probably could have been done via email. I'm a hands-on boss, and I pride myself on being approachable, but the leak has me spooked. Not to mention my possessive secret boyfriend putting ideas in my head.

Deborah pops her head in. "Sir, Mr. Blackthorn is here to see you."

I glance at Hayden. "We're done, right?" He spent the last five minutes telling me about his labradoodle's allergies, so I assume we have no more work to discuss.

He nods, but I don't miss the look of disappointment on his face. Maybe King is onto something.

I tell Deborah she can show my guest in, and he bounds into the room not a second later. His eyes go straight to Hayden, and he assesses my HR manager with a cool stare. "Hayden," he says, his tone clipped. "It's nice to see you. *Again.*"

Hayden stands, brushes an imaginary crease from his pristine suit pants, and gives a curt nod. "Same to you, King."

King bares his teeth, practically snarling, and I suppress a snicker at his unguarded reaction. In an attempt to defuse the tension, I wish Hayden a good evening, and he thankfully takes that as his cue to leave.

"Close the door, would you?" King says, and there's a hint of snark in his tone that I'm sure Hayden won't miss.

Hayden glances at me for confirmation, and I signal that he should do as King asks. As soon as the door is closed, King is across the room, his hand gripping my jaw.

He pulls me in for a rough kiss, then pulls back. "He wants you to fuck him, Mase. You need to be careful."

"I don't fuck my employees." I make a show of checking him out. He's wearing jeans and one of those ridiculously tight-fitting T-shirts, although I suspect they're not supposed to be all that tight. He simply happens to have the biggest biceps I've ever seen. "Although you do technically work for me."

His green eyes narrow. "No, I offer a service that you pay for. That's different."

I arch an eyebrow, resting my hands on his waist. "A service, huh?"

He runs his nose over my jawline, taking a deep inhale, and dips his hands inside my suit jacket. "Even you couldn't afford those kinds of services from me, Playboy."

"Is that why you give them to me for free?"

He hums against my skin, causing vibrations to travel through my entire body. "Yeah, you're a real charity case." He drags his teeth down the column of my neck and rocks his hips against mine. "You better be hard for me and not that douchebag who just walked out, baby," he growls in warning.

Why does his jealousy get me so fired up? "It's always for you."

"Good boy. Now, you want me to fuck you on your desk again, or shall I take you home?"

Damn, King's mouth should come with a health warning. It's been almost a week since he cooked me steak, and in that time, we've spent every spare moment we have together. I've barely seen anyone but him, and I blew off Sunday brunch with my family. Every night this week, he's shown up at my office a little after five to update me —an interesting way to describe him having his dick inside me. Because that's how it usually ends. Even if I start out topping, even when it begins with him on his knees sucking my cock, it ends the same goddamn way. And I've never been happier.

Can't happen tonight though. "As tempting as you make that sound, I have to go to my dad's for dinner tonight. It's my baby brother's birthday. I told you about it this morning."

His face falls. "Shit. Yeah, you did." He moves his hand to the back of my neck, gripping it possessively, exactly the way I like it. "How about you stop by my place after?"

I shake my head. "I promised Pop I'd stay over. He gets lonely in that huge house all on his own." King looks down, probably trying to hide his disappointment. I place my finger under his chin and tip his head back up so I can look in his eyes. "It's one night. Couldn't you use a break from me anyway?" I joke, trying to lighten the mood.

"Why would you think that? Do you need a break from me?" His face is calm now, his expression unreadable, but hurt bleeds into his tone.

"No. I didn't say that. But I can't miss my brother's birthday. Not even for you, Hotshot." I brush my lips over his. "You can spend one night without me, can't you?"

He presses his forehead to mine. "Yeah. But I don't want to."

I don't want that either. This is fucked up. I've dated plenty of guys, had dozens of relationships, and not once have I ever felt this attached to any of them. In fact, any relationship usually fizzles out after a few dates when they get too clingy. But King? I love how much he wants me because I crave him just as much. "Then come with me."

"To your brother's birthday party?"

"It's not a party. It's dinner. Mad is an incredible chef, and he loves to cook for new people. It would be like an extra birthday surprise for him."

"Your brother is cooking his own birthday dinner?"

I picture Maddox now, in Mom's old apron, surrounded by spices, vegetables I can't pronounce, and endless pots and pans—in his own nirvana. "Yeah. He loves it though. He's kind of an enigma, my baby brother. And you'll love him. Everybody does."

He sucks on his teeth, and I don't miss the way he inches away, creating a little distance before he can reject me. "But it's your family. Meeting them like this is a big fucking deal."

It is, but I really want to take him to dinner. More than that though, I want him to want it too. I'm just not sure he's ready. "You already met three of my brothers," I remind him. "But their wives will be there too, and my dad. And my nephew. It will be a lot. You don't have to come, but I would like you to."

His eyes bore into mine. "Your dad won't mind me spending the night?"

I bark out a laugh. "I'm thirty-five years old. He's not going to mind you spending the night."

He shuffles from one foot to the other while he wrestles with the decision. Damn, he's cute when he's nervous. "But ..." He shakes his head. "I'd be in the way. It's your family time."

It doesn't seem prudent to tell him that I've been known to take my one-night stands to my dad's for Sunday brunch, and on one occasion I invited a guy I'd just met to Thanksgiving. "They'll be cool with it. I can call ahead and let them know if that makes you feel better. But it's your decision."

He chews on the inside of his cheek, looking more adorably nervous than before. Now I really want him to come meet my family, and I could kick myself for not inviting him sooner. Maybe if he'd been given time to get his head around it ...

"Okay," he says with a definitive nod. "If you're sure it won't be a big deal."

I can't help the huge smile that spreads across my face. It's the biggest fucking deal ever, but I know that's not what he means. "It won't be."

"Do I need to get him a gift? Am I dressed nice enough for dinner?" He glances down at his clothes.

"No, he doesn't need a gift, and you're perfectly

dressed for dinner." I tug him closer and our chests collide. "Relax, it's going to be fun."

"I haven't been to your house in a long time, Mase. Not since ..." His voice cracks.

I seal my lips over his and slip my tongue inside his willing mouth. He wraps his arms around me and kisses me back like he might never get the chance again. I don't want to think about the last time he was in my childhood home. When he gave me that goddamn jacket and told me he'd wait for me when he went off to Harvard. It's all in the past now, and there's no room for it here.

THIRTY-FIVE

KING

I'm nervous as hell meeting Mason's family, at least like this. Drake is already a friend, and I know Nathan and Elijah well enough now. But this is different. This is me meeting the entire James clan—and doing it as Mason's boyfriend.

We climb out of his Lamborghini, and I look up at the house. It's a stunning two-story mansion with balconies and beautifully landscaped gardens. It would look more at home in the English countryside than New York. I haven't seen this place in eighteen years, but it looks as I remember it. This is where I spent the best nights of my life for eighteen precious months. I can hardly believe I threw it all away for the approval of a man I can barely stand to be around. From here, I can see the balcony of Mason's room, the same one I climbed up onto so many nights.

Mason slips his hand into mine, a present wrapped in silver-foil paper clutched under his other arm. "You okay?" he asks.

"It's ..." I swallow hard. "It's strange being back here."

He glances at the house, a wistful look in his eyes. "Yeah, I guess." Then he clears his throat. "Come on, it'll be fun. I promise."

I HAD ABSOLUTELY no reason to be nervous about Mason introducing me to his family. Every single one of them has been nothing but warm and welcoming.

Elijah was somewhat surprised about Mason's and my relationship, but only because he didn't pick up on it himself. There was no hostility from him. No negative feelings at all. In fact, he hugged me and pushed a glass of expensive Scotch into my hands.

Drake and Nathan seemed happy for us, and all the wives were eager to meet me. And I got to meet Maddox, the birthday boy and the brother I've heard so much about. I really like him. Of course there was Dalton too, and I was probably most nervous about meeting him. But the man is a real old-fashioned gent, and he reminds me a little of a younger version of Grampa. None of them were perturbed by Mason's request that we keep our relationship under wraps either.

Maddox cooked us all the most delicious Thai curry I've ever tasted in my life. The guy is a culinary genius.

And when I complimented him on his skill, he told me about his time traveling in Asia and Europe.

None of them seem to be aware that I visited this house countless times before, albeit via climbing through Mason's bedroom window rather than using the front door. I wonder if he ever told them about me without mentioning my name. Did he tell them how I broke his heart? I have no idea why, but I suspect he didn't.

A few years after I left, I read about his mom's death following a long battle with cancer. The dates suggested that she got sick soon after we broke up, and if I know Mason, I would bet that he hid the pain of his heartbreak for his family. That's the kind of person he is. Despite the shallow playboy persona he cultivates for the outside world, he's one of the most selfless people I've ever known. With his employees, with his family. With me.

The evening has been almost perfect. Almost because of Mason. He was fine when we got here, but he's barely spoken to me since dinner, and now he seems ... off.

"Unca Mase!" A child charges into the room and throws himself on Mason's lap. This must be Luke.

He was in bed sleeping when we arrived, but he woke up half an hour ago. Nathan went to settle him, but the weary look on the man's face as he trudges in behind his son tells me he must have given up.

Mason gives Luke a squeeze, and then the excitable toddler charges around the rest of the family, dishing out hugs and sloppy kisses before wandering over to me.

"Luke, this is Uncle Mason's boyfriend, King," his mom, Melanie, tells him.

"King," he declares triumphantly, flashing me an adorable toothy smile. Then, to my surprise, he clambers onto my knee and holds his toy airplane in front of my face. "Unca Mase, plane," he tells me earnestly.

"Did your uncle Mason give you this plane?"

Luke nods happily and giggles. "Luke plane."

"No plane tonight, little guy," Nathan says, taking a seat beside his wife. "You're supposed to be in bed."

Luke doesn't seem overly bothered by that and goes back to showing me his toy. He stays on my lap for the next thirty minutes, and his family declares it a feat for him to remain still for so long. I enjoy his chatter about planes and zoo animals, and when he stops to catch his breath, I tell him how much I like them too.

When he starts yawning, Nathan scoops him from my lap and declares he definitely needs to go back to bed.

"I'm tired too. I'm going to head to bed myself." Mason runs a hand through his hair, and while he does look tired, that tic in his jaw tells me he's pissed. I have no idea what's going on with him. Did something happen?

I place my glass on the coffee table. "I'll come with you."

"No," he says a little too quickly for my liking. "I'm worn out, so I'm gonna go straight to sleep. Stay with my family and have fun."

They all wish him goodnight, and he walks out of the

room. None of his brothers, their wives, or his father seem at all perturbed by his early departure. Elijah mentions how hard he's been working, and they all make sympathetic noises, but nobody else saw what I did. Mason kept that trademark smile on his face when he spoke to them, but he was upset about something.

Fuck, I'm such an asshole. Of course he's upset, seeing me sitting here with his family like I fit in. Having me back in this place—the same place where we used to make out on his bed while we listened to Green Day. The place where we first had sex. Where we secretly fell in love all those years ago. My memories of being in this house are all good because they all involve him. But I fucked up his memories of us when I broke his heart.

I shouldn't have come here with him.

I down my Scotch, wish everyone goodnight, and leave.

THIRTY-SIX

MASON

I can't get the sound of his laugh out of my head. The image of him sitting on the sofa next to Mel, bouncing Luke on his knee is burned into my mind. King was so at ease with my whole family. Like he belongs here with them. With me.

All of this should make me happy, so why doesn't it? Why does anger burn in my veins like my blood is made of fire? It makes no sense at all.

I unclench my fists and stare at the crescent-shaped grooves my clipped nails have left in the soft flesh of my palms. It's a pity I took down my old punching bag. I sure could use it. The urge to punch a hole through the goddamn wall is fierce.

There's a knock on my door, and my body responds the way it always does when he's near, sizzling with energy. But this time it's drowned out by my rage. "Mase, can I come in?" he asks.

Can't exactly say no. This is his room tonight too. I'll tell him I'm tired again. We can get some sleep, and maybe I won't feel like this in the morning. "Yeah," I grunt.

A few seconds later, he's standing in front of me. "Everything okay?" he asks.

I refuse to look up at him. "Yeah. I'm just tired."

He steps between my spread thighs. "You sure? Did I do something wrong?"

I look up and find him staring at me with concern. "You tell me, King."

"I would if I knew, but I have no idea. Seems you're pissed at me about something, baby."

"Don't call me baby," I snarl, and I'm shocked at the vicious edge to my tone.

"Then tell me what's wrong."

I jump up and push him out of the way. I can't stand him looming over me. Having him so damn close is only fueling my anger. "I don't fucking know."

He stuffs his hands into the pockets of his jeans. "Yeah you do."

I run my hands through my hair and shake my head.

He takes a few steps closer, invading my space once more. "You do, but I think maybe you're too scared to say it."

I snort. Is he fucking kidding me? "Don't fucking psychoanalyze me, King. I'm not a case you can solve."

His jaw tics and his shoulders tense. He looks like he wants to punch me in the mouth, and there's every possibility that's what I want too. Maybe that would make me feel better.

I take a step back, but he moves with me. I keep going until my back hits the wall and I have nowhere to go, and he's still there with me, his body inches from mine. My hands curl into fists at my sides, my blood thundering through my body. So much anger and hurt boil up inside me, a swirling vortex of emotion that I can't hold in for much longer. And if he doesn't get out of my way ...

"Just say it. Tell me why you're so pissed at me." His voice is low. Commanding.

I glare at him, every muscle in my body vibrating with pent-up rage. "You fit in here so well." I spit out the words. "You act like you care about them."

His eyes narrow. He inches closer. "They're all easy to get along with. And it's not an act. They're important to you, and they're easy to care about. You're easy to care about, Mase."

And there it is. The root of all my rage. "So why was it so fucking easy for you to stop caring?" I roar, pushing him hard in the chest. He staggers back a little before regaining his footing. "Why did you tell me it was all a lie? Why did you fucking leave me?" Tears are streaming down my face, and I don't bother wiping them away. This house is full of my memories of him. Memories I buried so deep because they hurt too much to recall. Every important sexual first I had was with him, right here in this room. And on one occasion in the den when nobody was home. I refuse to make him feel better by pretending this doesn't hurt. Let him see what he did. Let him see the damage he caused.

"Mason." He says my name like a plea, his green eyes dark with concern.

I push him again, harder this time, and although he staggers once more, he comes back to the same spot. "I'm sorry" is all he says.

But I can't bear to listen to his apology. I'm too overwhelmed by the pain, anger, and betrayal that I've kept buried for eighteen long years. I glare at him, and all I see is eighteen-year-old King, arrogant and cruel. His face twisted in a sneer as he told me how I disgusted him. How everything was fake. Part of me wants to slam my fist into his face, but the other part of me is too exhausted to move. "You fucking broke me." I slide down the wall, my legs unable to hold me up any longer.

Resting my head on my knees, I do nothing but sob. And I don't care that he sees or if he thinks I'm weak or pathetic. Too much of my life has been wasted craving his approval, and I'm done. I let it all go in a mess of tears.

I have no idea how long I've been sitting here, keeping my head buried so I don't have to look at him. He probably left anyway. Can't imagine he'd hang around to help clean up the mess that I've become. Thirty-five years old and sobbing on my bedroom floor like a kid. Even I know I'm pathetic.

But then I hear him moving, feel the heat of his body. He wraps his legs awkwardly around my waist, wedging one leg between my back and the wall, and crushes me to his chest, cocooning me in those huge biceps. My cheek rests against his chest, my tears soaking through his T-shirt. He rests his lips on top of my head. "You been holding onto that for a while, huh?"

I don't answer, and he doesn't speak again. He simply holds me until I stop crying and all the anger has bled out of me. Instead of the cruel King who humiliated and betrayed me, he embodies the version of himself I first fell in love with all those years ago. The one who always made me feel safe. Who made me feel loved.

I wriggle my head out of his hold and scrub at my wet cheeks. Gently, he moves my hands away and, cupping my face in his palms, wipes my tears away. "I know it's not enough, but I am sorry."

I swallow hard so I don't start crying again. "I know. I don't know where the fuck all of that came from."

"I get it. You saw me here in the same place we spent so much time together, playing happy family with your dad and brothers, and it brought it all back. That's under-standable."

"It wasn't only that. It was ..." I take a deep breath. "I saw you with them and saw what we could have had. We might not have made it, but we could have had something special." Fuck me, I sound like I'm in a rom-com.

"We did have something special," he says. "I fucked it

up, but that doesn't change what came before." His eyes are pleading with me to believe him, but I'm not sure I can.

"I'm sorry if I fucked up a perfectly nice evening."

He offers me a small smile. "You didn't. I had fun, and your brother seemed to have a good birthday. But this all had to come out sooner or later. It's not good to hold onto that kind of hurt."

He's right. I've spent my entire adult life convincing myself I was over him, not to mention what happened afterward, and that clearly wasn't true. "I'll take unresolved issues from adolescence for five hundred, Alex."

His grin widens and makes me smile in response. "I'll sit on this floor with you all night if I have to. But my ass is getting kinda numb and there's a real comfy mattress right there." He jerks his chin in the direction of the bed.

I groan as the pain in my spine makes itself known. "Yeah, the bed sounds way more appealing."

We both stand, and for some reason I feel like that awkward teenager again. Does he mean go to bed to sleep? I don't want to sleep, but I'm not entirely sure I want to fuck right now. King strips to his boxers and tosses his clothes on the floor. I do the same, except I fold mine and place them on the back of a chair. He's already lying under the covers with his arms behind his head when I'm done.

His gaze rakes over my chest. "Come here." The words lack his usual commanding tone.

I slide beneath the covers, and he rolls onto his side to

face me. He reaches out and strokes my cheek. "I regret the way things ended between us, Mase, and I wish I could take back those awful things I said."

"You were right—we were kids. I should have let it go a long time ago."

"No." He shakes his head. "Don't do that. I was eighteen and knew exactly what I wanted, but I didn't have the balls to fight for us. Not like you did. I was a fucking coward." He closes his eyes and sighs. "But what I regret more is never coming back and putting it right. That I let you carry that with you for so long is my biggest regret."

I cup his jaw and tilt his head up, leaving my hand there until he opens his eyes again. "Why didn't you come back?"

He shrugs. "I followed you in the news. I'd see the pictures of you online. I remember the day you were announced as COO of Jamestech. The suit you wore looked fucking incredible on you, by the way."

"Of course it did. It was Tom Ford."

A small smile plays on his lips. "You always looked happy. Free. I told myself that you wouldn't want me turning up here and ruining your perfect life. But I used that as an excuse. I was a fucking coward, and I couldn't bear to look you in the eye after the awful things I said."

And the awful things his father did. Does he know I came looking for him? I don't believe he does, and there's no point in bringing it up now. Everything is already so raw and vulnerable between us. "My life has been pretty good. And I'm sure it does look perfect from the outside. I'm incredibly privileged, and I know that. But yeah, it would have meant a lot."

He nods, his jaw working. "You know, mostly, I ..." His voice cracks. "I hoped that you'd know I couldn't have meant any of it."

Tears burn my eyes again.

"I'm not trying to make you feel bad. But in my head, it was one night. And then one deeply fucked-up phone conversation—"

"Then you ghosted me after," I remind him.

He nods. "I know. I'm not excusing it. I'm just telling you how I felt. I hoped that whenever you thought of me, you'd remember all the good stuff that came before."

The anger and hurt from earlier threatens to bubble to the surface again, and I take a deep breath. "I did remember. That only made it harder. Don't you get that? But what you said and what you did after—it negated everything good that came before."

His throat works as he swallows. "I understand that. The truth is, I was never good enough for you, Mason. I never will be." He slides his arm around my waist. "I'm not sure I can ever be the man you deserve."

My muscles tense, and I brace myself for the inevitable breakup speech. Ironic that I'm not usually on the receiving end of it. In fact, I never have been. Not with anyone except King, and here we are again. Fuck my life.

"But I lost you once, Mase," he says quietly. "And I'd

rather become a fucking monk and live the rest of my life in solitude than lose you again. I loved you then, I loved you all the days in between, and I still love you now. So fucking much. You deserve so much more than I have to offer, but if you'll let me, I promise to give you the best version of myself I can be."

Fuck, that was no breakup speech. My eyes swim with tears for an entirely different reason this time. When the fuck did I become a crier?

I have no idea how we'll navigate a relationship with him still in the closet, but we'll figure it out. There's a lot I'm unsure about where he and I are concerned, but there's one thing I'm completely certain of. "I love you too, King. And you are everything I need."

He smiles so wide it makes that cute-as-fuck dimple pop on his left cheek. " I have something to show you." He rolls over and grabs his phone from the nightstand, then pulls something up on the screen and hands it to me. It's the results of his tests from the sexual health clinic, proving he's clean. All I can think about is being balls-deep inside him. I toss his phone to the end of the bed and roll on top of him. "I got mine yesterday, but I was in a meeting and it slipped my mind." I rub my nose over the stubble on his jaw and inhale his masculine scent. "I really want to fuck you."

He grips the back of my neck and grinds his hips into mine, letting me feel every hard inch of him. Fighting makes us both hard. "Then do it."

"Let me grab my phone and I'll show you my results."

He shakes his head. "I trust you."

I trust him too—at least with my body. Not sure about my heart yet, as much as I'd like to be. "Are you only letting me top because you feel bad about my meltdown?"

He throws his head back and laughs, and it's an amazing sound. It rumbles through his chest and into mine. "No, baby. I'm letting you top because I love the way you fuck me." His green eyes grow dark, and he tucks a short curl behind my ear. "You're the only man I'd ever switch for, Mase."

"Same," I admit.

He groans softly. "I love that I'm the only guy who's ever fucked you." His grip on my neck tightens, and that possessive spark ignites in his eyes. "I'm the only guy who ever will. You got that?"

I push up onto my forearms. "I got it, Hotshot. Now turn over."

He does as I ask, his face turned to the side as I trail kisses over his powerful shoulder blades. "You do have lube here, don't you?" he asks.

I sink my teeth into the muscle at the base of his neck, leaving a satisfying red mark. "Would you let me fuck you without it?"

He presses his face into the pillow and groans before he replies. "I'd let you fuck me any way you want to, Playboy, but I would much prefer you use lube. Although I don't want to think about why you'd have some stashed in your childhood bedroom."

I press a kiss on the side of his neck. "I have lube, babe."

I jump out of bed and take off my boxers before grabbing it from the drawer. By the time I get back into bed, King is naked too. Straddling him, I knead the firm muscles of his ass. "Your ass is so fucking sexy."

He reaches back and squeezes my leg. "Then sink your cock into it, baby."

I squirt a generous amount of lube into my hand and work it over my hard length. When I'm done, I part his cheeks and add some to his asshole too. As soon as the cold gel hits his skin, he curses and I bite back a laugh. I settle between his thick thighs, nudging them wider apart with my knees. "You hungry for my dick, babe?" I tease him, notching the crown at his entrance.

He lifts his hips and barks at me to stop teasing him.

"So impatient." I edge the tip inside him. "And so fucking tight." His muscles squeeze around me, and white-hot pleasure sears my balls. Feeling him like this, without anything between us, is heaven.

"Christ," he groans.

I press my mouth to his ear and sink a little deeper. "You like that?"

"Fuck," he pants. "Yeah."

I give him another inch, holding back despite wanting to slide all the way inside him. I know all too well that urgent need to be filled and how incredible it will feel for both of us when I go balls-deep. Top or bottom, being with King is entirely different from sex with anyone else. It's more than a fleeting need for pleasure. It's a deep, carnal longing that floods every cell of my body. "Such a good fucking boy the way you take my cock."

"Fuck me, Mase."

I hold back, my muscles vibrating and my cock aching to drive all the way inside. While I love the way he fucks me, this is when I feel most myself. "You want all of me?"

His hungry moan almost makes me give into him.

My lips rest against the shell of his ear. "I want to hear you beg."

He lifts his hips, but I pull back, refusing to give him what he needs just yet. "Please, Mase!" he cries.

Oh, those words sound amazing on his lips. "You beg so fucking beautifully, babe."

He presses his face into the pillow while I go on sliding half my cock in and out of his tight ass. His body trembles, and in this moment, I own him.

"Tell me who this ass belongs to and I'll give you what you want."

"You!" he yells, and as promised, I drive all the way inside him.

We both groan at the sensation of my thick cock filling up his tight ass. "It feels incredible fucking you bare."

"Yeah," he grunts, pulling me as close as possible with his hand on the back of my neck.

I kiss the sensitive spot beneath his ear, and then I nail him to the bed. I fuck him so hard the headboard clatters against the wall. He sucks in a ragged breath and shudders. "Jesus, fuck! I'm gonna come." His muscles squeeze tight around my shaft. He sinks his face into the pillow and shouts my name.

"That's my good fucking boy," I growl, desperate now for my own release. It only takes a few more thrusts before my eyes roll back and my body lights up with pleasure. I grind my hips into his ass, filling him with my cum.

I lie on top of him, holding up some of my weight and resting my forehead between his shoulder blades. After I pull out of him, he rolls onto his side, forcing me to do the same so we're facing each other once more. Then he hooks his leg over mine and pulls me against his body and his cum-covered abs.

He flashes me a wink. "That was something, Playboy. You feel better?"

"Yeah. Sixteen-year-old me is feeling pretty damn pleased with me."

He does that thing where he tucks a strand of hair behind my ear and makes me feel like I'm the only person in the world who matters. "And what about thirty-five-year-old you?"

I dust my lips over his. "He's feeling pretty pleased with himself too, considering how hard he made you come."

He lets out a dark laugh. "Pretty sure I passed out for a second."

I rest my hand on the side of his neck, and we lie here, nose-to-nose, breathing each other in. When I look at him, I no longer feel any hurt or anger. Nor when I think about what happened between us all those years ago. I believe he doesn't know what his father did, and he'll never find out from me. But one thing I can say for sure is that I can finally let it all go.

THIRTY-SEVEN

KING

I will never take for granted getting to wake up with Mason's back against my chest, my arm wrapped around him, and my mouth tantalizingly close to his skin. Close enough to bite, lick, and taste whenever the hell I want to. I press a kiss on his shoulder blade, and he groans in his sleep.

And now I want him. Of course I do—I always fucking want him. How am I supposed to resist his naked body when it's pressed up against me? There's something cathartic about being in this room. The place I first kissed him. The first place we—

"Your cock is digging into my ass," he grumbles.

I nuzzle his neck and pull him closer. "I was thinking about the first time I fucked you. Is it any wonder I'm hard?"

He snorts. "You're always hard."

I nip his skin in warning. "Yeah, around you, as we established some time ago."

Laughing, he rolls onto his back, and his dark eyes bore into mine. "It was my first time, period. Not yours though."

True. I fucked plenty of girls before I met Mason. Fucked a fair few after too. I was a prize jackass. "My first time with a guy though," I remind him.

He traces his fingertips over my cheek. "I remember that you didn't seem a bit nervous, but I was shaking like a goddamn leaf."

The memory makes me smile. He was so fucking cute back then—a cocky fucker out in the real world, but when we were alone, he was all nerves and anticipation. Same as me. "I was nervous. I just hid it better than you." My first time with him was a bigger deal than losing my virginity to Penny Harper in the back of my car. A much bigger deal. I knew I liked boys from the age of twelve when I developed a huge crush on my fifteen-year-old math tutor. No girl had ever made me feel that way before, and none have since, no matter how much I tried to like them the same way I liked boys. The few boys I kissed before Mason cemented my preference.

That stopped when my father caught me. I was thirteen, and the punishment he doled out scarred me for life. So, like the good son I wanted to be, I did everything I could to bury those feelings deep. I was pretty good at it too. Until I met Mason. As much as I tried, I couldn't stay away from him. Couldn't deny the pull between us or do anything to stop the way being with him made me feel more alive than anything ever had before in my life. He's the first guy I ever did anything more than kiss. He scarred me too—left an indelible imprint on my heart and soul.

I roll on top of him and run my nose over his throat, inhaling the smell of his skin. His scent has always made my mouth water. Before him, sex was something I felt I had to do. It was a release, nothing more. "I remember how fucking good it felt to finally slide into your tight ass."

He groans. "Yeah, you made me wait for fucking months. Jerk."

I grind my dick against his, and he's as hard as I am. "Only until you were sixteen, baby."

He slides his hands up my back and wraps his legs around my waist. "So you were a responsible jerk, but still a jerk."

"Do you remember how good it was?" I drag my teeth over his Adam's apple. "How you moaned out my name when you came all over us both?" I fucked him like this after weeks of teasing and prepping him with my fingers, and I felt a euphoria like I'd never experienced when I sank my cock into him that first time. I can still recall the warmth of him, how tightly his muscles squeezed my shaft. Nothing between us as I emptied my load inside him. I'd never been stupid enough to fuck a girl without a condom and risk the continuation of the Worthington gene pool.

Mason slides a hand between us, gripping our cocks in one hand. "Yeah, I remember. And I remember how hard you came, King. I watched your eyes roll back in your head."

I hum my agreement. "Nobody has ever made me come as hard as you do, Mase." I reach for the lube and push myself off him long enough to lather up my cock.

"And nobody ever will, Hotshot," he says, and there's a possessive hint of warning to his tone that makes me harder for him. Nineteen years after the first time we did this and I'm as eager for him now as I was back then. Anxious, skinny teenage Mason, or cocky-as-fuck and built-like-a-Greek-god Mason—both of them do the same for me. Drive me feral with desire.

"I've waited a long damn time to fuck you bare again, Playboy." I drop to my forearms, and he wraps his legs around my waist again, guiding himself onto my dick. I love that he wants this as much as I do.

I inch the crown of my cock inside him and hiss out a breath before I push past the tight ring of muscle and into the heaven that awaits me. "Motherfuck! You feel so good like this." I grit out the words as euphoria shuttles around my body. He reaches for his cock, but I bat his hand away. "Nuh-uh, baby. Let me fuck it all out of you."

He groans, biting down on his bottom lip before he nods.

I sink all the way inside him. "That's my good boy."

He bands his arms around my back, and I rest my

weight on him, pressing my mouth into the crook of his neck where I can bite and lick and suck while I fuck him. And I can't help but think of those two kids, fucking for the first time, awkward and unsure, having no real idea of the heartache that was waiting for us.

But we're not kids anymore, and we know exactly what we're doing. He bears down, allowing me to sink deeper, and our bodies move in unison, slick with perspiration as we take what we need from the other. Our groans and moans fill the room along with the sound of my skin slapping against his. White-hot pleasure sizzles in every cell of my being. A tornado could tear through this house and I wouldn't stop this. Couldn't stop it. He is everything and everywhere. Flooding my senses until I'm made up of nothing but need.

"King, please?" He squeezes his eyes shut as he veers close to the edge.

I rest my mouth against his ear. "I know, baby, almost there."

His hard cock throbs against my abs, and I rub against his shaft with every thrust in and out of him.

"Fuck!" he shouts, and warmth spreads between our chests. Sticky and incredible.

I rest my forehead against his. "Such a good fucking boy the way you come for me."

"Yeah," he moans, and the sound of him undone, along with his tight ass rippling around my shaft, is enough to tip me into oblivion with him.

Dalton James's gruff voice snaps me from my thoughts. "Good morning, son. Did you sleep well?" He's at the counter with his back to me, pouring himself a coffee. I glance around the kitchen, expecting to see Mason, but it's only Dalton and me.

He must be addressing me. I clear my throat and answer, "Yes, sir."

"Sir?" He barks a laugh. "You make me feel old." He sits down at the table opposite me, his gray eyes twinkling.

"Old habit." I shrug, pushing down the memory of my father slapping me at the dinner table any time I didn't address him as sir.

He checks his watch. "It's not like Mason to not have left the house before eight-thirty. Did you two stay up late?"

Holy shit. He heard us fucking, didn't he? Thanking Christ for my poker face, I keep my expression neutral and pretend I don't give a shit that he knows I'm fucking his son. But I would prefer the ground to open up and swallow me whole right here. He sips his coffee and goes on watching me, and I realize I didn't answer his question. "Not really. It was just nice to sleep a little late."

"Ah," he says with a wistful sigh. "I can't recall the last time I slept past six. My body clock is a stubborn old gizzard and refuses to believe we've retired now." He carries on chatting about everything and nothing, and it's obvious that Dalton James doesn't give a damn if I was fucking his son all night. Not because he doesn't care about Mason, but because he truly doesn't care that he's gay.

Of course, I knew Mason's family accepted him for who he is, but it's another thing entirely to see it play out. I saw it last night too, but here, sitting with his dad who was raised in the same generation as my parents, casually chatting about the mundane, it feels all the more real and poignant. It's like a punch to the gut when I finally realize that this is normal. On some level, I always knew my family was fucked up, but now it's staring me right in the face.

Mason steps into the kitchen, looking edible in a fresh shirt and suit and smelling of that expensive cologne he wears. "I hope you saved me some coffee." As he walks past me, he stops to plant a quick kiss on the top of my head like it's the most natural thing in the world. And perhaps it is. It sure feels like it sitting here in this house, and I'm full of gratitude that the person I love more than anything in this entire goddamn world got to grow up in a place like this. It gave him the compassion to deal with someone like me.

Smiling, Dalton watches Mason pour a mug of coffee. "I know better than to take the last of the coffee when you're around, son. Like a grizzly bear with a hornet's nest up its ass."

Mason laughs and takes a seat at the table with us.

God, I love him so fucking much. I want to launch myself over the table and kiss him. What the hell has happened to me? "What are your plans for today, Pop?" he asks his dad.

"Maddox is taking me for lunch at that vegan place he's working at. He assures me it will make me renounce my love for meat." He pulls a disgusted face. "After that, Amber's taking me shopping. I need a new shirt or two." He pulls at the collar of the one he's wearing. "Then I'm going to get myself a haircut and a shave."

"A full day." Mason grins, leaning back in his chair. "You're going on a date, then?"

Dalton sips his coffee. "None of your beeswax."

"That means he is," Mason stage-whispers to me, shooting me a wink that does nothing to lessen my desire to have my mouth on him.

"One of us James men has to get out there." Dalton huffs a laugh. "Seeing as how all my sons seem to be falling in love and settling down."

I swallow hard, waiting for Mason to dismiss his father's claim, but he doesn't. Sure, he told me that he loves me, but that his family knows too feels like another huge step. "Mad hasn't," he says casually, showing no sign of unease at his father's assessment of our relationship.

"Well, Maddox is different. He doesn't date. But I have no doubt he'll find the right person for him." Dalton nods once. "He has an energy that attracts good people."

Mason hums his agreement, his eyes on me again. I

wonder what kind of energy Mason has that he attracted someone like me. The glutton-for-punishment kind? The life-full-of-secrets kind? Because as good as this feels, I'm worried it will all come crashing down around us again, just like it did before.

I only hope that if that does happen, I'll be strong enough to pick up the pieces and put us back together.

THIRTY-EIGHT

MASON

"You sure everything's okay there without me?" Elijah asks. "I feel bad about leaving again when we haven't found the leak yet." His face on my monitor is tan and relaxed, and the lines around his eyes are a little more pronounced than usual, but not because he's tired. He's smiling, and it looks like he hasn't stopped for months.

The old Elijah never would have considered leaving Manhattan during a crisis, but he's only having a long weekend in Charleston. It's not like he's off-grid, and he's right on the other end of the phone or a computer screen whenever I need him. I have to say I love this more relaxed version. He's still a workaholic and has managed to close another huge Korean deal from the comfort of his sun lounger. He's flying out there tomorrow to finalize everything and will be gone for another ten days.

"I have it all in hand, and King is making progress. He's confident he'll have our leak plugged soon. And I'll be interviewing for the new VP position Thursday and Friday. I'm planning to hand over a lot as soon as they start."

"Yeah, they need to be able to hit the ground running."

I nod my agreement. We have some stellar candidates, which is to be expected at the level we're recruiting for.

He smiles. "I'm proud of you, Mase."

I roll my eyes.

"I'm serious. I know I've taken a step back—"

"You deserve it, Elijah."

"I appreciate you saying that, but I was worried about putting more on you, and you've handled it all like a champ. Not to sound like the patronizing big brother, but I really am proud of you. And I know Pop is too."

My chest swells with pride. "Thanks, bro."

After we end the call, I stare out the window. I love this job and I always have, but I've enjoyed taking a more active role in the corporate side of things too. It feels good to know I'm not fucking it up. The only blot on my otherwise perfect horizon is the damn leak. Until we find out who it is, the whole company is on lockdown information wise. Basically, every single piece of information is on a strictly need-to-know basis. It adds to the pressure, but it also means we're not going to spring another leak.

There's a soft tapping on my door, and when I look up, King's standing there, looking all kinds of adorable and hotter than sin, in equal measure.

I wonder why he's knocking until I hear Hayden's voice and the unmistakable eager chatter of the new group of interns he's showing around this morning.

I risk a wink. "Come in, Mr. Blackthorn."

Grinning, he closes the door behind him. Instead of sitting in his usual seat, he perches on my desk in front of me, forcing me to scoot back a little to accommodate him. I love having his legs between my spread thighs. He leans down and seals his lips over mine. I slide my tongue into his mouth and deepen the kiss, but I'm the first to pull back. Hayden could knock at any moment to introduce me to the new interns.

King stuffs his hands into his pockets. "I've narrowed our suspects down to two."

"You have?" I ask. "Who?"

"Suspect one is Olivia Green."

I rack my brain to place her. "I know her name, but I can't remember what she does."

"She works in development, but she's pretty low on the ladder. And she's been passed over for promotion twice."

Now I remember her—I remember discussing her last interview with Hayden. "Yeah, she has. She's good, but she has no initiative. None at all, which is okay when you're a junior analyst and have three bosses who can tell you what to do, but not for the roles she was going for."

"Well, her emails suggest a couple of clandestine meetings that raised my suspicions. Could be she's hooking up with a married man or some other plausible explanation. But I'm running a sweep on any offshore accounts because her personal banking came up clean. However, she has motive and means."

I shake my head. "I can't see her having the savvy to do it. Who else?"

He winces. "You're not going to like this one."

"Who, King?"

He shrugs in a don't-say-I-didn't-warn-you way. "Hayden."

"Hayden? My head of HR? The guy you don't like because you think he wants me to fuck him?"

"First of all, he does want you to fuck him. But my dislike of the guy isn't a factor in this."

"Then what is?" I ask.

"He has more access to you than most of his colleagues. In fact, more than anyone else I've seen at this company. He could have somehow learned your passcodes or—"

"You think I'm that careless?"

He cups my jaw in his hand. "No, but why do you think I've spent so long in the office these past few weeks? After my initial sweep, I had around forty potential suspects. So I focused on them. Chatted over coffee, asked for help with my computer. People inadvertently reveal information about themselves. First car they drove. First pet's name. You know?"

"I'm not stupid enough to have my favorite pet as a

password clue, King. And besides, our security is a little more sophisticated than that."

"I'm not suggesting otherwise. I'm just saying, people who want to commit industrial espionage will find a way to use being close to you to get information."

Hayden is clingy and attentive, and he does spend an inordinate amount of his time hovering around me. But he's worked here for five years. He's a good guy. "What's his motive?" I ask.

"Money."

I shake my head. "That could be anyone's motive."

"No. Not everyone is motivated by money."

"And what makes you think Hayden is?"

"Have you seen the guy?" King says. "He drives a Lamborghini. Around Manhattan. The gas alone is astronomical, and I can't imagine what he pays to park it. Everything he wears has a designer label. Including his underwear."

"How the fuck do you know what underwear he wears?"

He smirks and cups my jaw again. "Oh, baby, I love it when you're jealous."

I bat his hand away. "I'm not."

"He keeps a change of clothes in his office."

I'm still not convinced. "I'm not sure that's enough to accuse him of espionage. I wear designer clothes and drive an expensive car around Manhattan."

He rolls his eyes. "Yeah, and you're a fucking billionaire, baby. Not a head of HR."

"He makes over half a million a year."

"Yeah, I know. There's some unusual activity in his banking too. Look, I'm going to do a full investigation. I won't come to you unless I have absolute proof, but these are the two people who work for you that stand out. And I've learned to trust my gut."

"What do you mean people who work for me?" It's odd that he used that choice of words.

He runs his tongue over his top teeth. "You're going to like this even less."

I can already tell I will. "Go on."

"What if it's someone not in the company?"

My hackles rise. "Like who?"

"Like someone who has a lot of unrestricted access to you and Elijah. To your family home. To your penthouse."

"The only person who currently fits that description is you."

He scowls.

"Obviously it's not you. But who the hell are you talking about? Not one of my sisters-in-law?" The thought of him accusing them makes me feel sick.

He licks his lips. "No, of course not. But what about Tyler?"

His words are a punch to the gut. "Tyler? My best friend? Melanie's cousin? The guy who doesn't have the faintest interest in tech?"

"He could easily get access to your and Elijah's computers. All he would need is a—"

"No," I snarl. "Tyler would never fucking do that. He would *never* fucking betray me like that."

King grinds his jaw. "People betray us. That's a fact of life."

I push my chair back, needing to get away from him. "No. That might be a fact of your life, but most people don't fuck over the people they claim to love."

This is no longer just about me and Tyler, and it probably never was. King growls. "You're telling me he loves you?"

I take a deep breath, desperately trying to get a hold on my anger, but it doesn't work. "Yes, he fucking does. And more than me, he loves his cousin Melanie. You know, Nathan's wife?"

"And do you love him?" he says, ignoring everything but my first sentence.

"What?" I blink at him. Jesus fucking Christ.

He walks toward me, and I register that we are once again squaring off against each other in my office. "I said do you love him?"

"Yes, I do, King. As a friend. He's my best fucking friend. Is that why you're doing this? Because you're jealous of my friendship with Tyler? A guy you met once, for barely a minute?"

His nostrils flare. "I'm asking you to consider that it could be him."

"Well, I fucking won't consider it. You don't get to accuse innocent people just because you're a jealous jackass."

His hand wraps around my throat, and he tugs me forward until my chest bumps against his. My treacherous dick stiffens in response. "Yeah, I am jealous. I can't help but be jealous of a guy that you trust the way you trust him."

My blood is boiling, and I want to take my anger out on King, preferably by fucking him senseless. But I can see this is coming from a place of hurt, so I take a few seconds and breathe through it. "He's never given me any reason to doubt him, King. That's how trust works. Have I ever given you any reason to doubt me? I love Tyler the way I love my own brothers. And full disclosure, there have been times when I've looked at him and wondered if there was something more, but I never acted on it. You know why?"

"Why?" His voice is strained.

"Because he's my friend, and I would have fucked up our friendship if I had. I've only ever been about shallow, meaningless hookups. And that's all Tyler and I would have been. Because I don't love him that way. For that kind of love, there's only ever been you. There will only ever be you."

He rests his forehead against mine, his breathing labored. "I'm sorry."

I place my hand on the back of his neck. "It's not him, King. Can you trust me on that?"

He loosens his grip on my throat and rests his fingers at the base of my neck, more like a caress than a hold. "Yeah."

"I love you, mi rey."

"I love you too, Mase. I'm always going to be a little bit of a possessive asshole when it comes to you though. You okay with that?"

Strangely, I am. "Yes. And I'm always going to be friends with Tyler. You good with that?"

I don't know what I'll do if he says no. I'm not prepared to give either of them up. And I know that as soon as the two of them get to spend some actual time together, they'll hit it off immediately.

"Yeah, I can handle that."

"That's my good boy," I tease, intending to break the tension. Instead, I create an entirely different, altogether more pleasant kind.

King growls, and the sound is impatient and feral. His mouth claims mine, and our hands work double-time exploring each other. Within seconds, I'm lost to him once more. King Blackthorn is my obsession. My darkness and my light, and all the shades in between.

THIRTY-NINE

MASON

K ing's fingers trail lazily down my abs as he lies next to me in bed. "I was thinking about how much I enjoyed our date that wasn't a date."

Yeah, I enjoyed it too, and I wish we could do it more often. I roll onto my side to face him. "What did you used to do? You know, like back in Chicago? Did you date at all?"

"I wouldn't call it dating, no. It was more ..." He runs a hand over the thick stubble on his jaw. "To be honest, it was just sex. Often with guys who were as happy to not be seen in public together as I was."

"So eighteen years of hookups? You've never been for dinner or a movie? Gone to a club?"

He arches an eyebrow. "You saw how out of place I looked in a club."

I suppress a laugh as I recall how awkward he was in

Xylophone, but only because I know him so well. He didn't look out of place though. "Not even a bar?"

He shakes his head. "Don't get me wrong, I wasn't as careful in Chicago as I am in New York. Being seen leaving a motel with a guy didn't freak me out as much as it would here, but I didn't want to do any of the dating stuff."

I suspect that's because of his father, but I don't want to bring him up and ruin this perfectly enjoyable morning. So instead, I smirk at him. "And I thought I was the king of casual."

"There were a few guys I saw regularly, but like I said, it was only for sex."

A pang of irrational jealousy spikes in my chest. "And you never caught feelings for any of them?"

He grins, no doubt aware of my motive for asking. "No. Feelings and me aren't exactly on good terms either." He trails his knuckles across my cheek. "Except where you're concerned, and then I feel everything, maybe a little too intensely. I think I never got over my first love, and I don't plan on ever trying."

"The feeling is mutual."

The moment stretches out between us, and I wish we could stay in this safe little cocoon we've built for ourselves. But the real world is out there waiting. And as much as I want to share that with him too, there's no sense in pushing him before he's ready.

"You think we could do the whole date that's not a date thing again?" he asks.

I can't stop my smile. This is a huge step for him—for us. "Do you have anything particular in mind?"

He shakes his head. "I wouldn't know where to begin. But it would have to be like last time. Just two guys …"

"Who look like friends. I get it." I press a soft kiss on his lips. "Leave it with me."

FORTY

KING

I answer Mason's call wearing the same smile I have on my face anytime I hear his voice. But nobody in this diner knows who I am or who I'm on the phone with, so I allow myself the simple pleasure of being openly pleased to hear from him.

"We have plans tonight, Hotshot," he says.

"We do?"

"That date that's not a date you asked for."

My smile grows wider. "Oh, yeah?"

"Pack an overnight bag and meet me in my office at seven."

Now I'm all kinds of intrigued. "Can I get a clue as to where we're going?"

"Somewhere nobody will look twice at us."

"At least tell me what I should wear."

He hums softly. "Smart casual. I have to run. See you at seven."

He ends the call, leaving me wondering what the hell smart casual consists of in Mason James's world. The waitress smiles and flutters her eyelashes at me. Fuck, I'm grinning like an idiot. Because I'm going on a date with Mason James. It's like I'm sixteen again, about to go meet this really hot guy who makes my stomach do a fluttery kind of thing that it's never done before.

Mason is waiting for me when I get to his office, with his overnight bag slung over his shoulder. He's wearing a dress shirt—the sleeves rolled up, showing off his toned forearms—and dress slacks. I'm glad I opted for similar attire.

"So, where are we going?" I ask him.

He smirks. "To the roof." He brushes past me and heads for the elevator. "You ever been in a helicopter before?"

I fall into step beside him. "Plenty of times."

He chuckles. "Good to know."

"Someone's flying us somewhere?"

He flashes me a cheeky wink. "Not someone. I'm flying us somewhere."

Will a single day go by without this guy surprising the hell out of me? "You can fly a helicopter?"

He winks at me. "I think you'll find there's no end to my talents, King."

Cocky fuck. There are a few employees working late, and that's the only thing stopping me from pinning him to the wall and sampling a few of those talents right now.

MASON IS A SKILLED PILOT. He's all serious business while he flies, and it doesn't take long for the twinkling lights of Atlantic City to come into view.

"We're going to Atlantic City?" I ask, peering out the window.

"Yup. Close enough to get there fast; far enough away for nobody to know us, and full of people too busy having fun to notice us even if they did. Seemed like the perfect place."

I can't argue with that. It's a perfect date that's not a date.

There's a concierge waiting at the helipad on the top of the hotel when we land. He greets Mason by name before handing him a room key. My stomach is bubbling with nervous excitement as he leads me toward the presidential suite. He's obviously been here before, but I don't dwell on that. I'm in Atlantic City with Mason, in one of the best casinos on the strip.

He drops his bag on the floor while I check out the suite, which is bigger than my apartment. He walks up behind me while I stare out at the incredible view of the ocean through the floor-to-ceiling window. "Would you look at that," I say, pointing at the incredible sight before me.

He runs his nose along the back of my neck and his hand over my ass. "I'm too busy admiring you to bother looking at the ocean," he says in a husky voice. "And I think it might be a good idea for us to get out of this hotel room before we end up not leaving it at all."

I spin around and grab his hips, tugging him closer. When I run my hand across his zipper, I find him already hard. "That doesn't sound like the worst idea."

His grin is wicked and wolfish, and I want to devour him. "We have all night. Would be a shame not to check out the casino, at least."

"I guess. What's the point of having a billionaire boyfriend if not to have him fly you to Atlantic City in his own private helicopter and watch him blow some of his fortune in a casino?"

He laughs darkly and grazes his lips over mine. "Oh, babe. I never lose."

FORTY-ONE

MASON

K ing is incredible at blackjack, and I enjoy simply watching him play. He quits when he's up by eight thousand dollars, and we step away from the table.

"What do you want to do now, Hotshot? Take me for dinner with your winnings?"

He brings his mouth much closer to my ear than he usually would in public. "I'll buy you dinner, Playboy. But how do you feel about room service?"

I feel all kinds of things, most of them in my cock. "I love room service."

We walk through the casino and take the private elevator to the presidential suite, and even in there, we refrain from touching. Sexual tension sizzles between us like it's a living, breathing thing, growing fiercer with every moment we deny it. By the time we get into the room, we're worked into a frenzy. As soon as the door closes, we clash, mouths hot and frantic for each other, bodies flush, hands grabbing and taking what we want. It's frenetic and chaotic and beautiful.

I pin him to the door, one hand fisted in his shirt and the other around his throat, holding him in place while I kiss him like he's the air responsible for my breath. He lets out a ragged groan that makes me smile against his lips. I love making him come undone.

"How does this date that's not a date compare to the last one?"

He arches an eyebrow, and we take a much-needed breath. "I guess it's okay, but I seem to remember there was dancing during the last one."

Fuck me, I love this playful side of him, and I'll do everything I can to bring it out of him more often. "I think I can fix that."

I take out my cell phone, connect it to the suite's Bluetooth speaker, and quickly choose a song.

He smirks at me when the opening beats of "Chasing Cars" begin to play. "Do you have a playlist of all the songs we used to make out to on there?"

I step closer, sliding my arms around his waist. "I do now."

He grabs my hips, and his body sways against mine as we resume our kiss, less hurried than before. This is sensual and sweet. A kiss born of knowing we have all the time we need.

When the song ends, we dance to the next one. Until King's stomach growls and a laugh bubbles out of me. "I believe you said something about dinner."

He nods. "Food, then fucking?"

"If you order the soufflé, we'll have time for fucking before food too," I tease.

We untangle ourselves from each other, and he grabs the menu before lying back on the bed, one arm tucked behind his head. "Fuck, I can't choose. This all looks good to me."

I straddle his hips. "Then order one of everything."

He drops the menu to his side. "That would be a waste and would wipe out all my winnings."

I pull off my T-shirt and toss it on the floor. "Then let me pay. What's the point of having a billionaire boyfriend if not to let him buy you an entire Michelin-rated menu?" I fall forward, and my hands land on either side of his head, but he plants his hands on my ribcage, stopping me from moving any closer.

His eyes narrow on my face. "I don't want your money, Mase. You know that, right? That's not why I'm with you."

I bend my head, pushing against the resistance of his hands, and dust my lips over his. "I know, mi rey. I was teasing you."

His warm breath mingles with mine, and he shifts his hips, rubbing his semi-hard cock against my ass. "And I'm supposed to be buying you dinner."

"Okay, buy me dinner. But I already have my dessert right here."

He slides his palms down to my waist. "Oh, you do?"

"Sure do." I take his lip between my teeth and bite down gently.

He digs his fingers into my hips and grinds me on his cock, making mine ache. "I really like the sound of that."

I rest on my forearms, trailing my teeth along his jawline and rubbing myself against him until he's groaning with need. "You know what I really want?" I whisper in his ear.

"What?" he grunts, his back arching.

I flick my tongue over the shell of his ear. "The lobster."

With a feral growl, he flips me and pins me to the bed, and I find myself laughing too hard to attempt to stop him. Grabbing my hands, he easily holds them above my head when I offer no resistance at all. "Food, baby boy," he rasps. "And then you're getting fucked."

He reaches for the phone on the nightstand with his free hand and dials room service. Still straddling me, he keeps me trapped between his powerful thighs and stares into my eyes while he orders us both the lobster.

"I REALLY NEED to fuck you, Mase." His voice is pained and desperate.

"Lube is in my bag," I pant.

He scrambles off the bed and goes to his bag rather than mine. Of course he has lube too. I told him to pack an overnight bag.

We enjoyed our lobster dinner, along with a few glasses of fine Scotch, and declared that the food portion of the evening had well and truly canceled out the fucking part. So we watched a movie, happy to simply lie with each other.

That all went to hell when we were brushing our teeth. First, our eyes met in the mirror. Then came the slightest brush of our fingertips. That was all we needed to reignite our feverish hunger for each other. We fell into bed, a tangle of limbs and tongues, kissing and grabbing and biting.

King crawls back over me, coating his cock in lube with one hand and nudging my thighs apart with his knees. He trails his tongue across my collarbone and growls. "You're fucking delicious."

I grab his hair and pull his lips to mine. "So are you, Hotshot. And I believe you're my dessert."

"Then you can have me, baby." He sinks all the way inside me with one smooth thrust that takes my breath away.

I cling to him, waiting for him to nail me to the mattress. But he presses his forehead to mine and pulls out in agonizingly slow motion before pushing back inside again, his shaft massaging my prostrate with every thrust.

Pleasure rockets through my body. My eyes roll back in my head. "Fuck, King."

He breathes heavily. "I love you, Mase."

I glide my hands down his back, kneading his taut muscles. "Love you too."

He pushes deeper, and a growl rumbles in his chest. "Tell me you're mine."

Holy fuck. My legs are shaking. "I'm yours, King."

"Only ever mine, baby."

"And you're only ever mine." I pant out the words, my cock aching between us with the need to come. I drag his mouth to mine, and he continues fucking me to the same deliciously slow rhythm. Our bodies operate on muscle memory, limbs moving in unison, skin gliding against skin. It's effortless and exquisite. My existence narrows, and I'm made of nothing but need. I dig my fingers into his muscles and wrap my legs around his hips, pulling him as deep as I can.

King rests a hand on the base of my throat. "I've only ever been yours." He kisses me again, his tongue lazily fucking my mouth as he takes us both to a long, brain chemistry–altering climax. The kind that shreds our souls.

I'll only ever be his. He is so much a part of me, he's in my DNA, and I wouldn't have it any other way.

FORTY-TWO

KING

T rub at my eyelids and reach for my coffee, hoping it will help me focus. But the glare of the screen is making my eyes burn, and I slam my laptop closed. I've followed every lead I dug up on the Cassidy Jones case and have come up with nothing. If she simply up and left like the cops concluded, then she's gone to a level of ass-covering that would make Jack Reacher proud.

And nobody in the real world is that good. I take another swig of my lukewarm coffee. Well, maybe a handful of people, but there's nothing to suggest Cassidy Jones had anywhere close to that level of knowledge or expertise.

Every instinct I have tells me she's dead. And that my father knows something about it. As cruel as he is, I can't bring myself to accept that he actually did it, but he definitely knows something. I call Curtis and give him a brief, uninspiring update and assure him I'll get him some answers eventually.

"I know I haven't paid you yet, but I'm waiting on a loan to come through," he says after thanking me for continuing to look into his daughter's disappearance. "Just give me a few more days."

"Don't worry about it," I tell him. "Consider this pro bono." He took out two bank loans using his car business as collateral to fund his previous PIs, and truth be told, this case has so many dead ends I can't help feeling I'm not giving it the time and attention it deserves. Not to mention the guilt I feel thanks to my father's involvement. Besides, I don't need the money. Even if my parents successfully contest my grandma's will, Grampa left me a few hundred grand. That's more than enough to put my retirement plan firmly back on track, and then some.

"I didn't know PIs did pro bono cases," he says.

"I do. I'll update you when I have something more."

He thanks me profusely, and it takes me a full minute to get him off the phone.

Sighing, I reopen my laptop. Mason's working late and won't be home for another hour, and I can't sit around and do nothing. There must be an angle I'm missing. A twenty-two-year-old woman doesn't vanish without a trace.

Except ... There are people like my father—people with enough money and power who can make anything happen. And they often do.

Sitting on this couch that cost more than the average

family income in a penthouse apartment that's worth more than most people make in a lifetime, it's hard not to draw parallels between Mason's family and mine. But the wealth is where it ends. Mason's family could buy mine fifty times over, but they don't act superior to other people.

A smile tugs at my lips when I recall the first time I met him. It was at some pizza place where kids from both of our schools hung out. This asshole rich kid pushed a waitress who knocked into Mason and spilled soda all over his shirt. Where a lot of the privileged little brats from schools like ours would have cussed her out, he only cared about whether she was okay. I don't remember what he said, but I do remember her smile. Her relief when he didn't make a fuss about the shirt that probably cost more than her week's wage. He made her feel special. Despite his success and having more money than god, he still makes people feel like that now. And that's why I fell in love with him.

My cell phone vibrates, signaling a text, and I groan when I see my father's name on the screen.

> Kyngston, we still need to discuss the outcome of your grandfather's will.

I type a quick reply back.

> Like my lawyer said, there's nothing to contest.

My phone rings in my hand, and I contemplate not answering it, but part of me wants to hear him squirm. Maybe Nathan was right about there being more to his and Mother's desperation to get their hands on Grampa's money.

I answer the call with all the civility I can muster.

"Kyngston, please. Can we at least discuss this like adults?"

"What's to discuss? The will is airtight."

"That is your mother's money, and you know it. Your grandfather had no right to give it to you."

"The money was intended for whomever looked after Grampa at the end of his life. And that was clearly not you or my mother."

He snarls. "We tried to get him to come home, and he would have if it wasn't for you and—"

"If not for your meddling kid?" I snort a laugh at my Scooby-Doo joke, but he is unsurprisingly not amused.

"Always the fool, Kyngston."

"A fool with twenty-five million in his bank account," I quip, unable to resist poking at him.

He's quiet, trying to rein in his temper, no doubt. "Can we please just discuss this? Come for dinner, and we can have a civilized discussion."

Civilized would mean he and my mother would have to remain mute the entire time. "Why do you care so much about Grampa's money? I know twenty-five million is a hell of a lot of money to most people, but Mother's art collection alone is worth at least half that. You're stinking rich, aren't you?" He clears his throat by way of answer, and it makes me wonder how desperate he truly is. "Now, if I thought you were in a bind, I might consider helping you out," I add.

It takes him a few seconds before he speaks again. "Actually, we do have somewhat of a cash-flow problem right now."

Wow. It must be a big fucking problem for him to have even considered admitting that to me. I put my feet up on the coffee table, enjoying this conversation all of a sudden. "What kind of cash-flow problem?"

"Not one I'd like to discuss over the phone. How about you come for dinner?"

I'd rather drive nails into my skull.

"Or we could go for a drink? Just you and me," he offers when I don't jump at his invitation. "Tonight?"

Things must be dire, but I have plans with Mason tonight. "Can't tonight."

"Tomorrow, then?"

I'm so close to breaking the Jamestech case that my time is going to be tied up with that tomorrow. "I'm really busy."

"Please, King?"

I swallow. He never calls me King. What the hell is going on that's making him this eager to meet with me? Curiosity makes me say, "Maybe I could meet you for one drink, but I have some work to tie up, so I'll let you know. If not tomorrow, then maybe this weekend."

"As soon as you can fit me in, son."

If only his desperation to see his only son was for anything other than needing money. Wouldn't that be something. Pity it will never be the case.

FORTY-THREE

MASON

K ing's triumphant grin fills me with anticipation and a little trepidation. He asked me to invite Elijah in for this meeting, so he obviously has news.

"I've found your leak," he declares.

Elijah edges forward in his seat. "Who?"

"Olivia Green," King announces proudly.

I'm surprised but glad it's not Hayden. That would make me a terrible judge of character, and despite his clinginess, he's good at his job. "Wow. I honestly didn't think she had the initiative to pull off something like this."

Elijah nods in agreement.

"Well, she's no mastermind. But she did meet Astyn Bartley around sixteen months ago at a yoga retreat in Virginia. Afterward, they kept in touch via email. None of the emails contain anything incriminating, but they've met a total of four times since then. All of those occasions have coincided with Spartan launching some new tech that Jamestech was also developing. And the last two meetings took place the week before your patent was hijacked."

"And you have evidence of this?" Elijah asks. I'm certain he trusts King's research and his judgment, but I also know he's envisioning the potential for some negative publicity in our future, if not a lawsuit for wrongful termination.

"Evidence of their meetings, yes," King answers. "Security footage of them leaving a restaurant. Credit card receipts for parking, as well as the emails confirming their meetings, which aren't admissible in court, but I assume you're not looking to go down that route."

"We'd rather not," Elijah replies.

King nods his understanding. "While the emails don't come signed from Astyn, I traced the IP to one of his company computers."

"And all in less than three months," I say with a smile, unable to hide my pride in him.

He winks at me. "Told you I was good."

Elijah hums. "We should get HR in here and get Drake to look over her contract. We need to be fully satisfied that we handle this properly. No scandal and no grounds for her to accuse us of anything untoward."

King smirks. "Or we could get her in here and make her crack," he suggests.

Elijah leans forward, intrigued. "Crack?"

"My research on her suggests she's only in this for the money. She's weak. Lacks initiative."

"Her personnel file confirms that," I add.

"All you have to do is confront her with the evidence, and I would bet my Kawasaki Ninja that she'll crack like an eggshell," King says.

A range of emotions flicker over my brother's face before he nods. "Then let's get her in here."

OLIVIA'S LOWER LIP WOBBLES. Elijah confronted her with the evidence King found, and she denied it initially, which wasn't unexpected. Then King detailed every meeting she had with Astyn Bartley—dates, times, locations. I provided the dates of the suspected leaks from Jamestech.

We're all staring at her, waiting for her to crumble.

"I-I ... It wasn't— He said that ... He was so insistent ... My cat needed an operation, and I didn't have the money." She sobs loudly.

I feel a twinge of sympathy, but Elijah rolls back his shoulders. "Collect your things, Miss Green. Leave without a fuss, and we won't prosecute you for industrial espionage."

And that's why he's the CEO. My brother's a good guy, so he's definitely sympathetic to her situation. But she sold our company secrets, several times, and he isn't going to risk the company our father built from the ground up on sentiment. She's lucky she's not going to jail.

She dabs at her eyes. "What will I tell people?"

Elijah's eyes narrow. "Tell them you were fired for gross negligence, or tell them you left because you couldn't handle the pace—I really don't care. But if I ever hear that one bad word left your mouth regarding this company and your treatment here, I will come after you with the full extent of the law. Do you understand me?"

She nods.

"Now, get the hell out of our building," he says.

Olivia leaves in a mess of tears.

"You sure about not prosecuting?" King asks as soon as she's out the door.

"It would be a long, drawn-out case," Elijah answers. "Spartan would have their own legal team, and there's no way they'd readily admit to stealing our tech. I'll pass the information along to their board, and Bartley will be out by the end of the week. Even with Olivia as a witness, prosecution would be messy and complicated, and I can think of a whole boatload of better things to do with my time."

"Same," I add, thinking about the impromptu trip King and I took to Atlantic City. I could use a hell of a lot more of that in my life. "And I don't need the extra work all the negative press would bring either."

Elijah stands and shakes King's hand. "But you did a great job, man. Thank you."

King smiles, and that dimple pops. "You're welcome."

"I'll recommend you to everyone I know. And if you're ever short of work, we can always find you something here at Jamestech." Elijah looks at me. "So long as that's okay with you?"

I nod. "All good with me."

Elijah smiles. "I'm going to call Amber and Dad and give them the good news. Can you let Nathan and Drake know?" He checks his watch. "And then how about drinks at O'Shaughnessy's at six to celebrate?"

King and I had plans to spend the evening together, but he motions for me to agree. "Sounds good," I tell my brother.

It's a loud and joyous celebration at O'Shaughnessy's, with all of my brothers and their wives in attendance, along with Dad. At eight-thirty, Mel starts yawning, and Nathan declares he's taking his wife home to bed. She protests a little, but he wraps his arms around her and whispers something in her ear that makes her laugh and melt into his arms.

"We'd better go too," Drake says.

I sneak a glance at Amber. She and Elijah can't have kids, which is something she really struggled with for a long time. Our difficult history aside, I love her and would hate for her to be hurting. But she's smiling at her sisters-in-law with nothing but love on her face. Nathan gives her a hug goodbye, and it's good to see them putting their differences behind them too. My cheeks ache from all the smiling I've been doing tonight, and I can't believe how good life is right now.

The party broken up, we all decide we have other places we'd like to be. Maddox agrees to go home with Dad while Elijah and Amber make plans for a late dinner.

"You still okay with staying at my place?" King asks me quietly. That was our original plan for tonight before we had our impromptu celebration.

"Are you still going to cook me a steak?"

He smiles. "I believe I promised you steak, sex, and *The Sopranos*."

"You did."

"And I'll deliver. I always do."

It's at times like these I wish he were out so I could kiss him in the middle of the street, or hug him, or even just hold his hand. But I settle for a smile, content enough that I'll get all of those things and more as soon as I get him alone.

FORTY-FOUR

After we got to his place, King realized he'd forgotten to get butter and broccoli from the store earlier and had to go back, so I took care of putting the potatoes in the oven before grabbing a shower. I'm still drying off when there's a loud knock at the door. I pull on a clean pair of boxers and head out into the living room.

"Did you forget your kcy, babe?" I call.

But when I pull open the door, it's not King standing in front of me. The entire world freezes, and my knees buckle. I grip the doorframe to stop myself from crumpling into a heap.

"Who the hell are you?" His face is twisted in a confused sneer. I would recognize those cruel features anywhere. He's barely changed in eighteen years. It seems the sick fuck doesn't recognize me though. All the breath leaves my lungs in a rush.

"I'm looking for my son," he says, looking over my shoulder before his eyes land on me again. Revulsion written all over his face, he looks me up and down. "Who are you?" he asks again.

I want to say, "I'm his boyfriend, you disgusting piece of shit," but I'm not about to out King to his father, so I swallow down all the things I want to say and tell a partial lie. "I'm a friend of King's."

His lip curls. "A *friend* who prances around his house half naked and calls him *babe*?"

I lift my chin and roll back my shoulders. Kyngston Worthington III might have terrified me once, but he doesn't intimidate me in the slightest now. "Your son isn't here right now. How about you come back some other time when you're welcome?"

Bristling, he makes a fresh assessment. I'm an inch or two shorter than him, and not as wide in build but over twenty years younger. He might be questioning whether he can take me. Any doubts he might have don't stop him from scowling at me like I'm something he stepped on in the street.

His cruel taunts come back to haunt me. *Disgusting little pervert. Unnatural. Should have been smothered at birth.* I recall the smell of him. The acrid taste. The sensation of his flaccid dick hardening in my mouth. The pain in my throat. Gagging. Tears rolling down my face as I choked on his length. How he laughed. How much he fucking enjoyed it.

He gives me a final once-over. "Disgusting pervert," he mutters, turning to walk down the hallway.

Eighteen years I've held onto what he did to me. Hid it like it was something I had to be ashamed of. Buried it so deep that it was never supposed to reach the surface. And now he's judging me like I'm the one who's fucked up. I snap. "What the fuck did you say to me?"

He spins around, face still twisted up. "I said you're a disgusting pervert."

"You really don't remember me, do you? You hypocritical piece of shit."

That gets his attention. His scowl deepens, and he comes back to the doorway, staring at me intently. Inspecting me like I'm some kind of exhibit in a freak show. His narrowed eyes flicker with a hint of recognition. His lips twist in a cruel sneer. "You're that dirty little deviant who seduced my boy."

His words are like a lit match to a pool of gasoline, causing rage to explode inside me. So intense I'm blinded by it. He anticipates the punch I aim at his jaw and ducks before it can connect. Using all of his body weight, he barrels into my midsection and pushes me back into King's apartment. I land on the rough carpet with him on top of me.

He straddles me, raining blows down on my head while he spews vile, hateful words. Because of who he is, the words hurt more. Because of what he did to me. I keep my arms over my head and feel myself revert back to that seventeen-year-old kid who was too weak to stop him.

But I'm not weak. I'm not a kid.

I hook my leg over his and roll us over so he's pinned underneath me. Blood drips from a cut above my eye, peppering his cheeks with red droplets, and I wrap my hands around his throat and squeeze. "You raped me, you sick fuck! I was a fucking kid, and you raped me!" Squeezing his throat tighter, I watch his face turn purple.

Everything happens so fast. He's clutching at my wrists with one hand. His other hand appears. There's a glint of metal. A flash of movement. He's got a fucking gun.

King's voice rings in my ears. "Mason!"

I'm on the floor, blood thundering in my ears. It all plays out like a movie.

Beside me, King and his father wrestle for the weapon. King comes out the winner and brandishes the gun. He stands over his father, his chest heaving, the gun in his hands pointed down. "Give me one fucking reason why I shouldn't pull this trigger."

Fighting through the fog of anger and confusion, I jump up and place my hand on his forearm. King keeps his finger on the trigger and his glare trained on the piece of shit on the floor. My voice firm but gentle like my touch, I say, "Because if you shoot him, there's every chance you will go to prison. And he is not worth it, King. He is not worth giving up your life for."

A muscle tics in his jaw. "I heard what he did to you. He brought this gun here. He was gonna use it. I can say it was self-defense."

I hate that he heard what his father did to me. It was easier to pretend it never happened when he didn't know. It was easier for me to forget that part of myself. I look down at Kyngston. A dark patch has spread across the crotch of his gray suit pants, and he's trembling violently, hands held up in surrender. "Look at him," I say. "He's a pathetic piece of shit. You'd really throw your whole life away—throw our life away—for him?" I place my hand on his cheek and turn his face so he's looking at me instead of his father. "He's not worth it. You know that better than anyone."

He stares at me for a few beats, his green eyes swimming with tears. Then he draws a deep breath before redirecting his attention to his father. "Get the fuck out of here. But if you ever come near either of us again, I will fucking kill you." He lowers the gun, and Kyngston scrambles to his feet and runs from the apartment like the coward that he is.

After closing the door, King locks the deadbolt and puts the gun down. "Why didn't you tell me, Mase?" he asks in a low voice, his back to me.

"And when would I have done that? You fucking ghosted me, and then you walked back into my life after eighteen years. Eighteen fucking years, King. And what? I'm supposed to drop that into conversation? 'Hey, babe, do you fancy Thai or pizza for dinner—and by the way, your dad forced his cock down my throat.'" I can't fucking stand the tremor in my voice. I knew this would come between us, that he'd find a way to blame me. I knew it would fuck everything up. The truth has a way of doing that.

I'm spiraling fast, and I don't know how to stop it. This isn't King's fault, but he's here and he's talking to me like … like what? Like he feels sorry for me. Like all he sees is that pathetic little kid who couldn't stand up for himself. Who couldn't stop what happened.

King turns around, his cheeks wet with tears. He scrubs them dry and places his hands on my hips. "I'm sorry."

Sorry? I swallow down the pain, anger, and sadness blocking my throat. "Would it have made a difference? If you'd known what he did? Would you have come back for me?"

His lower lip wobbles, and he bites down on it but doesn't answer.

"King?" I bark his name.

"I wish I could tell you that it would have made a difference," he says, pulling his hands back and looking down at his shoes. So now he can't even look me in the eye?

Stepping back, I suck in a breath that doesn't reach my lungs.

I can't breathe. Can't think beyond my rage. So much fucking rage. It bubbles up inside of me, fighting to be let out. And I feel King's pity too. Is it pity? Or does he feel as much guilt and shame as I do?

I'm too overwhelmed to know what the fuck is going on right now. I need to go. Need to find space to breathe. Room to think.

"I have to go." I grab my clothes from my overnight bag and get dressed. He doesn't try to stop me, and I fucking hate him for it. When I get back to the living room, he's sitting on the sofa with his head in his hands.

Still, he doesn't look up. He doesn't ask me to stay.

"You were right, King. I do deserve better."

My heart splits in two when I walk out the door. It shatters into a million pieces when I step onto the elevator and the door to his apartment remains closed. Once again, the only man I have ever loved has failed to fight for us.

Outside, it's pouring, and I tip my face to the sky and let the rain wash away my tears. I don't want to go home to my empty penthouse. But I also don't feel like unburdening myself to my brothers, which is what will happen if I turn up on any of their doorsteps in this state. I love them all dearly, but my older brothers are overprotective and will immediately go into destroy-every-Worthington-who-ever-lived mode, and Maddox is working.

I hail a cab and give the driver Tyler's address. Outside

of my family, and at least for now, he's the safest place I know.

"Holy fucking shit." Tyler blinks at me from his seat on the armchair across from me.

I blow out a breath and down the Scotch he poured me when I got here twenty minutes ago. He asked me what was up, and I unloaded everything. "I know."

"I can't believe you've held that in for all these years."

"Actually, I had extensive therapy. Then I held it all in." I laugh, trying to ease the tension.

"What a degenerate piece of shit." He shakes his head and downs his own Scotch. "Why didn't you ever tell your brothers?"

Immediately, my hackles rise.

He holds up a hand. "There is absolutely no judgment from me, Mase. I get why you didn't tell me, but ... You're all so close. I assumed ..."

I tell him about the day it happened, how determined I was to tell my family and ruin Kyngston Worthington III, and then how we were all shattered by my mother's news. "I couldn't do that to them, Ty. They needed me. Mom needed me. If she'd known what he did ..." I pour myself another drink from the bottle on the table. "You never met her, but my mom was the kindest, toughest woman on the planet. She could make grown-ass men tremble with fear."

I smile, recalling the time she chewed out our pediatrician in front of an entire waiting room full of patients for misdiagnosing my strep throat as attention-seeking. "Sick or not, that woman would have torn Kyngston Worthington III a new asshole before slitting his throat and burying him in our garden. I kid you not."

"Sounds like an incredible mom."

She was the best, and I wish he'd known her. "Yeah, she was."

He gives me his undivided attention, his eyes never leaving my face. "What about later? After your mom passed?"

I take a gulp of the Scotch and relish the familiar burn in my throat. "You mean did I think about telling anyone? Yeah, a few times, but after Mom died, there was the whole thing with Mad, and ..." I shrug. "There never seemed to be a good time to open up that old wound, you know? I was dealing with it. At least I thought I was."

He nods. "I get that."

"And also ..." I swallow hard. This is hard to admit, even to myself. "I felt ashamed, Ty. As a rational man, I know I have absolutely no reason to, but it's not easy telling people I was raped by my secret boyfriend's dad and that I couldn't do a damn thing to stop him."

"I get that too, buddy."

He sits quietly, letting me process. One of the many things I love about Tyler is that he only gives advice when it's asked for. "Wise men don't need it, and fools won't heed it," he told me when I asked why he's like that. Although he did once give Nathan a piece of advice that my older brother still thanks him for whenever he's had a Scotch too many.

"You think I did the right thing keeping it to myself?" I ask.

His bright-blue eyes narrow. "I think you did what you needed to do to survive, and how can that not be the right thing?"

"And King?" I wince. "I walked out on him, Ty. He just found out his father is a rapist piece of shit, and I up and left." I drop my head into my hands.

"You had every right to leave, Mason, and you know that."

"I feel like this whole mess has fucked everything up." I sigh and lean back against the comfy sofa.

Tyler comes to sit beside me, placing a comforting hand on my thigh. "While you weren't wrong for leaving, it sounds like King had a lot to process. And yeah, maybe he could have handled it differently and begged you to stay. But would you have?"

"I have no fucking idea. But it felt like he gave up on us so easily. Again." Pain lances through my chest.

"It couldn't have been easy for him to hear what his father did to you. Maybe he was doing what he needed to do."

"No." I shake my head. "He couldn't stand to look at

me. Every time he looks at me now, all he'll see is what happened to me. What his father did."

"You don't know that."

"What if that's what I see?" I say, admitting a deeper fear. One I've been afraid to admit aloud until now, and I can't help wondering if King is thinking it too. "What if the next time I'm on my knees for him all I see is his father's disgusting fucking face?"

"Has that ever happened before?"

I sink deeper into the chair with a heavy sigh. "No. But I could always separate them before. It was like there were two different versions of me, and now King knows both of them."

Tyler wraps his arm around my shoulder and drops a kiss on top of my head. "It will all look better in the morning, buddy. I promise."

"Yeah?"

He winks at me. "Things always do."

FORTY-FIVE

KING

The hatred I feel for my father is so intense I have trouble breathing. It's like I'm trapped down in that basement again. Chained up like a dog. Treated worse than a dog. Beaten and starved, all under the guise of curing me of my "sickness."

Until I finally got it. I understood. I was fourteen when I finally realized all I had to do was hide who I was, not change. Because I couldn't change, no matter how hard I tried. I liked boys. So I fucked every girl who smiled at me, and though I got no satisfaction at all from it, it pleased my parents. It earned my father's approval. And that was enough.

Until I met Mason James. From the minute I saw him, it was fireworks—like staring into the center of a supernova and knowing you'll get burned but sticking around anyway.

And I thought I was still doing a good job of hiding it. I really did. But my father found us in the back of Mason's Jeep parked in the middle of nowhere. Sneaky fuck had followed us. And he lost his shit worse than I'd ever seen before. I'd never been so scared. Not only for me, but for Mason too.

So I told the biggest lie of my life. I told him that it was all fake. That I lured Mason there to humiliate him, and that's why he discovered me with him. Not because we were together. Not because I loved him. And then I doubled down, saying all those vile, hateful things, words that burned when I spoke them. But I was protecting myself. Trying to make it all better again. The pain on my boy's face almost broke me, but I did it. And then my father dragged me home, and he beat me so hard I could barely stand. And the next day when he stood over me while I told Mason more horrible lies—it was after that when I decided I couldn't do it anymore.

And now I find out he went after Mason too. Forced his filthy cock into Mason's perfect, innocent mouth. Fucking raped him! And the man I love has lived with that for all this time. Not telling anyone because he felt—what? Ashamed? He has nothing to be ashamed of. My fingernails dig into my palms, biting into the skin. I'm going to fucking kill my father.

A siren blares from the street outside as a police car drives past.

Mason left. I let him go.

I couldn't bear the idea of him looking at me and seeing that sick piece of shit. I pull out my phone and bring up his location, hoping to see him at his penthouse or with one of his brothers, but it shows him at an apartment in the Meatpacking District. Fucking Tyler.

I don't know what breaks my heart more—that I let him down so badly eighteen years ago or that I did it again tonight. Finding out he sought comfort from Tyler is the final blow that makes it shatter into a million pieces.

Jealousy, anger, and shame burn through me, each fighting for domination and all of them getting their turn at the wheel. By the time the sun rises, I'm torn between driving to Tyler's house and ripping off his head or dropping to my knees and begging for Mason's forgiveness. Thankfully, something in me stops me from doing either. I replay my conversation with Mason a few weeks ago, when he swore that he and Tyler would never be more than friends. And I trust him—no matter how much I hate that it's Tyler who's there for him and not me. I'm self-aware enough to know that's a problem of my own making. I should have begged him to stay last night. I should have comforted him in whatever way he needed.

I let him down.

Again.

Well, this will be the last time. I will burn in hell before I ever let anyone hurt him again. Especially me.

It's time to stop hiding from the world. Time to stop

courting the approval of a man so vile and despicable that I am ashamed to share his DNA.

Looks I'm about to come out of that closet I've been hiding in for far too long.

CHAPTER
FORTY-SIX
MASON

"Mr. Blackthorn is here to see you, sir," Deborah says, poking her head into my office.

My heart leaps into my throat. While I was hoping he'd show up, I've also been dreading it. I have no idea how the fuck this is going to play out, and it scares the hell out of me. Nothing about my relationship with King is easy, but maybe that's what proves it's worth saving.

Regardless of how this is about to go down, I'm a grown-ass man, and I'm capable of having grown-ass man conversations. I take a deep breath. "Show him in."

A second later, he walks through the door, and it closes with a soft click behind him. He looks like he's barely slept. Despite everything, it makes my heart ache for him.

"You don't work here anymore" are the first words out of my mouth.

And "Did you fuck him?" are the first out of his.

What in the ever-living fuck? Now I'm angry and defensive. Great! "Fuck who?"

"Tyler. I know that's where you went last night."

How did he ...? Son of a bitch is tracking my phone. I stand so fast my chair topples to the floor. "Yes, I went to Tyler's, you fucking jackass." We stalk toward each other, and I'm pretty sure the scowl on his face is mirrored by my own. We stop when only a few inches separate us. "And you want to know why? Because I felt like being with someone who wanted me around. Someone who doesn't feel sorry for me. Someone who could bear to fucking look at me and not see ..."

His green eyes narrow on my face. "Not see what?"

I take a breath, keeping a lid on my rage. "Not see what he did."

His tongue darts out and he licks his bottom lip, his gaze never leaving mine. I look away first, unable to stand the pity in his eyes any longer. Then his strong hands are planted on either side of my neck, his thumbs rubbing the skin beneath my ears as he forces me to look at him again. "I don't see him when I look at you. I see me. If I wasn't looking at you last night, it was because I was so fucking ashamed."

I go to reply, but he cuts me off. "I'm ashamed that my father did that to you. I'm ashamed of the way I treated you. And when you asked me if it would have made a difference, it reminded me of what a coward I was. I never should have said all those awful fucking things to you when he caught us, but I was scared shitless of my father, and I still would have left the way I did. That is what I'm most ashamed of. You were always so much fucking braver than me."

His pain guts me. "It's easier to be brave when you have a whole family who loves you for who you are," I remind him. I can't imagine the torture of growing up with parents who hate a fundamental part of you.

He gives me a faint smile. "You'd have been brave anyway. It's one of the things I love about you."

God, I fucking love him too. So much it scares me. "Well, I am very lovable."

His smile grows a little wider, and his grip on my neck tightens. "But I don't look at you any differently, Mase. I hate what he did to you, but I don't feel sorry for you if that's what you're worried about. I want you as much as I always have. I love you more than I ever have. I'm terrified that all you'll see is him when you look at me, and if that's something we have to work through together, then I'm begging you to let us try." He steps closer and presses his forehead to mine.

"When I walked in and saw your lip bleeding, and then he pulled that gun ..." He shudders. "My entire world stopped turning, baby. I was in shock, and I didn't know how to handle it. I should have begged you to stay. I wasn't sure I had any right to ask. But I do know that I can't live without you."

Fuck me. Being with this guy is like living life on a rollercoaster. But I wouldn't choose a life that didn't have him in it. "I never want you to live without me, King." I pull back and level him with a look. "But for future reference, you should have led with all of that when you walked in here instead of asking me if I fucked my best friend."

He winces. "I'm sorry. I had every intention of keeping my mouth shut about him, but then I saw you and it all went out the window. I trust you, but I spent most of the night picturing you with your hands on him and drove myself fucking crazy. For future reference, I'm still going to be a jealous, possessive asshole and will sometimes react like a complete fuck-knuckle. But I will always trust you, baby boy."

My knees tremble and need spikes in my core. "Fuck, you know I love it when you call me that."

He runs his nose along my jawline and down to my throat. "Yeah, I know."

"Did you jerk off while you were imagining me fucking Tyler? I bet it made you hard."

The growl that comes out of him has me fighting to suppress my laughter. "I swear to god, Mase, one of these days, I am going to fuck all that attitude out of you."

I wrap my arms around his neck. "While that sounds hot, I think you secretly love my attitude."

He sinks his teeth into my neck and sucks hard.

I bite back a groan. "I have a meeting in ten minutes. Don't leave a mark."

Heeding my warning, he stops. "It makes me hard leaving my marks on you. What if I want everyone to know you're mine?"

I arch an eyebrow. "Everyone, huh?"

His expression turns serious. "Yeah. Everyone."

I take a step back, but he follows me, keeping our bodies flush. "You want to come out?"

He nods.

Wow.

I'm torn between elation and anxiety. Is this a knee-jerk reaction to what happened last night? Because if that's all it is ... "This is a big step, King."

He presses a soft, all-too-brief kiss on my lips. "I know it is. But it's what I want. I've spent far too long living half a life—and for what? The approval of two people I despise? You are the only person who matters to me, and your opinion is the only one I truly care about."

I place a hand on the back of his neck, holding his face close to mine. "I'm really happy that you're doing this. And although I'm fucking thrilled about what it means for me, and for us, I'm happiest that you're doing this for you, King. You deserve this. You deserve to be who you want to be without judgment from anyone."

"You're the one who gave me the courage to do it."

I dust my lips over his. "I love you. I'm gonna try to wrap up my meeting in half an hour. Will you hang around and wait for me? We can grab lunch. Or go back to my place and spend the day in bed."

His grin is wicked and sexy, but it fades when he checks his watch. "As tempting as that offer is, I have some things to take care of." He clears his throat. "But can I see you tonight?" As if I didn't just ask him to spend the day in bed with me, his tone is pleading, his expression filled with anticipation. As if there's a world in which I would say no to him.

"My place?" I suggest, not particularly wanting to spend time in his apartment.

That gets me a huge smile that makes his dimple pop. "I'll be there around six. That work for you?"

I nod. "That works."

His mouth crashes against mine, and he tangles his fingers in my hair as he tongue-fucks me like he owns me. I grind against him, feeling his cock stiffen against my own. With a Herculean amount of effort, I pull away, breathless. "It's now seven minutes to my meeting, and I really don't want to meet my potential new clients with a raging hard-on."

He glances down at the outline of my very hard dick in my suit pants. "No, I guess that's not the best first impression." His eyes are twinkling when they meet my gaze. He brushes his lips over mine. "Time to think unsexy thoughts, Playboy."

"Then you need to get out of here, Hotshot."

He brushes his knuckles over the bulge in my pants,

and my cock twitches at the brief contact. "Tonight, baby boy. We'll talk, okay?"

With that promise hanging in the air, he walks out of my office. I blow out a breath and push all thoughts of him from my mind, focusing instead on the clients I'm about to meet. Thankfully, we're discussing new AI software that writes systems maintenance code for waste treatment plants, which is the most unsexy thing I can think of.

CHAPTER
FORTY-SEVEN

KING

I wipe my sweaty palms on my jeans and try to swallow past the lump in my throat, but it feels like it's swollen shut. This is the last time I will ever come to this house. And if I can help it, the last time I will ever speak to either of my parents again. I've seen my future, and they're not in it, and I couldn't be happier about that fact.

I press the doorbell and wait, my heart hammering against my ribcage. I'm determined to keep a lid on my rage, say my piece, and leave. That goes straight to hell the moment I see his face.

All I see is what he did to Mason. To the boy I loved. The boy I gave up for his approval. I see seventeen-year-old Mason—who was nothing but goodness, light, and kindness—being violated by this piece of shit.

I push him full force in the chest, and he staggers back.

"You disgusting piece of shit!" I roar, over twenty years of rage and hatred pouring out of me at once. I advance on him, and he retreats down the hallway.

Did Mason cower like that?

"Why?" I shove him again. "I can almost understand why you hated what I was. Your own father fucked you up, and you married a sociopath incapable of feeling, so I can wrap my head around that even if I don't agree with it. But how could you ..." I punch him in the jaw, and he falls to the floor.

"Kyngston Worthington!" My mother's shrill voice echoes down the hallway. A hallway I now notice is empty of the antique furniture that usually resides here. "How dare you."

I spin to face her. "How dare I?" I roar. "Do you know what he did? To a seventeen-year-old boy? He fucking raped him. Did you know that?"

"It was a very long time ago," she says, deadpan.

"So fucking what. He raped the man I love."

She blanches. "How dare you," she says again.

"That's what gets the reaction from you? That I told you I loved a man—not that your husband raped a seventeen-year-old boy?"

Her lip curls, but she doesn't respond.

"Kyngston, son?" My father pleads, his voice soft and calm. "Think about what you're saying."

I turn my anger on him again. "I know exactly what I'm saying. I. Am. Gay. Despite the torture and your efforts to *cleanse* me, I love dick. Specifically, I love Mason James's dick. I love him. And you ..." I point a finger in my father's direction and then have to take a breath to calm my temper before I beat him to a pulp with my bare hands.

I change the subject. "What did you do to Cassidy Jones? Where is she?"

His lip wobbles, but it's my mother who answers. "That silly little whore."

I gape at her. "You know about her too?"

She waves a hand in front of her face. "I know about all of them, darling. Do you think I'm stupid?"

"So what happened to Cassidy?" I ask.

She shrugs. "How should I know?"

"I already told you I had nothing to do with her leaving," my father adds.

"Good riddance. Silly girl." Mother snorts. "She probably felt deeply embarrassed thinking your father would ride off into the sunset with her. Getting that trashy little tattoo."

Something clicks into place. "You saw her tattoo?"

"Emmeline," my father growls.

Her eyes dart away from my face. "Y-your father told me about it."

"You saw it, didn't you? She came here before she disappeared."

My mother stares at me, unspeaking, refusing to dignify my question with an answer. She truly is a sociopath.

I try my father again. "If she saw that tattoo, then Cassidy must have come here before she disappeared. What the hell did you do to her?"

His right eye twitches.

"Is she still here?" My eyes dart around the hallway. "No." I shake my head. "You killed her, didn't you?" I can barely believe the accusation leaves my mouth, but they're hiding something from me.

"Don't be preposterous, Kyngston," my mother says, but there's a tremor in her voice.

My father drops his head into his hands. "Son, it was an accident. Please. You have to believe me."

"What kind of accident?" I ask, horrified.

He looks up, his eyes wide. "There was a struggle. She hit her head. Nobody intended for her to be hurt."

"So ... What? You just let her die?"

A sharp, brain-splitting pain lances through my head and down my spine.

Then nothing.

My head is throbbing. It's dark, but maybe that's because I can't open my eyes. The smell is familiar and terror-inducing. My parents' basement. I drift back into unconsciousness.

"You expect me to murder our own son, Emmeline?"

I desperately want to hear the rest of this conversation, but I black out a second time.

"... POWERS OF PERSUASION." My mother's voice comes once more, followed by the sound of chains hitting concrete.

My father speaks now. "If he would just give us the money..."

"It's your fault we're about to lose the house, Kyngston. You were always useless with your own money."

"If they repossess this house..."

I'm frantically clinging to consciousness when I fade out again.

ICE WATER DRENCHES ME, and it's like a defibrillator to my brain. I suck in deep breaths as my body goes into shock.

"See, I told you he was fine," my mother says cruelly.

I try to move, but I'm chained to the floor. "W-what the fuck?"

"It's for your own good, son," my father says, his voice taking on an annoyingly saccharine tone like he actually believes that bullshit.

"I'm not a kid anymore! This shit won't work." I pull on the chains again, my anger giving me a burst of adrenaline. Pity there's not a lot I can do about it. I spent a decent part of my teenage years chained in this cold, dark basement. A few days every few months, to stop me from being tempted into sin. It was where they kept me for four whole days after he caught me and Mason. I left as soon as he let me out, but I still remained their good little boy, didn't I?

"Take a few days," my mother says. "I'm sure you'll come around to our way of thinking."

"What? Give you Grampa's money so you don't lose this house and nobody ever finds Cassidy's body, is that it?"

"It was an accident," my father repeats. As if that somehow makes what they've done okay. Given what I've learned about him in the last twenty-four hours, I'm not sure I believe it was an accident.

"Then you should have called for a fucking ambulance. Or the police!"

"He won't see sense yet, Kyngston, but he will. He always did in the end." She must be referring to how, after a few ice baths and a couple days without food, I would usually tell them with my whole chest that I wasn't gay and that boys who liked other boys disgusted me. Fuck, does she not understand I would have told them the earth was flat if it could have gotten me out of here?

But if she thinks there's a chance I'll cave, I might just be able to get out of here after all.

CHAPTER
FORTY-EIGHT
MASON

I keep checking the time, but it doesn't change the fact that King is thirty minutes late, which is unlike him. When he does get caught up, he calls, and I haven't heard from him since he left my office this morning.

His phone goes straight to voicemail, and I tell myself that he could be somewhere he can't get a signal. There are all manner of explanations to explain his tardiness and his lack of contact.

He could have been in some kind of accident and be bleeding out in a gutter somewhere.

I tell myself to calm the fuck down, but that doesn't stop me from calling every hospital in the state of New York to see if he's there. It's after seven-thirty by the time I've confirmed that nobody by the first name of King or

Kyngston or the last name Blackthorn or Worthington has been admitted today.

Something's happened to him. There's a sinking feeling deep in my gut that I've learned to trust over the years. After what happened yesterday, I'm certain that he intended to confront his father once he left my office, and I can't imagine any scenario where that visit will have had a positive outcome. The best-case scenario is that he's gone somewhere to cool off.

But he would have called.

Every instinct I have tells me King went to confront his father and something bad happened. Fuck, I have no idea what I'll be walking into, but I have to do something. He could be hurt—he could have hurt his father. Or something worse.

I need some kind of backup. We have plenty of security on staff, but they're all personal bodyguards or building security. I'm going to need a different kind of expertise for this.

I dial Nathan.

He picks up and says cheerfully, "Hey, Mase, what's up?"

"Nathan, I need some help."

It must be the tone of my voice, because he immediately switches into ice-cold defense-attorney mode. "What's happened, and what can I do?"

"It's King, and it's a long story, but I'm sure he's in some kind of trouble."

"He needs a lawyer?"

"I wish it were that kind of trouble. But no. I think he's in danger. I can't get ahold of him, and I think he's gone to see his father ... And, well, like I said, it's a long story. But I don't particularly want to face Kyngston Worthington on my own, and—"

"I'll be right there. I'll call Drake and Elijah—"

"Thanks, bro," I say, cutting him off. "But I think this calls for a different kind of help. Besides, if King does need a lawyer ..." *Or god forbid, if I do.* I take a breath. "Then you need to be as far away from the situation as possible."

"Mason," he says, sounding increasingly frantic. "What the hell is going on? Are you okay?"

"I'm okay. I can't explain it all right now, but King's father, well, he's a piece of shit. And I think King has gone to confront him, and I need ... I need you to put me in touch with your clients. I could really use their help."

"Fuck, Mase. You really want to fuck around with the Ryan brothers?"

I've met the Ryans a few times, and they all seem like nice guys. Mikey and I in particular get along well—we bonded over our similar sense of humor. But I'm under no illusions regarding the kind of men they are and the kind of shit they do.

"They are the exact people I need tonight, bro."

· · ·

387

Iᴛ's Conor Ryan I get ahold of. From the background noise when he answers, he must be in their club, The Emerald Shamrock. He's expecting my call, as Nathan promised he would be.

"Hey Mason, what can I do for you?"

"I don't know how much Nathan has told you but ..." I screw my eyes closed and go for it. "I think my boyfriend's in trouble. He went to his parents' house earlier, and he didn't come back. His dad is a real piece of shit, and I'm sure something bad has happened. I have no fucking clue what I'm doing here, Conor, or what I'm walking into, and ... I guess I was hoping you could help. Or that you might know a couple of guys who could."

"Right now?" he asks.

"Yeah."

He's quiet for a minute, then he says, "I mean, I have a few bouncers who are handy, but we generally take care of our own business, you know?"

I can imagine.

"Who is this guy? The father?"

"Kyngston Worthington III."

He huffs a dark laugh. "The investment banker?"

"Yeah," I reply, unsure if his laugh is good or bad.

"That fucker tried to have us shut down," he growls. Seems the evil laugh was a good thing. "Someone will be outside your building in twenty minutes."

After I hang up, I realize I didn't give him my address.

But people like Conor Ryan probably have plenty of ways to get that kind of information.

The black SUV pulls up twenty minutes later, as promised. I can't see the faces of the driver or the passenger due to the tinted windows, but when I climb into the back, I'm shocked to find Conor driving and his older brother, Shane, in the passenger seat. To be honest, I feel fucking honored.

"You okay?" Shane asks.

"No," I admit. "I feel like I'm going to vomit."

He grins at me. "It'll pass."

"Don't throw up in my new car," Conor warns, which doesn't help at all. "So we're going to the Worthington estate, right?"

"Yeah. I think that's where he is."

Conor drives like he knows where he's going, and I don't question him. I wouldn't be surprised if he knew where every person of interest in New York lives, though the thought is mildly terrifying. As are the two eldest Ryan brothers, who sit in silence. "Thanks for doing this," I say, if only to fill the awkward silence.

"Happy to help." Conor meets my eyes in the rearview mirror and nods.

"It was a quiet night," Shane adds. Then he rolls his shoulders. "And things have been a little too quiet lately."

Conor laughs like they've shared an inside joke. I know

from Nathan and Drake that the Ryans have settled down somewhat since they became fathers a couple years ago, and I can imagine the lifestyle they lead is not an easy one to step away from. No matter their reason for being here, though, I'm glad they are. My stomach is twisting itself into knots worrying about King and what we might find when we get to where we're headed, and I am beyond relieved to have them as backup.

FORTY-NINE

MASON

To all of our surprise, the gates are open when we arrive. Conor peers through the windshield like he's expecting something to happen as the car crawls along the gravel drive. Nothing comes.

"I would have expected them to have more security," he says to Shane, who hums his agreement. As we get closer to the house, I notice King's bike, and I'm filled with both panic and relief.

We climb out of the SUV, and Conor grabs a black gym bag from the trunk. I don't want to know what's in there, so I don't ask. My heart is already racing hard enough to explode. It goes on racing as we climb the few stone steps. So we're just going to ring the doorbell? Like regular visitors?

Conor does exactly that, and the three of us glance between each other while we wait for an answer. "Looks like they're not coming," Shane says after what feels like forever.

Conor shrugs. "I guess we let ourselves in?" He pulls a huge steel mallet-style hammer from the bag and starts smashing his way through the door, looking like a cross between Thor and Don Corleone—if the latter were Irish.

Shane draws a gun from inside his coat, and my hammering heart comes to an abrupt stop. But this is why I asked for their help. My gut assures me that this is exactly what King needs. A minute later, Conor has destroyed the lock enough to get us access.

All three of us step cautiously inside the house and are met by the twin barrels of a shotgun being held by Kyngston Worthington III. "Get the fuck out of my house," he snarls.

"Get King out here and we'll go," I say.

"He's not here."

Lying piece of shit. "His bike is outside."

"Don't give a fuck. I just told you he's not here. Now get the fuck out of my house before I shoot you all."

Conor snorts a laugh and pulls a gun of his own. Both Ryan brothers point their guns at Kyngston's head. "You could try, old man."

There's a movement from the other end of the hallway, and a woman calls out Kyngston's name.

"Stay the hell away, Emmeline," he shouts.

She wanders into the fray wearing a silk housecoat, seemingly unaware of her husband's command. One hand stuffed in her pocket and a glass of wine in the other, she stumbles into the no man's land between us all.

"Get out of the way, Emmeline," Kyngston orders. "Now."

Shane says, "Knee."

Deafening gunshots crack through the air. For a few seconds, I have no idea who fired and who was shot.

Kyngston wails in agony and crashes to the marble tile, clutching his knee.

Conor sprints to him and stands on said knee, and the sickening crunch of bone and cartilage fills the reception hall. "Where is he?" Conor growls.

Tears run down Kyngston's colorless face. "The b-basement."

Shane and I make our way to Conor.

"Where all dirty little boys go," Emmeline says, slurring her words.

As casually as he would pluck a piece of lint from his pants, Shane smacks her on the temple with the handle of his gun, and she slumps to the floor.

I step over her, my eyes locked on her piece-of-shit husband. "Where is the basement?"

He snivels, and Conor presses harder on his knee, causing him to shriek. Gasping, he jerks his head toward the sweeping staircase. "Behind there."

"Watch him, Con," Shane says. "We'll go find King."

We locate the door to the basement and find it padlocked. Shane shoots through it, and I wrench the door open. Cold, damp air rushes over us. I peer inside the dark and feel for a light switch on the wall, but I'm too impatient. Using the flashlight on my cell phone, I jog down the steps and shout King's name.

There's a metal jangling sound, and I shine my light in the direction it came from. Fuck, it's him. He scrabbles backward, his hand over his eyes as the arc of light from my phone reaches him. There's that distinctive metal sound again. Jesus fucking Christ. Are they ... chains? That motherfucker has him chained in the basement.

"King! King, it's me. I'm here." I run to him and crouch at his feet.

"Mase?" His voice trembles, his breathing labored. I place my phone on the ground and scramble around in the near darkness to figure out the quickest way to free him. Fucking chained, like some kind of rabid animal. What kind of person does that to another human being—least of all his own son?

Shane calls for me from the top of the basement stairs.

"He's here," I call back. "Can you see if you can find a light?"

Shane's heavy footfalls are the next thing I hear as he jogs down the basement steps.

My hands roam over King. His clothes are soaked and freezing cold, but when my fingers trace his skin, they meet something warm and sticky on his neck. "Shit. Are you bleeding? Where are you hurt?" Before I can pick up my phone again, the whole room erupts in stark white light.

"Found it," Shane announces.

I almost wish he hadn't. Nothing could have prepared me for the sight of my boyfriend lying on the concrete floor with blood pouring from a deep gash across his temple, his foot chained to a bolt in the ground.

But it's the way he's hugging his knees to his chest and shivering violently that tells me something is seriously wrong. Shane jogs over and drops to a crouch beside me. He immediately checks King's pulse. "Pulse is strong." Then he runs his hands down King's body, gently checking him over.

Thank fuck he seems to know what he's doing, because I'm so far out of my depth. All I know is I want to chain his father in this basement before we leave. Turn off the lights and leave him to rot. I'd do the same to his mom, too, if I thought she was sober enough to know what the hell was going on. "You bleeding anywhere that needs a hospital, buddy?" Shane asks.

"N-no. C-cold."

"Yeah, I know." Shane looks around for something. "You got yourself a nasty case of hypothermia."

Hypothermia? That sounds bad. The basement is cold and the floor is damp concrete, but that doesn't account for why King is shivering the way he is. Or why his clothes are soaking wet.

Shane grunts with frustration. "We need to get him

out of here and bring his body temperature up before he goes into organ failure."

"Organ failure? What the fuck, Shane?" I can't lose him. I won't.

"While he's still shivering, he's okay. Let's get him up," Shane says, snapping me into action. I can get answers and panic myself into a cardiac event later. Right now, the priority is getting King out of here. And I hold onto what Shane said—if he's shivering, he's okay.

Together, we hoist King up, and he winces when we touch his ribs. But he's so damn cold. His whole body quakes with the force of his shivering. "How can we warm him up fast?"

"He needs to lose the wet clothes. Body heat is the safest bet," Shane replies confidently. "Then get him somewhere warm. There must be a fireplace somewhere in an old house like this."

"N-no," King objects. "M-monsters. We n-need to l-leave."

I throw Shane a concerned look over the top of King's head. "It's the hypothermia, making him confused," he assures me.

"N-need to g-get out," King babbles.

Shane gives me a reassuring nod but speaks to King. "It's okay. We'll get you out of here."

When we get to the top of the stairs, Kyngston Worthington III is kneeling at Conor's feet with his hands behind his head and a grenade shoved in his mouth—yes, a fucking grenade. Only the pin protrudes from between his lips, and rivulets of blood run down his chin. He's whimpering and trembling all over, tears and snot dripping from his face.

Emmeline Worthington is still slumped in the corner.

"Hypothermia?" Conor asks, his eyes narrowed on King.

"Looks like," Shane answers. "We need to get him warm, but he wants out of here, so ..."

Conor nods, his eyes flicking to me for a beat. "We have blankets in the car, and I can turn up the heaters. We'll make it work." He redirects his attention to the piece of shit kneeling on the floor. "And what about this sick fuck? The grenade is to make sure he behaves. We can go a less messy way." His eyes glint as they meet mine. "I can make it look like a suicide. Heart attack? Home invasion? Professional hit?"

"Heart attack or suicide will be tricky to pull off now that you've smashed his kneecap to pieces and broken a few of his teeth, Con," Shane says, deadpan.

"How do you know he's broken some of his teeth?" I whisper.

"No other way to make the grenade fit," he replies coolly, and it's a stark reminder of the caliber of men I'm dealing with. I'm just relieved they're on my side. "Besides, you'll have to deal with the mother too," he adds.

Conor tips his head to one side, eyeing the sack of garbage at his feet with curiosity. "Home invasion, then?"

Kyngston wails around the weapon in his mouth, his face screwed up. I imagine if he could speak, he would be begging for mercy.

"N-no," King says. "L-leave them."

"We're here at your request, Mason. What's it to be?" Conor asks.

I glance at King and then back at his pathetic excuse for a father. Sniveling and crying like the coward he truly is. I hate him, but I'm not sure I'm prepared to have two lives on my conscience for him, especially as King doesn't want them dead. And my biggest priority is getting him out of here and into the Ryans' car so we can get him warm.

I shake my head. "Leave him to rot."

Conor shrugs, but then he grabs Kyngston by the jaw and squeezes hard. I wince, worried the pin on the grenade is about to pop out and blow us all to pieces. "Listen to me, fuckface. You ever go anywhere near any of my friends again, I'll be back. And next time I won't play so nicely. You understand me?" He taps the side of Kyngston's face, and the older man nods furiously.

King shivers.

"Let's get him out of here," I say, worry for him over-shadowing everything else now that the adrenaline of the rescue is wearing off.

We get him out of the house and bundle him into the

SUV. Shane nods to the back seat. "You need to get him out of those wet clothes."

Conor has been rustling around in the cargo space, and he shoves a couple of fleece picnic blankets into my hands. "He needs body heat. But if you warm him up too fast, he could go into shock. Take off your shirt and jeans, and then wrap both of you up in these. Okay?"

I nod my understanding and scramble into the back seat alongside King. Then I undress my boyfriend while the two most dangerous men in New York drive us home. King's teeth are chattering by the time I get him naked, which I remind myself is good. Shivering means he's okay.

I quickly pull off my T-shirt along with my sneakers and sweats and pull him into my arms so his cold back is pressed tightly against my chest and my legs are draped around his. I force the images of the bruises on his chest and back from my mind and concentrate on raising his body temperature. Like Conor suggested, I wrap one blanket around his front and the other around both of us.

His skin remains ice-cold, and I scrub my hands up and down his arms, warming him the best I can.

"Th-thanks, baby," he murmurs.

"You're sure we don't need to get him to a hospital?" I direct my question to Shane and Conor, but it's King who insists that we don't.

Shane studies him. "We'll have our doctor come check him over at your place."

"Can't someone go into cardiac arrest with hypothermia though?" I ask.

"I'm f-fine," King insists.

"Technically, yeah, but I think we got to him in time," Shane says. "He's still shivering, and he's warming up. But the doc will check on him and tell us if we need to take him in."

"What if I heat him up too fast or—"

King grabs for my hand. "I've d-done this p-plenty. You're doing g-great, b-baby."

He's done this plenty? As in recovered from hypothermia? When the fuck? Now's not the time to ask him about that though, so I hold him tighter and send up a prayer that he will be okay.

By the time we get to my building, King has stopped shivering and his lips are no longer blue. Apparently another good sign. He's still a little out of it, probably from a combination of the blow to his head and the hypothermia. Who knows what other injuries he might be suffering from. The sooner I can have a doctor look at him, the better I'll feel.

Dr. Lisa, which is the name the Ryan brothers affectionately call her, pulls off her latex gloves and wads them into a ball. She's already checked all of King's vitals and confirmed he seems stable and is unlikely to suffer any lasting effects from the hypothermia. And he doesn't appear to have any broken bones or evidence of trauma that would indicate internal injuries. She did recommend an x-ray, but King refused.

"He probably has a concussion, and I'd recommend bed rest for at least the next forty-eight hours," she tells me. "Plenty of fluids. Make sure he eats. I've given him something for the pain, and I'll leave some with you. Instructions on the bottle. And I'll call and check on him tomorrow. If he deteriorates at all, take him to the ER, but I expect he'll be feeling a hell of a lot better after a good night's sleep."

I shake her hand. "Thanks so much, Doctor. I really appreciate you making a house call so late."

She smiles. "It's no problem at all. Really."

Shane walks into the room with his cell pressed to his ear. "Of course I will, sweetheart. We'll be home soon." He ends the call and looks at his brother. "Jessie wants ..." He pinches the bridge of his nose. "No, she said she *needs* Cheetos and Sour Patch Kids. So we need to swing by somewhere that's open on the way home."

Conor squeezes his eyes closed and shakes his head. "Wife has the diet of a teenage boy."

Lisa chuckles. "How is my favorite patient?"

"She's fucking adorable," Conor says proudly. "But she's addicted to carbs and sugar, and she claims the baby needs them, so ..."

Shane smirks. "And even if they didn't, we'd get them for her anyway."

Conor smiles back. "True."

King's eyes are shuttering closed, and I usher everyone from the room. After offering another round of gratitude to Dr. Lisa and the Ryan brothers, I show them out. As soon as they're gone, the full events of the evening crash into me like a tsunami, and I double over, my hands on my knees as I struggle to catch my breath.

King in that dark, cold basement. Chained like a dog. His chattering teeth. His bloody face. The fear I would lose him. How close I came to ending his father's life.

Once the vise around my heart and lungs eases, I stand tall and suck in a deep, calming breath.

He's okay. We're okay. Nothing can touch us here.

"Mase?" King's raspy voice rouses me from the fitful slumber I fell into. I must have watched him sleep for hours before I dozed off myself.

His hand grasps for mine, and I link our fingers together. "I'm here, mi rey. You need anything? Water?" I check the clock on the nightstand and see it's a little after six a.m. "You can't have any pain meds until eight."

He rolls onto his side. "I don't need anything. I'm sorry I woke you."

I rest my palm on his cheek, and I'm relieved to feel his skin soft and warm. I'll never forget the ice-cold waxy feel of it for as long as I live. "I'm glad you woke me."

He smiles faintly. "We never got to talk."

"We can talk later. Rest."

"I'd rather talk now." The sadness in his tone makes

anxiety spike in my chest. Is this the part where he tells me he can't do this anymore?

I keep my tone even. "Okay. What shall we talk about?"

"I'm sorry about what my father did to you," he says.

Well, that's better than what I expected, but ... "That's not your apology to make, King. You didn't know. I am sorry I never told you though. I didn't want it to change the way you saw me," I admit.

"I can understand that, but it truly doesn't, baby. Does it change the way you see me?" His voice is so quiet and small—nothing at all like him. A fresh wave of hatred for his parents hits me. Whatever they did to make him doubt his worth is one more reason they deserve whatever is coming for them.

"No," I answer. "Not even a little."

His green eyes fill with tears. "Thank you for coming for me. Seems like I did need rescuing after all, huh?"

I press a kiss on his lips. "I will always come rescue you, mi rey. I'll be there whenever you need me to be, and you never have to thank me for it."

He turns his head and kisses the palm of my hand. "I told them I was gay. Then I told them that I was in love with you."

"That was really fucking brave. I'm proud of you."

He snorts. "Shouldn't have to be brave to tell your own parents who you really are. They could have been happy that I found someone I wanted to spend my life with.

Instead ..." A tear runs down his cheek, and I swipe it away with my thumb.

"You want to tell me what happened?"

He nods, and I listen while he tells me the hateful things his parents said. His mother's indifference. His father's anger. How he discovered they were broke and desperate for money and the reason why.

"Jesus fucking Christ, King. That's unthinkable. What the hell are you going to do?"

"I'm not sure yet. I don't know if I trust the cops after what happened when Cassidy disappeared, but I do know a detective. He's as decent as they come. I think if I give him the evidence ..." He pauses. "Alternatively, I could tell Curtis Jones what happened and let him handle it whatever way he wants to."

I trace my fingers over the gash on his head. I'd happily kill Kyngston Worthington III myself, but I'm sure life in prison is the more painful option for him in the long run. "Whatever you decide, I'll support you."

"Thanks."

"How'd you end up in the basement?"

He rubs the back of his head. "My father and I were arguing, and I heard my mother behind us ... Then there was this pain. Everything went black. My mother must have knocked me out with something. When I came around, I was in the basement. That's where I heard them talking about what happened to Cassidy, how they were worried about losing the house."

Emmeline Worthington is now on my list of people that need to rot. In hell or in jail—either will do.

King shivers. "I honestly thought I might actually die down there this time. I mean, it would have made sense. Getting me out the of way would have made them next in line for Grampa's money. I heard my father ask her if she expected him to murder me."

I hate that he thought for a second he was going to die all alone in that basement. I can barely comprehend that his own parents would do that to him. If I have anything to do with it, he'll never feel alone again a single day in his life. "You think that's what their plan was?"

He nods, and more tears fall. I wipe them away. "When we were in the car, you said you'd done this plenty. You've had hypothermia before?"

"Lots of times. When I was a kid, it was how ..." He swallows. "When my father found out I liked boys, he told me it was vile and unnatural and that I had a demon inside me."

Rage and despair swell in my chest, but I keep my lips pressed together and my hand on his cheek, letting him talk.

"I was about twelve that first time. They used to say the ice water would 'cleanse' me. It would happen once every few months, just to make sure I didn't 'stray from the right path.'"

"Holy fuck, King. I had no idea."

"Nobody did. I was a master at hiding who I really

was. From my parents and the rest of the world." His lips curve slightly. "Everyone except you."

His reaction to us being caught by his father makes so much more sense to me now. He must have been dying inside, and he's been carrying this pain around for years. My heart breaks into a million pieces for everything he went through at his parents' hands, not only as a kid but yesterday too. That anyone could treat their own child like that is beyond comprehension. It takes every ounce of willpower I possess not to jump out of bed and drive back to that house and burn it down with his parents inside. In fact, one quick call and I could make it happen. Right here from the safety of this penthouse.

Instead, I do the only thing he needs me to do—I listen.

HE LOOKS SO PEACEFUL SLEEPING. Serene. Unburdening himself of all the fucked-up shit he's carried around with him for most of his life was good for him. No matter how hard it was for him to say and how fucking devastating it was to listen to, he needed to release all that poison.

Before I fell asleep watching over King last night, I called Nathan and told him what happened, leaving out the history between King's father and me, and it took all my powers of persuasion to talk him out of calling the cops. He was appeased only by the confirmation that King and I were safe. And that we'd talk everything through in the morning.

Looking at King's face now, you'd never know he was almost killed by his psychopathic parents yesterday. When I think about how close I came to losing him, I feel like I can't breathe. There's no way I'd survive losing him a second time. We've come so far in a few short months, and I know with every fiber of my being that nothing will ever come between us again. He's it for me. All my years of fucking around with other guys and sticking to casual flings had nothing to do with not wanting commitment and everything to do with only wanting him.

My cell vibrates with a text from Mad, telling me that he and the rest of my brothers are on their way with breakfast. I should have known they'd arrive en masse after I agreed to Nathan's demand that he be allowed to come over first thing this morning. Honestly, I'm surprised they let the sun get all the way up first.

My stomach growls, and I contemplate waking King, but he needs as much rest as he can get. I manage to tear myself away from him, content that he'll be safe in here. I would die before I let his father anywhere near this place.

Fifteen minutes later, I'm sitting at the table, surrounded by some of the finest freshly roasted Colombian coffee I've ever tasted in my life from the vegan café Maddox works at, a tray overflowing with pastries, pancakes, and bacon—from a different café, obviously—a basket of fruit, and six different kinds of juice.

"You guys really went all out," I say around a large bite of cherry Danish.

Elijah grins. "Breakfast of champions."

Nathan, sitting next to me, places his hand on my shoulder. "You okay?"

I nod. Yesterday was possibly the most unbelievable day of my entire life, but I am okay. Better than, in fact. I feel lighter than I have in years. "Thanks for coming through for me."

His eyes narrow. "Always."

"And how is King doing?" Elijah asks.

Before I can answer, the man himself walks out of the bedroom wearing only a pair of my sweats. My eyes are drawn to the healing wound on his temple. His parents are lucky to be alive. For now.

King scrubs a hand across his head and blinks at all of us. "Sorry, am I interrupting?"

Goddammit, even beat up he's sexy as hell and no less adorable. "No." I pull out the chair next to me and indicate he should sit.

Maddox grabs him a plate and some silverware and passes it over. "We brought breakfast. What'll it be?"

"Shouldn't you guys be at work?" King asks, looking around the table. "It's after ten."

"Work can wait," Drake says.

"Yeah, this is more important," Maddox adds.

King rubs his eyes and shakes his head. "Breakfast is more important?"

Nathan takes a huge bite of a bacon roll, licks a little grease from his lip, and says, "No. Checking in on you and Mase is though."

"How are you doing, buddy?" Drake asks.

King eyes my brothers with what looks a lot like suspicion. Fuck. Is this too much for him after everything that happened? I know they're a lot, but they're my brothers. And this is how James men show our support. We're a big part of each other's lives. Hell, it's a lucky break that the wives and kid didn't tag along too. Not to mention Pop, who would be fussing over me and King and doing his damnedest to persuade us to get checked out at the hospital.

King spears a pancake with a fork and plonks it on his plate. "I'm okay, I guess. This is interesting. Kinda strange to wake up and have you all here eating a breakfast that would feed a platoon of soldiers." He scrubs a hand over his stubble. "Strange, but nice." He stuffs half the pancake into mouth, chews, and swallows before adding, "I could get used to it."

Elijah clears his throat, and it makes us all look toward where he sits at the head of the table. "Now that we're all fed, can we discuss the elephant in the room? What the fuck happened, and who do we need to kill?" Yup. There's that CEO energy we know and love.

FIFTY-ONE

KING

There's something about Elijah that leaves me with no doubt in my mind that he would do anything to protect his brothers, and the words he just uttered send a chill down my spine.

What if he thinks I'm not good enough for Mason? What if once he discovers that yesterday was all my fault, he decides I'm one of the people he needs to remove from his brother's life? Those familiar feelings of shame and guilt threaten to crush me, and I almost throw up the pancake I devoured. I hate what my father did to Mason. I hate what I did to him. I'm spiraling, and I'm doing it under the scrutinizing gazes of one of the most powerful and influential families in America.

Mason's hand lands on my thigh under the table, and he squeezes firmly, his fingertips digging into the taut muscle of my quads. With that one touch, he says everything: This is *our* story. Yes, there are parts of it that are shameful and full of regret, but it's still who we are. And whether his brothers hate me or not, he loves me, and that's all that really fucking matters.

"It's a really long story," Mason says, and he follows it up with a snort of laughter.

Maddox leans forward, his dark-brown eyes full of concern and ... I don't know exactly, but something tells me he has a lot of his own demons. "We got all the time in the world, bro."

Mason blows out a breath and looks at me. I nod my agreement. He needs to tell them the whole truth. He's carried it with him for far too long. And although my part in it will never be easy to hear, he deserves to tell his truth. They can judge me if they need to, but they can't possibly judge me as harshly as I judge myself.

I rest my hand on the side of his neck, and he leans into my touch. "Tell them everything, baby."

He bites down on his lip and takes a breath.

Mason's brothers listen to the story of our past, and when he glosses over my part in it, I fill in the gaps. I need them to know what I did, and I never want him to feel as though he has to hide anything because of me ever again.

I hold his hand while he tells them what my father did to him eighteen years ago. The fury in the room is palpable. But they let him talk, offering only words of reassurance and encouragement as he bares his soul. I'm so fucking proud of him.

And then we get to recent events, and I fill in some gaps about the kind of people my parents are and how nothing that happened yesterday should have come as a surprise. Still, it did. "That basement was a staple of my childhood, but I never expected they'd do that to me as a grown man. I'm ashamed that I wasn't strong enough to stop them," I admit, and the crack in my voice makes me feel weaker.

Mason squeezes my hand. "Because who fucking does that to their own kid? You were knocked unconscious from behind and chained in a basement. None of us are strong enough to withstand that."

I drop my head, wishing they'd all leave. The weight of their judgment is too heavy.

"Jesus fucking Christ, King." Drake whistles. "You're one tough son of a bitch."

My head snaps up, and I find him staring at me with awe. "What?"

"Putting up with all that as a kid. Having your parents treat you that way. Moving away and starting a new life on your own ..." He shakes his head. "I can't imagine being alone like that. Even when I was in Chicago, I knew any of these guys would be there in hours if I picked up a phone."

I shrug. "I guess I didn't know any different." I'm so fucking confused. They don't seem pissed at me at all.

"Having all of you, and Mom and Pop, be so supportive when I came out meant everything to me," Mason says. "It didn't matter if some asshole called me names or whatever, because I had my family. Home was always a safe place." He turns to me. "I hate that you didn't have that. Dealing with everything on your own makes you stronger and braver than you will ever give yourself credit for."

His brothers all voice their agreement.

I'm not sure I feel more uncomfortable with their pity than I would their judgment. Although it doesn't feel like pity—more like understanding. Whatever it is, I try to brush it off. "I don't know about that. And I'm not sure my shitty childhood is an excuse for the decisions I made as an adult."

Maddox shakes his head. "Nobody said it's an excuse. But bad shit like that affects your brain development. It wires you up differently. Makes you act in ways other people wouldn't." Maddox glares at his brothers. "That is scientific fact, assholes."

Elijah, Nathan, and Drake nod, and Mason holds his hands up in surrender. "I never said a word, bro."

Maddox narrows his eyes at him before returning his attention to me. "It also leaves a stain on your soul, and the only way to remove it is to let it out. Whatever way you choose to do it is up to you, but you gotta let it out. You can't keep all that to yourself or it will destroy you."

Mason reaches across the table and rests his hand over Maddox's, and Nathan, who's sitting beside him, wraps his arm around his youngest brother's neck and gives him a hug that resembles a headlock. It's obvious that Maddox is speaking from experience, but this isn't the time to ask him to reopen those wounds. I simply thank him for his insight.

Elijah clears his throat again. "Your father is a piece of shit, King."

I couldn't agree more. "He most definitely is."

He gives me a slight nod like he's pleased I'm in full agreement. "I would personally like to tear off his arms and beat him to death with them for what he did to Mason."

Again, I agree, and I tell him so.

"But I appreciate that this isn't my problem to solve, and Mason tells me that's not what either of you want." He loosens his tie.

"What do you want?" Nathan cuts in. "This isn't only about what happened to the two of you."

"Cassidy Jones." Her name makes us all pause for a moment. "You're right," I say. "My father knows I know the truth, and there's no telling what he'll do to try and destroy any potential evidence."

"So are you going to the cops, or are we handling this ourselves?" Elijah asks, and I could hug him for that. I've never known what it was like to have a family that would go to bat for you like these brothers do for each other. Except that's disrespectful to my Grampa. I'm sure his mind would have been on board even if his body wasn't.

Drake shakes his head. "There's a murder involved. Don't you think the cops are the safest bet?"

Elijah nods. "Just pointing out that we have options."

I've been thinking about what to do since Mason and I discussed it early this morning, and the only choice is to hand this over to the authorities. Cassidy and her father deserve that. Her memory deserves to be protected. "My father has a lot of influence with the NYPD, but I know a detective I can pass this on to. He'll make sure it's investigated."

"We have a lot more influence though, and we have some contacts in the DA's office," Nathan says. "Drake and I can pull some strings. Make sure a warrant is expedited."

I nod. "We'll go to the 25th precinct after breakfast." Charlie Evans is a divorced workaholic who lives at the precinct. He's also a moody son of a bitch before he's had his coffee and pancakes.

Mason offers me a reassuring smile. "Then that's what we'll do."

"And I'll go speak to Curtis Jones straight after."

Nathan makes a quick call, and when he hangs up, he fills us in on his conversation with the DA's office, and we all have to face the distinct possibility that my parents will get away with their crime if the police can't find solid evidence. But I am convinced Cassidy's body is somewhere in that house, or on the grounds at least.

"Whatever happens next, Kyngston Worthington III is finished in New York," Elijah declares. "In any part of the world where I have any influence at all, he is done. I will personally see to that. But more importantly, if your father isn't locked up immediately, are you both safe?"

"My father is a bully and a coward. He can't afford security these days, but even if he could, from what Mason told me, the Ryans scared the living shit out of him. There isn't a chance in hell he'd be willing to cross the Irish mob. And while he may still technically be breathing, he and my mother are very much dead to me. They pose no danger to Mason."

"And what about any danger to you?" Drake asks.

I'm touched by his concern for my safety, and it takes me a second to compose myself enough to answer. "They don't pose a threat to me either."

"You should beef up your security in here anyhow, Mason," Nathan says coolly. "I've been telling you that for years."

Mason rolls his eyes.

"I kind of agree, baby," I say, which earns me a scowl from him.

"Why are you on their side?" he huffs. "You just said your father is no threat to us."

"This has nothing to do with him, Mase. You're one of the richest men in America, and your security is nothing short of abysmal. You should have more cameras in your parking garage and at least one in the elevator. A panic room. At least half a dozen—"

"Okay, Sergeant Worst Case Scenario. I'll look into a little extra security."

Elijah looks pleased. "I'll hook you up with our security contractor, King, and you can come up with a plan—"

"King can come up with a plan? For *my* security?"

"Yes, Mason," Elijah answers. "Because if you won't listen to my recommendations, then King will force you to listen to his."

"Nobody better to set up security than your twitchy other half, bro," Drake says, laughing. "Amelia has our place locked up tighter than Fort Knox."

"Mel's the same," Nathan adds. "You can't take security lightly, Mase. What happened last night might have had nothing to do with your money, but there are fucked-up people out there who will do anything to get what they want."

"Jeez," Mason grumbles. "I thought this was supposed to be a fun let's-celebrate-the-fact-your-boyfriend-didn't-die-last-night breakfast."

Maddox chuckles. "Oh, the irony."

Elijah ignores Mason's griping and addresses me. "I'll send you his number."

"Great. Between us, we can cover all the bases and get an airtight plan in place."

Mason pushes back his chair. "I give up," he mutters. "Now, as much as I love you all meddling in my life, King needs to rest, and we have a cop to see before he can do that, so you all need to leave."

"You truly do love our meddling though, little brother." Drake grabs the last strawberry and tosses it into his mouth.

"It's our love language," Nathan says with a smirk.

For the next few minutes, I listen to the good-natured banter between my boyfriend and his brothers as they say their goodbyes and make plans for the weekend. They include me too, but I hold myself back enough to observe and soak it all in, enjoying being a part of this. It's new and strange but oddly comfortable.

A tiny voice in my head warns me not to get used to it because it can't possibly last. I tell that voice to go to hell.

FIFTY-TWO

As planned, Mason and I paid a visit to Charlie, and he was very interested to hear what I had to say. We also passed on the details of Nathan's contact at the DA's office, who had already been briefed on the situation. Charlie was confident he'd have a warrant by end of day tomorrow.

Afterward, we visited Curtis Jones. He sobbed in my arms when I told him what I'd discovered, and he's eager to witness the public downfall of the Worthingtons. He also swore he'd take matters into his own hands if the justice system failed him, and I can't say I blame him. While he was devastated about his little girl's murder, there was an underlying layer of relief that he finally knew the truth and that the world would soon know too.

It was a difficult day. Emotionally. Physically. Spiritually. It's not easy confronting the fact that your parents are murderers. I don't know how I would have gotten through it all without Mason. He's been incredible throughout everything.

We got back to his place a few hours ago, and he insisted on making me dinner. A delicious Moroccan lamb dish that Maddox taught him to cook, and he kindly dropped off the ingredients for it while we were out. I really could get used to this whole having brothers thing.

Mason is clearing the dishes now, having insisted I need to rest. I watch him press buttons on the dishwasher to find the right cycle and stuff my hands into my pockets —rather, his pockets, as I'm wearing his sweatpants—and admire him. The muscles in his back and shoulders flex with every move he makes, and his jeans cling to his perfect ass.

He is sheer fucking perfection. It's hard to believe I wasted so much of my life without him in it.

But perhaps we had to go through everything we did in order to end up right here. And despite my throbbing head and injured knee and the pain of everything we've endured, there's nothing I would change. I wouldn't risk a different outcome. The butterfly effect, I've heard it's called. I would do nothing to jeopardize my chance of being here with him at this exact moment in time.

He turns around and catches me staring at him. "See something you like?"

"I see everything I like, baby. Get your ass over here."

He strolls toward me, licking his lips. Tease. "I'm

pretty sure the doc said you should be resting today. No sudden or jerky movements." He smirks.

"She absolutely did not say that. Besides ..." I fist a hand in his hair and yank his head back. "I don't plan on any sudden, jerky movements." I skim my hand down his abdomen and squeeze his hardening length over his jeans. "They'll be slow and controlled, baby." I press my mouth against his ear and feel the shiver that runs down his spine. "It will be you who won't be able to control your movements when your cock is in my mouth."

He hisses out a breath. "Fuck." Shaking his head hard, he takes a step back. "But no."

"No?" I'm too shocked to say anything else. Is he being a brat, or is he actually refusing me?

He nods toward the floor. "Your knee is hurt, Hotshot. And you've already done more than you should have today."

Kneeling on this tile would hurt like a motherfucker, but I ache to make him lose control the way I can when I'm on my knees for him. However, he has a point. And a very comfortable bed. "I don't have to be on my knees to suck your cock."

He trails his fingertips down my cheek. "But that's how I want you, King. On your knees for me while I fuck your throat."

My stiff cock hardens further at the image he invokes.

"So until your knee is better, how about we switch?" He's already sinking to the floor, grazing his fingertips over my hard shaft. "Because this looks painful too." When he's in position, he pulls down the waistband of my pants, and my aching dick bobs free. With a flick of his expert tongue, he licks away the precum weeping from the crown and groans with satisfaction.

My hand still fisted in his hair, I hold his head in place and guide my crown to his lips. He kisses the tip before opening wide and letting me slip inside his warm, welcoming mouth, gliding his skillful tongue along the underside of my shaft.

Pleasure ignites in my core. "Fuck, Mase, you suck my cock like such a good boy."

He catches my eye and winks, and it's enough to make my knees tremble.

I cup his jaw while I fuck his perfect mouth, sinking deep into his throat. I wipe away any tears that are squeezed from his eyes with the pad of my thumb and watch his face, loving the way his eyelids flutter when I praise him. Losing myself in the contented noises he makes as he takes every inch of me.

"You're fucking perfect, baby. Fucking perfect and all fucking mine." I pull out and drive inside him. He swallows, and his throat muscles squeeze the tip of my dick, sending me hurtling over the edge. I come with a groan of his name, and my entire body spasms while I empty myself inside him.

Once he's all but sucked the soul from my body, he stands and wipes his mouth with the back of his hand before kissing me. Relishing the taste of myself on him, I tangle my tongue with his. When he pulls back, I'm left breathless and wanting more. "Are you up to being bent over this table and fucked?" he asks.

I want to be fucked over that table more than I've ever wanted to be fucked on or over anything in my life. Submissive or dominant, I'll take Mason any way, anywhere. "Hell yeah."

"That's my boy." His grin is cocky as fuck, but I love it.

He spins me to face the table and pushes me forward. I rest my weight on my forearms while he spreads my ass cheeks and spits on my hole, and my spent cock twitches back to life. Mason slides a finger inside me, and I groan at the intrusion. Despite what people think, spit is a pretty terrible substitute for actual lube. At least for a dick in the ass. A finger, I can cope with.

He works his finger in and out of me, massaging my prostate while he rubs his other hand down my back. "Fuck, King, this is such a tight ass."

He disappears, and I glance behind me to watch him take a bottle of olive oil from the cupboard.

I rest my face back on the smooth wood. "That better be extra virgin."

"Solo lo mejor para mi rey." He slaps my ass and rests his lips against my ear. "You know what that means?"

Warm oil drips down my ass crack, and all I can do is groan and shake my head.

"Only the best for my king. Because you are mine." He works a finger inside me. "Better?"

"Uh-huh." So much fucking better. I grind against him, and he adds a second finger. He teases me until it's no longer enough. "Fuck me, Mase."

He laughs. "So greedy for my cock."

A frustrated growl tumbles from my lips, and that only makes him laugh again. But he takes pity on me, and only a second later, his fingers are replaced by his slippery cock. He sinks all the way inside and mutters a curse in Spanish. "You're going to be so fucking messy when I'm done with you, mi amor." He presses his sinful lips to my ear, his chest bearing down on me and pushing me harder into the table. "Are you gonna let me take care of you when I'm through fucking you? I want to run you a bath and clean you all over."

He pulls out, and the sound I make can only be described as a whimper.

He slaps my ass again, harder this time. "Are you?"

I hate being taken care of, but for him, I can loosen the reins a little. "Yes."

"Buen chico," he growls, and fuck, it undoes me when he calls me good boy in Spanish. "You think you can come again for me?" He reaches around me and works me over while he fucks me on top of the table we ate dinner on. It doesn't take long before he coaxes another orgasm from me, and I spill cum all over his hand at the same time he empties himself inside me. My thighs are still shaking when he slides out of me and pulls my pants back into place.

I sink down on the chair beside us and pant for breath. "Fuck."

He crouches between my spread thighs and rests his hand on the side of my neck. It's covered in olive oil and my cum, but I'm past caring. "You okay, babe? Did I go too rough? You need some pain meds?"

I shake my head. "No. It was ..." I swallow down a knot of emotion. I feel so much of everything when I'm with him, and after years of conditioning myself to feel nothing at all, it's going to take some getting used to. "It was amazing. I just need to stop my head from spinning, that's all."

His face lights up with a smile. "Oh." He stands and gently kisses my forehead. "I'm going to run us a bath while you come back down to earth then."

He walks away with a smug chuckle, and I manage to swat his ass on his way past me. What happened with my father is still there, lingering in my thoughts like a dark cloud, but I know it will pass. I finally stood up for myself and for the man I love, and nothing Kyngston Worthington III can do or say will ever hurt either of us again. Today is the start of the life I should have always had but was too afraid to fight for.

FIFTY-THREE

MASON

"Are you sure you don't have to work today?" King asks.

"I'm sure." I toss a piece of popcorn into my mouth. "But that's the third time you've asked. Are you trying to get rid of me?"

"No," he huffs. "But I really am okay. You took all of yesterday off. There's no reason for you to stay here with me again today. I can watch movies on my own if you have more important stuff to be doing."

I roll on top of him and pin him to the mattress so our chests are pressed together. We only threw on boxers after we took a shower earlier and I insisted King go back to bed, per the doctor's instructions that he rest up, especially since he did so poorly at it yesterday, albeit for good reason.

His detective friend has kept him updated. A warrant

is likely to be issued today, and I want to be here with him when that happens, whatever the outcome. King insisted that if he's forced to stay home, he should at least get to watch movies all day, and I could be working in my home office, but I'm not going to pass up the opportunity to spend time with him in bed. "Listen to me, King—nothing, and I mean nothing, is more important to me than you. Work can wait. Everything can fucking wait."

He coasts a hand down my back, resting it above my ass. "I just don't want you to feel like you have to blow off work to look after me. I really don't need looking after."

"Did you hear a word I said?" I ask, and he bites down on his lip. So goddamn adorable, and now I want to do the opposite of letting him rest. "I'm not *looking after you*. I have nowhere else I would rather be. However, if you would prefer to watch this godawful *Road House* remake alone, I will—"

"I don't." He shakes his head. "I like you being here."

"Then will you stop asking me if I have to work?"

He nods, and I roll off him before my dick gets so painfully hard I have to do something about it. I promised to let him rest, and that's what I'm going to do. I focus on Jake Gyllenhaal's abs, which almost make this movie worth watching. But King has shifted onto his side and is lazily trailing his fingers up and down my abs. I can feel the heat of his eyes raking over my body. "You're supposed to be resting."

"I was also supposed to be resting earlier this morning when you fucked me in the shower."

I purse my lips to stop myself from grinning. "Exactly. Isn't that enough activity for you for one day?"

He drapes his muscular thigh over my hip. "I'm not sure there's ever enough *activity* where you're concerned, Mase."

I tip my head back and groan. "You're killing me, Hotshot. I promised Dr. Lisa I would make sure you got plenty of bed rest for forty-eight hours."

King shifts closer. "We are in bed."

I throw my hands behind my head and stare at the TV, pretending this remake is suddenly the most fascinating movie in the history of modern cinema. "I'm not sure what you're suggesting is restful in any way, mi amor."

He trails his hot mouth along my bicep. "Talking to me in Spanish really isn't helping matters." His hand drifts lower and grazes my semi-hard cock. It's safely encased in my boxer shorts, although I suspect not for much longer.

"Eres un diablo envuelto en el cuerpo de un dios, mi amor."

He groans. "Again with the Spanish. What the hell did you just say?"

I flip over and turn my head to the side, resting my cheek on my forearms so I can watch him. "I said you are a devil wrapped up in the body of a god, my love."

His eyes darken. "You are sinfully fucking hot, you know that?" As I suspected he would, he rolls on top of me and drags his teeth down the back of my neck. "I have no idea how I'm supposed to be able to keep my fucking hands off you."

"You don't even try."

He snorts and bites my shoulder. "Don't think I don't know the games you play, Mason James." He works my boxers over my ass. "Lying on your stomach so that this ass—" He slaps it hard. "This ass that belongs to me, is on full display. Begging me to fuck it."

He pushes himself up and straddles me so his thighs are pressed against mine. I can't move. I feel him reaching for the lube and coating his cock, and then a warm, slick finger works its way between my ass cheeks and into my asshole. "Fuck, that feels good."

"Yeah? You love me fucking you, don't you?"

He sinks in deeper, and I groan, pressing my face into the pillow. He leans over me and whispers in my ear, "Face out of the pillow, baby. I want to hear every dirty fucking sound you make for me."

I do as he asks, moaning loudly when he removes his fingers and swiftly replaces them with his thick cock. Then he cups my jaw and angles my face so he can thrust his tongue into my mouth at the same time he drives his entire length inside me. He swallows my gasp but lets me up for air. Resting his body weight on mine, he fucks me into the mattress and mutters dirty, possessive words in my ear.

I'm lost to the overwhelming sensations he wrings

from my body. He is everything—all-consuming. His scent surrounds me. The taste of his tongue dances on my taste-buds whenever he delves into my mouth. His skin against mine is soft velvet over the hard steel of his muscles. Pleasure races through my veins like lightning as he repeatedly hits that spot inside me.

"I love you, Mase," he growls, and I lose it, falling over the edge with him as he fills me with his release.

"Love you too, King." I manage to pant out the words and let him pull me into his arms, my back against his chest while his cum drips out of me. He nuzzles my neck, and I close my eyes.

Here, I feel safe. Loved.

Here—in the arms of the man I've loved for over half my life. The man I will go on loving for the rest of it.

FIFTY-FOUR

KING

Mason's cell phone vibrates, and he grabs it from the nightstand. "It's from Nathan. He says to turn on the news."

I grab the remote, anxiety bubbling in my stomach at whatever it is we're about to see. Charlie kept me updated until they executed the warrant, and I figure he's been busy since.

I flick to CNN, and the red banner across the bottom of the screen reads

BREAKING NEWS: PROMINENT NEW YORK BANKER AND HIS WIFE ARRESTED.

A reporter stands outside my parent's house, a large red umbrella protecting her from the rain. I snort at the irony that my mother has been reduced to his wife and not a person in her own right. It's misogynistic, and ordinarily I would hate it, but it's oddly satisfying.

The reporter's update is mostly speculation. She talks about human remains as if there might be more than one victim. After finding out about Cassidy, nothing would surprise me.

Mason links his fingers through mine. "You okay?"

I shake my head. Despite everything, it's not easy seeing my parents' heinous crimes splashed all over the five o'clock news. I grew up knowing they weren't good people, but I never would have believed them capable of murder.

"We can handle this," he says. "We can come up with a media strategy to make sure that you're not hounded, and I can help you write a statement and—"

"Baby," I cut in. "I love that you've gone straight to damage control, but this isn't work. You can switch off. There's gonna be questions, and I'll handle them, okay? I'm a big boy, and this isn't your mess to fix."

"I just want to protect you," he says.

"I know, and I love you for it. But they're the only people who've done anything wrong. We don't need statements or damage assessments or mitigation. Only the truth." I kiss his knuckles.

He wraps an arm around my shoulder, and we lie back and watch the rest of the news report. The photos they use of my parents are less than flattering, and I imagine my mother's horror at learning a picture of her with gray roots that makes her appear to have a double chin is being blasted all over the national news. It doesn't look like her at all. They must have worked hard to dig up that masterpiece.

As the report begins to repeat all the same information they've already revealed, my mind wanders and my emotions go to war, fighting for a turn at the wheel. But underneath all the negative ones, there's a whole lot of something I realize I haven't felt for a long time, and that's hope. It feels strangely karmic to watch a report on my parents being arrested while I'm in the arms of the man they convinced me it was wrong to love. The man who is one hundred times more decent, kind, loyal, and honorable than my parents ever were. It feels like a giant fuck you to the people who were supposed to love me unconditionally and instead made me spend over thirty years hating myself.

That chapter is well and truly over.

FIFTY-FIVE

MASON

K ing is going through his emails on his laptop, chewing on his lip and looking adorable. Thanks to Elijah's glowing recommendation, alongside the fact that my boyfriend is incredibly good at his job, he's been inundated with work and is able to cherry-pick the cases he wants to take on. While he's still recovering, he's agreed to focus on the less dangerous ones. No hunting down murderers for a while at least.

I zip up my hoodie and his head snaps up. "Where are you headed?"

I've been preparing myself for this conversation, but I'm still anxious about having it with him. And I have no idea why. I'm certain he won't have an issue with it. Maybe because I still don't identify as a "survivor of sexual abuse," or maybe because I should have told him before now. I drop onto the sofa beside him. "I'm going to my support group."

He blinks. "Support group?"

I nod. "It's for male victims of abuse—or survivors, I'm told is the appropriate term. I've been going for a couple of months. This will be my fourth one."

"And does it help?"

"Yeah. It does actually. And the guys I've met there are great. They listen and don't judge, and they made me realize ..."

King places a reassuring hand on my thigh, and I find the courage to finish that sentence. "That there was nothing I could have done to stop it from happening."

"I'm glad it's helped, baby."

"So you don't mind me leaving you alone? I'll only be gone a few hours, and I really could use some of their help right now. Finding out about Cassidy is bringing up all these feelings of guilt and stuff." I screw my eyes closed, hoping that me needing them doesn't make King feel like I don't need him.

"Of course. Do whatever you need to."

"They just get it in a way that other people don't and—"

"Mase!" He takes my face in his hands. "I understand. I can tell you one million times that you have nothing to feel guilty about, but I get that talking about it with people who've been through something similar must offer an entirely different perspective. You don't have to explain yourself to me. Whatever you need, whenever you need it."

"That goes both ways, King. I'm here for whatever you need too." I don't mention that I think he'd benefit from some therapy to deal with all the trauma from his childhood and what happened a few days ago. He needs time to process everything, and for now, he prefers to do that by keeping himself busy.

"I know." He kisses me softly. "Right now, you are all I need. I promise. Go to your meeting, and I'll be here waiting for you to come back and tell me how it went."

"I love you so fucking much, mi rey."

"Love you too, baby boy."

KING WAS RIGHT. Speaking with people who've been through a similar experience offers me a different perspective. After I shared the immense feelings of guilt that have been dredged up after discovering my abuser went on to hurt other people, many of them share comparable stories of their own.

"Abusers very rarely have just one victim," Peter tells me solemnly. The others in the group voice their agreement.

"Ain't nobody responsible for what he did but him,"

Chris, the guy who runs the group adds—a statement that is met with more fervent agreement.

By the time I leave the meeting, I feel much lighter. The same way I always do. I can see why Maddox still attends his support groups after seven years of sobriety.

But there's still one thing I need to take care of. I dial Nathan, and he answers after a few rings. "Hey, Mase."

"Nathan, I need a favor."

"Anything."

I brace myself and ask. "Can you get me into a jail?"

"A specific jail, or will any of them do?"

"Wherever King's father is being held. I want to see him. Can you make it happen?"

He answers me without pause. "I'll have to pull some strings, but consider it done."

That he doesn't tell me what a bad idea it is or try to talk me out of it is one of the many reasons he's such a good brother. "Thanks, bro."

"I'll let you know where and when. And if you need me to come with you—"

"Thanks, but this is something I have to do on my own," I say, ready to take this next step toward healing the boy I was and the man I am.

TWO DAYS after my call to Nathan, I find myself in the detention center visiting room in the Bronx. Kyngston

Worthington III hobbles in on crutches and is escorted to the chair across from me. He glares at me through the thick glass, and we both pick up our respective phones. "I was told I was seeing my son," he says with a snarl, revealing two missing front teeth. A gift from Conor Ryan.

"Nope. King won't come anywhere near you ever again, you piece of shit. Neither will I after today."

"What the fuck are you doing here?"

"I guess I just wanted to see you." I smile at him through the glass.

His scowl deepens. "You think I want to see you? You disgusting—"

"Little pervert." I finish for him. "Yeah, you've used that line before. You should really get yourself some new material."

He glances at the guard, who shakes his head. Kyngston bares his teeth like a cornered animal. I know Nathan arranged it so he was forced to take this meeting, and he'll remain here until I say he can leave. "Say your piece so I can go back to my cell," he demands.

I stare at him, his sparse hair peppered with gray, deep lines around his eyes and creasing his forehead. He'll likely die in a place much like this, which is no less than he deserves. He has a fresh bruise on his neck, peeking out from beneath his jumpsuit. Too fresh to be a gift from Conor Ryan, yet surprisingly, it gives me no pleasure at all to think of how he got it. "I have no desire to spend any more time in your company than is absolutely necessary. But I couldn't go the rest of my life without looking you in the eye and telling you that what you did didn't break me. You raped me."

His jaw tics.

"And I could spend hours arguing the irony of your narrative about me and your son being *disgusting perverts*, but I know I'd be wasting my time and energy. Your level of cognitive dissonance is astounding. You do know what that is, don't you?" I can't resist goading him a little.

His lip curls, but he doesn't speak.

"I did consider coming back to your house that night. I imagined how good it would feel to beat you to death with my bare hands. To take out every bit of rage and shame you made me feel on your smug face, but your son needed me, so ..." I shrug.

"Or you're a coward," he spits.

I simply smile, refusing to take his bait. "And then after you landed in here, I thought about how easy it would be to pay someone to do to you what you did to me, and what you did to Cassidy. And then I realized I'd be an idiot to waste my money on something that will happen naturally. You do know what happens to people like you in places like these, right?"

His Adam's apple bobs, and I suspect he's already experienced a taste of what life has in store for him. "But really, I'm here because I wanted to see you one last time. Remind myself what a pathetic waste of oxygen you are and tell you that your son and I are really fucking happy together. We are going to live an incredible life. And if you have any kind of love in your black heart for him, then you should take some comfort in the fact that he will never go another day of his life not knowing how loved he is. He'll have everything he ever wanted. I'll take care of him, Kyngston. I really will."

His eye twitches, and he mutters something under his breath that I don't catch, but I have no doubt it was some kind of homophobic slur. I truly don't give a shit.

Having said what I came here to say, I wink at him and hang up the phone. I leave the room without a single backward glance and finally close the door on that part of my life.

KING IS in the kitchen when I get home, and from the incredible aroma of spices, I'd guess he's making us curry for dinner. My stomach growls loudly.

He looks up and smiles, and I swear my knees go weak.

"Hey, baby. How was work?" he asks, wiping his hands on a dish towel. "Any problems for me to come take care of for you?"

I give him a brief kiss. "Are you telling me you miss working at Jamestech?"

"Actually, I think I just miss those late afternoon updates I used to give you." He flashes me a wicked grin.

I slip my arms around his waist and tug him close. "Well, you can give me any update you want right here."

He growls. "Yeah, I can."

"I went to see your father today," I blurt out before I get too distracted by that look in his eyes.

He blinks rapidly. "What? Why?"

I swallow my nerves. I probably should have told him beforehand, but he would have worried or tried to convince me not to go. "I had to look him in the face. He stole so fucking much from me, and I had to ..." I suck in a breath.

He rests his forehead against mine and palms the back of my neck, his grip possessive and calming. "I know, baby. How'd it go? Did it help?"

"Well, he was as pleasant as always."

He snorts. "Surely you didn't expect him to grow a conscience."

"No. And I didn't go there to try and make him understand anything, or even to gloat. I wanted him to see that he didn't beat me."

He dusts his lips over mine. "He could never beat you, Mase. It was brave to go see him."

"I also told him that I love you and that we are really happy. And I told him not to worry because I'll always take care of you."

His eyes narrow, filled with emotion. "You told him that?"

I nod, my fingers gripping his T-shirt. "It's true, mi rey. Always."

He kisses me softly. "What did I do to deserve you, baby?"

I pull him in for a kiss, taking what's mine. He's always been mine, and he always will be.

EPILOGUE 1

KING - THREE MONTHS LATER

I fidget with my bow tie, trying to get it to sit just right. I hate these things, and with good reason—they're ridiculous and pointless. The exception to that rule walks up behind me, his eyes on mine in the mirror. Of course his bow tie is perfect, and he looks fucking incredible.

Accepting defeat, I drop my hands and let the tie hang in a loose half-knot around my neck.

"Everything okay?" Mason asks.

"I hate tying these things," I huff.

A small smile plays on his lips. "So don't wear one, babe." He reaches around my neck from behind and unfastens the mess I've made. "Or better still, wear it like this." He leaves the two ends hanging loose and unfastens the top button of my dress shirt. "Looks good on you."

I study my reflection. He's right, it does look good. And it's infinitely more comfortable. "But it's black tie."

He skims his nose across the back of my neck. "And you're wearing a black tie."

Technically, yes, but I'm sure this isn't what the fancy invite meant when it specified the dress code. The gala dinner event is hosted by Amber's charity, and I've had nothing but pleasant interactions with the woman, but I know better than to get on the wrong side of her. Especially as this night represents so much more than a party for Mason and me. I want everything to go perfectly.

Aware of my unease, he wraps his arms around my waist and rests his chin on my shoulder.

"Relax, King. It's our party, and we can wear whatever the hell we like."

"It's your family's party," I remind him.

He smiles at me in the mirror. "And you're a James now, in all but name."

I answer without thinking. "I like your name."

"You can have it, mi rey. All you have to do is ask." He kisses my neck, and a shiver of excitement runs up my spine. "Are you sure you're not nervous about tonight for another reason?"

"I'm not nervous, Mase. I just don't like bow ties." I sound a little too defensive for the first part of that statement to be true.

"We don't have to do this tonight, babe. We don't have to do this so publicly."

I swallow down my anxiety. It was my idea that we

arrive at the event together. An idea that came to me during one of my therapy sessions. Me, in therapy! I was skeptical and certain I would never go back leading up to my first session, but I now go once a week. It's unbelievable how much progress I've made processing and reshaping the fucked-up thought patterns I carry from my upbringing.

Tonight's event will be attended by celebrities from all walks of life, and there'll be press everywhere, which is great for Amber's charity. It's also the perfect way to rip off the Band-Aid and let the entire world know Mason and I are together. At least it seemed like a good idea when I first suggested it to him.

"I could arrange for a pap I know to snap us in the park or something instead. Make it look natural, you know? We could borrow a dog from Mel's shelter for the day. How fucking adorable would that be? You'd look so fucking cute with a little beagle or something. They need dog walkers, you know? Hey, maybe we should adopt a dog. I've always wanted a dog—how about you?"

My anxiety level aside, I can't help but smile. It's obvious that I am not the only one feeling a little nervous about tonight. I turn around and slide my hands inside his tux jacket. "You are fucking adorable when you're nervous, baby."

He gives me a sheepish grin that only makes him look sexier. "Who said I'm nervous? Maybe I'm excited about our fictional dog."

I press a kiss on his lips. "What are we going to call her?"

"Call her? So we are getting a dog?"

His eyes shine with excitement, and I have to stop myself from telling him that we can get any number of dogs, cats, hamsters, goldfish, or whatever the hell else he wants. Anything to make him happy and put that look on his face. "I don't see why not."

His phone rings, and he looks at the screen and says he has to take it. "The tie looks great," he adds. "But if you'd rather go without, that's fine too." He gives me another quick kiss and answers the call.

Half studying my reflection and half watching him talk to Elijah on the phone, I decide to leave the tie as he arranged it. Sometimes I can hardly believe he's mine. I'm pretty sure he was teasing me about having his name, but what if …?

These past three months have been full of change for me. While tonight will be the first time we officially announce ourselves to the world as a couple, we go out on dates at least twice a week, and every time we bump into a friend of his, a possessive thrill runs through me when he introduces me as his boyfriend. We've also been snapped by paparazzi a few times already, but my name has never been given, and it's been nothing but speculation about whether New York's most eligible bachelor has a new love interest.

It's way too early to think about any bigger form of

commitment than confirming our relationship in the media, but still I find myself wondering what it would be like to call him my husband. I spent eighteen years of my life without him in it, and I've never been as sure about anything as I am about the fact that I want to spend the rest of my life with Mason James.

He's everything to me, and I want to share everything with him. Including his name.

"You okay?" Mason asks, looking pointedly at where I keep fastening and unfastening my left cuff link.

I turn my attention from checking out the limo to a more impressive sight. Nobody has ever filled out a tux better than Mason James. "Yeah. I was just thinking I've never had sex in a limo."

His laugh is deep and sexy. "How about we save that for the way home, Hotshot? We're almost there."

Less than five minutes later, the car rolls to a stop outside the event venue. A glance through the tinted windows confirms my suspicion—this event is a huge fucking deal. There's a red carpet, a horde of paparazzi, as well as a crowd of onlookers hoping to catch sight of a celebrity. A James charity gala is as big of a deal as a movie premiere.

All the moisture in my mouth evaporates. No, that's not true. It somehow travels straight to my palms.

"You sure about this, mi rey?" Mason's voice is soft and reassuring. If I asked him to, he'd tell the driver to get us out of here. And that's enough for me.

I give a firm nod. "Yeah, I'm sure."

He presses his lips against mine. "Then let's go hold hands in public, babe."

Happiness lights up my insides. This moment is long overdue. It's been twenty years since I saw him sitting in that booth at Nero's pizzeria. Twenty years since he first knocked me on my ass with that smile. I wish I'd had the courage to hold his hand in public back then. I should have shown the entire world he was mine two decades ago.

The door opens, and the sound of the crowd is almost deafening.

Mason laughs, totally unfazed by the attention we're about to be in the center of. "Wow, Amber knows how to throw an event, huh?"

I take Mason's hand in mine and climb out of the car. A flash of lights blinds me, and some people in the crowd shout his name. But I lace my fingers with his, and we stand together, and then I do what I should have done all those years ago: I kiss the man I love, and I don't give a single fuck who sees us.

EPILOGUE 2

MASON

"Hey, baby." King's deep, sexy voice fills my head, his soft lips grazing my ear.

I groan into my pillow, enjoying the vividness of this particular dream. It's so real I feel the bed dip beside me. King's smooth, skillful hand coasts down my back, his teeth nipping at the skin of my throat.

But King's in Chicago for the rest of the week, tying up all the loose ends on his business there and finalizing the sale of his apartment.

"Wake up, Mase. I have two hours before I have to get back on a plane."

My eyes fly open. "King?"

His laugh ruffles my hair. "Does anyone else have a key to your place and wake you up like this? Because if they do ..." His mouth is too busy playing over my skin for him to finish the question.

I roll onto my back, unable to keep the goofy smile from my face when I see the outline of his silhouette holding himself over me. "What the hell are you doing here?"

He drags his teeth along my jawline, and my cock hardens instantly. "I missed you. I spent eighteen years of my life without you, and now it seems I can't even go a few days without touching you." The words vibrate against my skin, sending warm currents of pleasure skittering through my body. He hurriedly tugs the duvet off and glides his palm over my chest and down my abs until he reaches the waistband of my boxers. His nimble fingers slip under the fabric, and my entire body comes alive at his touch. "Fuck, I can barely go a whole day without you. What have you done to me?"

He bites my neck, and I tip my head back, unable to answer. Not that I know the answer, but whatever it is, he has the exact same effect on me. He fumbles for the lube in the nightstand drawer, and no less than two minutes after he disturbed my sleep, he's sinking inside me and my eyes are rolling back in my head.

"Fuck, King." I grit out the words.

"I know, baby boy. I was born to fuck you, you know that?"

And fuck me he does, so thoroughly that my entire body is shaking from the strength of my climax. He rests his forehead against mine. "Fuck, Mase. I don't think I want to be your boyfriend anymore," he says, his voice strained.

My heart bottoms out of my chest, and I react on instinct. "What the fuck? Your dick's still inside me, and you're saying ..." I take a breath and tell myself to calm the fuck down. He didn't fly home from Chicago to break up with me, especially not right after he told me he can barely stand to be apart. "Just what are you telling me?"

He pulls back a little, staring down at me, his sinfully full lips twitching. "You're so fucking hot when you're pissed. Makes me want to push your buttons all the time."

I thread my fingers through his hair, which he wears a little longer now, and tug. Not hard enough to hurt, but enough to make him wince. "Stop being an asshole and tell me what you mean."

"I didn't mean I don't want to be with you, baby boy." He rocks his hips and pushes deeper inside me once more. "Haven't I spent the last half hour telling you, and showing you, how much I can't keep my fucking hands off you?"

God, I love being so full of him. My eyes want to roll back in my head, but I fight that instinct and stare at him. "So what are you talking about?"

"I've been thinking about doing this since the night of the charity gala." He gently slides himself out of me and rolls onto his side, his hand resting on my stomach—and in my cum, which he doesn't seem to care about.

I grab a tissue from the nightstand anyway and clean myself up before handing him some to do the same, but my deviant boyfriend licks his palm clean instead. I shake my head, pretending to disapprove, when in truth I fucking love watching him do that. And he knows it. I love every single thing he does. Love him.

He smirks. "You taste so fucking good. Why would I waste a drop?"

I direct him back to our more important conversation. "Been thinking about what since the charity dinner?"

He props himself up on his elbow, his green eyes twinkling. "I should probably do this in some big grand gesture kind of way, but you know that's not my style."

A grand gesture? What the hell is he talking about? My stomach ties itself into knots.

He brushes his knuckles over my cheek. "You said that night if I wanted your name, then all I had to do was ask."

Holy shit. My heart jumps to my throat. "Are you asking?" And exactly what is he asking?

"This might be the most unromantic proposal ever, but will you be my husband? Will you spend the rest of your life with me?"

Fuck. Me. That was honestly the last thing I expected him to say. "Are you serious right now?"

"I should have done it better, huh? I know you deserve a romantic proposal, but I was on the plane, and I thought why wait? I love you and want to spend every second of the rest of my life with you, and I thought—" He stops talking and chews on his lip.

I grab his face and kiss him. "You're so adorable when you're nervous, mi rey."

"Is that a yes?" he asks quietly.

"That's a yes. Although if you take my name, you'll be King James."

He raises his eyebrows. "King James-Blackthorn actually, and I won't lie, the prospect of being addressed like royalty has been the driving factor in my decision to commit the rest of my life to you."

I kiss him again. "Mason James-Blackthorn. I like that. Does this mean you're officially moving in? Or are you going to continue living here while you keep some clothes at your place under the pretense that you don't live here?"

He gives me a playful nudge in my ribs. "Yes, I'll move in while we look for our own place."

"Oh, we're buying a new place now too?"

"You think I'm going to have my husband live in this former fuck den?"

I laugh out loud. I can't help it, and I can't recall a time I have ever felt happier. "Okay. We can look for a new place."

I don't care where we live, just that we'll be living together. All the time. I should probably play this cool, but I can't stop grinning. "Wow. Getting married and moving in together—this has been quite the trip back for you, Hotshot."

He hums appreciatively. "Moving in with you definitely has its benefits." His eyes roam my body and stop to linger on one particular benefit that's already twitching under his gaze before trailing back up to my face.

I roll on top of him and pin his wrists on either side of his head, pressing him into the mattress. Then I dust my lips over his, teasing him with a kiss and grinding myself against his cock.

I kiss him hard, then pull back and ask, "What time is your flight?"

"Four a.m.," he pants, breathless.

"So, we have thirty minutes. I'm gonna need to spend most of that time with a part of me inside you, Hotshot. Now, you can suck my cock or I can fuck you. Which is it to be?"

"Fuck me, Mase," he groans.

"With pleasure, mi rey."

My King. My lover and best friend. My soon-to-be husband.

The place I feel safest and the only place that's home.

Still want more? You can get another delicious slice of Mason and King in the extended epilogue Here

Not done with the James brothers and want to find out more about the deliciously deep and mysterious youngest of the family? Then you can order Maddox's story, Made, right now:

Made

And you can find their older brother's stories here

Broken

Promise Me Forever

Rebound

ALSO BY SADIE KINCAID

If you'd like to know more about the famous Ryans and their wife, Jessie, you can find out all about them in the full New York Ruthless series. Available on Amazon and Kindle Unlimited

Ryan Rule

Ryan Redemption

Ryan Retribution

Ryan Reign

Ryan Renewed

And the complete short stories and novellas attached to this series are available in one collection

A Ryan Recollection

Have you tried Sadie's bestselling paranormal/ fantasy series yet? If you love possessive broody vampires, witches, wolves and all things magic, then try the Broken Bloodlines series here

Forged in Blood

Promised in Blood

Bound in Blood

The complete, bestselling Chicago Ruthless is available now. Following the lives of the notoriously ruthless Moretti siblings -

this series will take you on a rollercoaster of emotions. Packed with angst, action and plenty of steam.

Dante

Joey

Lorenzo

Keres

If you'd prefer to head to LA to meet Alejandro and Alana, and Jackson and Lucia, you can find out all about them in Sadie's internationally bestselling LA Ruthless series. Available on Amazon and FREE in Kindle Unlimited.

Fierce King

Fierce Queen

Fierce Betrayal

Fierce Obsession

Prefer a standalone to a series, then why not try Sadie's bestselling why choose billionaire romance

The Perfect Fit

If you'd like to read about London's hottest couple. Gabriel and Samantha, then check out Sadie's London Ruthless series on Amazon. FREE in Kindle Unlimited.

Dark Angel

Fallen Angel

If you enjoy super spicy short stories, Sadie also writes the Bound series feat Mack and Jenna, Books 1, 2, 3 and 4 are available now.

Bound and Tamed

Bound and Shared

Bound and Dominated

Bound and Deceived

About the Author

Sadie Kincaid is a dark contemporary and paranormal romance author who loves to read and write about hot alpha males and strong, feisty females.

Sadie loves to connect with readers so why not get in touch via social media?

Join Sadie's reader group for the latest news, book recommendations and plenty of fun. Sadie's ladies and Sizzling Alphas

Printed in Dunstable, United Kingdom

70353180R00272